THE DEATH MASK MURDERS

Jack Rogan Mysteries Book 7

GABRIEL FARAGO

This book is brought to you by Bear & King Publishing.

Publishing & Marketing Consultant: Lama Jabr
Website: https://xanapublishingandmarketing.com
Sydney, Australia

Cover Design by Giovanni Banfi

ISBN: 978-0-9876283-5-0

Signup for the author's New Releases mailing list to get a free copy of *The Forgotten Painting** novella and find out where it all began …

https://gabrielfarago.com.au/free-download-forgotten-painting/

* I'm delighted to tell you that *The Forgotten Painting* has received two major literary awards in the US. It was awarded the Gold Medal by Readers' Favorite in the Short Stories and Novellas category and was named 'Outstanding Novella' of 2018 by the IAN Book of the Year Awards.

Also by Gabriel Farago

Letters from the Attic
The Forgotten Painting
The Kimberley Secret
The Empress Holds the Key
The Disappearance of Anna Popov
The Hidden Genes of Professor K
Professor K: The Final Quest
The Curious Case of the Missing Head
The Lost Symphony

Dedication

For Joan, who always reminds me to *'either write something worth reading or do something worth writing'*.

Benjamin Franklin

The Death Mask Murders

Gabriel Farago

CONTENTS

Acknowledgements

Because of the draconian COVID-19 restrictions and lockdowns here in Australia, international travel – especially to South America and the Caribbean – hasn't been possible. This had a significant impact on my research because I like to visit all the major locations mentioned in my books to get a 'feel' for the culture and the people. That said, I have been fortunate in some unexpected ways.

To begin with, all the European countries and places featured in the book, I've visited before and know intimately. This was particularly helpful with the Bavarian scenes and Italian locations, especially Venice, Florence and Rome.

Many of my dedicated readers have joined my *Book Launch Team* over the years, and as members of that select group they have been closely involved with the publication of my books. On this occasion, I turned to them for assistance with the extensive research involved – especially the Inca period, the Spanish conquest, and the treasure trove of historical records in Seville.

Well, I was in for a pleasant surprise! I had no idea that among my readership there were so many experts in so many diverse fields, who generously gave of their time and offered guidance and advice on how to explore and master the many subjects and issues covered in the book. From university professors and lecturers, to librarians, archaeologists, criminologists and historians, I suddenly had access to a huge pool of knowledge and experience I was able to harness and draw upon in my research.

As there are just too many to mention by name, a big thank you must go to my *Book Launch Team* generally, and especially those members who so willingly reached out and became involved in this complex and exciting project. Without their assistance, this book just wouldn't have seen the light of day.

Preparing a book for publication requires many skills, especially during these uncertain times. It is a team effort. I've once again been very fortunate to have a group of talented and dedicated specialists on my team to help me deal with the many challenges of a rapidly changing publishing landscape.

As all my books are complex projects with multi-layered storylines, I work closely with my editor, Sally Asnicar of Full Proofreading Services, whose exceptional attention to detail and insights into the characters – old and new – and familiarity with all of my books have been invaluable in bringing this ambitious project to fruition.

In many ways, once the manuscript has been polished and finalised and is in all respects ready for release, that is just the beginning of the next crucially important stage. Because just writing a good book is not enough; you have to get it out there, make it visible, and ensure it connects with the market and your readers. This is a complex process that requires the skills of an experienced specialist.

Lama Jabr, my publishing and marketing consultant of Xana Publishing and Marketing, has been my adviser for many years and whose steady hand has patiently guided this project through the many challenges of a treacherous publication jungle. Her insights and expertise, especially when dealing with social media and complex publishing platforms, have been invaluable, and have made a huge contribution to the success of the *Jack Rogan Mysteries Series* and its worldwide popularity and appeal.

Who says we don't judge a book by its cover? In a way we all do, especially when surfing the Net for inspiration on what to read. In my view, an engaging cover and a clever design that reflects the 'spirit' of the book are essential components that give it visibility, and make it stand out in a fiercely competitive market.

In Giovanni Banfi I have a talented artist by my side who understands my work and knows how I want to present it. It is for that reason that the imaginative cover designs of my books and social media banners have attracted much attention and received many compliments over the years.

Sally, Lama and Giovanni are experts who always strive for excellence, and this is clearly reflected in the high quality of their work.

And finally, it would be remiss of me not to mention my wife, Joan, literary critic, researcher, patient sounding board and cheerful travel companion. Without her encouragement and unwavering support, this project just wouldn't have been possible, and the many literary awards and uplifting reviews belong as much to her, as they belong to me.

Thank you all for believing in me, and what I'm trying to achieve with my writing.

Gabriel Farago
Leura, Blue Mountains, Australia

Author's Note

Memories are the little gems that link us to our past. They can appear in surprising ways when we least expect it, and have a profound effect on the present.

I can still remember the fascinating little book very well. It was hidden beneath a set of dusty novels by Alexandre Dumas. Faded pages stained around the edges whispered 'Open me. Come inside and discover my secrets'. I found it by accident one afternoon after school, up in the attic of my grandfather's hunting lodge in Austria. I must have been about twelve or thirteen at the time, and the attic was a wonderland – especially for a young boy. Just to get to it was an adventure. I could only reach it by way of a narrow set of winding stairs, which always creaked.

Once I made it to the top, I was met by a low, wood-panelled door with solid, wrought-iron hinges. The attic, a narrow rectangular room at the very top of the spacious house, where a maze of massive exposed wooden beams held up a steep roof, became my secret world. It was a place where I could dream and let my imagination run free. And there was certainly a lot to stimulate the imagination – books mainly, hundreds of them – and a few fascinating, exotic artefacts from Africa and Asia to enchant a curious boy.

There were no shelves or bookcases; the books were all in old trunks covered in cobwebs. As a career soldier – a high-ranking officer in the Austro-Hungarian army – my grandfather travelled a lot. He was stationed in various parts of the Empire, often for years, and his most treasured possessions travelled with him in those trunks.

Sadly, I never met my grandfather – he died many years before I was born – but in that attic I believe I got to know him through his books. I became a voracious reader. After school, I headed straight to the attic. Not to do homework, but to read. It was my introduction to the wonderful world of books, a passion that has never left me and which today, more than ever, guides my life. I believe this was my grandfather's legacy; a gift to the grandson he never met: literature.

The most memorable feature of the little book in question was the picture on its faded cover. It was a picture of a striking golden Inca burial mask in the Prado in Madrid. I cannot remember the title of the book, but it mentioned a lost treasure and Inca gold. I can still recall sitting in my grandfather's leather chair, devouring the faded pages of this intriguing book telling the story of Atahualpa, the Inca king captured by Pizarro in Cajamarca, and the legend of a fabulous treasure hidden by Ruminahui, the Inca general who came to rescue his king, only to find that Atahualpa had been murdered.

Many years later I visited the Prado, and there in one of the glass display cases, I saw the golden mask. It was just as I remembered it. Surprised, I kept staring at it as memories of that little book I read up in my grandfather's attic all those years ago came flooding back, and my mind began to wander. What if that fabulous treasure hidden by Ruminahui did in fact exist and was still waiting somewhere to be discovered? What if ...?

These tantalising questions stayed with me and became the inspiration for this book.

Gabriel Farago
Leura, Blue Mountains, Australia

PART I
THE CURSE OF THE GOLDEN MASK

'There lies Peru with its riches;
Here, Panama and its poverty.
Choose, each man, what best becomes a brave Castilian.'

Francisco Pizarro

Prologue

Inca city of Cajamarca, northern Peru: 16 November 1532

It had begun to rain again. Low clouds and mist obscured an angry sky above the remote, almost deserted Inca city high up in the mountains. Francisco Pizarro looked up at a condor circling like a messenger of doom, the piercing call of the huge bird of prey making him uneasy. The battle-hardened commander could sense danger.

Consumed by ambition, lust for gold and riches, and yearning for glory and recognition, this illiterate, illegitimate son of a nobleman and an impoverished commoner from Extremadura – a western Spanish region bordering Portugal – was prepared to do almost anything to achieve his deep and dark desires.

When Pizarro with his band of one hundred and eighty profligate conquistadors entered the once beautiful and flourishing city of Cajamarca in November 1532, the timing couldn't have been better. A bloody civil war had weakened and torn apart the empire, and a fierce battle between Atahualpa and his brother Huascar had snuffed out the lives of thousands. Atahualpa had emerged victorious and had been proclaimed the undisputed king, or 'Inca', of the vast empire stretching southward from the Ancomayo in present-day Colombia, all the way to the Maule River in Chile. With an estimated population exceeding sixteen million, it was one of the four great pre-Colombian civilisations.

After the battle, Atahualpa was on his way to Cuzco with his army when news reached him that a strange band of foreigners from the north, with apparently supernatural powers that were feared by the priests, had entered his kingdom. His curiosity aroused, Atahualpa decided to meet them and see for himself what the unsettling rumours were all about. With an army of eighty thousand brave warriors behind him, he thought he had nothing to fear from a mere handful of men, however powerful and mysterious. This was a miscalculation that would cost him not only his empire, but also his life.

Alone and isolated in a strange, hostile land, Pizarro realised that any show of weakness would result in annihilation. Retreat was therefore impossible. Fighting an experienced army of this size in open battle, even if armed with only primitive weapons, was also out of the question and would end in disaster. The only alternative was to outwit his opponent and fight, but on his terms.

Pizarro sent word to Atahualpa that he would like to meet him in the great plaza, and was looking forward to making the acquaintance of the mighty Inca ruler he had heard so much about. Irritated by this arrogance, Atahualpa nevertheless agreed and decided to put on a show to impress. He entered Cajamarca surrounded by six thousand warriors, counsellors, and commanders, confident that he would capture the annoying interlopers and put an end to the rumours of supernatural powers, weapons that could kill like magic from a distance, and wild beasts that could trample seasoned warriors to death in battle.

Unbeknown to Atahualpa and his scouts, Pizarro had strategically positioned his men in fortified laneways and empty buildings leading to the central square, and were lying in wait, ready to attack. Concealed behind massive stone blocks and walls, Pizarro and his men watched in silence as the royal procession approached, oblivious of the deadly ambush awaiting them. Carried in a litter by eighty chanting noblemen and priests, and surrounded by hundreds of warriors and their commanders, Atahualpa looked like a god in his precious ceremonial cloak, heavy gold jewellery, and a magnificent headdress fashioned from exotic parrot feathers, which reflected the sunlight like a halo.

A veteran and cunning fighter, Pizarro knew the value of audacity and surprise. He also recognised the value of his reputation as a mysterious outsider from some faraway land, who commanded a small band of warriors armed with frightening weapons of supposedly supernatural powers that sounded like thunder and could kill from afar, and four-legged beasts that could paralyse an army of brave Inca foot soldiers and spread panic and fear.

As soon as the litter reached the centre of the plaza, Pizarro lifted his hand and gave the signal to attack. Several small cannons opened fire from all sides, causing mayhem, horror and death in the crowded square full of terrified warriors who couldn't see their attackers. Within minutes, hundreds lay dead or dying on top of one another, their maimed, blood-soaked bodies trapping the uninjured and making it almost impossible to fight back or escape. Their work done, the cannons fell silent, making way for the next wave of terror: the cavalry charge.

The Inca had never seen horses. They watched in awe as twenty-eight horses with heavily armed riders came charging at them from all sides, like an army of evil spirits carving trenches of destruction through the petrified crowd trying in vain to get out of their way.

Shouting orders, his sword drawn, Pizarro hacked his way unopposed through the confused multitude towards the litter. Paralysed by fear and confusion, the Inca warriors threw down their weapons and then fled in terror towards Pizarro's men waiting for them in the laneways with loaded arquebuses. The terrified nobles carrying the litter were cut down. Many had their hands or arms hacked off before the litter crashed to the ground and Atahualpa was captured by a jubilant Pizarro.

Mounting a surprise attack on Atahualpa and his army against all odds and taking the Inca king prisoner, was a stroke of genius. Audacity and courage fuelled by desperation had carried the day in a way no-one could have imagined. A small band of one hundred and eighty desperate men had managed to defeat an army of thousands, and in doing so had toppled a mighty empire and changed the course of history not only in the Americas, but in Europe as well. It marked the beginning of the famous treasure fleets crossing the Atlantic, with unimaginable wealth flowing into Spain, and ushered in a new era of international commerce on an unprecedented scale.

But everything has a dark side as well. Fabulous riches floating on the high seas presented extraordinary opportunities for the ruthless and greedy, eager to make a quick fortune. Enter the Golden Age of Piracy, a period between the 1650s and 1730s that gave rise to legends and buccaneers such as Pierre Le Grand, who made his mark by attacking galleons full of plundered treasure returning to Spain, and Henry Morgan, who audaciously raided Spanish ships and burned down Panama City. He was to be executed in England, but instead of a date with the noose he was knighted and made governor of Jamaica. And then there was Amaro Pargo, the legendary, womanising corsair who operated mainly in the Caribbean and gave rise to romantic fireside stories of piracy and fabulous treasure hidden in distant island caves. He is buried in San Cristóbal de La Laguna. Engraved on the headstone marking his grave is a skull with a winking eye and two crossbones.

In a desperate attempt to save himself, Atahualpa made Pizarro an offer he couldn't refuse. Well aware of the terrifying stranger's obsession with gold, Atahualpa promised to fill the chamber in which he was being held prisoner with gold in exchange for his freedom. Stunned by the enormity of the offer and its far-reaching implications, Pizarro agreed, and messengers were sent out by Atahualpa into every corner of the empire with orders to begin to assemble the ransom treasure consisting of countless tonnes of gold.

Cajamarca: 26 July 1533

During the weeks and months that followed, only small amounts of gold and silver began to arrive, and it became clear that it would take a very long time to fill the chamber as promised by Atahualpa, if at all. Pizarro and his men became increasingly suspicious and fearful that instead of collecting gold, Atahualpa was assembling a huge army to crush them and set him free.

Tired of waiting and aware of the impatience of his men, who became more restless and surlier by the day, Pizarro decided to act. Instead of waiting any longer for promised gold that may never arrive, he decided to execute Atahualpa as a sign of strength, thereby foiling any attempt to mount an attack to free him. Atahualpa was sentenced to death during a hastily arranged trial based on false charges, and then garrotted in public.

When the Inca priests approached Pizarro after this brutal and humiliating execution, to claim their dead king's body for burial, Pizarro noticed a magnificent gold mask being carried by Villaq Umm, the high priest, at the head of a solemn procession crossing the plaza. The heavy gold mask – a precious, ancient ceremonial object with magical powers – would protect the king from evil spirits and provide safe passage into the afterlife.

Mesmerised by the stunning beauty of the strange, priceless mask reflecting the setting sun like a promise of eternal life, Pizarro walked up to the priest and ordered one of his men to seize the mask, take it back to his quarters and add it to the meagre booty of gold and silver he had collected since taking Atahualpa prisoner.

Villaq Umm recoiled in horror and began to plead with Pizarro to reconsider. The interpreter used by Pizarro was only able to provide a very limited translation of the priest's lamentations, but it became clear that removing the mask and thereby depriving the king of his entry into the afterlife was not only a heinous crime, but would also result in a curse so powerful and severe that it would last for generations and bring untold misery and death to all affected.

Pizarro laughed and dismissed the priest kneeling at his feet, and was about to turn away when the priest took hold of a corner of his cloak in a last, desperate attempt to stop the evil deed. Annoyed, Pizarro was aware that all eyes in the crowded plaza were upon him, watching his every move. Pizarro realised a show of strength was needed to keep the angry crowd in check. He pulled his razor-sharp dagger from his belt, bent down and cut the priest's throat. Then he calmly turned around and followed the soldier carrying the mask, back to his quarters.

Had Pizarro waited just a little bit longer, things may have turned out differently. Unbeknown to Pizarro, just as Atahualpa was being executed, Ruminahui – the legendary Inca general – was approaching Cajamarca with the king's ransom treasure consisting of huge amounts of gold, being hauled up the mountains by hundreds of porters.

Upon hearing of Atahualpa's murder, Ruminahui ordered the porters to turn around and carry the treasure east to a remote, uninhabited part of the empire, beyond the reach of the treacherous invaders who had killed his king, and hide it. Rumours of a treasure hidden deep in the Llanganates Mountains soon began to circulate and reached the Spaniards, who mounted a desperate campaign to recover it.

The avaricious conquistadors and the forces of Ruminahui eventually met in the Battle of Mount Chimborazo. Ruminahui was defeated and captured. During a horrendous torture session that lasted days and would have made the Inquisitors look like amateurs, a defiant Ruminahui remained silent and refused to reveal the location of the treasure. The brave and loyal general took that information to his grave, adding further mystery to the already legendary treasure of the Llanganates that would haunt treasure hunters for centuries to come.

A few years later, on 26 June 1541, twenty heavily armed assassins – supporters of a rival conquistador, Diego de Almagro – stormed Pizarro's palace in Lima. Pizarro put up a valiant fight but was eventually overpowered and stabbed several times in the throat. Just before he died, he painted a cross in his own blood on the floor and asked for Christ's forgiveness. All his worldly goods and possessions were left to the Church, including the golden burial mask that had deprived a humiliated king entry into the afterlife. The curse of the golden mask had claimed its first victim.

After Pizarro's death, Almagro was appointed the new governor of Peru, a position he was able to enjoy for only a short time. He was executed the following year, after suffering a crushing defeat in the battle of Chupas.

1

Fleury-Mérogis Prison, Paris: 12 September 2018

Lying on a hard, narrow bunk in his tiny, claustrophobic cell, Maurice Landru was turning restlessly in his sleep. Covered in sweat and moaning, he clutched the top of the crumpled blanket with both hands to his chest like a drowning man holding onto a lifeline. Then something banished the bad dream that had tortured his feverish brain: an elusive flash of inspiration he had been desperately searching for since his conviction for murder five years earlier. It was the missing piece of a cruel puzzle that had haunted him for years, and almost sent him mad.

Instantly awake, Landru opened his eyes and sat up with a jolt. *Mon Dieu, that's it!* he thought and reached for the little notebook and pen he always kept under the mattress, to record fleeting ideas before they evaporated into the mind-numbing routine of prison life. Holding it with shaking hands, he got up, turned on the light, and wrote down two letters. Then he reached for Jack's book *The Lost Symphony*, which had just been released, and reread the passage he had underlined the night before. A broad smile spread across his face as he read the passage over and over. *No doubt about it, it works!*

Landru sat down on the bunk and reached for a bundle of papers on the little desk attached to the wall next to the toilet bowl. The loose, creased pages were covered in strange diagrams, symbols and calculations, with extensive notes in his spidery handwriting scribbled in the margins. The pages contained the work that had kept him sane all these years, and had nourished the flame of hope burning in his chest like an eternal fire that was keeping him alive.

Landru was certain he had just found what he had so desperately been looking for since his conviction, which could prove his innocence and set him free. Feeling elated, he brushed the notes and newspaper clippings aside, reached for a blank page, and began to write a letter to his lawyer.

2

Kuragin chateau: 24 September

Jack and Countess Kuragin sat in the conservatory overlooking the park-like grounds and the lily pond at the back of the chateau. Surrounded by potted palms and exotic plants, it was Jack's favourite place and where he did most of his writing when he was staying with the countess. The chateau just outside Paris had become his second home ever since he had found Anna, the countess's daughter, in outback Australia eight years earlier, and returned her to her pining mother's waiting arms.

For an intrepid, restless adventure junkie like Jack, who travelled most of the year, it was not only the place where he felt most comfortable and relaxed, surrounded by the warmth of a family he didn't have, but also a refuge from the harsh realities of life that seemed to follow him wherever he went. The chateau was a sanctuary where he could heal his emotional bruises, surrounded by the love of Countess Kuragin's family, who had welcomed him into their lives as one of their own. It was good-karma payback for a selfless act of extraordinary courage that had saved Anna's life and that of her baby son, earning him the friendship and gratitude of the countess.

'What now?' asked the countess, sipping her second cup of strong coffee, a teasing glint in her eyes.

'What do you mean?' said Jack, sitting back in his comfortable wicker chair.

'Well, you've just released your book about your Russian adventures, we've been to St Petersburg to return the famous Fabergé Easter egg to where it belongs, you've saved Professor Stolzfus – one of the great geniuses of our time – and you found your mother in Colombia. Have I left something out?'

'No, that's about it.'

'Then surely you see what I mean?'

17

Jack nodded. 'I was thinking of taking some time out. Finishing a book is always draining. As you know, writing is a struggle for me. I have to wrestle with myself to put words on a page. I'm much better out in the open, doing stuff.'

'Ah, is that what it is?'

'I haven't been back to Australia for a while now; this would be a good time to go to the Kimberley and pay my Aboriginal friends in Broome a visit, before the cyclone season begins.'

'Good idea. When are you leaving?'

'Soon.'

'Before another adventure you cannot resist finds you, and you have to drop everything?' teased the countess, smiling.

'Something like that. You know me too well.'

'You don't say. More coffee?'

'Yes, please.'

'It may already be too late for that,' interjected Claude Dupree, walking into the room. He had overheard the countess's remark. 'Cook told me I would find you here.'

Dupree, a retired French police officer, lived in the Gatekeeper's Cottage next to the chateau. He had become another member of the extended Kuragin family after a fire the year before had burned his home to the ground, killing his son. Dupree was severely burned and found himself with nowhere to live. The countess had offered the cottage without hesitation. Shortly after that, Dupree and Jack had collaborated in solving a notorious cold case concerning *Le Fantôme*, a cat burglar, and the Black Widow, a shady Paris art dealer and fence, which reached back to Dupree's detective days in the Paris Police Prefecture. These were all subjects explored in Jack's latest book – *The Lost Symphony* – which had become an overnight bestseller.

'Pull up a chair,' said Jack. 'Croissant?'

'Yes, please.'

Jack handed Dupree a plate and a cup of coffee. 'What do you mean, it may already be too late?'

'I just had a call from Lapointe ...'

Detective Chief Superintendent Marcel Lapointe was a senior commissionaire of the Paris Brigade Criminelle and one of Dupree's former junior colleagues and protégées. He reminded Jack of *Maigret*, the legendary fictitious Paris detective who featured in more than seventy novels by Georges Simenon. Lapointe, Dupree and Jack had collaborated in solving the sensational Ritz murder case the year before by linking it to the Black Widow, who had perished in dramatic circumstances in a deliberately lit house fire just before Lapointe could make an arrest.

'Oh, no!' said the countess.

'What was the call about?' asked Jack.

'An old case of ours ...'

'What kind of case?'

'The Death Mask Murders,' replied Dupree, lowering his voice as if just the mention of the controversial subject could bring bad luck and cause disaster.

'Never heard of it.'

'Not surprising; it was some time ago. Lapointe and I worked on it for years.'

'And this is relevant because?' said Jack.

Dupree took a sip of hot coffee and sat back. 'I'll tell you.'

'Here we go,' said the countess. 'I knew it. The Kimberley trip may have to wait a little longer.'

'Don't jinx it,' said Jack. 'Let's hear what Claude has to say.'

'The Death Mask Murders was without doubt one of the most complicated and challenging cases of my entire career,' began Dupree, 'and the most controversial. I still wake up at night from time to time, haunted by the memories and the unanswered questions.'

'In what way?' asked Jack.

'To begin with, we were dealing with a serial killer of a very different kind: sophisticated, clever, unpredictable, resourceful, and totally unique. None of the usual characteristics or patterns of behaviour applied. This was a dangerous criminal, out of the ordinary. Someone in a class of his own. No women involved, not even a hint of a sexual motive of any kind, only a bizarre signature. In fact, the absence of motive was one of our main problems in solving the cases. Random murders without obvious motive or connections are always a nightmare for the police. For years, the investigation was lost at sea without a rudder, in the middle of a media storm that pursued us relentlessly, screaming for answers and results. The pressure was enormous.'

'What kind of signature?' asked the countess.

'A death mask made of some kind of plaster of Paris was left at the scene of each crime.'

'Seriously?' said Jack. 'How on earth was that done?'

Dupree nodded. 'Good question. The killer prepared a death mask of the victim immediately after the murder before rigor mortis set in. He then removed the body, but left the mask behind. This must have been quite a process, but the killer knew what he was doing and was very good at it. Meticulous and resourceful.'

'How gruesome.'

'Perhaps, but in many ways he was quite an artist because the masks were perfect; expertly done. Quite beautiful and moving, in fact. A perfect replica of a face just after death. By the time we arrived at the scene, all we found was the mask and nothing else of importance we could use. The killer was fastidious in "cleaning up". He left no clues behind. Just the mask. It was like a game. He was playing with us, teasing us, throwing us a challenge. None of the bodies have ever been found except for the last one. We caught the killer in the act, so to speak. He was preparing the death mask as we arrested him. And one more thing: all the victims were killed in the same way.'

'How?' asked Jack.

'Garrotted. With piano wire.'

'How do you know this?'

'The death mask included the upper part of the neck as well and clearly showed where the wire had cut into the flesh. It even contained a piece of piano wire, obviously to tell us exactly how the victim was killed. It was like a signature.'

'How bizarre.'

'Oh yes. Everything about these cases is quite bizarre.'

'How many victims were there?'

'Three that we know of.'

'*Three?* There could have been more?' said Jack.

'Absolutely. We always suspected there were more. It was one of our most perplexing and difficult cases. All victims appeared to have been chosen at random – at least that was the thinking at the time – without any apparent links or connection to one another. That's why it took us years to catch the killer. We used a well-known profiler to help us, and even turned to a famous psychic the police had used before for assistance. That's how desperate we were.'

'Was this helpful?' asked Jack.

'Difficult to say.'

'Was the killer convicted of the other murders?'

'No, you put your finger right on it. Only the last one. And that's one of the main problems here. His name was Maurice Landru. We had no evidence to link him to the other crimes, except for the signature mask. And that was merely circumstantial, and certainly not enough without further compelling evidence. Especially without the bodies. What we needed was a confession, but Landru certainly wasn't the kind of man to confess to anything. On the contrary, he denied everything – even the killing of the last victim, despite all the evidence – and claimed that he had been framed.'

'Framed by whom?'

'The real killer, but he had no proof or leads of any kind to back this up. We dismissed this as fantasy, a fabrication of a desperate man, and we didn't take it seriously at the time. But now, after all these years?'

'What are you getting at?' said Jack, who had noticed a haunted expression on Dupree's face.

'I'm no longer that sure ...'

'That's quite something coming from someone like you,' said the countess.

Dupree didn't reply.

'Where's Landru now?' asked Jack, changing direction.

'Serving a life sentence in the Fleury-Mérogis Prison right here in Paris. There's a lot more about this case that is fascinating, and troubling.'

'Troubling?' said Jack. 'In what way? Apart from the fact that at least two bodies are still out there, their murders unsolved, I suppose.'

'I'll tell you another time.'

'Then, why are you telling us all this right now?' said the countess. 'You haven't told us what Lapointe's call was about.'

'Landru's lawyer contacted the Prefect of Police, the big man in charge of the Prefecture here in Paris.'

'What about?' asked Jack.

'New information, and a request. That's why the Prefect contacted Lapointe, who had worked on the case for years and knows the facts like no other. He was the one who arrested Landru and had him convicted.'

'What kind of information?' asked Jack.

'It's complicated,' said Dupree, sidestepping the question.

'And Lapointe called you this morning about this?' interjected the countess. '*Why?*'

'To be more specific, he called me about the request.'

Jack could feel the fine hairs on the back of his neck beginning to tingle. It was a familiar premonition that rarely let him down, and usually happened when a new adventure or challenge came hurtling towards him. *I have a bad feeling about this*, he thought. 'How intriguing,' he said. 'What kind of request?'

'The information and the request are linked.'

'Linked? In what way?'

'Landru asked for permission to meet someone, face to face.'

'How weird. Why?'

'He will only disclose this new information to the person he would like to meet.'

'Did he say who that was?'

'Yes.'

'Who?' asked Jack quietly, feeling his stomach begin to churn with trepidation and excitement.

'*You.*'

'What did I tell you? Here goes the Kimberley trip,' said the countess, shaking her head.

'Seriously?' said Jack, looking dumbfounded. 'This is nonsense, surely. I don't know anything about the man, or these cases you just told us about. And he wants to meet *me?* Are you sure? Why?'

'That's what we would like to find out. With your help, of course,' added Dupree, smiling, well aware that Jack wouldn't be able to refuse.

3

Gatekeeper's Cottage: 26 September

Once Jack got his head around the baffling Landru request and its potential implications, he had reluctantly agreed to meet the notorious killer, but only if access to all the police and prosecution files would be made available to him. He wanted to find out as much as possible about the Death Mask Murders and Landru's conviction before visiting him in prison.

A grateful Lapointe had personally delivered all the material within twenty-four hours, and Jack and Dupree had locked themselves away in the Gatekeeper's Cottage to trawl through the hundreds of pages to familiarise themselves with all the facts and fascinating aspects of the case.

'Well, what do you think?' said Dupree and poured Jack another Scotch. It was two in the morning and they had worked for more than ten hours straight, sustained by snacks and cheese platters delivered by the countess.

Jack rubbed his aching neck and reached for his glass. 'This case is unbelievable,' he said and held up a bundle of papers. 'More questions than answers, that's for sure.' It was a report by Professor Francesca Bartolli, an eminent forensic psychologist and well-known freelance criminal profiler who had worked on many infamous cases throughout Europe over the years, and had a reputation for being one of the best in her field.

'Ah, I thought you would home in on that,' said Dupree. 'That report has troubled me too over the years.'

'You must admit, looking at all the evidence in this case objectively – now from a distance – it does raise some serious issues and doubts, doesn't it?'

'It does,' conceded Dupree. 'But the pressure to convict was incredible at the time and, as is unfortunately so often the case, this can override objectivity and sound judgement.'

'Then let me ask you this: is it conceivable that the wrong man was convicted here?'

Dupree took his time before answering. 'While the evidence was rather overwhelming, it was perhaps a little too pat; too perfect and too convenient, if you know what I mean. Rarely seen in cases of this kind, which are usually quite messy and confusing, with numerous blind alleys and false leads and only the occasional evidence gem. However, everything here pointed clearly to Landru and this was, of course, seized upon by the police and the prosecutor at the time, desperate for results. After all, the accused was caught in the act, red-handed. Case closed.'

'I take this as a yes, then?'

Dupree shrugged.

'Especially in light of Professor Bartolli's report. She raised some serious concerns here that appear to have been completely ignored,' said Jack and pointed to the report on the table.

'She did.'

'Is she still around? Active?'

'She is.'

'Where?'

'In Rome.'

'I would like to meet her if possible. Before I speak to Landru.'

Dupree smiled. 'I was expecting something like that. But I have to warn you, she's quite formidable, as I remember.'

'Are you trying to scare me?'

'Not at all. Just a little warning.'

'You think she might try to profile me?'

'Now, there's a thought,' said Dupree, smiling. 'Unfortunately, she only does criminals, not incorrigible rascals. I'll talk to Lapointe and arrange it.'

'Good. I think this could be really important.'

'According to the prosecutor in charge of the case, the report was an inconvenient distraction, that's all,' said Dupree. 'He ignored it. But then, there was something else. Something totally unexpected ...'

'What?'

'You won't find it in these files because it happened a year or so after Landru's conviction. In fact, it happened only a few years ago, in 2014 when La Santé prison was closed for renovations and all the inmates were moved to other prisons.'

'I thought Landru was in the Fleury-Mérogis Prison?'

'He is now, but he was in La Santé after his conviction until the prison closed.'

'That infamous prison where Carlos the Jackal served time, and Michel Vaujour escaped by helicopter?'

'That's the one. Landru was held in the special VIP area for "personalities".'

'You don't say. A VIP area glamourising notorious inmates?'

'The media couldn't get enough of it. Visitors and cameras were actually allowed into the prison for a while after it was closed, and a curious public was given access to the inside of the empty and quite dilapidated prison that had seen so much: the dregs of society, the worst offenders, and many executions.' Dupree took a sip of Scotch.

'During the war,' he continued, 'nine political prisoners were executed by guillotine, and nine by firing squad in one single day: thirty April 1944. The last execution at the prison was a double beheading by guillotine in 1972. Quite gruesome.'

'Charming place.'

'It all happened just after the prison was closed.'

'What happened?'

'One of the obvious attractions was Landru's cell. A visitor left something behind for Landru. Anonymously, of course.'

'What?'

'An envelope addressed to Landru was left on his bunk. A reporter visiting the prison found it and took it back to his paper.'

'What was in it?'

'Something curious and quite sensational.'

'Are you dragging this out intentionally because you want to kill me with suspense?'

Dupree laughed. 'Nothing like that. I can't afford to lose you now, before we go and meet Landru. Lapointe and the Prefect would never forgive me. So you see, you are quite safe for the time being—'

'Then get on with it, for Christ's sake!'

'A handwritten note addressed to Landru, and a four-hundred-character cipher.'

'A *cipher* you say? How odd. Do we know what that was about?'

'Instead of handing the letter to prison authorities, as should have been done, the paper published the note *and* the cipher, which as you can imagine caused quite a stir and became a sensation. In fact, the paper referred to it as the Death Mask Cipher, and offered a huge reward to anyone who could crack the code. As you can imagine, the authorities weren't thrilled about this. It reopened a dreadful case and led to all kinds of questions and speculation. It put the spotlight once again on the two unsolved Death Mask Murder cases. Very embarrassing for the police.'

'Extraordinary. You said there was a note addressed to Landru as well; do you know what it said?'

'There was. All it said was something like this: "*All the answers you are looking for are right here*".'

'Fascinating.'

'It was more than that. Landru's lawyers demanded the case be reopened in light of this new information. Needless to say, the authorities would have none of this and dismissed the entire matter as a hoax, but it wouldn't go away. The paper fuelled the fire with the reward, and several prominent mathematicians and cryptologists joined forces to crack the code. The paper reported regularly on their progress and so kept the story alive for a long time and in the public domain.'

'And? Was it ever cracked?'

'No. Not even a supercomputer in the US, nor ingenious programs designed by professional cryptologists working for the FBI could come up with answers. Eventually, the public lost interest and the story died down.'

'Is that it?' asked Jack, suspecting there was more.

'Yes, until now.'

'What do you mean?'

'It's about that new information Landru has raised in his letter.'

'What kind of information?'

'Well, it's to do with this cipher, you see,' said Dupree, looking quite sheepish.

'Why didn't you mention this before?'

'I wanted to keep something up my sleeve in case you didn't want to become involved ...'

'I see. Isn't that a little devious? A few more juicy titbits to jolly me along if needed, and tempt the curious writer in me; is that it?'

'Another Scotch?' said Dupree, reaching for the bottle in the hope of deflecting the warranted rebuke.

'Did Landru say anything more specific about the cipher?'

'Yes,' said Dupree quietly as he refilled Jack's glass.

'What?'

'He claims to have cracked it and said that you helped him do it ... Cheers!'

4

Rome: 28 September

Jack crossed the Piazza della Minerva in front of his hotel next to the Pantheon, stopped briefly at Bernini's Elephant and Obelisk – one of his favourite statues in Rome – and then turned into a small side street leading to Armando al Pantheon, a Roman institution popular with locals, serving traditional Roman and Lazio fare. The reason Jack had chosen this small, intimate family restaurant for his meeting with Professor Bartolli was a comment made by Lapointe after he had arranged the meeting: 'Remember, like all good Italians, Professor Bartolli loves to eat. Make sure you take her to a nice restaurant. I told her all about you.'

As soon as Jack stepped into the crowded, wood-panelled room and was shown to his table, he felt instantly at ease. Run by the Gargioli family since the sixties, the restaurant radiated wellbeing and Roman charm, and the mouth-watering cooking aroma drifting out of the kitchen promised outstanding food for which the establishment was well known. Jack could understand why reservations had to be made weeks in advance to get a table.

Jack ordered some olives and a bottle of 2007 Illuminati Ilico Riserva Montepulicano d'Abruzzo, which he hoped his guest would enjoy, and then sat back soaking up the bustling, rustic atmosphere. He had almost finished his second glass of wine when Professor Bartolli walked in and looked around. Jack recognised her at once from the photos on her website and held up his hand to attract her attention.

Carrying a battered violin case under her arm and looking somewhat flustered in her tight-fitting leather jacket – her long, curly dark-blonde hair a little dishevelled – Bartolli didn't quite fit the image Jack had formed in his mind of the sophisticated criminal psychologist with a fearsome reputation, whose court appearances were legendary and performances under cross-examination formidable, instilling fear in those brave enough to question her opinions and findings.

'I am so sorry for being late,' said Bartolli, shaking Jack's hand, 'but despite my best efforts to leave the rehearsal before we finished, I was unable to do so. I play in a small chamber orchestra.' Bartolli bent down and pushed the violin case under the table, as there was nowhere else to put it. 'But the conductor would have none of it. "How would Vivaldi feel," he said, "if suddenly a number of key phrases in the concerto went missing?" I had nowhere to go after that. That's why I'm late, sorry. The last Friday of the month is practice night, only to be missed at the risk of being pilloried or, God forbid, *expelled*,' Bartolli prattled on. 'But Lapointe insisted we had to meet tonight. He said it was urgent. So, here I am.'

'You are a musician as well?' said Jack, trying hard to look serious as he watched the fascinating woman take off her jacket and scarf, tie back her hair and sit down. Tall and slim, in her early forties, with a prominent Roman nose and wide-set green eyes that didn't seem to stop smiling, she had an aristocratic look that reminded Jack of a painting of Lucrezia Borgia by Bartolomeo Veneto. He reached for the bottle and poured some wine into her glass. 'Looks like you could do with some wine.'

'Is it that obvious?' asked Bartolli.

'It is,' replied Jack, 'but no-one's looking.' They both burst out laughing. 'Salute!'

'Nice wine,' said Bartolli, pointing to the bottle. 'A 2007 Illuminati Ilico; good choice.'

'You like it?'

'What's not to like? Did you choose it because of the name?'

'Illuminati, you mean? The Bavarian secret society founded in 1776 to oppose superstition, curb religious influence over public life and abuses of power? No, I chose it because I was hoping you would like it. It's one of my Italian favourites.'

Bartolli looked at Jack, impressed. There was more to this guy than his good looks, reputation, and all the wild stuff about him on the internet suggest, she thought, and gave Jack her best smile. Instead of an evening she had viewed as a nuisance, she was beginning to relax. 'You did well; I love it. Shall we order? I'm starving.'

'Good idea. Discussing serial killers and controversial convictions on an empty stomach is never a good idea, especially after a demanding concert rehearsal,' teased Jack.

'You are absolutely right.' Bartolli opened a small leather handbag that had seen better days, took out a pair of glasses and put them on. Then she picked up the menu and began to study it with avid concentration, the old-fashioned, steel-rimmed glasses giving her an endearingly studious look that was somehow at odds with her casual, almost bohemian manner and appearance.

'I can strongly recommend some tomatoes with burrata to start, with some crusty bread, of course, followed by cacio e pepe. Then vitella arrosto con patate, perhaps? Do you like veal?' she asked.

'I understand it's a speciality of the house.'

'It is. You had a peek at the menu, no?'

Jack shrugged. 'Why don't you order for both of us? I've done the wine; it's your turn,' he said and closed his menu.

'Trusting someone you've just met with such an important decision? Is that wise?' said Bartolli, raising an eyebrow and clearly enjoying herself.

'I'm used to living dangerously.'

'I've heard. The internet is full of interesting stories about you.'

Jack waved dismissively. 'Exaggerations. You can't believe all that stuff.'

'I don't know. I heard some of the stories from Lapointe and Dupree, and I've found them both to be very reliable in the past. And I read your book *Professor K: The Final Quest* last night. Dupree suggested I should do that before I met you.'

'Ah. My Italian adventure two years ago,' said Jack. It was his turn to look impressed. 'You found time to read it?'

Bartolli rolled her eyes. 'It wasn't easy, I tell you. I live in controlled chaos with two teenage daughters, my mother – who rules us all with an iron fist – and a dog, Paulo. He's the only male in the household, and he knows it. I live in Trastevere, in an apartment above a busy market square. Paulo spends most of his day visiting the old codgers in the cafes, and the stallholders, who give him tasty morsels. He comes home at six and goes to sleep, just like my father used to do, after he was shot and had to retire from the Carabinieri.'

'He was a policeman?'

'Yes, a very good one. And before you ask, yes, he had a great influence on me and was one of the main reasons I studied criminal psychology.'

Jack nodded but didn't comment.

'My daughters are out most nights,' continued Bartolli. 'Driving the local boys crazy. You see, reading a big book like yours isn't easy in this environment, but I must say I did enjoy it, especially the parts about cooking and the pope. I read a lot about that in the papers at the time.'

'I can imagine.'

'I remember we all watched Lorenza da Baggio win that nail-biting *Top Chef Europe* final in Florence. It was amazing.'

'She's an extraordinary young woman. Married now, to Tristan Te Papatahi.'

'The other hero in the book. The one with the psychic powers?'

'Yes. Tristan can hear the whisper of angels and glimpse eternity.'

'What a wonderful thought. Do you believe in psychic powers?' asked Bartolli, watching Jack carefully.

'I don't like generalisations, but I do believe in what I see, and what I experience firsthand. I have known Tristan for more than eight years now. He was fourteen when we first met, confined to a wheelchair. Incapacitated, a vegetable. He spent several years in a coma after an accident, before he suddenly came out of it. His mother was a Māori elder. She too was a psychic, but his powers are stronger.'

'How fascinating.'

'Since then, I've seen him do some extraordinary things I cannot explain rationally.'

'You are close?'

'Yes, we are, but since his wedding a year ago, right here in Rome, actually, we don't see that much of each other anymore. Married life has taken over. He lives in Venice now, in the Palazzo da Baggio, which they run as a boutique hotel. Very popular—'

'Lorenza has a Michelin star restaurant there,' interjected Bartolli, becoming excited, 'Osman's Kitchen. I would kill for a meal there.'

Jack smiled. 'That could be arranged, you know,' he said quietly.

'They were married here in Rome, you say?' said Bartolli, changing direction.

'Yes, in the Sistine Chapel, by the pope himself,' said Jack casually, and refilled their glasses.

'You can't be serious!'

'But I am. The wedding had to be held early in the morning before the Sistine Chapel was opened for tourists. A small affair. Family only. They tied the knot right under Michelangelo's *Last Judgment*, with the pope's blessing. It was a thank-you gesture by a grateful pontiff for what Lorenza had done for him. In a way, she saved his life.'

'You *are* serious! Of course, the cooking in the Vatican, the Ottoman meal with its extraordinary medicinal properties. We read all about it. Incredible!'

'Yes, Hunkar Begendi.'

'The papers were full of it. We all prayed for His Holiness.'

'And the prayers were obviously answered because the pope recovered.'

'What an exciting life you lead. There could be some substance to all those stories about you on the internet after all, don't you think?'

'Perhaps. Who knows?' said Jack, a sparkle in his eyes. 'Ah, saved by dinner. Here comes our meal now.'

After their plates had been cleared away and they were well into their second bottle of wine, Jack broached the subject that had brought him to Rome to meet Bartolli. 'I don't know how much Lapointe has told you ...'

'Not much,' said Bartolli.

'I see, then let me start from the beginning: it all revolves around a mystery.'

'What kind of mystery?'

'Why would a convicted killer serving a life sentence want to talk to someone he has never met or had any contact with, and ask the authorities to arrange a meeting because he has some important new information about the case that is somehow linked to that person?'

'And that person is you?'

'Yes. Can you help me with that? I've read your report.'

'I understand there was a letter?'

Jack reached into his pocket, pulled out a piece of paper and placed it on the table in front of Bartolli. 'Yes, this is it here.'

Bartolli put on her glasses again and read the short, handwritten note aloud: *'After several years of frustration and despair, I have finally cracked the Death Mask killer cipher code, bringing new, vital information to light that has a direct bearing on my conviction. I hereby request that an urgent meeting be arranged with Mr Jack Rogan, the Australian author who was recently involved in solving the Ritz murder case. I will only disclose the information contained in the cipher to Mr Rogan, because he has helped me crack the code, and will therefore understand the full meaning and implications of this new information.'*

Bartolli took off her glasses and sat back, lost in thought. 'How strange,' she said, looking at Jack.

'It is. You know about the cipher?'

'I do. It was in all the papers. That too was quite weird and unexpected at the time, but to me it made perfect sense.'

'How so?'

'Because I always believed that the real killer wasn't Landru, but someone else. The sudden appearance of the cipher, which in essence is a puzzle, some kind of challenge, further supported my earlier views.'

'What kind of views?'

'That Landru's profile just didn't fit the facts of the case. Far from it. There were too many anomalies. The evidence in the case that ultimately convicted Landru appeared contrived; very cleverly so, I admit, but manufactured, nevertheless. But the French authorities didn't want any part of this. The pressure was enormous, especially on Lapointe, who was the arresting officer in charge of the case. Dupree had retired years earlier, but he had been closely involved with the murders, which straddled many years. As far as the authorities were concerned they had their killer, and that was that. My concerns were all in my report, which as you obviously know was brushed aside and my involvement terminated. I was shut out and told to go away.'

'Dupree told me.'

'He was the only one who had similar doubts about the case. While he was no longer with the police at the time – at least not officially – Lapointe brought him in, nevertheless, to assist with the investigation.'

'What do you make of this cipher? Do you think it's a hoax, or something more? Something relevant to the case, perhaps, as Landru seems to suggest?'

'Until we find out more it's difficult to say, but if you ask my opinion, I would be very surprised if it wasn't genuine.'

'Please, let me get this straight,' said Jack, looking intently at Bartolli. 'Landru isn't the killer in the Death Mask Murders case, but has somehow been framed by the real murderer. A year after Landru's conviction, the real killer leaves a mysterious cipher behind in Landru's cell with a note that suggests the cipher contains all the answers to the case. How am I doing so far?'

'Fine.'

'Why would the killer do this? Why revive the case by adding another chapter, or perhaps even risk exposure by calling Landru's conviction into question? I just don't get it.'

'That's a far more complicated question. Until we find out more about the cipher and what it says, it isn't possible to be analysing this constructively.'

'Fair enough.'

Jack reached for the bottle again and refilled Bartolli's glass. He knew the right moment had arrived.

'Would you be interested in becoming involved?' said Jack, asking the question that had been on his mind the whole evening.

'In what way?'

'Nothing to do with the authorities. Nothing formal. I would like to engage you personally, to help me solve this mystery and unravel this puzzle.'

'In my capacity as a …?'

'Professional profiler. I want to draw on your vast experience and your previous knowledge of the case.'

'Material for another book?'

'You see? That's why I want you involved. You've just met me and I'm an open book to you already.'

'I have to think about it. I would like to go over my old notes again first.'

'Understandable. I haven't given Lapointe my final answer yet, either.'

'What answer?'

'Whether I will meet with Landru. I wanted to talk to you first. And then there was one more thing.'

'What?'

'I want to track down the psychic who was consulted at the time and talk to him as well, before I give my final answer.'

Bartolli looked at Jack, surprised. 'Good idea. I can help you there.'

'You can?'

'Yes. The psychic you are talking about was one of the most extraordinary people involved in this investigation. In fact, as far as I was concerned he was the most fascinating aspect of the entire case.'

'In what way?'

'It's complicated. His name is Acrivos Papadoulis, a simple shepherd from Ithaca.'

'The home of the intrepid Ulysses?'

'Quite. I had come across him years before this case during my studies here in Rome. A most fascinating and unique man. Simple, pious, but with an extraordinary gift. One of our lecturers invited him to come to our tutorial and talk to us about his work. I've never forgotten the experience. It stayed with me ever since and taught me to always keep an open mind. And then I met him again, years later in the Death Mask Murder case.'

'What a coincidence.'

'Perhaps, or something more?'

'Destiny?'

Bartolli raised her eyebrows. 'I wouldn't have expected to hear this from you. But then again, it's all in your book.'

'You said you could help me here?' said Jack, trying to steer the conversation back to the most pressing question on his mind.

'Yes. I've kept in touch with Papadoulis over the years after the case. He's no longer doing this kind of work. In a way, he has withdrawn from the world of crime, but I know where you can find him.'

'You do? Where is he now?'

'He's a monk at Mount Athos in Greece.'

'Amazing. Do you think he would be prepared to see me?'

'Are you prepared to go there, just to talk to him?'

'Absolutely. The sooner the better.'

'I'll get in touch with him and let you know. It won't be easy, but I'll give it a go.'

Jack reached across the table and placed his hand on Bartolli's. 'Thank you. I really mean it.'

'This means a lot to you, doesn't it?'

'It does.'

'Why?'

Jack smiled at Bartolli. 'Destiny?' he ventured.

'Ah, that word again. What are you doing tomorrow?'

'Catching an early train to Venice.'

'Paying Tristan and Lorenza a visit?'

'Exactly. I haven't seen them for far too long.'

'Is that all?'

'What do you mean?'

'In some ways you *are* an open book, you know. At least to me. If Papadoulis should agree to a meeting, you will take Tristan along, right?'

Jack looked nonplussed. 'As you can obviously read my thoughts, you would also be aware just how grateful I am for—'

'Don't mention it. I had a fabulous evening, thank you. And I promise to let you know about becoming involved. Soon.'

Bartolli looked at her watch. 'Good heavens, is it that time already? I really must go! If I don't get home before my daughters' curfew, they will never let me forget it.'

'I understand. Do you have a car, or can I arrange a taxi for you?'

'No, thank you. But you can carry my violin case to my Vespa. It's parked just outside on the footpath. It's totally illegal, but everyone does it. I only hope no-one's pinched my helmet; this is Rome after all. I'll call you tomorrow.'

5

Venice: 29 September

Jack decided to catch the slower vaporetto rather than take a water taxi. Instead of calling Tristan to let him know he was coming, he had opted once again for surprise. This was typical Jack. After the four-hour early morning train ride from Rome, it felt good to take in the bustle of the Canal Grande, with all the excitement and usual tourist chaos on the busy waterways that were Venice. It also gave him some time to consider how best to approach the subject that had brought him to the floating city of canals. After last time, he had some misgivings about asking Tristan to accompany him to Mount Athos.

As the vaporetto approached the Rialto Bridge, his stop, Jack remembered his earlier visit that year. What had brought him to Venice on that occasion just a few months after Tristan and Lorenza's wedding in the Vatican, was Professor Stolzfus's dramatic abduction in London while attending the funeral of Steven Hawking in Westminster Abbey. What had followed was an extraordinary sequence of events that had taken Jack halfway around the globe and, but for Tristan's help, could have cost him his life.

However, it had also brought unexpected joy: in South America, Jack had found his long-lost mother whom he had been searching for in Africa. This had marked the beginning of a new, albeit somewhat unsettling chapter in his life. Suddenly, he was no longer alone. He had a family and a past to discover that he didn't know he had. For someone like Jack, this was a disconcerting realisation he was still trying to come to terms with.

As Jack stepped onto the familiar wharf, he realised that his visit would have its challenges. He was once again in Venice to try to enlist Tristan's help in solving a perplexing mystery. Unusual stories and challenges seemed to find Jack, not the other way around, and then drew him in, irresistibly, until he reached a point of no return.

Jack called it destiny; others called it the escapades of a hopeless adventure junkie hooked on adrenaline, who got high on exposure to extreme danger. The truth was most probably somewhere in between.

Jack was in two minds about approaching Tristan again so soon, and thereby intruding into his new life. He knew Tristan was restless, and Lorenza also knew this. But she also realised how much Jack meant to her husband and how much Tristan missed him. He was a different man when he was with Jack. Lorenza envied their closeness, but despite all that she was very fond of Jack and in no way resented him. As someone who loved Tristan deeply, she realised that Jack filled a need in him that she couldn't, and resisting it would be a grave mistake that could have dire consequences for their marriage. For that reason, she accepted their friendship and the fact that from time to time they needed to be together, because they had a special bond that ran very deep.

As soon as Jack walked into the elegant foyer of the sixteenth-century Palazzo da Baggio, with its magnificent paintings and tapestries that had been in the family for centuries, he remembered his last visit as he approached the reception desk. On that occasion, the haughty receptionist had given him the cold shoulder because she had no idea who he was; he didn't look like one of the well-heeled patrons who frequented the exclusive hotel. This time, however, she looked up and smiled as soon as she recognised Jack.

'Ah, the famous author returns. Don't worry, I won't make the same mistake again,' she said. 'Are they expecting you?'

'No.'

'I thought as much. Tristan has gone out, but Lorenza is in the kitchen. I'll tell her you're here.'

'No need. I'll tell her myself. I know the way.'

The receptionist shrugged. 'As you wish. A room with a view and a table for one, like last time?' she teased and gave Jack a coquettish look.

'Perhaps. But first let's see if I'm welcome.'

Hunched over a long marble kitchen bench running along the wall under the windows overlooking the canal, Lorenza had her nose in a cookbook and was furiously taking notes.

'Working on a new menu? Good. You can experiment on me. I'm starving!'

Lorenza looked up. 'Jack! What a wonderful surprise!' She walked over to Jack and gave him a kiss and a hug. 'It's so good to see you.'

Jack detected a hint of sadness in Lorenza and looked at her, concerned. 'Is something wrong?' he asked, sensing some disquiet and unease not only in her voice, but in her demeanour as well.

'You're just like Tristan. You pick up on moods and speak your mind.'

'Is that such a bad thing?'

'No. It's refreshing. Honesty is always refreshing. You're right. I'm worried about Tristan.'

'Why?'

'Later. What brings you here, unannounced as usual?'

Jack shrugged. 'You know what I'm like. I want to run something past Tristan.'

'Ah. As long as it isn't like last time. You said you wanted to borrow him for a few days, remember? And look what happened. He stayed away for weeks and both of you were almost—'

'I know.'

'Don't worry, Jack. You've come at a good time.'

'In what way?'

'Tristan is …'

'What about him?'

Lorenza looked at Jack, tears in her eyes. 'Unhappy,' she blurted.

Jack put his arms around Lorenza and held her tight. 'What makes you say that?'

'He's restless. He doesn't fit in here. This isn't him. This is my dream, not his. While we were renovating the place and setting up the restaurant, he was in his element. He loved it. But now …'

Jack gave Lorenza another hug, but didn't say anything. He knew this was a time to listen, not to talk.

'He and my father get on famously, but Papa's travelling now. He's rarely here. He still hasn't come to terms with losing Mama and my brother in what we now know wasn't an accident, but a Mafia hit—'

'Because your grandparents refused to cooperate with the Gambios in Florence with the property sale?' interjected Jack.

'Quite. I don't think he can get over that.'

'Understandable. It was quite a shock to find out what happened, and why.'

'Welcoming guests, playing the host, answering questions about his famous wife who people have come to see, it just isn't Tristan. You of all people must know that.'

Because Jack knew there was some truth to all this, he realised he had to choose his words carefully. 'Every marriage needs adjustment, especially a high-profile one like yours. Give it time. I know he loves you, that's what really matters here. Nothing else counts. I'm sure of it.'

'And I love *him*, more than I can express; that's why I so desperately want him to be happy.'

'We both want that.'

'I know. He's happy when he's with you. Surely you can see that.'

'I can. That doesn't mean he's unhappy with you.'

'I suppose not. It's just …'

'What?'

'He's a little lost right now. He was on such a high during the entire Stolzfus matter. He found it hard to adjust after that.'

'He wasn't the only one, I can tell you. I'll talk to him. Where is he?'

'He's working on a project.'

'What kind of project?'

'Because our guests always ask about our adventures, the abduction here in Venice and all the Mafia bits the papers wrote about, he decided to prepare a tour.'

'What kind of tour?'

'Well, since the release of your book about all this—'

'*Professor K: The Final Quest?*'

'Yes, there's been huge interest in the subject. Our guests want to visit all the places here in Venice mentioned in the book.'

'The Gallerie dell'Accademia, where you were abducted and Tristan attacked and left for dead under a bridge, and the Cimitero di San Michele where you were imprisoned in one of the crypts?'

'Yes, and quite a few more locations. And he wants to use his boat to ferry the tourists around and make it part of the tour.'

'The Riva Aquarama with the two-hundred-and-fifty horsepower Cadillac engines that James Bond would kill for? That should be a hit; great idea. And he has an arts degree from the Sorbonne. Could come in handy.'

'That's what I said. I hope it works and gives him some – how shall I put it? – purpose, I suppose.'

Jack nodded.

'I'll give him a call,' continued Lorenza. 'He'll be thrilled to see you. He's in St Mark's Square, working on the tour. He took the boat, so I can't drop you off.'

'No matter. I'll take the vaporetto and meet him at the wharf.'

'I won't tell him you're here. You can surprise him. I'll just tell him that someone wants to talk to him urgently and will meet him at the wharf.'

Jack smiled. 'He'll know as soon as you call him; watch.'

'All right, let's see.'

Lorenza reached for her phone and called Tristan.

'There's someone here who would like to talk to you urgently, darling. It's about what you—'

'*Jack!* He's here! I could feel it all morning,' interrupted Tristan, becoming excited. 'Right?'

Lorenza shrugged and looked at Jack.

As he whispered, 'I told you so,' Jack noticed a little smile creasing the corners of Lorenza's mouth.

Tristan could see Jack standing on the deck of the vaporetto, waving, as it approached the jetty. The melancholic mood that had taken hold of him over the past few days and had caused Lorenza such heartache, disappeared as soon as Tristan embraced Jack.

'I knew it!' said Tristan. 'I could feel it all morning.'

'You could feel what?' asked Jack. 'You look thin. Has Lorenza's cooking gone off?'

'No, of course not. I knew you would turn up today. And here you are. Come, let's have a coffee in your favourite place.'

'Caffé Florian?'

'Where else? Let's go.'

For Jack, the iconic Caffé Florian with its colourful history spanning three hundred years was the epitome of a Venetian meeting place. To see and be seen was the motto, and the justification for its astronomical prices.

'It's truly amazing to think that Goethe, Casanova, Charles Dickens and Lord Byron, to name but a few, sat here in the gallery outside just as we are doing right now, watching the pigeons and, no doubt, the girls parading past in St Mark's Square,' said Jack and pointed to a group of tourists taking photos.

'You are such a hopeless romantic,' said Tristan. 'What brings you here? Must be important. Let me guess ...'

Jack took a sip of his hot latte and looked expectantly at Tristan sitting opposite. 'All right. What do you think brought me here? You know, don't you?'

'Let's say I have a *feeling* about it, that's all; a hunch.'

'I've heard that often enough before, and I know just too well where those "hunches" of yours took us, and where we ended up.'

'All right. Let's see how close I am this time,' said Tristan, enjoying himself, and closed his eyes. 'I thought a lot about you during the last couple of days. You appeared even in my sleep. Once again, there was that aura.'

'What kind of aura?' asked Jack, a familiar sense of apprehension beginning to churn in his stomach.

Tristan took his time before replying. '*Danger*,' he said after a while. 'It's about a puzzle, isn't it?' he continued. 'And murder. Brutal murder.'

'What else can you see?'

'How can I explain this … I have these "flashes" of unrelated scenes. They are like little windows into the past. I've told you about this before. By themselves, they make no sense at all, but when you string them together, well, they actually tell a story.'

'Is that the case here?' asked Jack, leaning forward.

'I can't really say, but perhaps you can. There is this man sitting in what looks like some kind of cell. A tiny, crowded space full of papers. I can see barred windows, a heavy iron door, and something else …'

'What?'

'Something very strange. It looks like some kind of white face, motionless and rigid. A man's face without a body. The face is contorted, the eyes closed; scary. He looks dead. And wait, there's more … next to the face are some strange-looking symbols floating through what looks like fog.'

Jack reached into his pocket, pulled out a creased sheet of paper and put it on the marble table in front of Tristan. 'Like these here?' he asked.

Tristan opened his eyes and looked at the piece of paper. 'Yes, exactly like these,' he said, sounding surprised. 'What's this?'

'A cipher. It's at the heart of what I'm about to tell you. But before I do, what else can you see? This is important. Focus!'

'I can see gold. Lots of gold. Strange figurines, bracelets, jewellery. And all of it seems to be under water – on the ocean floor – because there are fish everywhere, and a bronze cannon like you see on pirate ships, and cannonballs covered in barnacles. Then I see men fighting. They are naked and have colourful feathers in their black hair. And wait, there's a huge sailing ship. Towering waves, lightning; a storm. And tall cliffs, men screaming, severed limbs, blood. The ship turns over, breaks apart and sinks into the waves …' Tristan opened his eyes and looked at Jack. 'That's quite something, don't you think?' he said.

'It is. Let's find out what it means. Interested?'

'You know me, Jack. Always.'

'Then come with me to meet a fascinating man who may be able to make sense of all this.'

'What man?'

'A monk.'

'Where?'

'Mount Athos.'

'Greece? Are you serious?'

'Absolutely.'

'If you clear it with Lorenza, I'm in.'

Jack smiled. 'Coward. I already have.'

'I know. Another coffee?'

6

Mount Athos, Greece: 1 October

Jack and Tristan stood on the outside deck of the small boat taking them to Dafni, the main port. It was early in the morning and Mount Athos, the legendary mountain dominating the peninsula, was shrouded in dense sea mist, adding to the mystery of this extraordinary place of spirituality and contemplation, with a monastic tradition reaching back twelve hundred years. Referred to by the monks as the 'Garden of Virgin Mary', Mount Athos with its twenty historical monasteries housing priceless collections of unique religious artefacts, books, and precious ancient manuscripts, was home to some two thousand monks devoted to study, spirituality, and a monastic life of piety, prayer and contemplation. As one of the largest monastery complexes in the world, it had no equal.

'You are very quiet,' said Jack. 'Penny for your thoughts?'

'It's this place,' said Tristan. 'Just look at that.' He pointed to a spectacular monastery complex melting out of the mist as they approached the tiny port of Pyrgos along the way.

'That's the Bulgarian Zograf Monastery. Impressive, isn't it?'

'How do you know this?'

'I've been here before.'

Tristan turned to face Jack. '*You have?* You never told me about that. When?'

'A few years ago. Just after I met you, and Will and I found Anna living with Aboriginal people in the outback, and we rescued her and her baby in the Kimberley—'

'And my mother died protecting Anna from that monster in the hospital in Broome,' interjected Tristan with sadness in his voice.

'Yes.'

'You came here, why?'

Jack took his time before replying. 'To find myself, I suppose. I was in bit of a mess after ...'

'Your friend Will fell to his death during Anna's spectacular rescue? Katerina told me all about it,' said Tristan and put his hand on Jack's arm in a gesture of friendship and reassurance. 'I know what that did to you, but what I didn't know was that you came here. For some kind of solace, no doubt.'

'Very perceptive of you, as usual.'

Tristan smiled but didn't reply.

'As you know,' continued Jack, 'only men are allowed here, and you need a permit to visit. The monks were very hospitable. They sensed my need and welcomed me. Took me in and looked after me.'

'In what way?'

'Apart from food and shelter?'

'Yes.'

'They looked after me spiritually and guided me until my wounds began to heal. They included me in their daily activities during my stay here. We went to church at two in the morning to pray, and stayed until six. Then we had a hearty breakfast – the food is outstanding here, the monks grow all their own stuff – and after that, we went to work in the fields until sundown.'

Tristan nodded. 'Can you feel it?' he said, holding up his hand.

'Feel what?'

'Difficult to put into words. Spirituality would be the closest. This place radiates a sense of peace, calm.'

'Or perhaps love?' ventured Jack.

Tristan was surprised. 'Yes, that's exactly what it is. You amaze me at times with—'

'Occasional insights? Not bad for an incorrigible rascal, you mean?'

'Something like that.'

'Will's death took a lot out of me, and then came that horror with your mother, and that showdown with the Wizard.'

'Dark times. The Wizard was the personification of evil. The cycle had to be broken, but that always comes at a cost. Someone had to pay.'

As Tristan was talking about something very painful and personal, Jack knew it was time to change the subject. 'Look. Here we are,' he said, as the boat approached the wharf at Dafni. Because it was the first boat of the day, there were only a few passengers on board. An elderly monk dressed in a simple black cassock approached Jack as soon as he stepped on shore, and introduced himself as Father Theophilos.

'Brother Acrivos is expecting you. I will take you to him,' he said. 'I will also show you to your quarters and be your guide while you are with us. We follow a strict protocol here. You will dine with me at the refectory of Pantokratoros. I will explain everything.'

'Thank you. I have been here before,' said Jack, 'and have benefited greatly from the hospitality in this remarkable place. And the guidance I received,' he added quietly.

Stroking his long grey beard, Father Theophilos looked thoughtfully at Jack and smiled. 'I hope that it will be the same this time. Brother Acrivos lives in a remote *skete* in Karoulia – a reclusive, pious community. All by himself in a cell on a cliff edge high above the sea. It's the most isolated part of Mount Athos.'

Father Theophilos paused, collecting his thoughts, a little unsure if he should continue. 'He has left monastic life behind and prefers to live as a hermit in complete isolation, far away from the distractions of everyday life here. He has been quite poorly lately; that's why he couldn't come himself and has asked me to take you to him. Access to his cell is quite difficult, as you will see. Come.'

The view from the clifftop was breathtaking. The morning mist had lifted, and the imposing mountain with its heavily wooded slopes reaching up to the summit some two thousand metres above sea level, inspired awe with its timeless beauty and majestic proportions pointing to heaven.

Jack looked down to the waves crashing against the rocks below. That's when he noticed three small lean-to-like dwellings wedged between crevices halfway down to the beach. They looked like swallows' nests clinging precariously to lofty rafters in a country barn. 'Is that where we are going?' he said and pointed to a narrow set of steep steps chiselled out of virgin rock.

'Yes, that's where Brother Acrivos lives,' said Father Theophilus. 'As you can see, the place is difficult to reach with all these ladders further down, and only a chain to hold onto for support. It's particularly precarious in the rain.'

'I can imagine.'

'That's why supplies are winched down in a large basket. Much safer that way, and faster. As long as you hold on to the chain, you will be fine,' said Father Theophilus. 'I'll go down first; come.'

Brother Acrivos was lying on a narrow wooden bed facing a window overlooking the sea. He propped himself up on his elbows and looked at his visitors. It was impossible to tell his age, but the grey streaks in his long hair and unkempt beard suggested a man well past sixty. Jack noticed that he was frightfully thin and the haunted look in his restless, feverish eyes reminded him of something he had seen before, especially during his days as a war correspondent in Afghanistan: approaching death.

'Ah, Mr Rogan and his young companion. Welcome to my humble lodgings,' said Brother Acrivos, his voice surprisingly strong for such a feeble-looking man. 'Forgive me for not getting up, but last night was particularly difficult for me. I'm on the end stretch, you see; cancer. Not long now …'

'I should go,' said Father Theophilos.

Brother Acrivos raised his right hand and pointed to Jack. 'Before you do, there's something you should know about Mr Rogan here, and his young friend.'

'Yes? What?'

'It was Mr Rogan who found Kazanskaya Bogomater and returned her to the Alexander Nevsky Cathedral in Yekaterinburg last year. We all saw it on TV, remember?'

Father Theophilos looked thunderstruck. 'Are you serious?'

'Absolutely. That's one of the reasons I've agreed to see him.'

Father Theophilos turned to Jack. 'It was *you* standing next to the pope and Patriarch Nicodemus in the Cathedral?'

Jack nodded.

'And it was you who carried the holy icon up to the altar, placed it on its pedestal and returned it to where it belongs?'

'Yes,' said Jack. 'That was me.'

Father Theophilos shook his head, unable to hide his surprise. 'That was history in the making. Would you mind if I introduced you during dinner at the refectory this evening? And perhaps you could say a few words about this to the monks? I know they would love to hear your story.'

'It would be my pleasure,' said Jack, always ready to oblige when storytelling was involved.

'You do know that we have a precious icon right here at Mount Athos?' said Brother Acrivos.

'Yes, the sacred eleventh-century icon of the Panagia,' replied Jack, 'known as the Axion Estin. As I understand it, the whole of Mount Athos is in fact dedicated to the Panagia.'

Brother Acrivos looked impressed. Few visitors knew that.

'Amazing,' said Father Theophilos and turned to leave.

'Before you go, there's something about the young man here you should know as well,' said Brother Acrivos.

Father Theophilos stopped and looked at Tristan. 'What?' he said.

'He can hear the whisper of angels and glimpse eternity,' whispered Brother Acrivos, 'just like me.'

Brother Acrivos's reputation as a psychic, who had worked with the police throughout Europe on high-profile criminal cases for years, was well known at Mount Athos. His psychic powers were questioned by many of the monks and viewed with scepticism, bordering on dismissive disdain. It was one of the main reasons he had withdrawn from monastic life and preferred to live in ascetic isolation.

'I don't think I'm quite ready for that just yet,' said Father Theophilos. With that, he took a bow. 'I will see you both this evening,' he said and stepped outside.

'A sceptic, as you can see,' said Brother Acrivos, smiling, and pointed to two chairs by the window. 'No matter, I'm used to it. Psychic powers are difficult to accept for monks here. I think they feel intimidated by them. They feel uneasy about things they don't understand and therefore threatens their faith. Yet, there's absolutely no need to feel threatened by these matters, isn't that right?'

Tristan nodded, watching the fascinating man on the bed in front of him with interest.

Taking a deep breath, Brother Acrivos turned to face Tristan. 'Francesca has told me a little about you. She said you have an extraordinary gift: psychic powers. Can you tell me about that?'

Tristan was a little taken aback by the unexpected question, and took his time before replying. 'Not everything around us can be explained in rational terms, my mother used to tell me. She was a Māori psychic just like her mother before her, living in New Zealand. What if psychic powers and insights are nothing more than a key to open a door to something that is perfectly natural, but hidden, and has always existed but not everyone has a key, or knows what to do with it?'

Brother Acrivos nodded, seemingly pleased with the explanation so far.

'What if,' said Jack, stepping in, 'all of us are part of a huge human memory bank, a repository of all of our experiences as a human race that can be tapped into by those who know how, and have the "gift"? While this may appear strange and far-fetched to some, why is this notion any stranger than, say, the recently discovered dark matter in our genome that appears to be a record of our entire evolution? Footprints, so to speak, left behind by nature for us to find and discover?'

'Very good. I was an illiterate shepherd boy on Ithaca, a small Ionian island with a turbulent history reaching back to ancient times,' said Brother Acrivos. 'According to Homer, it was the home of the mythical Odysseus. I discovered early on that I had the gift. My grandmother had it too, and taught me how to use it. It grew stronger as I grew older, and then came a day that changed my life: I helped solve a murder case on the island, and it all went from there.'

Jack pointed to a book on the floor next to the bed. 'I can see you are reading Carl Jung,' he said.

'Very observant of you,' said Brother Acrivos and picked up the book – *Synchronicity: An Acausal Connecting Principle* – and held it up. 'I am particularly interested in synchronicity, a fascinating concept developed by Jung that has resonated with me for years.'

'Please explain,' said Tristan.

'According to Jung, who as you no doubt know worked closely with Freud, synchronicity is a meaningful coincidence of two or more events where something other than the probability of chance is involved—'

'*Meaningful coincidence?*' interrupted Jack. 'But Jung believed in the paranormal, didn't he?'

'Oh yes, he did,' said Brother Acrivos and put down the book. 'But you didn't come here to discuss analytical psychology and hypothetical matters, but a specific case: the tragic case of Maurice Landru.'

'That's right.'

'Then please listen to what I have to say, as this is most likely the only time we will meet. I can think of no better example of synchronicity than you coming here today to talk to me about Landru. What is happening right now, here in this place, is nothing more than a meaningful coincidence with no apparent causal relationship, which is nevertheless meaningfully related. You will see in a moment exactly what I mean. Just consider how and why you came to see me here, today, to talk about Landru. That's a good start.'

Jack pulled his little notebook and pen out of his pocket, removed the rubber band and began to take notes.

'Before we begin, you should know that it was the Landru case that made me give up my work in crime investigation, withdraw from the world, and come here to Mount Athos. As it turns out, to die.'

'What was it about that case that made you do this?' asked Tristan.

'Two things. All of my findings and suggestions were stubbornly ignored by the authorities. They just didn't want to hear what I had to say, except for Francesca and Dupree.' Brother Acrivos looked dreamily out to sea. 'They understood,' he whispered.

'You said there were two things,' prompted Jack.

'Yes, that's correct. In all my years of dealing with criminal matters – some of them quite extreme, involving acts of violence and horror too difficult to envisage – I have never come across anything quite like it.'

Tristan could feel the back of his neck begin to tingle and his stomach contract. It was a familiar sensation he had experienced before, but only in situations of extreme danger.

'What exactly?' asked Tristan hoarsely.

Brother Acrivos turned to face Tristan. Their eyes met, and what Tristan saw reflected in those sad, hooded eyes shocked him. It was wide-eyed fear so intense that he had to look away.

'*True evil*,' whispered Brother Acrivos and closed his eyes.

'Could you please elaborate?' said Jack.

'I will, but I have to warn you. Once you hear what I have to tell you, there may be no turning back. I have tried, but it still consumes me. Even now.'

Brother Acrivos looked first at Jack, and then at Tristan. 'Are you sure you are ready for this?'

Jack nodded.

'We are,' said Tristan.

'Then I will tell you. Just give me a moment to compose myself.'

7

Montmartre, Paris: five years earlier

Acrivos Papadoulis was a light sleeper. He woke with a start and reached for his mobile on the bedside table. Instantly awake, he answered the call. 'Dupree! Do you know what time it is?' he said, looking at his watch. It was two in the morning.

'Yes, I do. *We got him*!'

'What do you mean?'

'You better get here before the body is removed. I want you to see everything just as we found it.'

'I'm on my way. What about Francesca?'

'I called her as well. She will be here shortly.'

Papadoulis paid the taxi and got out. The narrow Montmartre laneway was blocked off, and the lights flashing on top of the police cars in front of a dilapidated house looked ominous and eerie in the rain and the dense fog drifting up from the Seine.

Dupree saw Papadoulis speaking to a police officer, waved and walked over to him. 'Come, Francesca is already inside. We haven't much time. The Forensics guys have already gone to work and the cavalry isn't far away.'

Deep in thought, Bartolli stood by herself in a corner of the small, dimly lit room on the ground floor. She was processing the crime scene and taking in the finer details that might have escaped a less attentive observer. The shabby furniture and aimless clutter spoke of modest means and a disorganised lifestyle. The Forensics team was testing spotlights that had been set up earlier to illuminate the crime scene.

'I came as soon as I could,' said Papadoulis. 'What happened here?'

'Before I tell you what we have found out so far, what do you see?' asked Dupree.

'Or better still, what do you *feel*?' said Bartolli, nodding to Papadoulis.

'I see a well-built, naked man lying on the floor, face up. I cannot see his face because it is covered with what looks like some kind of gooey substance—'

'It's a negative casting material,' Dupree cut in, 'used for preparing death masks. Technically, it's referred to as dental impression cream. It's a powdery material you add water to, and then pour over the face. It takes about three minutes to set. It was applied shortly after death. It serves as a mould for the mask, which can then be prepared later, using plaster. When the patrol officers arrived and broke down the door, they found a man kneeling next to the corpse, apparently applying the material to the victim's face. His hands were covered in the stuff.'

'How bizarre. Caught in the act of making a facial cast of a victim who has just been brutally killed. It takes a special type of person to do this,' said Papadoulis. 'There seems to have been some kind of struggle. Look, an overturned table, broken glass, papers on the floor, syringes. Drugs?'

'Yes. Heroin.'

'And the limbs of the deceased are – how will I put this? – contorted. Unnaturally so. They look "arranged", wouldn't you say?' continued Papadoulis.

Bartolli nodded in agreement. She had come to a similar conclusion.

'And over there, next to the head, is what looks like a long wire with a piece of wood attached on each end; a garrotte?' she said.

'Yes, it certainly looks like one. Crude, but effective,' said Dupree.

'Lying in a pool of blood.'

'You told us what you see,' said Bartolli, turning to Papadoulis. 'Now please tell us what you *feel*.'

Papadoulis looked at Bartolli standing next to him just as the bright floodlights came on, making the room look like some kind of film set for a cheap horror movie. What Bartolli saw reflected in Papadoulis's eyes shocked her.

'I have felt this only once or twice before, but never quite this strongly,' whispered Papadoulis.

'What exactly?' asked Bartolli.

'Tell you later.'

'What are these two doing here?' said Lapointe as he stormed into the room – breathless, his face flushed – followed by the prosecutor in charge. He pointed impatiently to Papadoulis and Bartolli. 'Get them out of here at once!'

Dupree shrugged and turned to Papadoulis. 'Sorry,' he said. 'I hope you saw enough.'

'I did.'

'Enough for what?' asked Bartolli.

'To uncover what really happened here, not what we'll no doubt read in the papers tomorrow morning,' said Papadoulis and turned to leave.

Dupree hurried over to a doorway to get out of the driving rain, and lit a cigarette. 'Lapointe isn't thinking straight,' he said. 'He's been under enormous pressure lately. He believes he has caught his man at last. A lot is riding on this, as you can see.'

'Understandable,' said Bartolli, wiping her face with a handkerchief and shaking her wet hair. 'The question is, *has he?*'

'What do you mean?' asked Dupree.

'Got his man.'

'You are not convinced?'

'Before I answer that, tell us what you've found out so far.'

'Well, the local police received a call from a concerned neighbour hearing screams coming from the house here. A patrol car was dispatched to investigate. When the officers got here, a couple of excited neighbours were standing outside at the front door. To cut a long story short, the police broke down the door, went inside and found a confused man with his hands covered in blood and goo, kneeling next to the victim. We believe he was high on drugs. He's been taken to hospital, under guard, for testing. The rest you know.'

'I appreciate there hasn't been much time, but do we know anything about the victim?'

'As a matter of fact, we do. He's a male prostitute. Apparently, well known around here. It's that kind of neighbourhood.'

'And do we know anything about the man you arrested? Do we know who he is?'

'We do. He had his wallet on him with his driver licence, credit cards, the lot.'

'Very convenient. Who is he?' said Papadoulis.

'His name is Maurice Landru. He's a professor; lectures at the Sorbonne.'

'What in; do we know?' asked Bartolli, surprised.

'Not yet. But I can tell you he has no criminal record. Seems to be a pillar of society.'

'A crumbling one,' commented Papadoulis.

'Hm. Acrivos, what was it you could feel inside just before we were evicted?' said Bartolli. 'I saw your troubled face. You really scared me.'

Papadoulis took his time before replying and kept watching the rain. Then, taking a deep breath, he turned to face Bartolli. 'What I could feel, was a presence. The presence of evil, *true evil*—'

'Hardly surprising, bearing in mind what we've just seen,' interjected Dupree.

'You don't understand. I have seen many crime scenes before, some of them much more violent and shocking than this one. What I felt had nothing to do with the crime scene as such.'

'What then?' asked Bartolli.

'A lingering presence. A presence of pure evil filling the room with malevolent energy so strong that it made my head spin, and my heart miss a beat.'

'Could that have been left behind by the man who was arrested, do you think?'

'That's the really weird thing here. I don't think so. This evil force was still there, hovering.'

Dupree shook his head. 'I don't know what to make of this.'

'I do,' said Bartolli.

'You do? Tell me.'

'I think what Acrivos is telling us is this: there is another party involved here, apart from the victim and the alleged killer; isn't that right, Acrivos?'

Papadoulis nodded.

'How can he possibly know this?' said Dupree. 'Everything here points to—'

'That's exactly the problem here, can't you see?' said Bartolli. 'The circumstances don't fit the facts!'

'What are you telling me?' demanded Dupree. 'What facts?'

'What we've just seen. In there. I don't think the man who was kneeling next to the victim is the real killer here.'

'*That's absurd!*' Dupree scoffed and threw the cigarette stub into the gutter. 'How can you say that, after all you've just seen? Where's your evidence?'

'The profile we've built up by carefully examining the other cases does not work here. It doesn't fit. It looks as if it does, but once you—'

'Francesca's right,' interrupted Papadoulis, looking agitated.

'I'll prepare a report if you like, and set out my arguments and my reasons,' said Bartolli. 'Would you like me to do this?'

'Yes, please.'

'What about you, Acrivos?' asked Bartolli.

'I will do the same, although I suspect it will fall on deaf ears,' said Papadoulis quietly, shaking his head. 'The police seem convinced they have their man.'

'It's late. There's nothing more we can do here tonight. Go home and think about it,' said Dupree.

'We will, don't worry,' said Bartolli and put her hand on Dupree's shoulder. 'And you should at least try to keep an open mind.'

'I can't pretend that I like what you've just told me, but I will certainly do that, I promise. I'll ask one of the guys to drive you home.'

A man standing in the shadows on the opposite side of the lane watched the police car drive past with Bartolli and Papadoulis in the back. Then he turned up his collar, pulled the brim of his hat down to cover his face, and slowly walked to the end of the lane, where he turned left. Satisfied that his instructions had been followed to the letter, he melted into the rain like a ghost.

8

Fleury-Mérogis Prison, Paris: 3 October; first visit

Jack approached the meeting with Landru with trepidation. What Papadoulis had told him at Mount Athos about the case was not only unsettling, but went much further. Jack couldn't quite define the feeling, but a shiver of fear coated with some kind of irresistible curiosity came close. Jack could still hear Papadoulis's words ringing in his ears: *Once you hear what I have to tell you, there may be no turning back.*

Bartolli had called Jack the day before, but before giving him her answer, she first wanted to know how the meeting with Papadoulis had gone. Only after Jack had provided a detailed account did she tell him that she had decided to accept his invitation to become involved in the case. She also told him that she would like to meet Landru, if possible. A personal meeting, she argued, would give her a much better opportunity to evaluate the matter. Just like Jack, Bartolli was being irresistibly drawn into the mystery by a seductive magnet reaching out from the past, impossible to ignore. Also like Jack, she could sense that a big story was out there waiting to be discovered.

Dupree and Jack met Bartolli at the airport and drove straight to the Fleury-Mérogis Prison in the southern suburbs of Paris.

'The meeting is at three,' said Dupree. 'It's all arranged. One prison guard will be present. Rules. I won't come in, of course. Strictly no police, remember? He insisted.'

'How do you think he will react if I suddenly show up with Jack?' asked Bartolli.

'Not sure,' replied Dupree.

'I will make it clear to Landru that I will only listen to what he has to say if Francesca can be present,' said Jack. He looked at Bartolli sitting next to him in the car and smiled. 'I think I know how to persuade him to agree,' he said.

'If you say so,' said Dupree, unconvinced.

All prisons are intimidating. That's part of their function. The huge Fleury-Mérogis Prison with its four thousand inmates was no exception. As soon as Jack and Bartolli walked through the security gates, they stepped into a different, alien world, where freedom was a distant memory, relentless routine was king, and unquestioning submission to mindless rules that crushed the spirit and extinguished the last spark of independence, the only way to survive.

Although they were obviously expected and the purpose of their visit was known to the authorities, Jack and Bartolli were viewed with suspicion, bordering on resentment. They were seen as outsiders intruding into a place where they didn't belong, and were greeted accordingly: with curt and frosty politeness, disclosing only the barest of information and directives as to how the meeting would be conducted and how long it would last.

'I don't think we are welcome here,' whispered Jack as they followed the guard down a stark, dimly lit corridor smelling of cleaning fluid. 'What do you think?'

Bartolli shrugged. 'All prisons are the same: inward-looking and somewhat threatened by outsiders. Don't worry about it.'

'I can't help feeling uneasy about this.'

'Understandable. It's not every day you get to meet a convicted killer serving a life sentence, who wants to tell you something important about his crimes. For your ears only,' added Bartolli, sounding conspiratorial.

'That's what worries me; *why?*'

'You are afraid of what he might tell you? Of what you might find?'

'A bit. This reminds me of a prison visit in Fremantle in Western Australia a long time ago. I was trying to find out what happened to my father. That was back in 2002.'

'Your *father?* And did you?'

'It's a long story. He died in a prison fire during a riot.'

'I'm so sorry,' said Bartolli, shaking her head. 'You are a dark horse, Jack.'

'There's a lot more to all this. It's complicated. I'll tell you about it one day.'

'Were you alone when you visited the prison that day?'

'Yes, that's what reminded me of it. The same feeling.'

'Well, at least this time you won't be. Alone, I mean. We'll do this together.'

Feeling better, Jack shot Bartolli a grateful look as they stopped in front of a steel door, and the guard picked up a phone mounted on the wall.

'Thanks again for, you know …' he said.

'I'm just as curious as you are.'

'But do we know what we are letting ourselves in for?'

'We will soon; look,' said Bartolli.

As the guard put the phone back into its cradle, the heavy door opened silently from the inside. '*Après vous*,' said the guard, 'the prisoner is waiting,' and stepped aside.

Apart from a shiny steel table that had been relentlessly scrubbed clean for years and a few chairs, the stark room was bare. The table was divided in the middle by a thick glass partition with small holes, separating the prisoner from visitors. A bored prison guard stood by the locked door, staring vacantly into space, the harsh neon light giving the windowless space an unwelcoming appearance where not even one's thoughts appeared to be private.

The handcuffed man sitting at the table in no way resembled the notorious killer Jack had been expecting to meet. Clean-shaven, hair cut short, and sitting ramrod straight on a battered chair that was clearly uncomfortable, he looked more like a military man waiting for interrogation than an academic who had once held a prestigious position at the Sorbonne. Even his drab prison uniform looked tidy and hinted at a fastidious man who cared about his appearance, even in a notorious place like the Fleury-Mérogis Prison. In stark contrast to his intimidating surroundings, his demeanour radiated self-confidence and purpose.

'I thought I made it clear I wanted to meet with you alone, Mr Rogan,' said Landru, sounding strong and confident as Jack approached the table. Landru lifted his handcuffed hands and pointed to Bartolli standing next to Jack. 'Who's that?'

Jack took his time before replying. 'This is Professor Bartolli, a criminologist. At the time of your arrest, she was the only one who believed that you weren't the killer,' he said quietly. 'Her report is the main reason I agreed to this meeting. She stays, or I go. Your choice.'

For a while, Landru stared at Bartolli through his thick, rimless glasses as the tension in the room grew by the second. Jack realised the meeting was hanging in the balance, as the contest of wills that could tip the scales any which way was gaining momentum.

Looking relaxed and at ease, Bartolli confidently held Landru's gaze without showing any signs of intimidation.

'Very well,' said Landru at last. 'Please take a seat. We haven't much time. There are strict rules here, as you are about to find out. It would be best if you could just listen to what I have to say first. Questions may have to wait for another time. You'll see why in a moment. Any problems with this?'

Jack shook his head and without saying a word, put the letter Landru had sent to the prosecutor on the table. Then he pulled his little notebook and pen out of his pocket and carefully took off the rubber band holding it together.

Bartolli didn't plan on taking any notes. Instead, she kept watching Landru closely. She knew from experience that in a tense, highly charged situation like this, every gesture, every facial expression counted. Landru would have carefully prepared for this meeting and obviously had a game plan. The best she could do therefore in the circumstances was to listen and observe.

'Please listen carefully,' began Landru, sounding somewhat agitated. 'We haven't much time ...'

Dupree waited for Jack and Bartolli at the prison gates. The expression on Jack's ashen face told him this was not the time to ask questions. That would have to wait. Jack and Bartolli would tell him what happened in their own good time.

'A cup of tea and a slice of cook's apple cake back at the chateau might be the way to go; what do you think, guys?' said Dupree as he manoeuvred the car out of the prison car park and into the busy afternoon traffic.

'Good idea,' said Jack and reached for his notebook. Appreciating Dupree's tact, he put his hand on his friend's arm. 'I think a stiff drink might be a better option,' he said.

'That bad?'

'Astonishing would be the right word here; what do you think, Francesca?'

'It would.' Bartolli closed her eyes, let herself sink into the seat, and in silence went over the extraordinary encounter with Landru, her analytical mind recording every detail and storing it for later.

Jack opened his notebook and began to scribble furiously in the margin. He always did this immediately after an important meeting, before his memory began to fade and played tricks on him later. He smiled as a ripple of excitement washed over him and he realised that another great story had once again just found him. *Destiny in action*, he thought and closed the notebook, eager to hear what Bartolli had to say about it all.

By the time they arrived at the Kuragin chateau two hours later, Jack and Bartolli had both digested the extraordinary things Landru had told them and were ready to talk about it. Having so far controlled his curiosity, Dupree was eager to hear it, as he had the added pressure of Lapointe waiting for his report.

9

Kuragin chateau, 4 October

If Jack had thought that inviting Bartolli to stay at the chateau at short notice might be an imposition, he needn't have worried. Countess Kuragin and the vivacious professor from Rome hit it off from the moment Bartolli dropped her backpack on the floor of the foyer and began to admire the interior of the stunning chateau, while at the same time talking about Italian cooking.

Bartolli felt instantly at home in the chateau. Her natural charm and Italian exuberance drew people to her wherever she went, and those meeting her for the first time were invariably surprised to learn that she was a respected international criminal specialist, who had made it her life's work to delve into the dark recesses of the criminal mind. After quickly settling into one of the guest rooms and having a hot shower, she went downstairs to join the others for dinner. A splendid duck prepared by cook – who had been forewarned about the visitor's passion for food – was served in the dining room.

After dinner, everyone went to the music room.

Jack turned to Dupree standing next to him. 'Just look at those two,' he said and pointed to Bartolli and the countess sitting in front of the fireplace discussing the merits of a bottle of 2002 Chateau de Beaucastel Chateauneuf-du-Pape the countess had retrieved from her cellar earlier.

'It's very light on the palate,' said Bartolli, savouring the delicious wine. 'Well balanced. Good nose.'

'From the Rhone Valley,' said the countess. 'One of my favourites.'

'I can see why. You have a magnificent home. And so peaceful; not like Rome.'

'I love Italy, especially Venice. I would live there if I could,' said the countess, looking dreamily at her glass. 'I spent a lot of time there when I was younger. I was in love. It was magic!'

'Ah, love. That elusive treasure you often find when you least expect it. And when you do and want to hold on to it, it evaporates.'

'How right you are. And the biggest and most lasting treasure that remains is friendship. If you're lucky.'

'They look like old friends,' said Dupree and took a sip of brandy.

'I'm so glad Francesca came with me to the prison,' said Jack. 'She put it all into perspective. I can't wait to hear what she has to say about Landru. He certainly wasn't what I expected.'

'Why don't we ask her?' ventured Dupree, who had endured the entire dinner without even touching on the subject that was on everyone's mind. 'Lapointe called three times already ...'

'I understand, but we needed some time to digest what Landru told us before discussing it with you.'

'Fair enough, but—'

'I agree, it's time. Come, let's do it.'

Jack walked over to the fireplace, picked up the half-empty bottle on the coffee table and turned to Bartolli. 'Before we get too comfortable, I think Claude here deserves to know what we found out this afternoon, don't you?' he said.

Turning serious, Bartolli nodded.

'Would you mind telling us what you made of Landru, professionally speaking. Your impressions?' continued Jack and refilled the two glasses.

Bartolli settled back into the cushions and looked pensively at the glass of wine in her hand. 'A complex man. Highly intelligent, disciplined and very confident, especially when we consider the circumstances. Obviously gay. He was in complete control of the meeting. He called the shots, as they say. Not a mean feat when you are in prison serving a life sentence. He knew he had something we wanted, and wasn't going to hand it over without first making us listen to what he wanted us to hear.'

'He's been in jail for several years now, protesting his innocence,' added Jack.

'Exactly. In my view he put up quite a convincing argument, even after all this time, don't you think? He pointed out all the flaws in the case against him and suggested that soon, there would be more.'

'I agree, and it all revolved around one thing: that mysterious cipher left in his prison cell by an anonymous stranger,' said Jack. '*All the answers you are looking for are right here,* said the note. He obviously became obsessed with this.'

'Let's not forget, Landru spent the last four years trying to crack the code. That tells us a lot, doesn't it? This is a desperate man looking for answers. He *believes*, you see. He actually believes that he can find those answers in the cipher, if he cracks the code. That's what keeps him going. This is not the mindset of a guilty man who already knows the answers because he committed the crimes. What would be the point?'

Dupree nodded, hanging on Bartolli's every word. She had just articulated exactly what had troubled him all these years. 'And did he? Crack the code?' he asked, unable to contain his curiosity and impatience any longer.

'Yes, he did, but before we tell you what the cipher says, you should learn some more of the background, because it explains why Landru asked for me, someone he had never met. Francesca and I discussed this earlier.'

'That has puzzled me too. Why *you*, Jack? Do you know?'

'Partially.'

'What do you mean, *partially*?' demanded Dupree, becoming agitated.

'Landru didn't tell us everything. All he said was that he had carefully followed the Ritz murder cases in the papers. He also said that he had read *The Lost Symphony*, my most recent book about the Ritz murders and the whole Russian story, and that something in the book opened his eyes and helped him crack the code.'

'Did he say what it was?' said Dupree.

'No, not as such, but he did mention Malenkova, the Black Widow, and that all this had to do with her. But what really surprised me,' continued Jack, 'was that he also mentioned Mademoiselle Darrieux and hinted that she too was somehow involved.'

'Are you serious?'

'That's what he said.'

'Did he elaborate?'

'No. He said he would tell us later, when we were ready. Funny thing to say, don't you think? Instead, he took us through the complicated process of how he cracked the code, and why it had taken him so long. It was all very technical, confusing even, and almost impossible to follow, but we had to listen. He insisted.'

'How weird. What on earth did he mean by all that? Is he playing games, you think?' Dupree wanted to know.

'I don't believe so,' said Bartolli. 'I think he was deadly serious.'

'What could possibly be the connection here, do you think?' asked Dupree. 'The link between the cipher and Malenkova? She's dead now, gone, and so is her assistant, and ...' Dupree didn't complete the sentence and glanced at Jack. He could see the pain in his friend's eyes and instantly regretted having gone down that path, but it was too late. Memories of Anielka and what happened to her were obviously still raw, and the wounds left behind, deep.

'No idea,' said Jack, shaking his head sadly. 'But I'm sure it all revolves around the cipher; what it says.'

'Are you going to tell me, or do you want to kill me slowly with suspense?' said Dupree, introducing some levity to ease the tension.

'I believe prison has taught Landru something very important,' said Bartolli.

'What's that?' asked Jack.

'Patience. The way he conducted the meeting made that clear. To me, it seemed like a carefully orchestrated chess game, full of purpose and tactics,' said Bartolli. 'He was moving us around like pieces on the board. His board; his game. I have no doubt he wants to meet with us again, and in order to do that he knows he has to have something to offer. That's why he didn't tell us everything and kept us in suspense. Curiosity is a great motivator.'

Bartolli took a sip of wine.

'He also knows that Jack is a storyteller,' she continued. 'Always on the lookout for the next challenge, the next adventure, the next big story. His books make that clear—'

'He got that one right,' interrupted the countess, laughing. 'Jack's an adventure junkie. Trust me, I know, and he's also a hopeless romantic.'

'Landru wants us to do his bidding on the outside, as directed by him from the inside. Clever, don't you think?' said Bartolli. 'He's a classic manipulator, a very smart one driven by desperation, but he's no psychopath. He could be the victim here, not the perpetrator. He even promised Jack the story of a lifetime.'

'Did he now? And you believe him?' asked Dupree, frowning. 'Do you believe he's innocent and was wrongly convicted, and all of this is about finding the proof?'

Bartolli took another sip of wine and took her time before replying, the anticipation in the room rising, as this was the critical question on everyone's mind.

'Yes, I do,' said Bartolli quietly. 'I have from the very beginning.'

Dupree turned to Jack. 'What about you, Jack?' he asked.

'I want to take it a step at a time, but this may help.'

Jack reached into his pocket and handed a piece of paper to Dupree.

Dupree looked at it. 'What's that?' he asked.

'The decoded cipher.'

'*What?* Are you serious?'

'Yes.'

'But that's an address here in Paris.'

'Exactly. But read on.'

'*Deep down in the cellar is a wall. Behind it you will find all,*' read Dupree. 'How strange. Another puzzle?'

'Perhaps.'

'Are you suggesting that Landru spent four years trying to crack the code – unsuccessfully, I might add – until he read your book and found a clue?' said the countess. 'And this is the result?'

'Looks that way …'

'An address and a riddle; is that it?' said Dupree, looking incredulous.

'According to Landru,' replied Jack, 'it may contain all the answers to what he's been looking for all these years. Something that will prove his innocence, and clear his name.'

'But there was something else, remember?' interjected Bartolli. 'The strange thing he said on the way out.'

'You're right, I almost forgot. As the guard escorted Landru out of the room, Landru stopped briefly, turned around and said something curious.'

'What?' asked Dupree.

'"As you will soon see, there's more to all this than just my conviction". That's what he said.'

Dupree shook his head. 'Extraordinary. What now?'

'Isn't it obvious?' said Jack and handed Dupree a cognac.

'What do you mean?'

Jack lifted his glass. 'We check out the address tomorrow, break down the wall and see what's behind it; what else? And if there's no wall and we don't find anything, we forget about Landru and go somewhere nice to have lunch. Cheers!'

Bartolli reached for her glass and looked at Jack. 'Sounds like my kind of plan,' she said. 'Salute!'

10

On the outskirts of Paris, 5 October

The address in the decoded cipher turned out to be an abandoned, dilapidated house at the end of a narrow cul-de-sac in one of the poorest districts of Paris. Surrounded on three sides by an overgrown hedge, it was well shielded from prying eyes, and a crumbling wall with a rusty iron gate facing the street kept out uninvited visitors.

Lapointe sat in an unmarked police car parked in front of the house and looked again at his watch. *They're late*, he thought and lit his pipe. He had arrived early with a Forensics team, just in case. It was drizzling and an icy wind was blowing across from the Alps to the southeast, a chilly reminder that summer was well and truly over, and winter not far away.

Instead of entering the house upon arrival, Lapointe had decided to wait for Dupree and Jack. Not just out of courtesy, but because he wanted to hear firsthand what Landru had said during the interview. Methodical and cautious by nature, Lapointe realised that everything had to be done by the book, because if even just part of what Dupree had told him about the cipher was true, the house behind the wall could hold unwelcome secrets and surprises that could not only cast a shadow of doubt over Landru's conviction, but reopen the notorious Death Mask Murder cases. This in turn could quickly become an embarrassment for the police and the prosecutor, with unwelcome consequences further up the chain of command, which Lapointe wanted to avoid at all costs.

Dupree stopped his car, took a deep breath and looked at Jack sitting next to him. 'You can always rely on Lapointe. He has arrived with the cavalry. This could be interesting; ready?'

Feeling uneasy, Jack nodded and kept staring at the house, the morning mist giving it a mysterious, almost ghostly appearance. *Looks like a house of horrors*, he thought. *Straight out of* The Return of the Living Dead.

Dupree turned to Bartolli sitting behind him. 'Lapointe knows you're involved, but he doesn't expect you here, remember? Jack asked you to come along, not me. I don't know how he'll react.'

'Understood.'

'Leave Lapointe to me,' said Jack, turning up his collar. 'What do you make of the place, Francesca?'

'Theatrical. Almost too much so. It looks like a stage.'

'Planned, you think?'

'Carefully, I'd say.'

'That's what I thought too, as soon as I saw it. Right down to the ivy almost covering the front door. What does that tell you?'

'We could be in for a surprise.'

'Even after all these years? With no guarantee that the cipher code would ever be cracked, revealing the address? A long shot like that?' asked Dupree, shaking his head.

'If I'm right, we are dealing with a very different mind here,' replied Bartolli. 'Calculating and dangerous, but definitely with an agenda. The uncertainty and the gamble are part of the game. Part of the excitement. Time is not an issue; power over life and death is. This is a long game, but one with a specific purpose. A plan, of that I'm sure.'

'What kind of plan?' asked Jack.

'I wish I knew.'

Jack opened the car door. 'Then let's go and find out.'

If Lapointe was in any way surprised to see Bartolli, he certainly didn't show it. He greeted her politely and pointed to the house. 'Let's get out of the rain and go inside, shall we? Good to see you again, Jack. Thank you for helping us out and meeting with Landru. You must tell me about the meeting, but first let's see what this is all about.'

'Let's do that. What do we know about the house?' asked Jack, certain that Lapointe would have made enquiries overnight.

'It was bought quite a few years ago from a deceased estate by a company registered in Jersey in the Channel Islands, involved in some kind of security business. Usual web of complex trusts, smoke and mirrors. Typical tax avoidance stuff.'

'In short, we don't know who's behind it, nor are we likely to find out, right?'

'That's about it.'

'Was the house bought before or after the murders?'

'Good question. Just before.'

It took Lapointe's men just moments to break down the door. Lapointe was the first to enter the house, followed by Dupree, Bartolli and Jack. Inside it was almost dark, as the windows were covered with cardboard from the inside. Not surprisingly, the electricity wasn't connected. Lapointe turned on his torch.

The house was empty, without any furniture or furnishings of any kind, not even curtains, light fittings or blinds. The first thing Jack noticed was the smell: rising damp and mould with a hint of pungent rat urine. Layers of old dust covered the floor, scattered with rat droppings. It was apparent the house hadn't been entered for months, possibly years.

Lapointe walked quickly from room to room. All were empty. It was obvious he was looking for something. Remembering what was in the cipher, Jack suspected it was stairs leading into a cellar. He was right. Lapointe stopped at a set of narrow stairs and trained his torch down into the darkness below.

I wonder what's waiting for us down there, thought Jack, an icy shiver racing down his spine, signalling excitement and danger.

Lapointe turned to Dupree. 'Well, this is it,' he said. 'Let's see if this is some kind of practical joke, or something a little more sinister.'

One by one, they walked down the stairs, careful not to bump their heads against the low ceiling. The small, dark room at the bottom of the stairs was also empty. The floor was paved with uneven bricks covered in moss, making them slippery. Jack walked slowly around the room, running the tips of his fingers along the walls. 'Here, have a look,' he said and pointed to some cracks in the brickwork. 'Looks like an old doorway, bricked up.'

Lapointe came over, had a look and nodded. Then he turned around and signalled to one of his men holding a sledgehammer. 'Make a small opening here, but be careful. I want to have a look inside first, before we go any further.' The man stepped forward and began to swing the heavy hammer. After two strokes, the wall began to crumble and a few bricks fell to the floor. An opening appeared: an ominous-looking dark hole, beckoning into the unknown lurking beyond.

Holding up his hand, Lapointe walked over to the opening, bent down with his torch and looked inside. Everyone in the room froze and watched, mesmerised.

This was one of those occasions when time appears to stand still. Seconds can turn into agonising minutes brimming with suspense, when a moment of destiny is about to unfold. Holding his breath, Jack kept watching Lapointe's face. Illuminated from below by the torchlight accentuating his tense features, the police superintendent's expression looked like the face of someone who had just glimpsed the unthinkable.

'Stand back! This is a crime scene,' croaked Lapointe, barely able to speak. 'Everybody go back upstairs, *now*!'

Lapointe turned around and almost bumped into Jack, standing behind him. 'Well, are you going to tell us what you saw?' asked Jack.

'Not right now; later. Please go back to your car and wait for me.'

'That bad?'

'I need some time to find the words.'

Lapointe came out of the house half an hour later and got into the back seat of Dupree's car. He took off his wet hat and for a long, tense moment just sat there in silence. Then he turned to Bartolli sitting next to him. 'I owe you an apology, Professor. You too, Dupree.' Lapointe stared out of the fogged-up car window. 'You were right all along. Landru couldn't have done this. Certainly not alone.'

'What's down there?' asked Jack.

'A chamber of horrors, the likes of which I haven't come across in my entire career.'

'Care to elaborate?'

'Later. When we know more.'

'What about Landru?'

'He and the cipher are our best leads. At least for now. I would like you to meet him again, Jack, soon, and tell him what we found. He deserves that. He obviously trusts you. And you too, Professor. I would like you to help us here, if you are prepared to take on the case again and become involved, after all that's happened.' Lapointe looked at Bartolli. 'Please consider it?'

'I will. I don't like unfinished business.'

'How many?' asked Dupree.

'I counted six. There could be more.'

'Bodies?' said Bartolli.

'It's complicated,' said Lapointe, sidestepping the question.

'But we had only three murders here in Paris, and that includes Landru's conviction,' said Dupree.

'Exactly.'

'So, what's next?' asked Jack. He realised it was pointless trying to get more information out of Lapointe.

'It's up to Forensics now, the experts. This is huge. All I ask of you is not to talk to the press. We'll make a formal announcement once we know more. Can I count on you?'

Everyone agreed.

'That's about it. I'll keep you informed. Better go.'

Here it is again, thought Jack as he watched Lapointe get slowly out of the car, seemingly reluctant to go back inside. The haunted look on Lapointe's face reminded him of Papadoulis's expression at Mount Athos, when he had uttered 'true evil'.

11

Fleury-Mérogis Prison, Paris: 7 October

If Landru was in any way apprehensive or curious about the visit, he certainly didn't show it. He was confident the address in the cipher would have been investigated straight away, and the site carefully examined by the authorities. He therefore knew that the moment of reckoning had arrived and his entire future depended on what Jack was about to tell him.

Landru was waiting in the same stark visitors' room as on the previous occasion, and looked up when Jack and Bartolli entered. Bartolli noticed that he appeared calm and in control, without displaying any emotion, which was surprising in the circumstances.

'We came as soon as we could,' began Jack. He sat down facing Landru and looked at him through the glass partition. After briefly describing the house and the cellar, he came straight to the point.

'The police attended with a Forensics team and broke down a wall in the cellar revealing a concealed chamber. We were not allowed to stay and therefore didn't witness any of this firsthand. What I'm about to tell you is based on a briefing by Chief Superintendent Lapointe, who is in charge of this investigation. We met with him yesterday. As you know he was—'

'I know who he is,' interjected Landru calmly.

Jack nodded and pulled his little notebook out of his pocket. 'The briefing was comprehensive with lots of photographs, but we weren't given any copies. I will therefore do my best to describe what we saw.'

Jack cleared his throat and opened his notebook.

'In the middle of the chamber stood three sealed metal drums, each about the size of a large wine barrel. Carefully positioned on the floor in front of each drum was what looked like a white plaster death mask. In front of each of the masks was a sealed glass jar. Each jar contained a clear liquid, which turned out to be a potent embalming fluid, with a human ear and an eye floating in it.'

Jack paused to let this sink in and looked at Landru, who just sat there, motionless and silent. 'But this wasn't all,' he continued. 'There were three additional death masks in the chamber – all neatly laid out in a row – each with a jar containing an ear and an eye in front of each mask, but without drums or anything else standing near them. Otherwise, the chamber was empty.' Jack cleared his throat and then continued.

'Initial examination of the contents of the drums found partially dissolved human remains, apparently linked to the two unsolved Paris Death Mask Murder cases, and one other. Sulfuric acid and a cocktail of other chemicals were apparently used. The pathologists believe that the eye and the ear in the jars in front of each drum belong to the respective murder victims in the drums, but this still has to be confirmed. As for the other three jars, investigations are continuing.'

'I think I know who the other four might be,' said Landru, 'but not because I was in any way involved in the murders.'

Jack looked up. '*You do?*' he asked. 'How?'

'It's complicated, but you will find out soon enough,' came the cryptic reply.

Jack closed his notebook, exasperation on his face. 'I think it's time to put the cards on the table, Monsieur Landru. We are talking about seven connected murders here, only one of which appears to have been solved. The one that has brought you here and landed you in jail. We've done everything you asked. I don't like playing games. It's time to come clean or we walk away, *right now.*'

Landru smiled for the first time. 'That would be a big mistake.'

'Tell me why.'

'Before I do, I would like to hear what Professor Bartolli makes of all this.' Landru looked at Bartolli and ever so slightly raised an eyebrow, signalling a subtle challenge.

'What was found concealed in the cellar has been carefully prepared over a long period,' began Bartolli, anxious to keep Landru talking. 'Possibly years, and it was put on display in a very theatrical way. Calculated and precise. Someone went to a lot of trouble to create this scene. It looked like a gruesome exhibition in a house of horrors, but with a quite specific purpose. It was all *meant* to be found. Each item faced the doorway, for maximum effect, and obviously sends a message, especially the eyes and ears in the jars. No effort has been made to conceal the identities of the bodies involved. On the contrary, the death masks clearly identify the victims, and the body parts left behind will no doubt provide other compelling evidence as to identity. DNA ...'

'What does all this tell you about the perpetrator, or perpetrators, should there be more than one?' said Landru. 'As an experienced profiler, you must have formed a view.'

'Without knowing more about the victims and the circumstances of their murders, I am missing one critical element in my analysis. And the whole cipher issue is an added, rather baffling complication. However, what I can say with confidence is that none of this fits any specific pattern of criminal behaviour. This is all *outside* the textbook. There is no obvious motive to start with, which is always a problem. The police believe that the victims appear to have been chosen at random, yet there seems to be a clear underlying purpose to all this: a carefully prepared plan. The question is, what kind of plan and to what end?'

'Very good,' said Landru. 'I think you are absolutely right so far, except for motive. The motive is in fact very clear and precise, but understandably, you couldn't possibly know this.'

'But you do?' asked Bartolli.

'Yes. Once again, it's complicated.'

'Can you tell us?'

'One thing life in prison with its mindless routine gives you in abundance, is time to think. I've had plenty of time in here over the years to do just that, and I believe that I have used that time well. I have something to offer both of you,' said Landru. 'I believe it's an opportunity of a lifetime.'

'How so?' said Bartolli, looking at Landru with interest. To her, he was quickly turning into a fascinating subject, worthy of study. Landru had sensed this and decided to capitalise on it.

'For you, Professor, this could become the most significant case of your entire career. And I don't say that lightly or flippantly. A groundbreaking case for textbooks and lectures, which students and experts alike will talk about for years to come. Not to mention the impact on your reputation ...' added Landru, lowering his voice as he threw out the bait.

Landru turned to face Jack sitting opposite. 'What I can offer you, Mr Rogan, is something quite different: should I be able to persuade you to become more closely involved and take the next step in this saga, you will soon be drawn into one of the biggest adventure stories of your life. Bigger than Isis and the murder of her parents, bigger than finding the Ottoman recipes and saving the pope's life, and bigger than rescuing the genius Professor Stolzfus from the deadly clutches of that South American drug cartel, just to name a few.'

'You have obviously read all of my books,' said Jack.

'I have, and that's one of the reasons I turned to you with this in the first place. You are the only man I can think of who could rise to the challenge and pull off what it may take to solve this extraordinary case. Your recent Russian adventures have made that clear to me. You have the mindset, the intellect and, most important of all, the curiosity. You thrive on a challenge and never give up. But there is more to all this, much, much more ...'

'Care to elaborate? I need more,' said Jack, impressed by Landru's tenacity and arguments.

'All in good time. Another thing prison life has taught me is patience. And patience can be very rewarding and could go a long way here, as you could soon find out, Mr Rogan. It's up to you.'

He's playing cat and mouse, thought Bartolli, watching Landru carefully. *Very clever.*

'Give me at least *something*. Last time, you mentioned the Black Widow, and you also mentioned Mademoiselle Darrieux. Are you suggesting that they are somehow connected to all this?'

'Yes, I am,' said Landru, pleased to see that the conversation was heading in the right direction.

'How?'

'That too is complicated and will take time to explain, but I have put certain procedures in motion that will do just that.'

'More riddles,' said Jack, shaking his head.

'Patience, please! Hear me out. I believe that I have worked out who has committed all these murders, and I also know why. What I don't know is *on whose behalf* they were committed. That would be for you to find out because it may be the only way to solve this deadly riddle. I also believe I know why this bizarre display has been left behind for us to find, and the role of the cipher in all of this. You see, there's a much bigger picture here than meets the eye. This story started a long time ago. It was handed from generation to generation, and the last chapter hasn't been written yet.'

For the first time, Landru became somewhat agitated. The conversation was entering critical territory.

'Let's take this one step at a time,' said Jack. 'When and where did the story begin?'

'On sixteen November 1532, in the Inca city of Cajamarca,' came the reply.

'Are you serious?' said Bartolli, looking exasperated. 'How can you possibly be so precise?'

'That's the date Atahualpa, the last Inca king, was murdered by Pizarro,' said Jack.

Landru looked impressed. 'Very good. I knew you were the right man for this.'

'Next question. What's the role of the cipher in all this? You said you knew,' continued Jack, ignoring the compliment.

'I was set up and sent to prison for a murder I didn't commit. That happened for a reason. I was desperately trying to get out of an arrangement I was trapped in. It was like living in a cage with no way out. I was a hopeless drug addict by then. Heading for a nervous breakdown, doing irrational things. I had to be silenced because I had become a danger to—'

'A danger to whom?' interjected Bartolli.

'Later.'

'Here we go again.' Jack waved dismissively.

'Patience. By putting me away, the investigation into the Death Mask Murders was closed. The authorities hinted that I was responsible for all the Paris Death Mask Murders, despite the fact they couldn't prove it. The similarities were just too great, they argued. After that, I was effectively silenced and locked away for good. The public could feel safe again, and the police had what they wanted. Case closed. But by doing that, the quest came to a sudden halt.'

'What quest?'

'I have been on a quest for more than thirty years. My entire career, no, my entire *life* revolved around that quest. Still does. You of all people would understand what that means, Mr Rogan. You yourself were involved in something not dissimilar ... the Ark of the Covenant?'

'Can you elaborate?'

'Later.'

Jack shook his head.

'The cipher was given to me in order to reignite the quest, and by cracking the code, I did just that. And you, Mr Rogan, helped me do it. It was in one of your books! Serendipity. You would call it destiny.'

'This is crazy!' said Jack.

'Far from it. It's ingenious, as you will see in a moment. The cipher has guided us to that chamber of horrors as you called it, and as soon as the police release a statement about that – which they will – it will send a signal that the code has been broken, and the quest is back on. For certain parties watching, this will mean a great deal. That was the purpose of that chamber of horrors. One of them. There's another, more important purpose.'

'What purpose?' said Bartolli.

Landru took his time before replying. 'My release,' he said after a while. 'Once carefully examined and analysed, the objects in that chamber will make it clear that I am innocent and couldn't possibly have been the serial killer they portrayed me to be, and it will cast serious doubt over my conviction. It is, therefore, only a matter of time before I'm released. My lawyers are very confident. And once that happens, those who are behind all this know that I will resume the quest that I embarked upon such a long time ago.'

'What quest?' asked Jack.

Landru took a deep breath and looked intently at Jack. 'To find the legendary Inca treasure of the Llanganates,' he whispered.

'The enormous hoard of gold and other treasures assembled for Atahualpa's ransom, but hidden by one of his generals deep within the Llanganates Mountains after the king was murdered?' said Jack.

'You are well informed.'

'This is fantasy, surely,' scoffed Jack. 'Shrouded in legend.'

'Not at all. The treasure exists and I almost found out where it is, but I was missing a vital clue. That's where Malenkova comes into play, you see, and that's how I cracked the code. And they will once again be right there, watching my every step, I'm sure of that.'

'Who?'

'Those who are behind all this. Those who arranged all the murders while staying in the shadows, and spent a fortune covering their tracks. Just as in the Stolzfus matter,' added Landru quietly, dropping the first clue.

'The Stolzfus case? What could that possibly have to do with this?'

'You will find out in due course.'

'Are you suggesting this matter and the Stolzfus case have something in common?'

'Yes. And that's another reason why we were destined to meet, you and I, and are now destined to join forces.'

'Why should I believe you?' Jack almost shouted.

'Because of who you are! Because I know you want to find out.'

'Give me one reason why I shouldn't just walk away, right now. What possible link could there be between Stolzfus and this? This is absurd.'

'As I said before, I have put certain things in motion that will explain all this.'

'What kind of things?' asked Bartolli.

'I have kept a detailed journal here in prison. I have written down everything you need to know. The journal is with my lawyer. It is waiting for you, should you decide to come on board and join me on this journey. It will be dangerous, no doubt about it, very dangerous, but I'm sure this will come as no surprise.' Landru looked at Jack. 'And the rewards will be beyond your wildest dreams. That I can promise you!' he added quietly.

'Final question,' said Jack, trying to stay rational. 'Before I can give you my answer, I need to know one thing.'

'What's that?'

'The connection between the Stolzfus matter and this here. It seems too far-fetched.'

For a while, Landru stared into space, wrestling with himself, the pulsating veins on his forehead and the beads of perspiration on his brow the only signs of the struggle within. Should he drop the bombshell now, or save it for later? he asked himself. Then he lifted his gaze and looked at Jack sitting opposite. The expression on Jack's face told him that the matter was hanging in the balance; something significant was needed to get him over the line. '*Spiridon 4*,' whispered Landru, hoping that he had made the right decision.

Jack looked thunderstruck. 'What did you say?'

'Spiridon 4.'

'You can't be serious!'

'I am. Call my lawyer and he will give you my journal. It's all in there, and you can see for yourself. But once you do that, you have to give me your word that you will join forces with me. You are my secret weapon; in fact, my only hope. I can't do this without you, Mr

Rogan, of that I'm sure. The others are too powerful and too ruthless. And too clever. So, what will it be?'

Just then, the guard stepped forward, indicating that time was up. The meeting had to come to an end.

'I have to think about it,' said Jack and stood up.

'Fair enough. My lawyer's name is Lucien Doumer. He represented me at the trial,' said Landru as he stood and walked to the door.

'If I call him and pick up your journal, you know my answer,' said Jack, unable to hide the excitement in his voice.

Landru stopped at the door, looked back and smiled. 'I already do, Mr Rogan. Good day.'

12

Obersalzberg near Berchtesgaden: 8 October

Deep in thought, Ronan O'Hara sat at his workstation facing the wide, floor-to-ceiling window overlooking the stunning Bavarian mountain panorama. The morning fog had just lifted, revealing snow-covered peaks glistening in the bright sunlight like massive, timeless columns of rock pointing towards heaven. It was his favourite place of contemplation in the converted old farmhouse, where he did most of his creative thinking.

Looking like a command centre, the powerful computer with its three large, suspended monitors, and a communications system that would have been the envy of an aircraft carrier crew, allowed him access to almost every corner of the globe with the click of his mouse. With this, O'Hara had everything he needed at his fingertips. For a man like O'Hara, who thrived on power but craved anonymity and preferred to remain in the shadows, it was the perfect place from which to run his dark empire.

The spacious, three-hundred-year-old alpine farmhouse he had purchased almost thirty years earlier from a distant relative – an old aunt – and now rarely left, was the perfect domain. In his early seventies, diminutive in stature, completely bald and wearing thick glasses, O'Hara looked more like a retired headmaster than the secretive and shy billionaire businessman behind the Dark Net Bazaar.

The DNB, as it was known to the initiated, was an illegal, banned underground site pursued by almost every major security organisation around the world, trying in vain to shut it down. It was a marketplace where it was possible to buy just about anything imaginable, for a price. From a teenage slave girl in Kenya, to a state-of-the art rocket launcher, a jet fighter aircraft, or parts to build a nuclear power station, this site had something for everyone. It was also a place where it was possible to indulge one's deepest and darkest desires, from every drug imaginable, to snuff movies, real-time murder scenes, and the most perverse live pornography.

But O'Hara's biggest money-maker by far was gambling, connected to extraordinary computer games that he designed personally. A mathematics genius who carried complex algorithms and equations around in his head like other people might carry around recipes for pies or curries, his extraordinary mind could conjure up ideas and combinations for complex computer games with a few strokes on his keyboard that would have taken an advanced university think-tank months, if not years, to develop.

The games were each unique and combined had a huge international following, turning over millions every month. Payment was in bitcoins through a secure app on the dark web.

The reason these games were so sought after and popular was the blurred link between illusion and reality. In these games, traditional cartoons rubbed shoulders seamlessly with live scenes, which added a totally different dimension of excitement and reality to sex, extreme violence and death, the hallmarks of these ingenious games. And by gambling on the outcome of the action in certain scenes, the observer became a personally involved participant with an opportunity to influence the game and win huge sums in seconds.

For these reasons, the interactive games were very addictive and players regularly spent days glued to their computer screens, spending large amounts of money in the hope of securing that big prize. Once that happened, the winner was 'written' into the game and became one of the characters in the action. This too was a huge incentive, as it added prestige and 'dark web fame', and allowed the winner to gamble at much better odds. In addition, the winner received regular cash bonuses to keep him or her motivated. O'Hara had perfected this approach into a winning formula that had made him a fortune.

Looking at the picture-postcard farmhouse surrounded by dense forest – mainly tall, gnarled fir trees that had weathered many a harsh alpine winter – no-one would have guessed that these idyllic surroundings were hiding a dark, sophisticated operation below ground, directly under the hoofs of a herd of contented cattle grazing peacefully in the lush meadows.

Located just a kilometre from the Obersalzberg – Hitler's alpine fortress where the Fuehrer had spent a lot of time during the war and planned some of his most ambitious campaigns and diabolical 'solutions' – O'Hara's complex had become the HQ of a different empire. A cyber empire with elements of potent evil that would have rivalled the Nazis, and in many ways made their concentration camps look tame by comparison. In fact, O'Hara's converted farmhouse and the neighbouring properties he had bought up over the years didn't look all that different from Hitler's beloved 'Berghof' complex. Of course, nothing remained of that or any of the other buildings on the Obersalzberg except for an extensive, fortified underground bunker network that still criss-crossed the area like a maze. Everything else had been destroyed after the war.

O'Hara looked again at the French newspaper headline article he had printed off earlier, and smiled. It was an announcement by the Paris police about a sensational find in a deserted 'house of horrors lurking in the suburbs' as the paper called it, reviving the notorious Death Mask Murder cases that had haunted Paris five years earlier, and dominated the headlines for weeks. Landru was specifically mentioned, his conviction put once again under the spotlight and questioned.

So, he cracked the code at last, thought O'Hara. The missing piece of the puzzle had been found, and it was falling into place. The quest could now resume! All that remained to be done was to get Landru released.

The Death Mask Murder cases had been part of O'Hara's most successful and lucrative computer games, earning him a fortune. Each of the murders had been recorded live and posted on the dark web, with millions being wagered on the outcome of certain scenes and actions leading up to, and including, the murders.

Apart from serving as a most unique and unimaginably brutal subject for a series of computer games, the Death Mask Murders had a separate, much deeper purpose, and it all related to another of O'Hara's passions: treasure hunting.

O'Hara had come across the legend of the Inca treasure of the Llanganates by chance thirty years earlier, and was instantly hooked. Since then, he had used his considerable resources to find out if the treasure really existed and, if so, how to retrieve it. That was how he had come across a paper published by Professor Landru of the Sorbonne. In that paper, Landru had carefully set out the history of the treasure and put forward persuasive arguments, supported by credible evidence, suggesting that the treasure was real, and even hinting at possible locations where it might be found. To O'Hara, who deep down was as addicted a gambler as his cyber-punters, this was irresistible.

That was when O'Hara formulated a brilliant plan. He would use Landru and his extensive knowledge of and passion for the subject that bordered on obsession, to lead him to the treasure – if it did in fact exist as Landru seemed to suggest.

In addition, O'Hara came up with another ingenious idea. He developed a sophisticated computer game about the Llanganates treasure-legend that could be used to 'draw out' additional information about the treasure and its history. By putting the subject 'out there' on the dark net, and setting targets and challenges as part of the game, he could harness thousands of minds to see if someone knew something useful, or saw a connection that he could use in his quest. That was how the Death Mask Murders had been conceived.

Once Landru was released, he would continue his quest. Of that, O'Hara was sure. He was just as passionate about it as O'Hara. And after what Landru had been through, there was nothing else left for him do to in life. O'Hara, a master manipulator with an uncanny understanding of human nature, always knew which buttons to press to get what he wanted from people. He therefore knew exactly what to do to get Landru released. He would send something sensational to Chief Superintendent Lapointe's private email address that would do just that.

O'Hara scrolled through some of his secret, encrypted files until he found what he was after. Then he retrieved Lapointe's email address, which he had hacked into a long time ago, and attached the explosive file. For a moment he looked up and watched the majestic Watzmann, the tallest mountain in the district, emerge in all its glory out of the mist.

Here we go, he thought, feeling a wave of excitement. *Let the final stage of the quest begin, and see where it takes us.* O'Hara smiled and pressed the send button.

13

Paris Police Headquarters: 9 October

'We are almost there,' said Dupree as he approached Police Headquarters at Place Louis-Lépine, 1 rue de Lutèce. It was early in the morning and the traffic was diabolical as usual. The trip from the Kuragin chateau had taken almost three hours. 'I haven't been here in years. I used to love this place.'

'Lapointe didn't give you any hints?' asked Jack, sitting next to Dupree in the car.

'No. All he said was it was urgent and asked us to meet him here. He sounded quite agitated, which is unusual for him.'

'The announcement in the paper yesterday about that "house of horrors" must have caused quite a stir and ruffled more than a few feathers.'

'You can say that again. The Landru case could quickly turn into a major embarrassment. I'm sure that's what this is all about.'

'Let's find out,' said Jack. 'Here we are. One good thing ...'

'What's that?'

'The office of Landru's solicitor is quite close. I'm going there after our meeting.'

'So, you've made up your mind then?'

'Of course I have. There wasn't really much to think about, and Landru knew it. I'm hooked.'

'You don't say,' teased Dupree and parked the car.

Looking like a man who had worked through the night without sleeping a wink, Lapointe met them in the corridor outside his office. 'Thank you for coming so quickly. I really appreciate it. I wouldn't have asked if it wasn't important. We have a problem ...'

Lapointe ushered them into his office and closed the door. 'Come, I have something to show you, but before I do, you must promise to keep this to yourselves for the time being. You'll see why in a moment.'

'Goes without saying,' said Jack.

'Please take a seat.' Lapointe turned his computer screen around. 'Watch,' he said and pressed the play button.

For the next three minutes everyone in the room watched in silence, mesmerised by the horror unfolding on the screen.

'Where on earth did this come from?' asked Dupree, looking shocked, after the screen had gone blank.

'It was sent to me yesterday from a server we can't trace. Anonymous and secure. Typical dark web; professional stuff.'

'This is unbelievable,' said Jack. 'Is it authentic?'

'The experts seem to think so, but are still looking into it,' said Lapointe.

'A brutal murder recorded live on video. Who would do something like that, and why?'

'Exactly,' said Lapointe. 'And why send it to me now, after we've just discovered that chamber?'

'To set the record straight?' ventured Dupree.

'I doubt it,' said Lapointe. 'This is part of a plan.'

'Could we see it again, please?' said Jack, moving his chair closer to the screen.

'Sure.'

The short video opened with a scene showing Landru, apparently comatose, slumped in a chair. His eyes were closed, his mouth open. There was no sound to the video, which made what was to come even more chilling. On a small table next to the chair were a hypodermic needle and other drug-taking paraphernalia. Kneeling on the floor next to Landru was a naked young man. Someone standing behind him was holding a gun to his head.

Then the camera swung around and a dark figure standing in a doorway came into view. Blurred at first, and difficult to see in the gloom.

Then the camera moved closer.

Wearing a black suit, white shirt, a large polka-dot bow tie and white gloves – the face hidden behind a mask of a grinning clown – the figure walked slowly into the room and stopped in front of the camera.

Lapointe stopped the video. 'The young man kneeling on the floor is the male prostitute we found garrotted in his flat in Montmartre five years ago. This video was taken there, no doubt about it. Everything fits. The surroundings, the furniture, everything, right down to the last detail. Many of the items are still in our evidence archives.'

The rest of the video showed the grinning clown garrotting the young man from behind with what looked like a wire. The camera zoomed in on the young man's contorted face and bulging eyes full of terror until blood could be seen oozing out of his open mouth, and his body went limp.

The final scene showed the clown walking slowly towards an open door at the back of the room. As he reached the door, he stopped, turned around and waved, before disappearing into the darkness.

'This is grotesque!' said Jack.

'Perhaps so, but what it *means* is that Landru didn't commit the murder, and I don't have to tell you what that implies. The consequences are too awful to contemplate.' Lapointe paused, a troubled look on his face.

'Gentlemen, we now have seven unsolved murders on our hands and we know of only three, committed right here in Paris. As for the others, who knows? We are contacting Interpol right now to see what they can come up with. These murders were committed a number of years apart, and except for the three Paris murders, they most likely occurred in other countries.'

'An international serial killer team?' said Jack. 'There are at least three people involved here apart from Landru and the victim.'

'I don't know what to think right now,' said Lapointe. 'The Prefect isn't even returning my calls at the moment. Apparently, he was speechless when he heard the news. So, here we are.'

'I can imagine,' said Dupree.

For a while Jack just sat, deep in thought. Something at the end of the video just before the screen went blank had caught his eye.

'Could you please play the very last bit again? Just before the clown walks through the door and disappears. There was something ...'

'Sure,' said Lapointe and adjusted the video.

Jack got up and walked over to the screen for a closer look. 'Please stop the video as soon as I ask.'

Lapointe nodded and pressed the button.

The clown had just turned around and was waving. Just before he disappeared into the darkness and the screen went blank, part of a left hand came into view.

'Stop!' Jack shouted. The image froze. '*There*,' he said and pointed to the screen.

Lapointe stood and walked around the desk to have a better look. Dupree came closer too. 'What are we looking at?' Dupree asked.

'There's something here, at the back of the wrist; look!'

'I can see it,' said Lapointe. 'It looks like some kind of tattoo. A *number*? Thirteen ... something?'

'That's what I think,' said Jack, a broad smile spreading across his face as he remembered Landru's last words just before he left the interview room. 'The hand is quite small, don't you agree, guys?' continued Jack.

Dupree nodded. 'Could be a woman's hand. She must have been recording the whole thing. She's holding the camera with her right hand, I'd say, and is about to turn it off with her left. Her index finger is pointing at the camera.'

'Makes sense,' said Dupree.

'And why is this significant?' asked Lapointe.

Jack took his time before replying. 'Because I think I've seen this tattoo before,' he said quietly.

Lapointe and Dupree stared at Jack, stunned.

'You can't be serious!' said Lapointe, breaking the silence. He lit his pipe and watched Jack carefully. After Jack's recent involvement in the notorious Ritz murder case, Lapointe knew better than to just dismiss this comment as fantasy.

Jack held up his hand. 'Before I can tell you more, I want to be absolutely sure,' continued Jack, pre-empting the barrage of questions that was about to erupt.

'And you think you can do that?' asked Lapointe, looking incredulous.

'Yes,' said Jack quietly. 'I believe so.'

14

Kuragin chateau: 10 October

Countess Kuragin tightened the belt of her dressing gown and walked into the conservatory. It was three in the morning. Earlier, she had observed from her bedroom window that the light was on – a sign that Jack was still working – and decided to find out what was keeping him up all night.

Jack sat in his usual place by the window, surrounded by the indoor palms, open books, and bundles of loose pages covered in handwriting. His laptop was open and he was staring at the screen. Empty coffee cups and a cheese platter with a few grapes and broken crackers on the windowsill were the only evidence of any sustenance consumed during a long night of sleuthing.

'Do you know what time it is?' asked the countess.

Jack looked up, surprised. 'No idea, but what I can tell you is this …' Jack held up a small folder like a trophy. 'This is without doubt one of the most extraordinary things I've read in years.'

The countess smiled. She had seen it all before, but Jack's enthusiasm was infectious. 'And what might that be?'

'Landru's journal I picked up from his solicitor yesterday.'

'Ah. A serial killer's diary?' said the countess, a teasing glint in her eyes.

'It's a lot more than that.'

'I tell you what. Let's go down into the kitchen. We'll have a cup of tea and you can tell me all about it. What do you say?'

Jack closed the folder and stood up. 'You're on.'

After the conservatory, where he did most of his writing, the spacious, vaulted kitchen in the basement with the long wooden refectory table in front of the fireplace – a leftover from earlier days – was Jack's favourite place in the chateau, where he had spent countless hours with the countess over the years. It was an informal place of wellbeing where he felt totally at ease and free to share some of his most intimate thoughts, and fears, with the countess, who had not only become a close friend, but his confidante as well.

'How I love this place,' said Jack and pointed to the large, ornate samovar on the kitchen table. '"A tea urn warming generations" you called it. And to think that it all began with Anna …'

The countess reached for Jack's hand and squeezed it. 'I can never repay you for what you've done. You brought my only daughter back to me and saved my grandson. Without you, both would have perished.'

'You've repaid me many times over, you know,' said Jack, changing direction. 'You gave me a home, a sense of belonging when I needed it most. Will's death took a lot out of me.' Jack looked pensively at the samovar. 'Part of me died with him in the Kimberley that day,' he added with sadness in his voice.

'Well, you are part of the family now, like it or not. Tea?'

'Yes, please. I'm a little worried about Tristan.'

'In what way?'

'Difficult to say, but he's not …'

'Happy?'

'Spot on. I don't think married life at the fancy palazzo in Venice is for him.'

'Married life is an adjustment for everyone, especially someone like Tristan.'

'I suppose so. He's a different person when he's with me.'

'Hardly surprising,' mumbled the countess and handed Jack a cup of tea. 'Now, tell me about this journal.'

Jack sat down on the bench and opened the folder he had brought with him. 'Fascinating stuff,' he said. 'And it all began with an Inca khipu.'

'What on earth is that?'

'The Inca had no written language. Therefore, no written records of any kind to tell us about their culture and their history except for these mysterious khipus. Khipus are knotted cords that recorded information. Strings that speak.'

'Fascinating. How do they work?'

'It's complicated and to us, used to writing, quite alien. Unfortunately, this unique Inca recording system remains largely undeciphered. However, a few years ago, Landru, who as you know was a history professor at the Sorbonne specialising in the Spanish conquest of Peru and the fall of the Inca Empire, teamed up with an anthropologist and ethnohistorian in Germany to decipher a famous khipu in the Ethnological Museum in Berlin, the Morales khipu.' Jack sipped his tea and continued. 'Mainly made of cotton and Llama wool, khipus were produced by master weavers in a complex, traditional weaving process, and consisted of warped threads made into multicoloured knotted chords, which conveyed information in surprisingly sophisticated and effective ways. The Morales khipu was discovered in Lima in 1655 by Father Ignacio Morales, a powerful Jesuit. And judging by what I've read so far, that event marked the beginning of this extraordinary story, culminating in the bizarre Death Mask Murders,' added Jack quietly.

'Seriously?'

Jack reached for Landru's journal on the table in front of him and opened it. 'Oh yes,' he said. 'Listen to this …'

Lima Cathedral: 2 February 1655

Dressed in simple, modest robes that belied his lofty position, Father Morales was on his knees in one of the side chapels of the cathedral, praying for guidance. An imposing edifice begun by Pizarro more than a hundred years earlier, Morales had spent the best part of his adult life building the cathedral into one of the most impressive and powerful visual representations of Catholicism in South America. A symbol of faith and European religious power, this extraordinary achievement had only been possible because of close collaboration between the Spanish Court and the Church, especially the Jesuits.

A consummate diplomat and shrewd negotiator who understood human nature, greed, and the insatiable lust for power that were the hallmarks of the representatives of the Spanish Crown in Lima, Morales had used his considerable influence back in Spain to further the cause of the Church in South America in ways no other before him had been able to achieve. However, to be able to continue to do so, he desperately needed more than influence. He needed money.

Morales made the sign of the cross and was about to stand up when a monk walked up to him from behind. The monk stopped, unsure of what to do. Morales noticed his shadow and turned around. 'What is it?' he asked.

'Forgive the intrusion, Father, but one of our missionaries has just returned from the mountains and is asking for you—'

'Can't it wait?' snapped Morales impatiently.

'No. He's dying and wants you to hear his confession.'

'Where is he?'

'In the monastery.'

Morales and the monk hurried back to the monastery, which was just behind the cathedral.

'We put him in there,' said a monk waiting at the door and pointed to a small cell. 'He's in a bad way.'

The first thing Morales noticed was the foul smell. *Decaying flesh*, he thought and covered his nose with his sleeve as he walked slowly over to the dark shape lying motionless on top of a bunk. At first he didn't recognise the gaunt face hidden by an unruly beard and long, sweaty hair, but when he looked into the man's feverish eyes burning with zeal, recognition dawned.

'*Diego*? Is that you?' asked Morales, unable to hide his surprise and disbelief.

'It is,' said the man, his voice weak and barely audible.

'It's been more than three years. We thought you were dead.'

'All the others are. I'm the last one. With the Good Lord's help I made it back, just. As you can see, I'm dying. We haven't much time, yet there's so much I have to tell you ...' Diego's voice trailed off and he began cough, blood oozing from the corners of his mouth covered in sores.

'Water!' shouted Morales. 'Give the man water.'

A monk came running with a pail of water and helped Diego to drink.

Feeling better, Diego looked at Morales. 'We found it,' he whispered.

'What are you saying?' demanded Morales.

''We made it all the way to the volcano. Ruminahui's legendary treasure exists.'

'Have you seen it?' asked Morales, his voice trembling with excitement.

'Not as such, but I brought you this.' Diego reached into a deep pocket in his torn cloak and pulled out a stunning ceremonial knife of solid gold. 'This is a *tumi*, a sacrificial knife. There are hundreds of them in the cave.'

'What cave?'

'There's a secret cave at the base of the volcano. A deep tunnel reaching down into the fiery throat of the mountain, haunted by spirits. That is the place where Ruminahui hid the treasure after Atahualpa was murdered by Pizarro in Cajamarca. The cave is guarded by a tribe. Only the chief and the Inca priests know the exact location of the cave, which is high up in the mountains. They are descendants of the porters who carried the treasure into the mountains and hid it from the invaders. We spent several months with the tribe and I befriended the chief. He even converted—'

'What about the treasure?' interrupted Morales, well aware of the importance and urgency of the moment. '*Do you know where it is?*'

'We were not allowed to visit the cave. I tried, but it is forbidden. I only saw a few pieces of gold kept by the priests in the village as ceremonial objects. They are all part of the treasure. This here is one of them.'

'Then, it was all for nothing? It's an impenetrable wilderness out there.'

'Not entirely,' said Diego, gasping for breath.

'What do you mean?'

'When it became clear that we wouldn't be taken to the cave, I tried a different way.'

'What way?'

'While we were there, the chief became very ill and was dying, just like I am right now. I told you I was able to convert him ...'

'What of it?' asked Morales, becoming increasingly frustrated.

'I told him that if he wanted to enter the kingdom of heaven, he had to repent. When he asked me what that meant, I told him that he would have to deliver the treasure to God as a sign of his submission and faith.'

Morales looked at Diego, impressed. This was exactly the kind of thing he would have done. The fear of damnation was a powerful tool he had used many times before. '*And?*' he asked.

'The chief was too weak by then to even get up, and there was no way the priests would have taken us to the cave, so he did the next best thing.'

'What?'

'He told me where it was.'

'Are you serious? *How?*'

'He gave me this.'

Diego reached into his pocket again and pulled out what looked like a knotted bundle of coloured cords and held it up, his hand shaking.

'What's that?' asked Morales.

'This is a khipu.'

'Ah, yes. I've seen these before. They record stories, numbers, quantities for trade goods, things like that.'

'Yes, but not this one.'

'What do you mean?'

'According to the chief, this khipu records the exact location of the cave. It is a guide, using ancient landmarks known to the natives living there. It is like a map that will take us to the treasure. After he gave me this, I gave him absolution and he died. I now ask you to do the same for me,' said Diego, and closed his eyes.

* * *

'What at story,' said the countess and refilled Jack's cup. 'I can see why it kept you up all night. You mentioned a murder. Something to do with this?'

Jack opened the folder again. 'Landru certainly seems to think so, and it would seem with good reason, especially in light of what was found in that chamber of horrors the other day.'

'Care to explain?'

'The anthropologist Landru was working with on the Morales khipu at the time – a man called Gerhard Blumenthal – disappeared mysteriously while working at the museum. The Morales khipu disappeared with him. At first, the authorities treated this as some kind of theft, but the day after Blumenthal's disappearance, the police found what is believed to be a plaster death mask left on the steps of the museum.'

'How bizarre.'

'No trace of Blumenthal or the khipu have been found. Until now, perhaps,' added Jack quietly.

'I don't know how these cases seem to find you, Jack, but this is definitely up your alley,' said the countess, smiling. 'I suppose you and Claude will be working on this?'

Jack nodded, closed the folder and stood up. 'You must admit, this is irresistible.'

'To someone like you, definitely. Almost as good as your recent Russian adventure, I'd say.'

'I would love Tristan to join me in this. His instincts would be invaluable.'

'Why don't you ask him?'

'It's not quite that simple. I would hate to, you know, interfere with his marriage … *again!*'

'I understand. Just think about it. Perhaps Lorenza wouldn't mind?'

'You think so? Because she understands that he needs this?'

'No, because she loves him.'

15

Rome: 12 October

Jack got out of the taxi and, shielding his eyes from the glare, looked across the busy market square teeming with morning shoppers. Buying their fresh vegetables for the weekend, they haggled excitedly about the price with the stallholders, as was expected. It was a classic Roman shopping ritual that brought a smile to Jack's face. As he walked slowly past a stall selling tomatoes, zucchinis and artichokes, trying in vain to find house numbers, he looked up to see Bartolli standing on a balcony above him on the first floor, waving.

'Wait there, I'll come down,' shouted Bartolli.

Wearing an apron and her hair tied back with a scarf, Bartolli pushed through the noisy throng towards Jack. 'I should have warned you. Friday is market day and always chaotic around here. Welcome to Travestere.'

'I'm glad you saw me; no house numbers.'

Bartolli shrugged. 'I need some more tomatoes. Lunch is almost ready. Stay right here. I won't be long.' Bartolli returned moments later with a bag of tomatoes and took Jack by the hand. 'Come, follow me.'

Jack had arrived earlier that morning from Paris and had suggested they meet at a restaurant, but Bartolli insisted he come for lunch at her place instead. 'I hope you didn't mind coming here,' said Bartolli as they walked up the stairs.

'Not at all. This is absolutely delightful. I love all the bustle. Thanks for inviting me.'

'Mum wanted to meet you. She's read all of your books ...'

Jack stopped on the landing and looked at Bartolli. 'Now you tell me ...'

'She's a fabulous cook. She's cooking lunch. Bucatini all'Amatriciana, her speciality.'

'Ah.'

Bartolli burst out laughing. 'You are so predictable, Jack: *food!*'

'Is it that obvious?'

'Yes, it is.'

Bartolli and her mother looked more like sisters than mother and daughter. Same striking facial features, same curly dark-blonde hair, same smile. Jack felt instantly at home in the kitchen as he watched them put the finishing touches to the pasta with much flair and lively gesticulation.

'You can set the table on the terrace outside, if you like,' said Bartolli. 'In this household everyone pitches in, except Paulo.' Bartolli pointed to the old dog sitting on a mat in the corner, looking longingly at the stove.

Jack took off his jacket and walked out onto the terrace. 'What a view!' he said, letting his eyes roam over the cupola of St Peter's in the distance and across to the iconic ramparts of Castel Sant'Angelo. He set the table, then opened the wine he had brought, poured two glasses and took them inside into the kitchen.

'A 2007 Illuminati Ilico Riserva, like last time,' said Bartolli. 'Very thoughtful of you. How did you manage this? You came straight here from the airport, no?'

'Secret,' said Jack and handed a glass to Bartolli and one to her mother.

'I could easily get used to this,' said the mother, giving Jack her best smile. 'Salute!'

After a splendid lunch on the terrace, washed down with a copious quantity of red wine, Bartolli's mother excused herself and took Paulo for a walk.

'She's amazing. I can't believe she's your mother,' said Jack.

Bartolli smiled. 'That's what everybody says. She had me when she was eighteen. Same age as I had my first daughter. You are lucky my girls aren't here. Otherwise, there would have been pandemonium. Teenagers!'

'Where are they?'

'Picnic with their cousins. Now tell me what brought you here that you couldn't tell me over the phone.'

Jack put down his serviette and looked at Bartolli. 'The deeper I delve into the Landru case, the more astonishing it becomes.'

'His journal?'

'Yes. That's certainly part of it, but what really rocked us was that anonymous video sent to Lapointe that I mentioned.'

'Go on.'

Jack reached for his briefcase, pulled out his iPad and turned it on. 'Here, have a look.'

'I'm glad you showed this to me after lunch,' said Bartolli after she had watched the video in silence.

'According to Lapointe, this could get Landru out of jail – soon.'

'And so it should. According to this, he's definitely not the murderer. I said it all along, but nobody listened.'

'No, but *who is?* And more importantly, why all this theatre? A series of almost ritual killings. This must have a purpose.'

Bartolli shrugged, took a sip of wine and looked at Jack. 'Any ideas?'

'Perhaps.'

'Care to tell me about it?'

'Seven bizarre, unsolved murders. Same modus operandi but seemingly unconnected, except for the death masks. Yet, there seems to be a very precise pattern here; a clear, premeditated purpose.'

'Can you be more specific?'

'Dupree and I are working on it,' said Jack, avoiding the question.

'Come on, Jack.'

'It's too early for conclusions. We are barely in a position to ask the right questions. And there are so many unanswered questions here.'

'I see.'

'Yet one thing is becoming very clear.'

'What?'

'Landru didn't commit any of the murders, yet he's *connected* to all of them. There's a common thread.'

'What kind of common thread?'

'A quest.'

'*A what?*'

'You heard me.'

'What kind of quest?'

'A quest to find one of the greatest lost treasures imaginable.'

'Are you serious? A *treasure hunt?* Sounds a bit far-fetched, don't you think?'

'That's what I thought at first, but the evidence uncovered so far is compelling.'

'Tell me about it.'

'Dupree and I are still trying to piece it all together, but I can tell you a little about what we've found out so far.'

Bartolli sat back in her chair and looked expectantly at Jack.

'As you can imagine, Dupree and I pored over Landru's journal, line by line, word by word. It's a very clever, carefully constructed document. It provides enough information to create interest, but does not provide all the answers. It's designed to draw us in. Get us involved; hook us.'

'And has it done that?' asked Bartolli.

'What do you think? I'm here, aren't I? So far, Landru is holding all the cards. He's a smart operator who's had a lot of time to think about all this. To plan ...'

'He's a desperate man with an agenda.'

'He certainly is that, and we are part of that agenda. Whatever he has in mind, he can't do alone. For some reason I haven't quite worked out as yet, he needs me.'

'Oh, I can tell you why that is so,' said Bartolli, smiling.

'You can?'

'Sure. He needs you because of who you are. Because of what you do, and how you do it. Your profile, your networks. It's all in your books; simple.'

'You think so?'

'Jack, it's obvious. And then, of course, there's some kind of connection he mentioned. A link. Something to do with the cipher, remember? With this new information disclosed by the cipher – the house of horrors, and now this video – he has all he needs to deal with the authorities and prepare the way for his release. His lawyers will see to that. But obviously, there's more, much more. And for that, he needs *you*. And from what I've seen so far, he's doing an excellent job to get you involved. To draw you in.'

'You are right; and does that include you?' asked Jack, a sparkle in his eyes.

'It does. I'm also hooked. And besides, I want to see this case through.'

'Good, because I don't want to do this alone. No, I *can't* do this alone,' Jack corrected himself. 'Dupree and Lapointe are working on the obvious bits. The forensics stuff, looking into the other murders using Europol and Interpol. They are policemen, doing police work. As you can imagine, they are both under enormous pressure to get results.'

'But that's not for us, right?'

'No. There's a much bigger picture here, and that's where we come in.'

'Any ideas of what that might be?' asked Bartolli.

Jack took his time before replying, looking dreamily across the terracotta rooftops shimmering in the midday sun.

'Perhaps. We are dealing with a desperate, middle-aged, gay man, a highly intelligent, well-educated academic who has been ruined. I can't imagine what he had to endure in jail, yet he hasn't been defeated. He certainly hasn't given up. On the contrary, he's coming out fighting. You saw him. Remarkably confident and strong.'

'And what do you think he's fighting for? Apart from the obvious: vindication and being set free?'

'At least part of the answer can be found in his journal. From very early on in his career, he's been obsessed with one specific subject.'

'What subject?'

'The legendary Inca Llanganates treasure. And that's what got him into trouble in the first place and ultimately landed him in jail, convicted of a murder we now know he didn't commit. It all began with the publication of a paper that caused quite a stir in academic circles when it was published quite a few years ago.'

'I'm impressed! You *have* done your homework. Do we know anything further about that paper?'

'Not all that much at the moment, but I'm working on it. The paper was called *The Navarro Chronicles*, after a seventeenth-century manuscript of the same title written by a Spanish monk, which Landru discovered in a monastery library in Spain. I have tracked down a copy and am about to read it. That's what started it all and, according to Landru, was the reason behind the first Death Mask Murder.'

'*What?*'

'You heard me. Dupree is looking into it right now, but I am following a different trail.'

'What kind of trail?'

'I want to find out who's behind all this, and *why*. And, of course, that's what Landru wants me to do. Focus on the bigger picture and leave the murders to the police.'

Bartolli shook her head. 'This is amazing. Any leads?'

'Possibly. That's why I am going to Florence this evening. On the five-thirty train.'

'To do what?'

'I have a meeting tomorrow morning with Chief Prosecutor Grimaldi, and Cesaria Borroni, the acting chief superintendent of the Squadra Mobile. I know them both quite well. Mafia stuff from the past ...'

Bartolli looked impressed. 'Friends in high places. A meeting about what?'

'A tattoo, and a hunch.'

'You are a dark horse, Jack Rogan. What kind of tattoo?'

Jack pointed to the iPad on the table. 'A tattoo I saw in this video.'

'And this is relevant because?'

'It's a long shot, but if I am right it could lead us to whoever is behind all this.'

'Can you be more specific?' asked Bartolli, sounding excited.

'Not yet. But if I *am* right, I would like you to come with me to talk to someone in prison here in Italy. A notorious criminal. Interested?'

'What a silly question. First you wind me up, and then you ask me *this*?'

'Sorry. I just had to be sure first. Not all of my hunches turn into bullseyes.'

'I understand. If you want to be on the five-thirty train, you better get going.'

'I suppose so.'

'I could take you to the station if you like.'

'On the Vespa?' asked Jack, looking alarmed.

'Only if you're game, of course,' teased Bartolli.

'I'll take a taxi, if you don't mind.'

'Coward!'

16

On the train to Florence: 12 October

Jack loved trains, and preferred train travel to flying. To him, it was a wonderful way to relax and experience at least a little of the countryside. He settled back into his comfortable seat and watched the outskirts of Rome glide silently past as the train turned north on its way to Florence.

Jack opened his briefcase and pulled out the Landru journal. He wanted to go over the section dealing with the discovery of *The Navarro Chronicles* again, which according to Landru had marked the beginning of the tragic Death Mask Murders saga that had just taken such a dramatic turn with the discovery of that chamber of horrors in Paris.

What could possibly motivate someone to commit such atrocities over a period of so many years? Jack asked himself as he kept reading. What kind of mind could come up with such an evil yet ingenious plan and, more importantly perhaps, implement such complex, carefully staged murders without getting caught? This required not only courage and dogged determination, but careful planning and extraordinary resources as well.

Landru had come across *The Navarro Chronicles* by accident through a friend he had met in a Paris nightclub. He was in his early thirties at the time, working on his PhD. Eager to make a name for himself, he saw in *The Navarro Chronicles* the opportunity he had been waiting for.

Buried deep in the archives in a forgotten corner high up on the shelves in a place where they didn't belong, *The Navarro Chronicles* was an extraordinary eyewitness account of a secret expedition financed by the Spanish king into a remote part of the Andes. The expedition was a search for a lost Inca treasure hidden by Ruminahui, an Inca general, after the murder of the Inca king Atahualpa in Cajamarca in 1533.

Written by Father Sebastian Navarro, a *mestizo* – he had an Inca mother and a Spanish father – the chronicles turned out to be the only credible documentary evidence not only of the fact that the fabulous Inca treasure did exist, but more importantly that it was actually found hidden in a remote mountain cave, and recovered.

Landru wrote a paper on the subject that instantly propelled him to the academic prominence he had craved, and secured him a coveted teaching position at the Sorbonne. Little did he know at the time that this moment of triumph was also the beginning of his long and devastating downfall.

Jack pulled out of the back of the journal the copy of Landru's paper he had quickly downloaded from the internet that morning, put on his glasses and began to read.

Llanganates Mountains: June 1659

Father Morales saw a shaft of sunlight penetrate the dense jungle canopy ahead, like a guiding beacon showing the way through the wilderness, and held up his hand. 'Let's stop over there,' he said and pointed to a small clearing. Exhausted, his parched throat crying out for water, Morales got off his mule and began to rub his stiff legs. That's when he saw it.

'There!' he shouted. 'The volcano!'

Father Navarro hurried over to him and had a look. 'I think you're right,' he said. 'That must be it. At last!'

The party, consisting of ten heavily armed soldiers on horseback and two dozen local porters with mules, had left Quito a week earlier. Officially, the purpose of the expedition was a religious one: to bring the word of God to one of the tribes living in a remote mountain area in the east. The presence of the two Jesuit priests made this believable, but the real purpose of the journey was something quite different known only to the two priests, and the two senior officers in charge of the soldiers acting as escorts. Forays like this into the unknown hinterland were by no means uncommon, and therefore hadn't attracted undue attention.

No-one looking at the pitiful party struggling up the mountain would have suspected the real intentions behind the expedition. It had taken Morales four years; a long, arduous trip halfway around the world; and all of his diplomatic skills, influence, and powers of persuasion to make this mission a reality.

The breakthrough came when, after months of waiting, he was finally granted an audience with the king, Philip IV of Spain. After presenting the stunning golden tumi and the khipu that Diego had brought back from the mountains to His Majesty as evidence that the legendary Ruminahui treasure was real, Morales was able to persuade the king that an expedition to retrieve the treasure was warranted. What Morales couldn't have known was that his timing was most opportune.

With his treasury almost drained by costly wars, and therefore always short of money, the king saw in Morales's proposal a possible way to replenish the coffers of his impoverished empire. If only part of what Morales had described was true, then such an expedition was certainly worthwhile.

Not only did the king finance the expedition, he also provided two of his most trusted officers to lead it, and promised Morales and the Church a share of the treasure. A week later, armed with the king's letter of instructions to the Viceroy of Peru, Morales set sail with the two high-ranking officers, and returned to Lima to arrange the expedition.

Morales spread out the khipu, which was supposed to lead them to the treasure cave, on a rock, and turned to Navarro. 'What do you think?' he said, watching Navarro carefully. The reason he had asked Navarro to accompany him on this expedition was his extensive knowledge not only of the language, Quechua, but also as a mestizo he was familiar with local customs and most importantly, knew how to 'read' and interpret khipus.

'I think we are getting close,' said Navarro and pointed to the mountain. 'I can recognise a number of features described here in these strands. We should approach the mountain from the south, and then follow that ridge over there.'

Five hours later, they reached what looked like an overgrown entry to a large cave at the base of the steep mountain they had sighted earlier. It was the entry to a complex system of multilevel lava tubes, formed by a pahoehoe flow of very fluid lava under a congealing surface crust thousands of years ago. For hiding a treasure, these huge tubes that reached for several kilometres into the mountain, like shafts and tunnels of an underground mine, were perfect, but without some kind of map it would have been futile to begin searching for a hiding place in this confusing and dangerous underground maze. That's where the khipu came to the rescue as it provided much-needed directions on how to navigate the complex system without getting lost, and ultimately locate the hiding place of the treasure.

Just before they entered the cave, one of the officers walked up to Morales. 'We are being watched,' he whispered. 'There are eyes everywhere, even up in the trees. We are surrounded. I believe some kind of attack is imminent.'

'What do you suggest we do?' asked Morales, looking around anxiously.

'Get into the cave and take cover, and leave the rest to me. Quickly!'

As Morales and Navarro made a dash for the cave, the officer turned around, drew his sword and barked some orders. His men dismounted immediately and formed a protective line in front of the entry to the cave. Their loaded arquebuses at the ready, they were waiting for the attack. Moments later, it came – suddenly and from all sides at once, even from above.

It began with a hundred hostile voices chanting ancient war songs to spread terror and intimidate the foe, the strange, high-pitched sounds echoing eerily through the dense vegetation hiding the attackers. This was followed by a barrage of arrows and spears raining down from above, before the first wave of half-naked warriors attacked with clubs. Two of the porters who hadn't made it into the cave in time were beaten to death, their panicked mules stampeding into the forest.

The officer lifted his sword and shouted, 'Fire!' Ten arquebuses fired all at once, the sound of the shots rolling like thunder through the mouth of the cave behind the soldiers. The first wave of warriors lay dead or dying on the ground, blood gushing from huge wounds. Stunned, the warriors coming up from behind looked on in terror. They had never seen or heard gunfire before, nor had they seen horses, which to them looked like some strange spirit-beasts belonging to another world.

After the barrage, the officer stepped forward and plunged his razor-sharp sword into the chest of a young warrior who came running towards him, killing him instantly. The soldiers next to him, all war-wise veterans, attacked, continuing the slaughter, the war clubs and wooden shields of their opponents no match for their own superior weapons made of steel.

Then abruptly, everything went silent. The chanting stopped and the beaten attackers retreated into the bush, leaving their dead behind. The officer held up his hand. 'That's enough,' he said, realising a pursuit would be futile and dangerous. 'Well done, men. I don't think they'll be coming back in a hurry. Let's secure the entry to the cave and go inside.'

Holding a candle in one hand and the khipu in the other, Navarro followed the directions imbedded in the knotted threads with the certainty of a somnambulist. The first clue that they were getting close came when they stumbled upon a mound of human bones.

'Here, look!' said Navarro and pointed to three crushed human skulls on the ground in front of him. 'The threads tell us that Ruminahui and his warriors killed the porters who carried the treasure into the cave. I believe we have just found them.'

Morales nodded, barely able to control his excitement. He too could sense they were getting close. Then something caught his eye: a golden face wedged between two rocks was staring at him out of the gloom like a messenger from the afterlife, trying to warn off unwelcome intruders.

'Over here!' he cried out and knelt down on the ground. 'Come, give me a hand.' The soldiers following behind formed a semicircle and held up their torches. As they came closer, spreading the light, Navarro pointed to the golden face. 'This is a ceremonial mask of the Sun god Inti,' he whispered, as a chill of fear raced down his spine, triggered by distant memories of his Inca ancestry. 'We are entering a different world here. We must be careful.'

Ignoring the warning, Morales cleared away a pile of small rocks in front of the mask. An opening appeared. Morales bent forward and looked inside.

'Can you see anything?' asked Navarro.

'Yes, wonderful things!' replied Morales, his voice hoarse.

What he was looking at was the lost treasure of a defeated civilisation that had desperately tried to save its king, and failed.

Jack slipped the pieces of paper back into Landru's journal and closed his eyes. *What an extraordinary story,* he thought, and let his mind drift back to Morales and the treasure cave. *I wonder what happened to all the gold?* Feeling relaxed and sleepy, Jack began to doze off, but just before he fell asleep, the loudspeakers crackled into life and a cheerful voice announced the train's imminent arrival in Florence.

17

Florence: 13 October

Jack went down to the breakfast room in the small hotel he had checked into the night before, near the Firenze Santa Maria Novella railway station. He was one of the first guests to arrive, and carefully chose a particular table near the buffet.

The choice of hotel had been quite deliberate. It was conveniently located near the station, and close to the Squadra Mobile HQ. But there was another, more important reason for the choice. It was the same hotel Jack had stayed in only a few months earlier during the Stolzfus matter. It had been the place of his dramatic abduction by Spiridon 4 – a notorious hit squad engaged by the Mafia – which had taken him all the way to South America, and almost cost him his life.

But the choice of the breakfast table had another, more immediate relevance and urgency. It was the very same table where he had been sitting when he spotted the wrist tattoo he thought he had recognised in the Landru murder video. And that was the reason he had come to Florence to talk with Chief Prosecutor Grimaldi and Chief Superintendent Borroni, who had been in charge of the Giordano case and had broken that family's hold on the drug supply in Florence.

Jack sat down at the table, ordered a cafe latte and tried to remember that fateful breakfast just over three months ago. As he sipped his coffee, he let his mind drift back to the morning that had changed everything. Satisfied that his memory hadn't played tricks on him, he finished his breakfast and prepared himself for the meeting arranged for eight am in the chief prosecutor's office.

Before going into the familiar building he had visited several times before, Jack crossed the road, went into the small trattoria he knew was Grimaldi's favourite, and bought half a dozen *cornetti*. Jack didn't want to arrive empty-handed. After all, this was Italy, and food an important part of interacting with friends.

Grimaldi greeted Jack like an old friend, gave him a hug and patted him on the back. 'Wonderful to see you again, Jack, and so soon. I hope this visit to Florence will not be as eventful as the last one.'

'Shouldn't be. After all, most of the villains we were after are either dead or in jail.'

Grimaldi nodded, but as one of the most successful Mafia hunters, who had himself survived several assassination attempts, he knew just too well that the real world was different. 'Unfortunately, not all of them,' he said, looking pensively out the window as the familiar church bells began to toll, announcing the hour. 'Cesaria should be here any moment. Coffee?'

'Yes, please.'

Even before the bells of Santa Maria del Fiore, which were always a little behind the others, fell silent, the door opened and Cesaria Borroni, the acting chief superintendent, burst into the room. Grimaldi, Borroni and Jack knew each other well, having closely worked together in 2016 on the notorious Giordano assassinations and the bloody fight against the Mafia in Florence, and then again more recently in the Stolzfus matter.

'Have one of these,' said Jack and pointed to the paper bag on Grimaldi's desk. 'Still hot.'

'Don't mind if I do. I started at five this morning.'

Borroni helped herself to a *cornetto* and, munching happily, looked expectantly at Jack. 'What brings you here this early? You said it was urgent.'

Jack opened his briefcase, pulled out his iPad and turned it on. 'This here,' he said. He called up the Landru murder video, put the iPad on Grimaldi's desk and pressed the play button.

Cesaria stopped eating and stared at the screen. 'That's quite something. And we think the Mafia's bad. Where did you get this?'

During the next few minutes, Jack provided a brief summary of the Landru case, his curious involvement in the matter, and the meaning and potential ramifications of the video.

Grimaldi shook his head. 'No doubt about you, Jack. You seem to become entangled in the strangest cases.'

'And in the weirdest ways. But why are you showing us this?' asked Borroni. 'Now?'

'Because of this.' Jack rewound the video and stopped it at the frame showing the hand with the wrist tattoo.

Borroni leaned forward for a better look. 'The tattoo?' she asked.

'Yes. I've seen it before.'

'Seriously?' said Grimaldi. 'Where?'

'At breakfast in a hotel not far from here, on the morning I was abducted.'

After a moment of silence Borroni said quietly, 'Looks like a woman's hand.'

Jack nodded. 'It is.'

'Teodora?'

'Yes—'

'But Teodora's dead. She died in that car accident at Lake Como,' interjected Grimaldi.

'I know.'

'So, why is this relevant?'

Jack held up his hand. 'Please hear me out. I contacted Izabel Santos. She lives in Milan. As you know, Teodora and Izabel were lovers. She confirmed it: Teodora had a number tattooed on her wrist. We can only see a one and a three, but the whole number was 1389, a year.'

'What kind of year?' asked Borroni.

'Thirteen eighty-nine was the year of the Battle of Kosovo,' said Jack. 'Historically, it was a decisive battle between the Catholic Serbian Prince Lazar and Sultan Murad, the ruler of the powerful Ottoman Empire. Both Lazar and Murad were killed during the battle and both armies suffered huge losses, but the Serbian army was annihilated. This defeat marked the beginning of Ottoman rule and the arrival of Islam in the Serbian principalities. To Muslims living in the area, this date has huge significance to this very day, and the recent bloody conflict and persecution of Muslims can be traced back to that battle.'

Grimaldi lit a small cigar. 'What are you suggesting here?' he asked as the implications of what Jack had just said began to sink in.

'What I'm suggesting is this.' Jack pointed to the screen. 'If Teodora was present at this killing and took the video, as this picture here seems to suggest, then it follows that the Spiridon 4 were most likely involved and carried out the murder.'

'Not an unreasonable assumption,' said Borroni, 'but an assumption, nevertheless. Teodora is dead and so is her twin sister, Nadia. That means two members of Spiridon 4 are no longer with us.'

'But two, namely Aladdin and Silvanus, are. And we know where we can find them.'

Grimaldi watched the smoke from his cigar curl towards the open window. 'We do. They are both in the Pagliarelli maximum-security prison in Palermo.' Grimaldi looked at Jack. 'Mainly thanks to you, and Tristan.'

'What's on your mind, Jack?' asked Borroni.

'I would like to talk to them.'

'You are joking, surely,' said Grimaldi, looking alarmed.

'No. I'm deadly serious. As we all know, Spiridon 4 were hired guns. Perhaps the most sophisticated and expensive – and successful – hit squad in the business. Just think back to the Stolzfus matter. Can you think of another group who could have pulled off that kidnapping, and what followed?'

Grimaldi shook his head.

'If Spiridon 4 carried out this killing, then someone hired them to do it, and paid a small fortune for their services.'

'And you want to find out who?' interjected Borroni.

'Yes. As I told you, there are seven unsolved murders involved here. All seem to be connected and have great similarities.'

'Are you suggesting that Spiridon 4 were somehow responsible for them all?' Grimaldi reached for a small ashtray on the desk in front of him and stubbed out his cigar.

'A reasonable conclusion, wouldn't you say? If I'm right, then someone paid millions over a period of several years to have these murders carried out in a carefully choreographed manner. Ritual killings, you could call them. The question is *why*, and on whose instructions.'

'And even if a meeting with Aladdin and Silvanus could be arranged,' said Grimaldi, 'do you really think they would talk to you and tell you about these matters? *You* of all people? The fact that you and Tristan were willing to testify against them was one of the main reasons they pleaded guilty, and there was no trial. They got twenty years, and for that we are all in your debt. Trials are notoriously unreliable. Anything can happen. We've seen it many times, haven't we, Cesaria?'

Cesaria nodded.

'Oh, I think they would talk,' said Jack.

'What makes you say that?' said Borroni, unsure where Jack was coming from.

'They will talk, trust me, if we offer them the right thing in return.'

'*We?* Come on, Jack. This doesn't make any sense. Why should "we" go along with this and offer them anything? My superiors would never agree to this. We have a conviction. The matter is closed.'

Jack took his time before replying. 'I'm calling in a favour,' he said quietly. 'You said yourself, in this very office by the way, that you, no, *Florence,* owed me a big favour. Isn't that right, Cesaria?'

'It is. I was there.'

Looking distinctly uncomfortable, Grimaldi lit another cigar. 'Before we go any further with this, there's something you need to know first. We were about to contact you and tell you, but since you're here ... Cesaria, please tell him, but this stays strictly between us, understood?'

Jack nodded.

'We've heard from one of our Mafia informers that Alessandro Giordano is planning something,' began Borroni.

'Planning what?'

'Some kind of revenge attack. The fallout from the Stolzfus matter has all but ruined him and his family. The lucrative South American drug supply came to an abrupt end, and the only reason he isn't in jail is because nobody is talking, but he has lost a lot of face. And in Mafia circles that's bad. Really bad. And the only way to regain face and respect is by hitting back.'

'What are you getting at?' asked Jack, frowning.

'We know that Venice is part of what used to be Giordano territory. The family still has a lot of influence and business interests there.'

Jack felt his stomach begin to churn as a wave of fear washed over him. *Venice*, he thought. *Oh my God!*

'And who lives in Venice?' continued Cesaria. 'Who played a major part in bringing about the Giordano family's downfall?'

'*Tristan*,' whispered Jack, turning pale.

'Exactly.'

'Are you saying he's in danger?'

'We are not sure. But you know how these things work. Rumours like this don't start without a reason, and our sources are usually very reliable.'

'Jesus, Cesaria, what do you suggest we should do?' asked Jack.

'Not much you can do, except take this seriously and be careful, and that goes for you too, Jack. Your books have trodden on many toes, and embarrassed the Mafia. You are not a popular guy in certain circles here in Italy, that's for sure. But for now, you must warn Tristan. We can't, but you can. After all, this is only a rumour that officially doesn't exist because of where it comes from and why, if you get my drift.'

'I do.'

'Now, what about Aladdin and Silvanus, and calling in that favour you mentioned?' said Grimaldi, 'Would it perhaps be fair to say that I no longer owe you anything, or doesn't this warning count? What do you think?'

'I want to think about it. Can we discuss this another time? I have to go to Venice. Right away.'

'I understand,' said Grimaldi, sounding relieved, and stood up, signalling that the meeting was over.

'I'm sorry it has come to this, Jack,' said Cesaria as they walked down the stairs together. 'Don't be too hard on him, but you must take this seriously.'

'I am.'

'What exactly did you mean by offering Silvanus and Aladdin something in return?'

'This is not the right time ...'

'But you have something in mind, don't you?'

'Yes, I do.'

Cesaria reached for Jack's arm and squeezed it. 'I understand. We've been through a lot together. You know you can always count on my support, night or day.'

'Thanks, Cesaria, I know.'

'Grimaldi is under a lot of pressure right now. A lot of it is self-inflicted. He hasn't forgiven himself for not being able to nail Alessandro for his part in the Stolzfus matter ...'

Jack shrugged. 'He's done his best.'

'Often for a man like him, that's just not enough. He feels responsible.'

'For what?'

'For this threat. Didn't you see it? He was embarrassed.'

'I could never hold him responsible for this threat. He's achieved more than most.'

'Perhaps. But we are talking about Chief Prosecutor Grimaldi here. A legend. And he's a changed man since his friend's death in Istanbul.'

'Conti?'

'Yes.'

'That changed you too, didn't it?'

'Yes, it has. Conti saved my life. You were there and saw it all. There are certain things you can never forget.'

'That showdown in the cisterns in Istanbul?'

Jack nodded. 'Yes.' He too had been deeply affected by Fabio Conti's dramatic death two years earlier. Conti had been Borroni's superior officer at the time, and they had a close bond. They had been hunting down a notorious Mafia hit man, Luigi Belmonte, working for the Gambios – another Florentine Mafia family – and had cornered him in the Basilica Cisterns, where everything came to a dramatic climax and left two men dead.

Borroni embraced Jack and kissed him on the cheek. 'Good luck, Jack, and give my regards to Tristan and Lorenza.'

'I will.'

'I'm sure this isn't the end of this Landru case of yours.'

'No, it isn't.'

'I didn't think so. Take care of yourself.'

'I will do that too,' said Jack and hurried to the door.

18

Venice: 14 October

Jack stepped out onto the terrace on the first floor of the Palazzo da Baggio, and looked pensively down to the Grand Canal below, bustling with early morning traffic. It was just after sunrise. With the stage-like facades of the palazzos on the opposite side of the canal still shrouded in morning mist, it was a timeless scene that hadn't changed for centuries. A scene that would have prompted painters like Canaletto, Bellini or Carpaccio to reach for their sketchbooks to capture a fleeting moment of perfection.

Jack had arrived by train from Florence late the night before and, feeling exhausted, had gone to bed early. The palazzo was full of guests and Tristan and Lorenza were both busy working in the restaurant – Osman's Kitchen – which as usual was booked out.

Jack hadn't slept well. In fact, he had hardly slept at all. Grimaldi's warning had kept him awake and Jack was trying to work out how best to talk about the warning to both Tristan and Lorenza, on the one hand without alarming them, and on the other playing down the threat and making it appear far-fetched and trivial. *Then again*, he thought, *there could be a little silver lining in all this*. Suggesting that Tristan should come with him for a few days to help him with the Landru case might not be such a difficult subject to broach after all, and may well be supported by Lorenza in the circumstances.

As Jack watched the first rays of morning sun melt away the mist and climb slowly up the moist, moss-covered walls like ghostly fingers reaching for the sky, he remembered his conversation with Izabel about Teodora on that very same terrace only a few months earlier. A strong believer in destiny, Jack shook his head. Izabel had been telling him about Teodora, her new lover she had only just met, and the first shoots of happiness she had felt after the tragic death of Soul, the jazz singer and love of her life, whom Jack had saved in Central Park in New York years before.

No-one could have imagined on that idyllic morning what was to come. A few weeks later, Teodora was lying dead in the wreck of her Lamborghini Centenaro at the bottom of Lake Como, Izabel was trying to mend a second broken heart, and Jack himself had only escaped death because of the fortuitous intervention and support of friends who cared.

Instead of soaking up the sun and feeling calm and relaxed in the stunning, familiar surroundings, Jack felt uneasy, unable to shake off an unsettling sense of foreboding. And it had to do with one word in Grimaldi's unexpected warning that refused to go away: *imminent.*

'You're up early,' said Lorenza, walking out onto the terrace.

'So are you,' said Jack, grateful for the interruption.

Lorenza tossed back her lush hair and looked at Jack. 'The relentless siren call of the kitchen. A true chef can never stray far from the stove.'

'I suppose not, especially when you are running a restaurant like this, with adoring guests devouring the last crumbs on their plates, hoping for more.'

'Every dream has its price.'

'I know all about that.'

'I know you do.'

'How is he?' asked Jack, changing the subject.

'Better. You saw him last night. He's very good with the guests.'

'Good. I'm sure he'll settle in. Just give him time.'

'I hope you're right.'

'I'm sure I am. You know why?'

'Tell me.'

'Because he loves you; simple.'

Lorenza walked over to Jack and gave him a peck on the cheek. 'You always find the right words, don't you?'

Jack shrugged. 'It's never the right time, but I have something important I want to talk to you about.'

'Oh? What?' Lorenza pulled a chair across to the table and sat down facing Jack.

'I don't want to alarm you, but something's come up. Something important we can't ignore.'

'Oh? Tell me! What is it?' asked Lorenza, unable to suppress a sudden shiver.

'A warning.'

'*A warning*? What kind of warning?'

Jack reached for Lorenza's hand and, holding it tight, told her about the Alessandro rumours and Grimaldi's warning.

Lorenza listened without interrupting. She felt a wave of fear like an icy wind on a bleak winter's morning as she remembered the death of her mother and brother. They had both been killed in a car crash, which it was strongly suspected had been caused by the Mafia as a warning gone wrong.

Jack could see the pain on Lorenza's face. 'I know,' he said softly. 'Unsettling echoes of the past, but I had to tell you. And I wanted to tell you first, alone.'

'Thanks Jack. Very thoughtful of you. What do you think we should—'

'Look at you two,' said Tristan cheerfully as he stepped out onto the terrace. 'Holding hands. And so early in the morning. I hope I'm not intruding.' He was carrying a tray with a steaming plunger and a basket of fresh pastries, a tantalising aroma of fresh coffee hanging in the air as he put the tray on the table. 'If I didn't know better, I would now have to question my wife about the attractive man she's with, while at the same time trying to control a jealous rage without spilling any of this. Coffee anyone?'

Jack looked at Tristan gratefully, the unexpected humour a most welcome interruption to the earlier tension.

Lorenza let go of Jack's hand, got up and embraced Tristan. Then she kissed him passionately on the mouth.

'Wow! What have I done to deserve this?' Tristan looked at Jack and winked. 'Italian wives. Who can ever work them out, eh?'

'Sit down. Jack has something to tell you, darling.'

'I can't. I have to go and pick up the Carrigans. They're on the early overnight train from London, remember? I'm late as it is.'

'You stay; I'll go.' Lorenza took off her apron and put it on the back of the chair. 'I haven't had a spin in the boat for far too long anyway. Will do me good before we prepare for lunch.'

'As you wish. I'll stay with Jack and have breakfast, then.'

'You do that – and listen carefully to what he has to say.'

Lorenza blew Jack and Tristan a kiss and, adjusting her hair, hurried to the door.

Lorenza fired up the two powerful two-hundred-and-fifty-horse-power Cadillac engines of the Riva Aquarama, enjoying the throb of the engines roaring into life. She guided the sleek boat away from the mooring under the palazzo, and then past moss-covered stone walls and through an iron-studded gate opening straight onto the canal. Once outside, the cold early morning air hit her like a blast from a freezer. Lorenza reached for Tristan's green parker that he always kept under the steering wheel, and put it on. Slipping on the hood to keep warm, she waited for a gap in the traffic and then put on speed.

The man watching the palazzo on the opposite side of the canal put down his binoculars and smiled. Then he reached for his phone and made a call.

'He's just come out and is on his way. If he takes the usual shortcut, we'll do it now; clear?'

'Understood. Everything's in place. We are ready.'

'You know what to do.'

'I do.'

How Lorenza loved that boat. It had belonged to her late brother and she had given it to Tristan as a wedding present after he had fallen in love with it. He could now drive it almost as skilfully as she. Enjoying the spray hitting her face, her wet cheeks glowing with excitement, Lorenza steered the boat expertly through a flotilla of small boats taking vegetables to market. Smiling, she ignored the rude hand signals of the boys sitting on the crates, and even waved back.

I'll take the shortcut, she thought, looking at her watch as the powerful boat roared past gondolas and vaporetti packed with morning commuters. Overtaking a water taxi at high speed, Lorenza lined up the boat for a sharp right-hand turn that would take her into a narrow side canal, which normally cut several minutes off the journey to the train station, especially during the chaotic morning traffic. The turn was a little tricky because she would have to navigate around a massive bridge pylon with only centimetres to spare, but Lorenza, an excellent driver, had done this countless times before and knew every inch of the way.

'Here he comes now!' the man standing on the bridge shouted into his phone. The man standing in the wheelhouse of a barge with a large crane on top, lowered the arm of the crane, virtually blocking the narrow entry into the canal next to the pylon. By the time Lorenza turned the corner and saw the steel arm in front of her, it was too late. With nowhere to go, the boat crashed at high speed into the massive piece of steel. Almost cut in half, the boat veered to the left, collided with the bridge pylon and burst into flames.

Moments later, the man on the bridge made another phone call. 'Done!' he said. 'There's nothing left of the boat. No-one could have survived this.'

'I knew I could count on you, Bohdan,' said Alessandro and hung up.

Satisfied, the man joined the crane driver, who had abandoned the stolen barge, and together they walked away from the inferno under the bridge.

19

The funeral, Venice: 19 October

Lorenza's sudden death had rocked Venice to the core, and a sense of gloom descended on the city that could be felt everywhere. People were shocked and found it difficult to accept the fact that Lorenza da Baggio, celebrated *Top Chef Europe* winner and pride of Venice, was no more.

The official word was that Lorenza had been killed in a tragic boating accident. However, the authorities working frantically behind the scenes had a different view, but were reluctant to make it public until solid evidence was found to link Lorenza's death to foul play. Instead, the city fathers proposed a traditional Venetian funeral with all the trimmings, to provide the grieving population an opportunity to say goodbye, and give Lorenza a memorable send-off befitting such a famous and much-loved local celebrity.

Draped in a flag embroidered with the da Baggio family's coat of arms, Lorenza's coffin stood on a makeshift bier in the middle of the grand salon on the first floor of the palazzo. It looked like an island of sadness in a sea of spectacular flowers. Above the two marble fireplaces facing each other, the tall mirrors reaching up to the ornate ceiling decorated with precious frescoes made the room look twice the size.

It was eleven in the morning and the last of the mourners filing past the coffin had left, leaving Jack and Tristan momentarily alone in the silent room. The pallbearers were due to arrive in half an hour to take the coffin down to the funeral gondola, which would take the coffin along the Canal Grande to the official service in the Church of San Giorgio Maggiore, due to start at noon. Situated on an island in St Mark's basin, this stunning Renaissance church had seen several funeral services for members of the illustrious da Baggio family over the years.

Contrary to tradition the coffin was closed, because Lorenza's face was so badly disfigured by the horrific injuries sustained in the accident – especially the fire – that she was virtually unrecognisable. Instead, a lovely photo showing a smiling Lorenza in her beloved kitchen stood on the lid, a sobering reminder of the precious, fleeting moments of life, and the certainty of death.

Tristan stared at the coffin in silence.

'How are you, mate?' asked Jack and reached for Tristan's hand.

'Numb. I can't feel anything. And when it really mattered the other day, I couldn't feel anything either. Nothing. I couldn't even warn her! How do you explain that?'

'I can't. But things don't work that way, do they? We are but instruments of fate, aren't we? You of all people know that.'

'Little comfort right now.'

'I suppose not.'

'It's difficult to comprehend that only a year ago, Lorenza and I stood here in this very room after our wedding in the Vatican. Married in the Sistine Chapel by the pope himself on the same day, surrounded by friends and family. It was all like a fairytale.'

'It was that,' said Jack, remembering that extraordinary day in September the year before. They had just returned from Rome after the intimate, private wedding attended by only close family. The wedding – a thank-you gesture by a grateful pontiff – had to be held early in the morning, before the tourists arrived to admire Michelangelo's timeless masterpiece.

Dressed in his Sunday finest, the gardener had met them at the jetty near Marco Polo airport with the very boat Lorenza had been killed in. The boat, and two others borrowed from friends, had been decorated with colourful garlands, giving the ride home along the Grand Canal the festive air of a wedding procession, Venice-style. Yet a few moments from now, Lorenza would begin a different journey along the same canal. It would be her last journey, taking her to her final resting place next to her ancestors in the Cimitero de San Michele.

'I still can't quite believe this is happening,' said Tristan. 'It's like a bad dream, and I will wake up in the morning after a restless night, covered in sweat, but relieved that the nightmare is over. Only this time, the nightmare is real and just beginning.'

Jack squeezed Tristan's hand. 'We'll get through this. Today will be the worst. The funeral service with all those people in the church will be tough. The pope even sent one of his cardinals to officiate. That's how much he thought of Lorenza.'

Tristan looked at Jack standing next to him. 'Thanks, Jack.'

'What for?'

'For being you.'

Jack gazed at Lorenza's coffin. Momentarily overcome by the sadness of the moment, tears began to well up from somewhere deep within, clouding his vision. His vision may have been blurred, but something he had felt for a long time couldn't have been clearer: he realised that time was precious and life uncertain at best, and certain things had to be said before it was too late and the opportunity lost forever, overtaken by the relentless march of time.

'I've wanted to say this for a long time,' said Jack quietly, his voice quivering with emotion.

'Say what?'

'Thanks, Tristan.'

'What for?'

Searching for the right words, Jack took his time before replying. He realised that these would perhaps be the most important words he would ever say to Tristan.

'For being the son I never had.'

'Is that how you see me?' whispered Tristan.

'I do.'

Without saying a word, Tristan turned to Jack and embraced him. Banished by love, the crushing pain and sadness that only moments earlier had all but overwhelmed Tristan, began to lift. The healing had begun.

Because it was almost time to leave, Countess Kuragin had been looking for Jack all over the palazzo, to finalise the funeral arrangements. She had arrived the day after the accident and taken charge of the situation. Leonardo da Baggio, Lorenza's father, had been walking the Camino de Santiago, the ancient pilgrimage trail in Spain, at the time, and had been difficult to contact. He arrived a day later, devastated, and was greeted by a grieving household preparing for a funeral.

The countess opened the heavy wooden door leading into the salon and was about to go inside when she saw Jack and Tristan locked in a silent embrace in front of Lorenza's coffin. Deeply moved, she stopped, tiptoed out of the room and quietly closed the door.

Expertly manoeuvred by six oarsmen, the large, ornate black funeral gondola with its sad-looking wooden angel at the prow, slowly approached the palazzo and tied up at the front steps. It had rained during the night and a dense fog hovered over Venice like a shroud, giving the facades of the palazzos along the canal an ethereal, ghostlike appearance. Moments later, the heavy medieval, iron-studded wooden double doors leading into the palazzo opened as the bells of Venice began to toll, giving the signal for the funeral procession to begin.

Carried by six pallbearers – Tristan and Lorenza's father at the front, followed by Jack and three of the chefs, all close friends of the family, working in Lorenza's beloved restaurant kitchen – the coffin left the da Baggio home and was carefully lowered onto the funeral gondola to begin its final journey first to the church, and then to the cemetery island.

Surrounded by hundreds of spectators, Cardinal Borromeo and his entourage of senior clergy – all dressed in ceremonial finery – waited in front of the church for the gondola to arrive. This was a great honour bestowed on the deceased, who was clearly held in high esteem by the Church.

Those familiar with Lorenza's role two years earlier in saving the pope's life, would not have been surprised. Nor would they have been surprised by the presence of Cardinal Borromeo, because the cardinal had been instrumental in facilitating the pope's treatment and recovery. He was the one who had brought Lorenza to Rome and had persuaded her to cook for the pontiff. The ancient Ottoman dish with its medicinal properties – Hunkar Begendi – which had saved the pope's life and had become an overnight culinary sensation, still featured as a signature dish in Lorenza's restaurant, because taking it off the menu would have caused diner outrage and a serious patron riot.

First, Cardinal Borromeo blessed the coffin as soon as it arrived, and then led the funeral procession into the church packed with mourners. Venetians loved pomp, and had arrived in droves just after daybreak to secure a place inside the church, and so be part of what was viewed as a rare, historic occasion not to be missed.

As expected, the music inside was uplifting and impressive. A chamber orchestra and large choir supported the booming organ as the cardinal entered, walked slowly down the aisle, and then opened proceedings by reading a personal message from the pope himself. This raised the ceremonial bar to dizzying heights, which all fortunate enough to witness this recognised instantly.

After excerpts from Mozart's *Requiem*, and a moving eulogy by Lorenza's grieving father, which had many reach for their handkerchiefs to wipe away tears, the coffin left the church. Followed by the cardinal and his entourage, it was carried down the stairs to the waiting funeral gondola to begin the final leg of its journey to the isle of the dead. Many choked with emotion as they watched the cardinal make the sign of the cross before the funeral gondola was slowly rowed away, and disappeared into the mist.

As soon as the gondola was out of sight, excited chatter and joviality erupted as the mourners returned to the realm of the living and prepared to go to lunch, as tradition demanded. They would lift a glass or two in memory of the deceased, who had just been farewelled in such a spectacular fashion, and celebrate her life. In Italy, funerals and food were inextricably intertwined. This was especially the case when the deceased was a famous culinary icon like Lorenza.

Back at the Palazzo da Baggio, the restaurant staff had insisted on putting on a wake – a spectacular lunch that would have made Lorenza proud. The Osman's Kitchen dining room had been transformed into a festive reception area fit more for a wedding celebration than a wake, with long tables for ten or more, and abundant flowers to add cheer to the occasion.

Cardinal Borromeo and numerous city dignitaries had been invited, and several members of the chamber orchestra had agreed to provide the music in return for lunch, and copious quantities of excellent wine brought up from the da Baggio cellar.

The countess walked up to Jack, who had just handed a glass of champagne to a bishop. 'Can you believe this?' she said and took him aside.

'Only in Italy. But isn't it great? Lorenza would have loved this. Sadness and joy, surrounded by food to ease the pain.'

'I agree. Just look at them. How is Tristan?'

'Coping. He knows how to deal with loss.'

'And so do you.'

Jack shrugged. 'Such is life.'

'I saw you two embrace in front of Lorenza's coffin,' said the countess quietly. 'I didn't want to intrude ...'

'It was a special moment.'

'I could see that.'

'How's Leonardo coping?' said Jack, changing the subject.

'Not well. This is a catastrophe. He's now lost both of his children. And in such dramatic circumstances.'

'Will you stay with him here for a while?'

'Oh, yes. I can't leave him alone; not now. And I've asked Anna to come here with Billy. Will do her good and help her cope with the grief. She and Lorenza were close. She couldn't face the funeral.'

Jack looked at the countess and nodded. 'I understand. Strange, how tragedy can make you see things clearly.'

'What do you mean?'

'Another time, but I think this may apply to both of us.'

'You think so?'

'Definitely. Look, there's Cesaria. She made it after all!'

'Yes. She was late and came directly to the church. Go and talk to her.'

Jack walked over to Cesaria, standing in front of the fireplace by herself, away from the others. 'I'm so glad you could come,' he said and kissed her on the cheek.

'I'm so sorry, Jack. I can't express how I feel about this.'

'I know, neither can I,' said Jack and pointed into the room. 'That's why this here, is perhaps the best way to cope.'

'You could be right. This is classic Italy. Grimaldi couldn't come.'

'I didn't expect him to.'

'It's not what you think. He was devastated by the news. He couldn't come, not because of work, but because he couldn't show his face. Not here, not now.'

'Come on ...'

'I'm serious. You and I both know what happened here, and why. The local authorities are pussyfooting around at the moment, but sooner or later it will come out. This was a Mafia hit, arranged by Alessandro, and that's why Grimaldi couldn't come. He feels responsible.'

'That's nonsense.'

'Not to him. Does the family know?'

'Only Tristan.'

'Good.'

'I couldn't possibly tell Leonardo. Not now,' said Jack.

'I understand.'

'Grimaldi sends his sincere condolences.'

'He called me. He called Tristan as well.'

'I know. But that's not all; there's more.'

'What do you mean?'

'Before we get stuck into lunch and drown our sorrows, you should know this ...'

'Oh? What?'

'Grimaldi has arranged for you to meet Aladdin and Silvanus in jail.'

'*What?* Are you serious?'

'He thought a lot about what you said. Like you, he can see a possible connection here, and is keen to pursue it. That's one of the main reasons I'm here. He actually sent me to talk to you.'

'This could be a game changer.'

'Perhaps. I would like to know what you meant by offering Aladdin and Silvanus the right thing to make them talk.'

'Ah. Over lunch. Let's sit down. I think the first course is on its way. You are staying the night, of course?'

'If I'm invited.'

'Come on. In this place, you are as much part of the family as I am. Come, I feel like getting drunk. Never fun on your own.'

'What is it that Countess Kuragin keeps calling you?'

'I have no idea what you are talking about.'

The countess, who had overheard the remark on her way to the table, put an arm around Cesaria. '*Incorrigible rascal,*' she said quietly. 'But keep this to yourself.'

20

Palazzo da Baggio, Venice: 20 October

'I thought I would find you here,' said Cesaria as she walked into the salon, the flowers – now past their prime – the only reminder of the outpouring of grief and sadness the day before. The makeshift bier had been removed, and most of the furniture put back where it belonged. 'I knocked on your door to say goodbye, but you weren't there.'

Jack sat in front of one of the fireplaces and looked up. 'Couldn't sleep. Got up early.'

'Me too. I have to get back to Florence, early train. How are you?'

'I have been better.'

'That was some wake last night.'

'It numbed the pain, but only temporarily. There's always the morning after. Everything has its price.'

'Tell me about it.'

Jack pointed to the photo in front of him on the marble coffee table. It was Lorenza's coffin photo from the day before. 'She'll be forever young, you know,' he said. 'Just like Marilyn Monroe and Princess Diana.'

'A hell of a price to pay for eternal youth, don't you think?'

Jack nodded and pointed to a chair opposite. 'It doesn't come with a choice. Come, sit with me. I have something to tell you.'

Cesaria sat down and looked at Jack.

'Firstly, thank you.'

'What for?'

'The prison visit. You must have persuaded Grimaldi?'

'I may have put in a word or two but ultimately, it was his decision. He came round.'

Jack picked up the folder on the table in front of him and held it up. 'This is without doubt one of the most extraordinary stories I've come across for a long time. Explosive stuff!'

'What is it?'

'Landru's journal.'

'Ah. The one you told me about that he wrote in prison?'

'Yes. And gave to me. Exactly why is still a bit of a mystery, except for one thing he said.'

'What was that?'

'He claimed that there's a connection between these horror murders and the Stolzfus matter.'

Cesaria looked up, surprised. 'Did he say what it was?'

'Yes. Spiridon 4.'

'Did you believe him? Did he explain?'

'No. And for that reason, I dismissed this as nonsense. At first that is, but then came that video I showed you.'

'Teodora's wrist tattoo.'

'Exactly. I can't just dismiss that. That's serious evidence, and no longer just speculation. And we both know how little things like that can quickly turn into major leads that ultimately solve the case.'

'I can see that. I can also see where you are going with this.'

'I know you can. And for that reason, thanks again for the prison visit.'

'It was Grimaldi,' said Cesaria.

'Sure.'

Cesaria looked at her watch. 'The water taxi should be here any moment. I better get going.'

'Sorry I can't take you.'

'No matter. I suppose you'll be following those breadcrumbs of destiny you always keep talking about,' said Cesaria, a coquettish expression on her face.

'You know me too well. And I want to take Tristan with me. He needs to get away from here. Otherwise ...'

'Good idea. And those breadcrumbs will take you to Palermo, I suppose?'

'They will. How quickly can you arrange that prison visit?'

'Just tell me when you want to go.'

'As soon as possible.'

'I thought so. I'll get onto it and call you. I'd better go.'

Jack stood up and embraced Cesaria. 'You know what the real treasure is in life? The only thing that really counts in the long run?'

'Yes. You told me in Istanbul after Conti was killed.'

'Ah. You remember.'

'Of course, and I agreed with you.'

'You did. *Friendship*,' whispered Jack and kissed Cesaria tenderly on the cheek. 'Have a good trip.'

Because it was still early and no-one seemed to be stirring, Jack settled back into his chair. He did some of his best thinking early in the morning before the distractions of a new day intruded and replaced contemplation of the important, with urgency of the trivial. Jack reached for Landru's journal and opened it where he had earlier underlined a certain passage:

While The Navarro Chronicles *were of huge importance, especially in academic circles where they were seen as the first documentary evidence of note supporting the view that the Llanganates treasure was real and had been retrieved, they were also the source of great frustration, because the account stopped abruptly without giving any clue as to what happened to the treasure after it had been removed from its hiding place in the cave.*

For almost two years, this is where the matter rested, until an unexpected intervention of fate changed everything: I went on a pilgrimage in Spain.

For the next hour, Jack kept reading, but instead of providing answers, Landru's account raised only questions and possibilities. Jack suspected this was deliberate and part of Landru's clever strategy to draw him into his quest. However, he revealed some tantalising titbits of information that would have to be followed up and addressed another time. These titbits revolved around some crisis in Landru's life and an intriguing pilgrimage in an attempt to resolve it.

Jack opened his notebook, reached for his pen and began to jot down some thoughts: *Landru has some kind of breakdown relating to his homosexuality and goes on a pilgrimage in Spain in an attempt to deal with it. He spends three weeks walking the iconic Camino de Santiago and ends up in Santiago de Compostela. There he visits the shrine of the apostle Saint James the Great, and while praying in the cathedral meets an old monk, who takes him to the archives of the cathedral and shows him something of great significance to do with the Llanganates treasure. Unfortunately, Landru doesn't say what it was, but hints that it changed the entire direction of the quest.*

Jack paused as he listened to what sounded like the bells of San Giorgio Maggiore conjuring up images of the funeral service the day before.

Then he wrote down one more sentence – *Address with Landru during next meeting!* – underlined it and closed his notebook.

For a while Jack just stared at Lorenza's coffin photo on the table in front of him. *How terribly unfair*, he thought, more determined than ever to follow his breadcrumbs and solve the mystery. Because a stubborn little voice inside his head that wouldn't be silenced, kept whispering that Lorenza's death and the Death Mask Murders were somehow connected.

PART II
THE LOSS OF THE GOLDEN MASK

'If you do not accept the yoke of the Church and the King of Spain, I will make war on you everywhere in every way that I can. The death and destruction will be your fault.'

'I have not come here for such reasons. I have come to take away their gold.'

Francisco Pizarro

<h1 style="text-align:center">21</h1>

Pagliarelli Prison, Palermo: 25 October

Built in 1980 in the Pagliarelli neighbourhood of Palermo, the notorious maximum-security prison had a fearsome reputation as one of the most severe and brutal places of incarceration in Italy, if not the whole of Europe. Built of steel and reinforced concrete, this large, forbidding complex was designed for long-term incarceration of inmates who were classified as the most violent and dangerous in the prison system, and therefore posed the highest security risks.

In a way, it was a prison within a prison. Contact with the outside world was almost non-existent, and solitary confinement was used extensively for long periods to punish prisoners and at the same time protect them from themselves and one another. It was a place where prison guards had a great deal of authority and independence when it came to discipline and punishment, often without accountability, or outside scrutiny or review. This was deemed necessary, because the prisoners assigned to this prison were considered a serious threat not only to law and society, but to the institution itself.

Grimaldi had to pull many strings in high places, use his influence and reputation as one of the most respected Mafia hunters in the country, and call in some very special favours, before he finally managed to get permission for Jack and Tristan to visit Aladdin and Silvanus in prison. Permission for Bartolli to accompany Jack had been denied by the authorities, but there had been no objection for Tristan to go along with Jack instead.

As the last two surviving members of Spiridon 4 – one of the most ruthless and violent international hit squads, with strong Mafia connections and wanted in several countries – Aladdin and Silvanus were two of the star prisoners at Pagliarelli. Almost revered by other inmates for their violence and legendary crimes, their apprehension and conviction were two of the biggest feathers in Grimaldi's prosecution-cap by far, and had considerably elevated his reputation as a fearless Mafia hunter. For this reason, Grimaldi was at first reluctant to facilitate a prison visit. This was further complicated by the fact that Aladdin and Silvanus refused to cooperate and agree to a meeting with Jack, which, strangely, was one of their few rights in that brutal place. This had quickly turned into a major obstacle that threatened to derail the entire plan, and it was only after Jack had sent a personal message to them through Grimaldi that they finally agreed to a meeting.

The message, which consisted of only a number – 1389 – had at first perplexed Grimaldi. But once Jack explained what it represented, Grimaldi understood it could make all the difference, and be the circuit breaker to the frustrating impasse they had been hoping for. He was right. Aladdin and Silvanus changed their minds, and a prison visit was arranged.

It had taken Jack and Tristan almost two hours to navigate the complex security arrangements and strict red tape that governed access to the prison. This consisted of a full body search, including in some very private places, and a meticulous examination of their clothing while they stood naked in a cold, stark room. Compared with this, Jack's recent visit to Fleury-Mérogis Prison to talk with Landru was like visiting grandchildren at pre-school.

Looking like a windowless, underground concrete bunker, which Jack thought it most probably was, the small, dank meeting room was both claustrophobic and intimidating. No doubt intentionally so. Wearing grey boiler suits, Silvanus and Aladdin sat on metal chairs, their hands and feet chained to the moist wall behind them.

The first thing Jack noticed when he saw them through the iron grille separating them from visitors like exhibits in a zoo, was how pale and gaunt they looked. Sunken, restless eyes suggested spirits crushed by boredom and mindless prison routine. The boiler suits – several sizes too large – hung limply from their haggard frames, no doubt the result of a poor diet lacking in nourishment and variety. A far cry from the lavish lives of luxury and great wealth Silvanus and Aladdin had enjoyed for years. All financed by an almost endless litany of daring, ingeniously executed crimes – many of them paid for by the Mafia – that very few in the business could have attempted.

Silvanus was the first to speak.

'I must give you that,' said Silvanus, looking at Jack, 'you have balls.' He turned to his brother sitting next to him. 'Don't you think so?'

Aladdin nodded.

'What does this tell you?' continued Silvanus.

'They want something.'

'Quite.' Silvanus looked again at Jack, and then at Tristan, his penetrating gaze disconcerting. 'Don't you wonder what two witnesses whose evidence led to our conviction could possibly want from us, here, in this wretched place?'

'I can't imagine.'

'Can you perhaps enlighten us, Mr Rogan?' said Silvanus, looking expectantly at Jack.

That's one dangerous man, thought Jack as he realised that Silvanus's spirit was far from broken. He may have looked thin, perhaps even emaciated, but the way he spoke and conducted himself in an almost unthinkably brutal and humiliating situation, spoke of a man who would never give in, and never give up. Only fight. *Good,* Jack thought. *Exactly what I've been hoping for.*

Instead of replying, Jack signalled to one of the prison guards standing behind him. The guard stepped forward and placed Jack's iPad on a small table facing the two prisoners. This had been previously arranged with the prison authorities, who had given permission for Jack to show a video to the prisoners, but only after it had been viewed by the guards and a copy retained.

Without saying a word, Jack pressed the *play* button and watched Silvanus and Aladdin carefully while the silent video of the brutal

Landru murder was playing. Their faces and body language gave nothing away, but their eyes were glued to the screen, watching the video like two mesmerised children watching cartoons after school.

'Fascinating, Mr Rogan. You came all this way to show us *this*?' said Silvanus.

'The number 1389 obviously means something to you, otherwise you wouldn't have agreed to see us,' said Jack, calmly. 'And I believe I know what it means to you, and why.'

'You speak in riddles,' scoffed Aladdin.

Jack held up his hand. 'Please, let's not insult each other.' Jack picked up the iPad, called up the frame showing the wrist tattoo and put the iPad back on the table. 'This is Teodora's hand, isn't it?' said Jack.

'I have no idea what you are talking about,' said Silvanus, shaking his head. Teodora and her sister, Nadia, had been the other two notorious members of Spiridon 4.

'Oh, I think you do,' Jack countered, undeterred. 'The number 1389 was tattooed on the inside of Teodora's right wrist. I know that for a fact. Izabel, Teodora's former lover, confirmed it. And it's not just any number, but a number with a specific meaning to a young Muslim woman whose parents were brutally murdered during the Kosovo war. Isn't that right? Thirteen eighty-nine is the date of the Battle of Kosovo, which marked the arrival of Islam in Serbia and the beginning of a long, dramatic struggle ending in recent persecution and rivers of blood. Right?'

'I have no idea what you are talking about, but thank you for the history lesson, Mr Rogan,' said Aladdin, his voice thick with sarcasm. 'Teodora is dead. Her body was cremated. Her sister, Nadia, is dead too, buried at sea. So, what is the possible relevance of all this?'

'This may help,' said Tristan, stepping in. 'Allow me to tell you what I can feel.' Jack noticed he'd deliberately said *feel* instead of *see*.

'*Feel?* What on earth do you mean?' asked Silvanus, sounding impatient.

'Tristan is a psychic with a special gift,' said Jack, well aware that Romani gypsies like Silvanus and his brother believed in such things and took them seriously. It was in their blood. 'He can feel and see things others can't.'

'When I close my eyes, I can *feel* your presence,' said Tristan, closing his eyes. 'When I looked at this video for the first time, I could feel the same thing.' Tristan opened his eyes. 'I believe you were both present when the murder was committed. Teodora and Nadia were there too. Landru didn't commit the murder he was accused of and sent to jail for; you did—'

'This is absurd,' interrupted Silvanus. 'This meeting is over.'

'When I saw photos of that chamber of horrors in Paris a couple of weeks ago, with all the death masks and grizzly remains displayed like trophies,' continued Tristan, undeterred, 'I had the same feeling. It was the four of you who committed those murders, not Landru. It was the work of Spiridon 4, no-one else.'

Silvanus looked at his brother. 'This is nonsense. We should leave.'

'Before you do,' said Jack, 'please just listen to this; there's a lot riding on it for you.'

Looking disinterested, Silvanus shrugged. 'If this is some stupid, clumsy attempt to entice us to admit to something we didn't do, forget it. Go back to where you came from, Mr Rogan, and let us go back to our cells.'

'Nothing could be further from what we have in mind.'

'*In mind?* You have something in mind?' said Silvanus.

'Yes. Something I know you will be interested in.'

'I doubt it.'

'Please hear me out.'

Silvanus shrugged.

'We didn't come here to ask you to admit anything. We simply told you what we know, and what we believe happened. And Tristan told you what he *feels*. That's all. But all of this is only the background to what I am about to propose.'

'You have a *proposal?*' said Aladdin, looking bemused. 'Seriously?'

'Yes, seriously.'

'You are full of surprises, Mr Rogan. What kind of proposal?' asked Silvanus, suddenly interested.

'All we are after is information in exchange for—'

'What?' interjected Silvanus.

'Certain benefits.'

'What kind of benefits?' asked Aladdin.

Jack held up his hand. 'Later. Now that you know what we think about the Death Mask Murders and who committed them, you will understand my next question.'

'Go on,' prompted Silvanus.

'We want to find out who was *behind* all these bizarre, staged killings, and why. Let's assume for the moment that Spiridon 4 did in fact commit at least some of the more recent murders, as we believe they did, they would have done so as hired guns for someone else, who paid a small fortune for their services. The question is *who*, and *why*. If you can help us with this, we are in a position to offer you something valuable in return.'

'Something puzzles me,' said Silvanus. 'Why are you so interested in all this?'

'That's my business.'

'As for offering us something of value,' continued Silvanus, 'my brother and I will spend most likely twenty years in here before we are then extradited to the US to face trial on other serious matters, which, if we are convicted, will keep us in jail for the rest of our lives. Surely you see our dilemma. What could someone like you, therefore, possibly offer us that would be of some value in our situation? Hypothetically speaking, of course.'

Jack stared at Silvanus for some time, collecting his thoughts. He realised that the meeting had reached the pointy end, and everything depended on how he answered the question.

'You have summed up your own situation accurately. There is very little we can offer you in here, except for a few small privileges, like internet access and the like. The real benefit, which is far more valuable, is somewhere else.'

Silvanus waved his hand dismissively. 'More riddles.'

'Not really. It's actually quite simple. What I can offer you concerns your families,' said Jack quietly.

Silvanus sat up as if stung by a hot needle from behind. Both Silvanus and Aladdin were married with families. According to Grimaldi, both families were currently under investigation, their assets frozen and under threat of confiscation as possible proceeds of crime, which if successful, would leave them destitute and in disgrace.

'Go on,' prompted Silvanus.

'If you can help us identify who was behind all these murders and financed them, then we can offer you a deal.'

'What kind of deal?'

'A negotiated settlement of the pending proceedings concerning your families. A settlement that would at least leave your families with something to live on, and get on with their lives without facing certain ruin. Interested?'

'What guarantees are you able to give us? Should we be able to help you, that is?'

'Only my word.'

'You are joking, surely.'

'No. I'm deadly serious. This is a matter of judgement and trust. This is the only chance you have. Once we walk away from here, the deal is off the table and we'll never come back. Your call.'

Silvanus looked at Aladdin. 'I have to talk to my brother, in private.'

'No problem,' said Jack and stood up. 'We'll wait outside, but remember, the train only stops at this station briefly. Once it leaves, it will never return. Please consider that.' Jack stopped at the door and turned around. 'Which one of you is the clown in the video, I wonder? Is it you, Silvanus, or perhaps you, Aladdin? I suppose we'll never know, will we?' said Jack, and followed the prison guard outside.

22

O'Hara's alpine fortress, Obersalzberg: 26 October

O'Hara looked at the encrypted text message sent to him by one of the prison officers in his pay at the Fleury-Mérogis Prison, and smiled. It was a brief report about the visitors Landru had recently received. *He's on the move. Excellent*, thought O'Hara, *it's time*, and turned off his computer. Then he walked over to the large window and watched the morning sun light up the stunning mountain panorama, rising out of the mist like the opening scene of a Wagnerian opera heralding epic drama and bloodshed.

Feeling energised, he took his private lift down three storeys to the underground basement of the complex, where part of an abandoned WWII bunker had been converted into a large, secret, fortified network of chambers, where O'Hara kept his dark web server and stored his most precious encrypted records and prototypes of his lucrative computer games. This was also the place where he conducted his private conference calls and sent encrypted messages to his operatives in various parts of the world. It was O'Hara's private domain, his sanctuary, accessible only by his most trusted assistants and technicians, mainly when work was needed on the priceless, unique server, and only with his express permission. The security access code was changed regularly and was only known to a privileged few.

O'Hara glanced at his watch. There were still a few minutes before the conference call he had arranged the day before. Enough time to have another brief look at the precious documents and artefacts he had painstakingly collected over the years. These items were the clues left behind over several centuries, his 'footprints of destiny' as he liked to call them that would ultimately, he firmly believed, lead him to the elusive treasure that had been taunting him for decades and had become a consuming obsession. O'Hara knew he was finally getting close, but he also knew that the last step was always the hardest.

This was further complicated by the fact that Spiridon 4, the hit squad he had used for years and relied on for his most important and sensitive assignments, was no more. What this meant was that a new solution had to be found quickly, and that was always risky and a challenge. The imminent conference call was all about that.

O'Hara punched the security code into the pad on the door that opened a steel cabinet. A wave of excitement washed over him as soon as his eyes fell on the precious objects arranged on glass shelves in chronological order, like pages of a children's story book. Each object told part of a story that had begun in 1533 and was still going strong, its ultimate outcome uncertain. The first item was a copy of *The Navarro Chronicles* – Landru's paper that had started it all. The next item was the intriguing Morales khipu, which had unlocked many secrets and cost Gerhard Blumenthal his life in Berlin.

Bohdan Petrinko, a broad-shouldered, muscular man in his forties wearing army fatigues, sat in a dimly lit room on the first floor of the Cossack House in the heart of Kiev, the Ukrainian capital. The Cossack House was the main recruitment centre for Azov, a far-right Ukrainian militant group that had played a major part in defending Ukraine against Russian military aggression. For the past two years, Petrinko – a veteran resistance fighter – had worked as a senior Azov recruiter operating a vast network of global contacts stretching from Canada to New Zealand, offering far-right extremists military training and combat experience. This was how he had come to the attention of the Mafia in Florence, who were always on the lookout for mercenary hitmen with military experience, addicted to violence and danger, and motivated by greed and access to easy money.

Nervously drumming the tips of his fingers against the armrest of his chair, Petrinko kept staring at this watch; it was almost time. If the man he had heard so much about did call, this could be the opportunity he had been waiting for. It was time to once again get out of Ukraine, change direction, and make some money.

At seven am precisely, his mobile rang. Petrinko reached for his phone on the table and answered it.

'Riccardo Giordano told me a lot about you,' said O'Hara without introducing himself. 'He speaks very highly of you and that's the reason we are talking right now.'

'I understand,' said Petrinko, eager to prove himself and grateful for another chance after the recent embarrassing blunder in Venice that had killed Lorenza da Baggio instead of the intended target.

'I have very specific needs—'

'What kind of needs?' interrupted Petrinko impatiently. The phone call wasn't going quite as he had expected.

'I need someone devoid of fear and without scruples of any kind, who is prepared to follow precise instructions to the letter, and that includes killing without hesitation. No questions asked. Are you such a man, Mr Petrinko?'

'If Riccardo Giordano has recommended me, you have your answer, surely, Mr …?'

'My name is unimportant. We'll never meet.'

'Understood.'

'Is that a problem?'

'No.'

'Tell me about yourself.'

'I'd rather not. My past is unimportant. What counts here is the present.'

O'Hara chuckled. He liked the answer. 'Very well,' he said. 'Then let's turn to the present and leave the past in the shadows.'

'Let's do that.'

'Something small to begin with, but important. Surveillance.'

'Fine by me.'

'That could quickly escalate without notice?'

'No problem.'

'When can you start?'

'Right now.'

'Is France a problem?'

'No.'

'All your instructions will come from me, over the phone. Clear?'

'Absolutely.'

'So, please listen carefully.'

'I am.'

Satisfied, O'Hara put down the phone and looked pensively at the open steel cabinet. One item, the most important one, was still missing, but he was certain that Landru had worked out what it was and, if it did exist, where to find it. Cracking the cipher had made that clear. He was also certain that Landru – a driven man just like himself – was designing a plan right now, and reaching out to the very people who could help him make it work. And if this was indeed the case, O'Hara wanted to make sure he was right there next to him every step of the way. With Spiridon 4 no longer involved, making that a reality was a challenge, and O'Hara was hoping that in Petrinko he had found the right man to help him achieve it.

O'Hara reached for what he considered to be the most important item in his collection after *The Navarro Chronicles* and the Morales khipu. It was an exquisite scrimshaw whale tooth – not full size, but a miniature one. The tip of the tooth had been sawn off and made into an amulet that could be worn around the neck. *If only this could talk*, he thought, letting his mind drift, *what amazing stories it could tell*. O'Hara closed his eyes and ran his fingertips along the tiny, heart-shaped map engraved on the smooth surface of the ivory, hoping that very soon he would be able to finally unlock its secrets.

23

On the *San Cristobal*: 23 June 1664

Father Morales stood on the pitching deck of the *San Cristobal*, a large Spanish galleon, and took a deep breath. He shielded his eyes with his hand from the blinding sun as he watched the billowing sails of the huge ship leaving the port of Portobelo on the east coast of Panama, with its precious cargo.

Because the cargo consisted almost exclusively of silver mined from the legendary Cerro Rico Mountain high up in the Andes near the mining town of Potosi, the *San Cristobal* had been provided a special escort – a Spanish man-of-war – to protect it from pirates on its way to Havana. There, it would reprovision and join the *Flota de Indias*, the Spanish treasure fleet specifically designed by admiral Pedro Menéndez de Avilés to transport precious cargo safely back to Spain. The fleet assembled twice a year in Havana Harbor and travelled to Seville in convoy to avoid the ever-circling pirates always on the lookout for vulnerable stragglers, or ships separated by storms from the safety of a fleet protected by patrolling warships.

Morales had waited a long time for this opportunity: a safe passage back to Spain to keep his bargain with the king.

'We made it, Father,' said Navarro, feeling safe for the first time since leaving Lima. The cumbersome trip across the isthmus by mule train had been particularly arduous and dangerous. It had been the most vulnerable part of their journey so far.

Morales looked at Navarro and nodded. 'We couldn't have made it without you.'

Navarro had been invaluable. Not only did he speak the native language, he was also able to read the khipu and interpret its subtle messages linked to the landscape. All this had finally allowed them to locate the Ruminahui treasure five years earlier, hidden in a cave deep in the remote mountain wilderness. But finding the treasure and transporting it back to Quito had been the easy part.

'Can you believe it has taken us almost five years to reach this point?' said Morales.

'Greed and lust for gold make monsters out of men.'

'How right you are.'

Rumours that the legendary Inca treasure hidden in the mountains by Atahualpa's general had been found and was on its way back to Lima spread like wildfire through Peru, sending shivers of excitement and speculation through the colony. Every tavern, every boarding house was abuzz with wild stories of unimaginable wealth, there for the taking if one had the courage and resolve, and knew where to look. The few by-now exhausted soldiers protecting the porters struggling under the weight of the gold had been attacked several times even before reaching Quito. After suffering heavy losses, the expedition managed to limp into Quito and the relative safety and protection of the Church.

It was only because of the bravery and ingenuity of the Jesuits that the treasure hadn't been lost. The Jesuits used their network of trusted supporters to secretly transfer the gold to Lima by sea, where it was hidden for several years in an underground chamber next to the dead buried below the church, until the rumours died down and the corrupt officials, cutthroats and brigands lost interest, and it was considered safe to transfer the treasure to Spain.

Joining the mule train across the Isthmus of Panama with a huge silver delivery had been a stroke of genius. It had provided the cover needed to transport the gold from Lima to Panama by ship, and from there by mule train and porters across the isthmus to Portobelo.

Only Captain Diego de Medina knew that the legendary Ruminahui treasure, consisting of several tonnes of solid gold, was on board and was travelling back to Spain as part of an annual silver shipment from the Potosi mines. This made the cargo on his ship the most valuable in more than a century and explained why a man-of-war, a powerful frigate with hundreds of sailors and one hundred and twenty-four guns, was escorting the galleon to Havana under sealed orders from up high: the admiral.

Normally, the galleon would carry sugar, spices, tobacco, silk and pearls in addition to timber and agricultural goods, but not on this occasion. This time, the cargo consisted almost exclusively of silver and the secret Inca treasure, under the protection of the king himself.

Medina walked up to the two Jesuits and bowed. 'Gentlemen, we can relax,' he said and pointed to the impressive man-of-war sailing a short distance behind them. 'Apart from our own guns, we have the firepower of one of the best-equipped warships in the fleet, under the command of one of the most respected captains in the land, protecting us. There isn't a pirate in the Caribbean who would dare attack us, and once we rendezvous with the treasure fleet in Havana, we will have even more protection.'

'Have you ever encountered pirates on your journeys, Captain?' asked Navarro.

'I have. They are the scourge of the Caribbean and never far away. One has to be always vigilant. They are excellent sailors and usually very well equipped. Fast ships. Being able to outsail other vessels is their main advantage. Apart from that, they are daring, ruthless and desperate. When you know that the end of a rope is waiting for you should you ever be caught, you will fight to the death, and they do. Trust me, I've seen it.'

'We must be grateful for our escort then,' said Morales, looking pensively across to the impressive man-of-war travelling under full sail. 'Very reassuring.'

Medina nodded.

'We are indebted to you, Captain,' said Navarro. 'We feel safe and in good hands. I have no doubt that the dangerous part of our journey is behind us. And besides, our best protection is the cover of secrecy. As long as no-one knows what travels with us in those trunks, we are surely safe.'

'Quite so,' said Medina. 'I would be both honoured and delighted if you would join me for supper in my cabin this evening, gentlemen. I have some splendid wine from my family's vineyards.'

'Where are they?' asked Navarro.

'Near Zaragoza.'

'Mazuelo grapes?'

'You know your wine, Father. Yes, we cultivate this ancient variety on our estates. Actually, it originated in our area around the ninth century and spread from there throughout Western Europe all the way to North Africa.'

'Says it all,' observed Morales. 'A toast to a safe journey would be most appropriate; wouldn't you say, Captain?'

'Quite so. Until tonight then, gentlemen. Duty calls, I must go.'

For a while, Morales and Navarro watched in silence as the sun sank slowly into the calm sea like a blood-red fireball, casting long shadows across the deck as the ship changed course and headed north-east towards Cuba.

For some reason he couldn't quite explain, Navarro felt uneasy and saw this as an ominous sign of things to come.

24

'Mad Dog' Regan. Near Havana: 23 June 1664

Captain 'Mad Dog' Regan stood on the quarterdeck of *The Templars Revenge*, a brigantine he had captured from the British during a daring mutiny two years earlier, and surveyed his domain. Arms crossed behind his back, his sturdy, buckled shoes firmly planted on the slippery timbers of the pitching deck, he watched the keelhauling about to start.

A flamboyant dresser, aware that appearances mattered – especially in front of a crew like the one assembled on deck to watch the punishment – Regan took great care with his attire. Looking impressive in his embroidered, red-velvet dress coat, tricorn hat complete with ostrich feather, gold-fringed sash, and a heavy leather bandolier with several brace of loaded pistols, he looked more like a prosperous merchant prince of the high seas than one of the most feared and ruthless buccaneers roaming the Caribbean for plunder.

What could have given him away, however, was his face. Once handsome but now disfigured by a missing ear and a nasty cutlass scar running down his left cheek that his bushy beard couldn't hide, it had become a callous face that had seen too much violence and death. Wanted in several countries, with a huge price on his head, he had managed to outfox, outgun and outsail numerous sorties trying to capture him.

As a former boatswain in the British Navy, he knew that iron-fisted discipline was the mother of obedience, and without obedience no ship could function properly, especially one like *The Templars Revenge,* which depended on a motley crew of lawless cutthroats and brigands to stay afloat and fight.

Naked and shivering, his hands and feet tied to a long rope, the young sailor who had disobeyed an order by the bosun to adjust the sails during a storm, was ready to face his punishment. Regan looked at the quartermaster and nodded. The quartermaster lifted his hand and gave the signal for the punishment to begin. Moments later, the hapless wretch was thrown overboard to be dragged along the keel of the ship.

Keelhauling was one of the most severe and brutal punishments meted out on the ship because more often than not, it resulted in death. Not only did the sharp barnacles encrusting the keel inflict horrendous injuries by ripping the skin to shreds, but drowning was also a real prospect depending on the time spent under water, the ship's speed and the wind. Instead of feeling sorry for one of their own, the boisterous crew shouted and cheered and wagered on the outcome. On a ship like *The Templars Revenge*, there was no such thing as compassion or mercy, only survival.

After a few minutes, the sailor's limp, lifeless body – his contorted face cut to shreds – was dragged out of the water. The quartermaster walked over to the body and examined it. Assured the man was dead, he cut the rope attached to the feet with his dagger, and stepped back. Two men came forward, lifted the man off the deck and threw him overboard. The punishment was over.

Satisfied, Regan turned on his heels and was about to return to his cabin when the quartermaster walked up to him. 'I think he's ready to talk,' said the quartermaster.

Regan nodded and followed the quartermaster below deck.

The man sitting on the floor tied to one of the four-pounder guns was barely conscious. His face was badly swollen, his unkempt hair blood-encrusted, and blood dribbled from the corner of his open mouth. He had been beaten to within an inch of his miserable life. The swelling had closed one of his eyes and his nose had been broken. A bare-chested, burly man stood next to him, rubbing his knuckles.

'What have you got?' asked the quartermaster.

The burly man tipped a bucket of water over the motionless wretch. 'Tell the captain what you've just told me,' he growled.

Regan, who was fluent in Spanish, knew that reliable intelligence was the key to creating opportunities for an ambush or a raid, and vital for keeping a step ahead of the enemy. For that reason, Regan operated an elaborate network of spies in all the major ports, including Portobelo, together with a sophisticated communication chain that would have been the envy of the British Navy. In his cabin he also had some of the best charts available at the time. This allowed him to carefully plan an ambush or intercept, and to use location, speed and timing to his best advantage.

The man being interrogated had been overheard by one of Regan's spies boasting in a tavern about a mule train transporting a hoard of gold for the Jesuits. After leaving the tavern, dead drunk, the man had been abducted by Regan's men and was taken to a concealed cove close to Portobelo, where *The Templars Revenge* was waiting under cover of darkness.

'How do you know about this mule train?' asked the quartermaster.

'I was in charge of it.'

'How do you know about the gold?'

'I saw it.'

'*You did?* How? Where?'

'One of the mules fell down a ravine and we had to climb down to retrieve the chest it was carrying. It had broken in half. That's when I saw it.'

'Saw what?'

'Vessels, figurines, masks, jewellery, all of solid gold. A Jesuit priest came up to me and told me that it belonged to the Church and to keep this to myself.'

'What happened to the chest?'

'We loaded it onto a ship together with everything else we were carrying, mainly silver from the Potosi mines but ...' The man stopped talking. He was drifting in and out of consciousness.

'*What?*' pushed the quartermaster impatiently and kicked the man in the chest.

The man opened his good eye. 'There were several other chests that looked just like the one we retrieved from the ravine,' he whispered. 'They were different from the silver chests – bigger, stronger.'

'What are you suggesting?'

'More gold.'

'*What ship?*' said Regan, bending down to hear better.

'The *San Cristobal*, bound for Havana.'

Regan smiled and turned to the quartermaster. Suddenly something that had puzzled him made sense. 'Tell him when he comes round that he has a choice: he can join us, or he can join Davy's locker. His call.'

Regan returned to his cabin and began to pore over the charts spread out on his desk. The quartermaster, a seasoned campaigner and Regan's trusted right-hand man, joined him moments later. 'What do you think?'

'This explains why the *San Cristobal* has been given a man-of-war as an escort. For one galleon? Hardly. There had to be more to this than just silver from the mines. Now we know, don't you think?'

'I agree. The Spanish are very frugal when it comes to money, and the Jesuits are secretive and influential in all the right places. They wouldn't send a ship like that to protect just one galleon without good reason. They could have provided a far less expensive escort. And the presence of the Jesuits is also telling. Devious bastards!'

It was well known that Regan hated the Catholic Church with a passion. He could trace his ancestry right back to the Knights Templar, who had been deviously dispossessed by Pope Clement V in 1312. Many of the impoverished and disgraced Templars, including Regan's ancestors, took to piracy as a new way of life. It was the reason he had named his ship *The Templars Revenge*.

Regan turned to the chart in front of him. 'They will take the most direct route to Havana. The fleet is already late and hurricane season is almost upon us. Time's running out. That means they should be about ... here.' Regan stabbed his right forefinger at a point on the chart.

'Agreed. So, what's on your mind?'

'We are much faster and can easily catch up with them during the night.'

'There's no way we can attack two ships like that,' argued the quartermaster. 'We'd be blown out of the water!'

'Of course not. But we can do what we always do. Watch and wait. Just like a pack of wolves. You never know, something can happen. This has served us well in the past. Opportunity favours the brave, right? The weather has become very unpredictable lately, and there are many hidden reefs along the way.'

'Sure. And besides, the boys need some excitement. It's been too long.'

'I agree. We'll tell them in the morning. In the meantime, full speed ahead. I even know a little shortcut the *San Cristobal* wouldn't be able to take. Here, between these two islands. A narrow channel. It's a little tricky, but we should be able get through, even at night.'

'I'll see to it,' said the quartermaster, looking adoringly at his captain. Regan never disappointed when it came to the daring and the unexpected. That's why the men on board would follow him without hesitation to the gates of hell, and beyond.

25

Florence: 26 October

Grimaldi and Cesaria had an early start. They were eating breakfast in the chief prosecutor's office when the security guard admitted Jack and Tristan. It was just after seven in the morning and the office staff hadn't arrived yet. Grimaldi walked around his desk and embraced Tristan. 'I am so sorry for your loss,' he said, his voice trembling with emotion.

Cesaria looked at Grimaldi in surprise. This was a rare show of affection by a man who had seen unimaginable violence and cruelty, was dealing with the most dangerous criminals in the land on a daily basis, and was known for his reserve and iron-willed self-control.

'Thank you for the warning; you did what you could,' said Tristan, a little embarrassed.

'It was too late, and for that I'm deeply sorry.'

'No-one could have done more,' said Jack, trying to diffuse the awkward moment.

Grimaldi shook his head. 'I should have.'

'What matters now is to bring those responsible to justice,' Cesaria weighed in and turned to Jack. 'How did it go?'

'An extraordinary encounter, to say the least,' said Jack. 'The body search was quite an adventure ...'

'I bet,' said Grimaldi, smiling. The ice was broken. 'You are among the very few without a life sentence, or two, to have seen the inside of that prison. Pagliarelli isn't visitor-friendly and neither are my superiors. They were less than enthusiastic about your visit. Anything useful?'

Jack turned to Tristan. 'Tristan, your impressions?'

Tristan's extraordinary abilities were well known to both Grimaldi and Cesaria, and both took them seriously because of Tristan's previous track record and astonishing results. Cesaria looked expectantly at Tristan.

'I have no doubt that both Silvanus and Aladdin have been involved here, not just in the Landru murder, but most likely in several of the Death Mask Murders.'

'What makes you say that?' asked Grimaldi and lit one of his small cigars.

'I could feel it, and hear it.'

'*Hear* it?' said Cesaria, frowning.

'Yes. When we showed them the video and during the conversation that followed, I could hear things. Most of the time it isn't what's actually said that counts, but what *isn't*. Silence can speak. I could hear what *wasn't* said, and it was quite revealing.'

'Care to elaborate?' said Grimaldi.

Tristan shook his head. 'At first, both of them were quite arrogant and dismissive and denied everything, just as we expected, but once Jack mentioned a possible deal involving their families, everything changed.'

'You obviously chose the right approach, Jack,' said Cesaria.

'It would appear so. Needless to say, I made no promises. Everything depends on results. I made that absolutely clear.'

'And they went along with this?' asked Grimaldi, raising an eyebrow.

'They did.'

'That tells us a lot.'

'It does. They even went a step further and made a "down payment", they called it, to keep us interested. Perhaps a significant one, considering the circumstances.'

Grimaldi looked at Jack, surprised. 'What kind of down payment?'

'The question on the table was simple enough: I wanted them to help us identify who was behind the murders. In short, who engaged Spiridon 4 to commit these extraordinary crimes; who paid the bills.'

'And?' prompted Cesaria.

'Before giving us an answer, the brothers wanted a word in private. We left the cell.'

Grimaldi blew some smoke towards the open window and looked pensively at Jack. 'And?'

'We returned a few minutes later and they made the down payment I mentioned,' continued Jack.

'What kind of down payment?'

'Three words,' replied Jack, smiling.

'Ah, you want another crostini before telling us, is that it?' joked Grimaldi and pushed the plate with the crostini towards Jack.

'Not at all, but thank you.' Jack took one and began to munch happily, to let the tension grow. 'In fact, we need your help with the down payment.'

'How so?'

'Because it may mean a lot more to you than to us.'

'Oh? How curious. Three words you said?'

'Yes: "Ask Don Lorenzo".'

Grimaldi looked thunderstruck. Collecting his thoughts, he stubbed out his cigar and for a while, just listened to the church bells.

For whom the bell tolls, thought Jack and kept watching Grimaldi. He could sense this was another moment of destiny. Tristan too had his eyes firmly fixed on Grimaldi, aware that the entire Landru matter rested on those three words.

'This is quite extraordinary, especially in the circumstances,' began Grimaldi, speaking softly.

'How so?' asked Jack.

'You'll see in a moment. Not many people here know this. In the early fifties, a young peasant boy from Calabria came to Florence to make his mark. Within a few short years, he had clawed his way to the top of the criminal tree by forming strategic alliances and eliminating his enemies. During the sixties and seventies, he was the undisputed king of the Florence underworld. That's when he was given a nickname, as so often happens in Mafia circles: Don Lorenzo, after Lorenzo de Medici, the fabulous Renaissance ruler of Florence and head of the Medici family.'

'You obviously know who we are talking about here,' said Jack.

'I certainly do, and so do you.'

'*Seriously?*' said Jack.

'Oh yes, and in light of what has just happened in Venice and who we suspect was behind it, this is even more remarkable.'

'Care to enlighten us?'

'During the eighties, Don Lorenzo became Don Riccardo. He preferred to use his own name by then—'

'As in Riccardo Giordano?' interrupted Jack.

'Uh-huh.'

'Alessandro's father? *The* Alessandro you warned us about?'

'Yes.'

'This is crazy!' Jack looked at Tristan. 'Can you believe this?'

'Oh yes, I can. In a way, I'm not surprised. The threads of fate are coming together to form a tapestry of violence and death spreading like cancer. It all fits. I could feel it in Palermo, and I can feel it right now.'

'Where is Riccardo now?' asked Jack.

'He went back to Calabria after the Stolzfus matter blew up and just about ruined the family. He left everything, or to put it more accurately, all that was left of the family business, to Alessandro and went to live on the old family farm just outside Lamezia Terme, home to the richest and most powerful crime syndicates in Europe.'

'Could we go and see him, do you think?' asked Jack hopefully.

'That may not be such a good idea,' said Grimaldi, chuckling.

Cesaria was smiling too. She knew all about what was happening in Calabria right at that moment. One of the largest criminal trials in Europe was about to get underway. Three hundred and fifty of the most notorious Mafia crime bosses, the *capi*, were about to go on trial in a fortified concrete bunker, built as a security measure especially for the occasion. The biggest Mafia trial in Italian history was about to begin.

'Riccardo's retirement to the farm was short-lived and didn't quite turn out as planned.'

'How come?'

'Bad timing; very bad.'

'In what way?'

'Cesaria, why don't you tell us?'

'All right. Allow me to do what Jack usually does: tell a story. This story is all about women, Mafia women who'd had enough. It all started with a movement under the banner of "*Vedo, Sento, Parlo*", "I see, I hear, I speak". And boy, are they speaking out! What had always protected the Mafia heavyweights, the *capi*, from prosecution and conviction was *omertà*, the code of silence. Based on fear and relentless punishment and retribution, no-one dared to talk or go to the authorities, until now.'

Cesaria paused and looked at Jack.

'The women are coming out of the shadows and beginning to talk,' she continued, becoming quite animated. 'They will be the star witnesses in these trials. Mothers, wives, ex-wives, daughters, lovers. They've had a gutful of the violence, the fear, the intimidation. Enough of their sons being expected to follow in their father's blood-soaked footsteps, leading to a relentless cycle of secrecy, violence and crime. The picturesque rolling hills and villages of Calabria hide a dark secret. No-one looking at some of the men working in the fields, tending their crops and livestock, would believe that they may be looking at one of the most powerful and ruthless members of the *'Ndrangheta*, "Men of Honour", the Calabrian Mafia, controlling a large part of the European cocaine trade, human trafficking, cybercrime and the lucrative, illicit arms supply to anyone able to pay.'

'Wow!' said Jack. 'That's quite a story. And Giordano's involved in all this?'

'Oh yes. He may be in his seventies, but he's still one of the key players in Calabria. Powerful, respected, influential. Right now, he's waiting for the trial to begin while his son Alessandro lives the high life on a yacht on the Riviera,' said Grimaldi, the bitterness in his voice clear. 'And all because of this wretched code of silence. But that will change. Everyone trips up sooner or later and when he does, I will be there. You can count on it!'

'What do you make of Silvanus's three words?' asked Jack.

'I would definitely take them seriously,' said Grimaldi. 'Spiridon 4 was an expensive, exclusive hit squad, and Giordano was well known for being a shrewd facilitator; a go-between who made money out of providing such services for those who had deep pockets. We've seen this firsthand in the Stolzfus matter. He provided not only a deadly service, but a cloak of anonymity protecting the principals. For a price, of course. A high one.'

Jack nodded. 'While Silvanus and Aladdin may not know who actually hired them, or why, Giordano would. At least up to a point—'

'He would certainly know a lot more than Silvanus and his brother,' Cesaria cut in. 'He was always very circumspect about the way he did business, and with whom. That's why he's survived this long.'

'Do we know where he is right now?'

'We do,' said Cesaria. 'He's sitting in a steel cage in a concrete bunker in Lamezia Terme, waiting for the trial to start.'

'How nice. Could we go and talk to him?' asked Jack.

'No point,' said Grimaldi and lit another cigar.

'How come?'

'Let me answer this,' said Cesaria. 'I can tell you for a fact that under no circumstances would Giordano talk, no matter what happens. As far as he is concerned, this case is all about *omertà*, the code of silence. The only reason these high-profile Mafiosi operating in the shadows are going on trial is because *omertà* has broken down: the Mafia women are talking. And that's a real problem for the *capi*, the men in charge, because the women know a lot about Mafia business, and are prepared to take the stand in court and testify. They will spill the rotten Mafia beans. Unheard of!'

'A dead end, then?' said Jack, disappointment in his voice.

'Not necessarily,' said Cesaria with a knowing smile.

'What do you mean?'

'Giordano may not be prepared to talk, but *Giuseppina* might.'

'Who's Giuseppina?'

'Giordano's wife. She's one of the star witnesses in the trial.'

'Seriously?' said Jack, looking incredulous.

'Yes.'

'And you think we could meet her?'

'I don't see why not. I know the prosecutor,' said Cesaria. 'We helped her prepare the case and provided a lot of information about Giordano just recently. She owes me.'

'Where is Giuseppina now?'

'In a safe place somewhere in Calabria. Under witness protection.'

'Another body search then, I suppose?'

'Quite possibly.'

'Oh dear.' Jack turned to Tristan. 'We are getting quite good at this lately, don't you think, mate? First the Fleury-Mérogis Prison in Paris, then the Pagliarelli in Palermo, and now a safe house in Calabria.'

'All good intelligence has its price, Jack,' said Tristan.

'I suppose so. I need another coffee.'

26

At sea. Somewhere on the way to Cuba: 24 June 1664

The storm blew in from the north during the night with unexpected fury, and intensified just before sunrise. Regan hadn't slept a wink. He had spent the night watching the direction of the storm and interpreting the currents, and carefully studying his charts for clues.

'This would have slowed down the *San Cristobal* and blown her off course,' he said to the quartermaster standing next to him. 'I reckon she should be about here.' Regan prodded an index finger at a point on the chart and looked at his quartermaster. 'If the gods of the deep are with us, perhaps she got separated from her escort during the night,' he continued, a crooked smile spreading across his scarred face, 'leaving her vulnerable.'

'Could be,' said the quartermaster, well aware where this was heading. If the galleon was off course without her escort and they should somehow manage to find her, then there was a real chance of taking the ship. *The Templars Revenge* could outsail and outgun the *San Cristobal*, and the two hundred ferocious, loot-hungry pirates on board their ship could easily overwhelm her crew.

'Assemble the men,' said Regan, pushing the map aside, 'I want to talk to them.'

'Straight away,' said the quartermaster, itching for some action. 'If we pull this off, it could be the prize of the century.'

'It would be that. But more importantly, we would deliver a heavy blow to the Church and make history,' said Regan, grinning. To him, robbing the Jesuits was more important than adding more loot to the pirate coffers. Yet the promise of gold was still the best way to motivate the rapacious crew and whip them into a plunder-frenzy.

Spellbound, the crew listened to their captain painting a picture of a vulnerable Spanish galleon within their grasp, groaning under the weight of silver and gold beyond their wildest dreams. Standing on the quarterdeck in the driving rain, his drenched red coat flapping in the wind like dragon wings, Regan looked exactly like the legendary, invincible buccaneer the whole of the Caribbean was talking about, instilling fear and panic every time *The Templars Revenge* hoisted the dreaded Jolly Roger, the pirate flag, and pounced on its prey.

Regan reached for his cutlass and turned to face the huge seas rocking the ship. 'The *San Cristobal* is somewhere out there, and we will find her,' he shouted and pointed to the north. 'And when we do, we will take her! *Are you with me?*'

'Yes!' roared the men.

'Then, let the hunt begin! Quartermaster, change course now!'

The lookout high up in the crow's nest on top of the main mast saw it first: white sails on the horizon. Regan smiled when he heard the news. The *San Cristobal* was exactly where he thought she would be. The crucial question that would determine his next move was this: was she alone, or was her escort close by? If so, he couldn't risk a confrontation. But should she have been separated from her escort during the storm, which was possible, then he had his once-in-a-lifetime chance.

Regan turned to the quartermaster. 'Until we know for sure, we must try to stay out of sight, but close in at the same time.'

'How are we going to do that?'

'Ah. Easy. Here, look.'

Regan picked up the map and pointed at a group of small, uninhabited islands that lay directly ahead. 'We are much faster than the *San Cristobal*. We can sail around these islands without being seen, and intercept her here.' Smiling, Regan tapped a forefinger on the map.

It was a brilliant plan. The islands would act as cover. 'By the time we come to this point here, we'll be almost upon her. If her escort is close by, we retreat; if not, we engage. I know these islands well. They will not risk a pursuit in these treacherous waters. And besides, we are faster.'

The quartermaster looked in awe at his captain as he left the cabin to give the orders for the ship to change course.

The San Cristobal had been badly damaged during the storm. One of her masts had broken in half, crushing the deck area below. Three seamen had been killed. The carpenters were desperately trying to repair the damage in order to keep the limping ship manoeuvrable.

At first, Captain Medina thought that the frigate emerging out of a channel between two islands in the distance was his escort. Relieved, he reached for his telescope to make sure. Closing one eye, he pressed the telescope against the other, and paled. It wasn't his escort, but something ominous: a large ship without a flag, coming towards him under full sail. Holding his breath, he kept staring at the ship when suddenly, a flag was hoisted: the dreaded black skull and crossbones; the Jolly Roger. *My God, The Templars Revenge*, thought Medina, well aware what this meant.

'Pirate ship ahead!' he shouted, pulling himself together, and began to bark orders to prepare his ship for battle.

Regan turned to the quartermaster standing behind him. 'She's damaged, a sitting duck,' he said and put down his telescope. 'And no escort in sight. This is our day! Prepare the guns. We'll give her a broadside first to cause panic and confusion, then we board.'

Every man on *The Templars Revenge* knew exactly what do to. Within moments, the guns were primed and ready, the grappling hooks prepared for boarding, and the excited men – armed to the teeth – were standing by, the razor-sharp blades of their cutlasses reflecting the morning sun like a deadly army, ready to march into battle and fight to the death.

27

Searching for the *San Cristobal*: 25 June 1664

Captain Cordoba, commander of the *Santo Cristo de Tobar*, knew the area well but had searched the whole day for the *San Cristobal* without success. Separated during the night by the storm, he had kept his ship well away from the islands and their deadly reefs that flanked the route he had chosen to Havana because he was in a hurry, anxious to make it to Cuba before hurricane season began. Relatively easy to navigate on a calm day, the reefs became very dangerous during a storm, and experienced sailors like Cordoba stayed well clear of them.

Fearing the worst, Cordoba took another pass through a narrow channel the *San Cristobal* could have drifted into during the night, when one of his men saw some debris floating in the calm sea ahead.

The half-submerged barrels, pieces of rope and splintered decking timbers told a tragic, all-too-familiar tale of a ship wrecked, most likely on a hidden reef during the storm. Survivors seemed unlikely because few sailors could swim, but Cordoba decided to keep searching the area just in case, as long as daylight allowed. Just before sunset, one of the lookouts began to wave his arms. 'Over here,' he shouted and pointed to a large piece of timber with some canvas and rope attached, floating by with what looked like several men clinging to its side.

One of those men was Navarro, who licked his parched lips and stared at the ship towering above him. Trying to focus, he lifted his aching arm and began to wave like a man possessed.

Cordoba couldn't believe his luck. One of the men plucked from the deadly grip of the sea appeared to be none other than the feared 'Mad Dog' Regan, the notorious buccaneer. The scar, the missing ear, the diamond earring and the red embroidered coat all pointed in the right direction. He was barely alive when they lifted him onto the ship and it was only after the ship's surgeon went to work on him that he began to drift back into the world of the living, albeit, thought Cordoba, for a limited time. Regan's date with the hangman seemed a certainty once they reached Havana.

The other two survivors were Navarro, and a deckhand from *The Templars Revenge*, a boy of about ten who, as a lowly powder monkey, helped load the guns during combat. Both had only survived because they had strapped themselves to the piece of floating timber with a rope from the rigging, and so managed to keep their heads above water. Two others also strapped to the timbers were not so lucky. They had drowned during the night.

Wrapped in a blanket and holding a mug of brandy with shaking hands, Navarro sat on a stool in the captain's cabin. No longer cold and shivering, he thanked the Good Lord for his miraculous rescue. He tried to stand up when Cordoba swept into the cabin, looking impressive in his uniform.

'Don't get up, Father,' he said and reached for the brandy bottle on the table. 'A little more?'

Navarro shook his head, bracing himself for what he knew was to come: an interrogation.

With his arms folded in front of his chest, Cordoba looked sternly at Navarro. 'Please, Father, tell us what happened.'

'As you know, the storm came out of nowhere,' began Navarro, a natural storyteller. 'It must have been just after midnight when the wind began to howl, and huge seas began to pound the ship. We were told to stay inside and batten down. Outside, the crew was desperately preparing the ship in the hope to ride out the storm. Visibility was almost non-existent in the driving rain. About an hour later, I heard a loud crash. The whole ship began to shudder and we feared it must have hit a reef, but fortunately, that wasn't the case. When I looked outside, I saw that one of the masts had broken in half and fallen onto the deck, bringing down the rigging and trapping several sailors under its massive timbers. There was a lot of shouting.

Then, just before daybreak, the seas finally calmed. The storm had gone, and the *San Cristobal* was drifting in what looked like a lake surrounded by small islands.' Navarro stopped and looked dreamily into the distance.

'Go on,' prompted Cordoba.

'The ship had been badly damaged during the night and was barely seaworthy. Captain Medina had managed to keep his ship away from the treacherous reefs, but he had been unable to protect it from the ferocious wind and mountainous seas. The carpenters went to work to repair the damage. That's when it happened.'

'What happened?' asked Cordoba.

'A ship appeared out of nowhere. At first we thought it was you, but soon we realised that wasn't so. The Jolly Roger flapping in the wind told us that. Pirates! Captain Medina, a courageous man, realised at once what was happening. He prepared his ship the best he could for the inevitable. But,' Navarro paused, 'he did have something rather extraordinary up his sleeve ...'

'What?' asked Cordoba.

'A brilliant surprise.'

'What kind of surprise?'

'Once he realised that we were under attack by *The Templars Revenge*, Regan's notorious pirate ship, he knew that without your support, we were doomed. Regan didn't take prisoners and this was going to be a fight to the death. That's when Medina knew he had to do something special, and he did.'

'Did what exactly?'

'He carefully positioned his ship between two reefs in a way that placed a partially hidden, deadly obstacle into the path of the attacking ship, which, if luck was on his side, could have devastating consequences should its captain fail to notice the looming danger in time. And that is exactly what happened.'

Navarro took a sip of brandy.

'Can you elaborate?' asked Cordoba, fascinated by the account. He knew that the circumstances of the loss of the *San Cristobal* would have a significant bearing on his reputation and future in the Spanish Navy.

'Realising we were trapped and helpless,' continued Navarro, '*The Templars Revenge* closed in rapidly, with hundreds of screaming marauders lining the decks, cheered on by their larger-than-life captain standing on the quarterdeck, brandishing his cutlass. In the excitement of the chase, they failed to notice the telltale signs of a shallow reef, and headed straight for it, just as our captain had hoped. The trap was about to close. We watched in silence as the pirate ship came bearing down on us. As soon as it was almost within range, Medina gave the signal to fire – merely as a distraction, I suspect – and then our ship retreated a little further into the channel behind us. Moments after the guns went off, most of them missing their target, *The Templars Revenge* hit the reef side on at full speed. The impact failed to stop the ship, but pushed it slightly off course, the razor-sharp reef gouging a huge hole into its side. The ship began to take on water, but continued towards us, nevertheless. A few minutes later it was close enough for the grappling hooks to be thrown across, but before that happened, *The Templars Revenge* fired a broadside at close range, causing enormous damage to our ship. After that, the jubilant pirate crew came on board as the two ships were joined in a deadly embrace. The rest was hand-to-hand combat. Slaughter, severed limbs, rivers of blood, death.

'What about Regan? Did you see him?'

'Yes. He was one of the first to come on board. Firing his pistols and fighting like a madman, he was hacking his way towards our captain, who was directing his men from the quarterdeck ...'

'And?'

'The men stepped back as Regan climbed onto the deck and confronted Medina. Moments later, the two captains were locked in a ferocious duel. A fight to the death.'

'What happened?'

'At first, they appeared evenly matched, but soon Regan, the superior swordsman, gained the upper hand. When he inflicted a deep cut that almost severed Medina's left arm, the valiant captain of the *San Cristobal* was, just like his ship, doomed. Bleeding profusely, he sank to his knees and the naval short sword fell out of his hand. Just before Regan delivered the coup de grâce and cut off his head, Medina turned to the quartermaster fighting close by, and with his voice failing, gave an order. Moments later, there was a huge explosion below deck as the powder kegs were ignited by the crew and set the ship on fire. By the time Regan realised what was happening, it was too late. The *San Cristobal* was sinking and the fire spread quickly to the sails and the rigging and across to *The Templars Revenge*, setting it on fire as well.'

Cordoba nodded, well pleased with what he had just heard. Captain Medina had made sure that the precious cargo of silver did not fall into the hands of the pirates, and his men didn't die in vain, but with honour, and took the pirate ship and its crew down with them into their watery grave.

'What happened then?' asked Cordoba.

'The fighting stopped and it was every man for himself. Most jumped overboard to escape the flames. That's what I did. I managed to climb on top of a floating piece of timber just before the *San Cristobal* disappeared into the deep, taking *The Templars Revenge* with it.'

'Captain Medina died with honour,' said Cordoba, 'and turned defeat into victory. And thanks to you, Father, his story will now be told and recorded in the annals of history.'

With that, Cordoba took a bow, turned and left the cabin, satisfied that his own reputation was not only safe, but would soon be considerably enhanced when he delivered 'Mad Dog' Regan, the dreaded pirate, into the hands of the authorities in Havana, and Father Navarro, a respected Jesuit, gave his eyewitness account of what happened to the *San Cristobal*.

28

A secret location near Catanzaro, Calabria: 27 October

Cesaria looked at her watch and turned to Jack sitting next to her in the plane. 'Not long now,' she said. 'We should land in Catanzaro in less than half an hour.'

'I can't believe you pulled this off so quickly,' said Jack.

'It wasn't easy, I can tell you, but we owe you, Jack, especially after your help in the Stolzfus matter, and what happened in Venice. And besides, this could assist in the court case.'

'I understand.'

Cesaria reached for Jack's hand. 'I'm glad you didn't bring Tristan along.'

Jack nodded. He had persuaded Tristan to return to Venice, rather than come along to meet the mother of the man suspected of having arranged the hit in Venice meant for him. 'It would have been a mistake. He tries to hide his pain, but things are too raw at the moment. But I do miss his intuition. You know what he's like. He can see things we can't.'

'He can hear the whisper of angels?'

'He can. And what's really surprising is …'

'Yes?' said Cesaria, watching Jack carefully.

'What those whispers are all about. Not always angelic.'

'Fallen angels?'

'Some of them definitely are.'

'You think so?'

'Oh yes.'

'The eternal conflict? Good and evil?' Cesaria speculated.

'Sometimes almost impossible to tell apart.'

'I know what you mean. This Mafia court case is a bit like that. Good and evil sitting side by side at the kitchen table; sleeping in the same bed.'

'What's Donizetti like?' asked Jack, changing the subject.

'Tough, like Grimaldi, and just as determined. A very courageous woman. We call her the Iron Lady. There have been several attempts on her life. She lives under constant police protection.'

'I can imagine.'

Once again, Grimaldi had to use all his contacts and influence to get permission for Jack to meet with Giuseppina Giordano, one of the star witnesses in the upcoming Mafia trial. But what had finally made it all possible was Cesaria's relationship with Nicola Donizetti, the lead prosecutor, and head of the investigation that was behind the sensational trial due to start in Lamezia Terme.

Cesaria and Donizetti had worked closely together for several months, collecting intelligence and evidence about the Giordano family's operations in Florence and other parts of Italy. In fact, it was Cesaria's secret collaboration with Giuseppina after her son's assassination that had finally persuaded the wife of one of Italy's most notorious Mafia bosses to turn against her husband and her family, break the code of silence, and agree to testify about the Mafia and its complex web of corrupt business interests and influence in high places, which not only protected the criminal empire, but also made it possible.

This in turn had been the beginning of the *Vedo, Sento, Parlo* – I see, I hear, I speak – movement, which had assumed momentum once Giuseppina's cooperation with the police, and the reasons behind it, had become public. Suddenly, dozens of Mafia wives, mothers and daughters turned against the Mafia that had ruled their lives for generations, and said 'enough is enough!'

'But everything comes at a price,' continued Cesaria as the plane prepared for landing. 'The Mafia hit back with ruthless acts of violence that ripped families apart and left mutilated bodies of mothers and grandmothers lying in the fields and on the steps of churches after Sunday mass. Instead of cowing the rebellious women into submission, this only hardened their resolve, and more women came forward and joined the movement.'

'How fascinating,' said Jack, finding it difficult to believe the picturesque capital of Calabria that looked so peaceful and inviting from above, hid such dark secrets.

Prosecutor Donizetti met them at the airport with two heavily armed police officers by her side, and quickly ushered them into a secure corridor leading to another part of the airport where an army helicopter – its engines running – was waiting.

'I want us to get away from here quickly,' she said, handing Jack and Cesaria bulletproof vests. 'Here, put these on. Airports are dangerous places, difficult to control. Especially now.'

Impressed, Jack watched Donizetti – a petite, energetic woman in her fifties – climb into the helicopter while the two police officers stood guard. Moments later, the chopper took off and turned north towards the hills.

After a short flight, the helicopter descended and landed next to a remote farmhouse on top of a hill. Armed police met the chopper and stood guard while everyone got out and hurried into the house, the whole operation taking only a few minutes.

'You can take these off now,' said Donizetti, undoing her flak vest. Inside, the farmhouse was welcoming and cosy. Giuseppina, a stocky woman in her seventies, was in the kitchen, cooking. 'I made us some lunch,' she said, embracing Donizetti and Cesaria. 'Almost ready.' It was clear the women had formed a close bond during difficult times, and appeared totally at ease in each other's company. Donizetti introduced Jack and began to set the table. Cesaria poured some wine into a rustic jug and rummaged around for some glasses in the old kitchen dresser next to the stove.

'I hope you like pasta,' said Giuseppina, speaking passable English with a heavy Italian accent. She took off her apron and looked at Jack with interest.

'What's there not to like, when it smells so good,' said Jack, smacking his lips. 'What are you making?'

'Ravioli Calabrese. Ravioli filled with – how do you say? – a mix of Provola cheese, soppressata salumi and pecorino, with a spicy tomato sauce.'

'I can't wait.'

'Good. First we eat, then we talk.'

'Fine by me.'

'Cesaria told me what happened in Venice,' said Giuseppina after Jack had finished a second helping and devoured half a loaf of bread. 'My heart, it bleeds.'

Jack put down his spoon and looked at Giuseppina. 'Lorenza was an outstanding cook, just like you. She would have loved your pasta.'

Giuseppina nodded, sadness in her eyes. 'Somehow, we must break free from this violence. That's why you are here, no?'

'Yes,' said Jack.

'One of my sons is dead. Gunned down in the middle of Florence. The other is lost to me as well. As for my husband ...'

Cesaria stood up, walked over to Giuseppina and put an arm around her shoulders. It was a spontaneous gesture of comfort and empathy between two women who knew pain and loss. 'You have already taken the first step,' she said. 'It will get easier from now on.'

Jack was wondering what Tristan would have made of all this: The mother of the man, who most likely arranged the hit – ordered by his autocratic father while sitting in a Calabrian jail – denouncing violence and talking about loss. A hit that was meant for Tristan, but had killed the love of his life instead.

There are no winners in this, thought Jack, searching for a way to introduce the subject that had brought them to Calabria to meet this extraordinary woman. That's when Donizetti came to his rescue and met the subject head on, well aware that the helicopter would return shortly and take them to the airport so that Jack and Cesaria could catch their flight back to Florence. The less time they spent in Calabria, the better. The eyes and ears of the Mafia were everywhere, and mortal danger just around the corner.

'Giuseppina, you know a lot about the matters we talked about,' she said. 'Is there anything you can tell us about Spiridon 4 and these Death Mask Murders?'

Giuseppina stood up, walked over to the dresser and took a notebook out of a drawer. 'Yes, I think there is. At the time, none of this made any sense, but after we spoke the other day, all the pieces fell into place,' she said in Italian, sounding alert and strangely energised.

The helicopter landed just as the passengers began to board the flight to Florence. Jack and Cesaria were cutting it fine, but this was intentional, as Donizetti wanted them to spend as little time as possible at the airport, which she considered high risk and dangerous.

'Thanks for everything,' said Jack and shook Donizetti's hand. 'Let's see where all of this takes us.'

'Please keep me informed,' shouted Donizetti, trying to make herself heard over the roar of the rotor blades. 'You must hurry, your plane is leaving shortly. Follow me!'

'Will do.' Jack and Cesaria climbed out of the helicopter and looked around. Flanked by two armed bodyguards, Donizetti walked quickly across the tarmac towards the terminal. Jack reached for Cesaria's arm and followed close behind.

The trained eye of the bodyguard on Donizetti's right saw it first. A man pushing a baggage trolley stopped, unzipped a sports bag and pulled out what looked like a sawn-off shotgun. 'Gun! Two o'clock!' shouted the bodyguard and reached for the gun in his shoulder holster.

Years of working on the front line as a war correspondent in Afghanistan had taught Jack how to react to imminent danger. Without thinking, he hit the ground and pulled Cesaria down with him. Moments later the shotgun went off, followed by several shots from a handgun.

As Jack looked up, he could see the man with the shotgun slumped against the baggage trolley. The shotgun had slipped out of his hands, and half his face was missing. Gun at the ready, the bodyguard was walking towards him and kept firing. When Jack looked ahead, he could see Donizetti lying on the ground. He was unable to tell whether she was dead or alive, but the other bodyguard lying next to her was bleeding from a huge wound to the back of his head.

'We must get out of here!' shouted Jack and pulled Cesaria to her feet. 'There could be others.'

'Where's Donizetti?'

'Over there!'

Cesaria ran across to Donizetti and knelt down next to her. She could see she was bleeding from a shoulder wound. 'Get on that plane! Quickly!' said Donizetti.

'I can't just leave you!'

'You must. I'll be fine; just a scratch,' said Donizetti and pointed with her chin to the dead bodyguard lying next to her. 'He took the bullet meant for me. Now leave! This is an order!'

Despite the commotion on the tarmac outside, and the chaos and confusion inside, the plane took off on time. The airport had been sealed off, and dozens of police rushed to the scene. Siren's blaring, ambulances kept arriving.

'Can you believe what has just happened?' said Jack as the plane began to climb and turned north, heading for Florence.

Cesaria just stared out the window, her face ashen. Jack reached for her hand and squeezed it. 'I need a drink; what about you?'

Cesaria nodded but didn't reply.

Jack knew from experience that in stressful situations like this, humour was the best way to deal with the unthinkable.

'One of the best pastas I can remember, served in a stunning location guarded by armed police, and prepared by the wife of the man who most likely ordered the murder of a close friend of mine. And then we almost get killed at the airport. Some breadcrumbs, eh? I don't think Calabria is for us, what do you reckon?'

Slowly, Cesaria turned and looked gratefully at Jack, a hesitant little smile creasing the corners of her mouth. 'Thanks, Jack.'

'What for?'

'For reacting so quickly. God knows what would have happened if—'

'Hush. We are both here, and Donizetti will be fine.'

'I hope so. I told you, she's special.'

'Courage always is.'

'Do you think it was worth it?' asked Cesaria. 'Coming here, I mean?'

'Giuseppina gave us all she could.'

'That's not what I asked.'

'I know. Well, let's have a closer look: she overheard only snippets that could, I stress *could*, be relevant.'

'Go on.'

'There's no doubt that Teodora was the go-between. She visited the Giordano villa in Florence often; we know that. Spiridon 4 was involved, so much is clear. The question is, what were the assignments all about? Were the Death Mask Murders part of it and, more importantly, *who was behind it all?* Who was the client paying the bills? Right?'

'Yes. But there was more,' said Cesaria.

'There was. This intriguing video she mentioned.'

'Exactly. Remember what she said? She walked into the study to serve lunch to her husband and her son—'

'That's when she saw it,' interjected Jack.

'A gruesome video of a shocking murder.'

'And overheard the one thing that could help us here.'

'Correct. Something about making money on the dark web through gambling involving death?'

'Ritual murder. What does that remind you of?' asked Cesaria.

'*Ars moriendi?*'

'Exactly! It's very similar, don't you think? Theatrical killings just like those we witnessed at that farm outside Florence in the Gambio and Belmonte matter. Gambling and violent death.'

'You are right,' said Jack as he remembered the evil life-and-death game involving real people, which they had raided on that fateful night in June two years earlier. It was the night they had rescued Tristan and Lorenza from the deadly grip of the Mafia.

'I wonder what all this means?' said Jack. 'Making money on the dark web?'

Cesaria reached for Jack's hand. 'I'm sure you'll find out, Jack. If anyone can, it's you, and I know just the person who could help you do it.'

'You do? Who?'

'Someone you've met before.'

'I'm intrigued.'

'Someone who helped us trace Tristan in Venice that time after he had been abducted.'

'Clara Samartini!'

'Exactly.'

'How did Conti introduce her; can you remember?' said Jack. 'I think he called her the youngest and brightest member of the Florence Forensics team.'

'That's her. Now, let's try to relax and have that drink, shall we?'

'Coming up! Let's make it a large one.'

'I'll call Dr Samartini as soon as we arrive in Florence and arrange a meeting,' said Cesaria, feeling better.

'Good idea. I can't wait.'

'You and your breadcrumbs,' teased Cesaria and squeezed Jack's hand. 'You live a dangerous life, Jack Rogan.'

'I wouldn't have it any other way; would you?'

<h1 style="text-align:center">29</h1>

Havana: 2 July 1664

Captain Cordoba knew how to impress. As soon as the *Santo Cristo de Tobar* – a spectacular man-of-war displaying the maritime might of Spain – sailed into Havana Harbor in the morning and docked, word about the capture of 'Mad Dog' Regan, the feared pirate, spread like wildfire through the town.

Soon, cheering crowds lined the shores, hoping to catch a glimpse of the notorious buccaneer, who had terrorised the Caribbean for years and made a mockery of the authorities trying in vain to capture him, and bring him and his cutthroats to justice.

Cordoba didn't disappoint. Looking beaten and dishevelled, his red coat in tatters, Regan was marched off the ship by a contingent of armed sailors. With his hands tied behind his back and a rope around his neck, Regan certainly did look like a beaten man. But looks can be deceptive. Deep down, Regan was far from beaten, and anyone taking a closer look would have noticed the defiant expression on his scarred face, and the hatred and danger lurking in his eyes. The crowd erupted in cheers when Cordoba and his officers came ashore in their splendid uniforms looking like sea battle-hardened victors, radiating confidence and success.

Cordoba couldn't have timed his arrival better. The annual treasure fleet returning to Spain had already assembled and was ready to depart. Hundreds of sailors and merchants were in town, preparing for the journey, their ships loaded with precious cargo: emeralds from Colombia, gold and silver from the Andes, and mahoganies from Cuba and Guatemala.

Havana, designated the 'Key to the New World and Rampart of the West Indies' by the Spanish Crown, was not only a wealthy trading port, its fortified harbour also provided much-needed protection from marauding pirates. Pirates were a constant threat and challenge to the authority of the Captain General, the Spanish governor of the island who was responsible for the safety of the city, and the protection of its lifeblood, commerce.

Guarded by impressive fortifications like the Castillo San Salvador de la Punta, which protected the west entrance to the bay, and the Castillo de los Tres Reyes Magos del Morro – Morro Castle – which guarded the eastern shore with a chain strung across the mouth of the harbour to the fort at la Punta, Havana provided a safe destination for the hundreds of trading ships bringing New World treasure to Cuba for the journey back to Spain.

Cordoba went straight to the governor's residence to present his report.

As soon as the governor heard that the notorious 'Mad Dog' Regan – a thorn in his side for years – had been captured, he was overjoyed. A quick trial followed by a public execution, just before the fleet was due to depart, was exactly what was needed to give his reputation and standing a much-needed boost, and instil confidence in the safety of the treasure fleet travelling back to Spain under the protection of the navy and courageous captains like Cordoba.

The loss of the *San Cristobal*, while disappointing, could be blamed on a storm, and not on a pirate attack. The sinking of *The Templars Revenge* was an added bonus, which could be attributed to the valiant fight put up by Captain Medina and his crew, who had sacrificed their lives for the common good. That would be the official version of events recorded in the relevant dispatches going back to Spain with the fleet.

'You must be congratulated, Captain,' said the governor. 'This is an outstanding result under difficult circumstances. And you say there is an eyewitness who saw it all and can testify?'

'Yes, Your Excellency. Father Navarro, a Jesuit priest. A well-connected one as it turns out,' said Cordoba. 'According to Captain Medina, he even had a letter of introduction from the king himself ...'

'I see. Not only respectable and reliable, but well-connected in high places as well. In short, the perfect witness. There were no other survivors?'

'Not as far as we could tell. Apart from Regan and Father Navarro, only a boy from the pirate ship.' Cordoba shook his head. 'After a storm like this, it's a miracle anyone survived.'

'Quite. I will prepare a report, and no doubt so will Father Navarro. You can rest assured, Captain, that you and your crew will be appropriately mentioned and your exemplary conduct duly acknowledged.'

Cordoba took a bow, well pleased with himself. 'Thank you, Excellency.'

'Where is the wretch now?'

'Where he belongs. In chains. In a dungeon in Morro Castle.'

'Excellent.'

'A quick trial then, and a very public execution. We must make a spectacle of it. The people will love it!'

'I agree.'

'As a deterrent, of course, and to show the world that Spain rules these waters, no-one else.'

'The admiral will be pleased, Excellency, and no doubt so will the king.'

'I expect so,' said the governor, stroking his beard.

Regan sat up as soon as he heard the key turn in the lock. He slipped the amulet he had been working on into his pocket, and hid the nail he had found on the floor of his cell, in the rotting straw of the rat-infested bedding. Shielding his eyes from the cone of light creeping into the dark cell, Regan looked at the burly gaoler towering above him.

'Stand up!' commanded the gaoler.

Regan stood up.

'He's ready. You can come in now.'

A man wearing a leather apron came into the cell and began to measure Regan's height.

'What's going on?' asked Regan.

'Can't you see? He's taking measurements,' said the gaoler, grinning.

'What for?'

'Your rotting corpse, of course, you miserable wretch. You have an appointment with the noose. You will end your life by dancing the hempen jig at the end of a rope. And once you're dead, your corpse will be enclosed in an iron cage and left hanging to rot,' he added, laughing. This was a common deterrent intended as a grisly, public warning against future acts of piracy.

'When?'

'Soon. Very soon.'

'In that case, I want to see a priest. The Jesuit who gave evidence at my trial. I spoke to him and asked him. He said he would hear my confession.'

The gaoler nodded. This was a condemned prisoner's right.

'I will let him know,' he growled and followed the other man out of the cell, and then locked the heavy door.

Smiling, Regan took the little amulet – the tip of a whale's tooth he usually wore around his neck – out of his pocket, and then searched through the straw for the nail. As soon as he found it, he went to work, well aware that he had to finish the engraving before the shaft of moonlight reaching through the barred opening in the wall disappeared.

Three days later

Navarro followed the gaoler down the slippery stone steps leading to the castle dungeons. 'In here,' said the gaoler and pointed to an iron-studded wooden door with massive, rusty hinges. 'Just call out when you're finished. I'll come and get you.' The gaoler unlocked the door and pushed it open.

Navarro nodded, stepped into the cell and looked at the man standing in the shadows. Instead of finding a man cowering on the floor, crushed by the prospect of soon facing a horrible death, he found Regan standing upright in his chains, radiating composed confidence, bordering on arrogance, Navarro thought, and authority.

'Thank you for coming, Father,' said Regan, his voice surprisingly strong. 'There isn't much time, so I'll come straight to the point.'

'I thought you wanted me to hear your confession.'

Regan laughed. 'I am more interested in this life than the next, but a confession it will be. Of sorts.'

'I don't understand.'

'You will in a moment. I would like to suggest a deal,' said Regan, lowering his voice.

'A *deal?*' asked Navarro, looking incredulous. *Perhaps he's lost his mind?* he thought, searching for an explanation for the baffling comment.

'What kind of deal?'

'I have something of great value to you and your Church, and you can help me with something I have to do before I depart this world. Interested?'

'You speak in riddles. Please explain.'

'I know that the legendary Ruminahui treasure was on the *San Cristobal.*'

'How can you possibly know this?' said Navarro, looking astonished. 'Not even Captain Cordoba knows.'

'I have spies in every port, eyes and ears in every tavern.'

Navarro nodded, but didn't respond.

'What would you say if I were to show you a way to retrieve that treasure?'

'This is fantasy, surely.'

'Far from it. The *San Cristobal* is resting on a reef in shallow waters. The treasure would be quite easy to recover,' Regan paused for effect. 'If you know where to look, that is,' he added quietly.

Regan watched Navarro carefully. The expression on Navarro's face told him all he had to know.

'Seriously?' said Navarro, sounding hoarse.

'Absolutely.'

'Are you suggesting that *you* know where to look?'

'I do. As you can imagine, I know these waters like the back of my hand. I had some of the best charts available on my ship. I know exactly where the *San Cristobal* is right now with all that gold ... within reach.'

'And you are prepared to tell me in return for what?'

'Excellent. We understand each other. It's about that boy from my ship who was rescued with us.'

'James Mascarino, the young powder monkey?'

'Yes. Do you know what will happen to him?'

'According to the law, he's a pirate just like you, albeit a very young one. You heard what was said during the trial.'

'I did. I know I will hang, but they didn't say what would happen to him.'

'And this matters to you?'

'It does.'

'May I ask why?'

'This is all part of my confession, right?' asked Regan, ignoring the question.

'It is.'

'Therefore, the seal of confession applies here?'

'It does. Nothing you tell me as a penitent can be disclosed by me to anyone. Canon 21 of the Fourth Council of the Lateran made that absolutely clear in 1215. It is binding on the whole Church.'

'It matters to me, because James is my son,' said Regan quietly. 'Mascarino is his mother's name. She was Portuguese.'

Navarro looked at Regan in silence for a while, and then nodded. Suddenly, it all made sense. 'They are reluctant to hang him because he's so young. He'll probably stay in here for the rest of his life, I suspect. In a cell just like this one. Forgotten. Or they may hang him later.'

Regan nodded. 'If you were to intercede on his behalf, could this perhaps change?'

'Perhaps. You mean if I were to take him into the care of the Church, for example, for the purpose of reforming him?'

'Something like that.'

'I think the governor may listen to this. I have friends in high places, and he knows it ...'

'Excellent. Here's the deal. If you promise to do all you can to save my son, I will show you exactly where to find the *San Cristobal*.'

'How will you do that?'

'On a map. One was presented by Cordoba as evidence during the trial, remember?'

Navarro nodded.

'To show roughly where my ship attacked and went down with the *San Cristobal*,' continued Regan. 'Except Cordoba got the position all wrong. He was guessing, of course.'

'But you know exactly where she is?'

'I do. And if you were to bring the map here, I could show you. Do you think you could do that? Bring the map in here, that is?'

'I think so.'

'Do we have a deal?'

'I ... I want to think about this,' stammered Navarro, somewhat taken aback.

'*There's no time!* You have to give me your answer now. And there's one more thing,' added Regan quietly, introducing the most important part of the proposed bargain.

'What?'

'I would like to see my son before I go to the gallows. I want to spend a few moments with him alone. In here. To say goodbye. Do you think you could arrange that?'

'I suppose so. It's not too much to ask in the circumstances. And as a priest and your confessor, I would have—'

'Do we have a deal?' Regan interrupted impatiently, aware that time was running out.

Navarro looked at Regan, his mind racing. If what Regan was proposing was real, then this was an offer almost too good to be true.

In any event, he had nothing to lose by making a promise to save the poor boy's life in return.

'We have a deal,' said Navarro.

Regan held out his hand. Navarro shook it. The deal was sealed. 'Then you better get going, Father, and bring me that map,' said Regan, smiling.

30

In front of Morro Castle, Havana: 7 July 1664

Gallows had been hastily erected just outside the castle gates during the night. The execution would take place in front of Morro Castle, a symbol of Spanish power. The imposing fortifications would provide a fitting backdrop to the hanging of one of the most notorious pirates, who had humiliated the governor for years, captured countless merchant vessels, and made a mockery out of the navy trying to protect them.

Word of the hanging had spread quickly through the city, and a huge crowd had assembled at first light in front of the castle, eagerly waiting for the spectacle to begin and enjoying the carnival atmosphere.

Standing on top of the ramparts, the governor shielded his eyes from the glare of the rising sun and looked down at the throng in front of the gallows, surrounded by armed guards under the command of Captain Cordoba. Satisfied, the governor began to stroke his beard and turned to Navarro standing next to him.

'This will send a strong message to the wretched buccaneers out there, don't you think, Father?'

Navarro nodded.

'And tell them that it is only a matter of time,' continued the governor, 'before they are blown apart by our warships and face the end of a rope, just like Mad Dog Regan, their "invincible" hero. I am sure your superiors in Spain will be pleased to hear that.'

'They will indeed, Excellency,' said Navarro, well aware of the subtle hint. 'I will certainly mention this in my dispatch.'

'Excellent. Your interest in the prisoner's spiritual needs is to be commended, Father,' continued the governor. 'Especially as he's the man responsible for the sinking of the *San Cristobal* and the death of Father Morales.'

'The condemned man will be judged by a higher authority for his sins; I am only ministering to his immortal soul. As his confessor, I will be by his side when he takes his last breath and meets his maker.'

'Very noble of you. And so is your interest in the boy. I must say, I wasn't quite sure what to do with him. He deserves to hang, of course, but one so young?' The governor shook his head. 'Your proposal could solve my dilemma, and for that I am grateful. Let's hope something good comes out of this terrible business.'

Smiling, Navarro bowed his head, but didn't reply.

'And don't forget, the boy must witness the execution. It will serve as a stark reminder not to follow in the footsteps of his evil captain.'

'Quite so, Excellency. I will make sure he stands right next to me during the execution and sees it all.'

'Very well. You better go then, Father, it's almost time.'

Blinded by the bright sunlight as he stepped into the courtyard on his way to the gallows, Regan closed his eyes and braced himself for what was to come. With his hands tied behind his back and a chain attached to a heavy iron collar chafing at his aching neck, he almost stumbled as he was dragged towards the castle gates by a contingent of jubilant prison guards, enjoying their part in the spectacle. Squinting, Regan opened his eyes just before they reached the gates and stepped outside.

The excited crowd began to cheer as soon as the hated pirate, who had caused so much death and destruction, walked through the gates, signalling the beginning of the gruesome pageant that had brought them to the castle so early in the morning.

If they expected to see a beaten man begging for mercy, they were surely disappointed as Regan walked confidently towards the waiting gallows, his bearing almost regal despite his tattered coat, the expression on his face defiant. He might soon lose his life, but deep down he knew he could leave this earth a winner with the last laugh, should Navarro have been able to persuade the governor to spare his son.

So far, Navarro had kept his side of the bargain. First, he had arranged that all-important meeting Regan had asked for. Regan had spent several precious minutes alone in his cell with his son. This had given him enough time to tell the boy all he had to know about his daring plan, and instruct him how to implement it. But most important of all, he had been able to give his son something precious that made it all possible, and would allow the boy to continue the Templars' revenge, long after his father had gone.

After that, Navarro had brought the map to Regan's cell, and Regan had confidently pointed to a spot where he claimed the *San Cristobal* was resting in shallow waters on a reef. For someone who loathed the Church and what it stood for, Regan had put on a convincing performance that completely fooled Navarro, who saw contrition and repentance, where there was only treachery and deceit.

As he walked towards the gallows, Regan could see his son standing demurely next to Navarro, waiting for him with the masked hangman by his side. For an instant, Regan felt a wave of sadness and regret, as nagging doubts began to claw at his heavy heart. What if Navarro had been unable to convince the governor, he asked himself, and James would spend the rest of his life in the dungeons, or worse? If so, his carefully laid plans would fail and it would all have been for nothing.

Forever the optimist, Regan banished the dark thoughts and kept walking. Ignoring the roar of the crowd as he slowly climbed the wooden steps leading up to the gallows on top of the dais, which looked more like a macabre stage set than a place of execution, Regan kept watching Navarro for a sign.

As his confessor, Navarro was allowed to be present and talk to the prisoner just before the execution. The hangman was about to place the noose around Regan's neck when Navarro held up his hand. 'Please give us a moment,' he said. The hangman stepped back.

'The governor agreed,' whispered Navarro. 'Your son will come to live with me in the monastery and receive an education.'

Relieved, Regan nodded, his scarred face creasing in a smile as Navarro made the sign of the cross over him and then withdrew.

Regan watched his son as the hangman placed the noose around his neck and fastened it. James, his face ashen, held his father's gaze and pointed with trembling fingers to the amulet he wore around his neck, which his father had given him earlier that day. Suddenly, the crowd fell silent, realising that the crucial moment had arrived. The hangman looked up at the governor standing at the ramparts above.

Slowly, the governor raised his hand like a Roman emperor about to decide the fate of a defeated gladiator in the arena.

The last thing Regan saw before the trapdoor opened under his feet, was the amulet around his son's neck with the tiny map he had engraved that pinpointed the exact location of the *San Cristobal*, with Ruminahui's legendary treasure waiting at the bottom of a shallow sea.

Just before the noose tightened around his neck and broke it, Regan began to laugh as he remembered the spot on the map he had shown to Navarro. Of course, it was nowhere near the *San Cristobal*, but somewhere out in the ocean, far away from the sunken treasure coveted by the Church.

PART III
THE ALLURE OF THE GOLDEN MASK

'The conquistador has no real appreciation of the new, wanting only to make his fortune and return to build an ugly palace towering the pigsty of his birth, but not before he does his best to transform the Indies into the nightmare they left behind.'

John Caviglia, *Arauco*

31

Florence: 28 October, morning

Rising early, Jack went for a walk along the banks of the Arno and had breakfast in his favourite trattoria near the Ponte Vecchio. He was preparing himself for what he sensed would be a pivotal meeting, showing the way for the next important step in the Death Mask Murders investigation. The phone call he had received from Dupree the night before had made that clear. Enjoying his second latte, Jack was going over his notes he had prepared since his first prison meeting with Landru at the beginning of the month.

Because so much had happened so quickly, Jack was drawing up a timeline of events he knew would be essential if he wanted to put all the crucial elements into perspective, and work out a meaningful strategy going forward. He also knew from experience that there would be only one opportunity to do this with all the key participants present. Satisfied, Jack finished his latte, closed his notebook and slipped the old rubber band over it. Then he paid the bill and hurried to the chief prosecutor's office on the other side of the river a short distance away.

By the time Jack arrived at Grimaldi's office, Cesaria and Dr Clara Samartini were already waiting for him.

'Just in time, Jack,' said Grimaldi and pointed to the whiteboard behind his desk. 'I heard what happened. Dreadful business. Donizetti will pull through. She's recovering in a military hospital in Naples. You had a lucky escape.'

'Extraordinary woman. At least that's good news.'

'Now you know why I was reluctant to arrange the meeting.'

'I had no idea Calabria was that dangerous.'

Grimaldi shrugged and pointed to Samartini.

'Clara has made excellent progress during the night, as you will see,' he said, 'regarding the new information you obtained from

Giuseppina Giordano yesterday. Well done, by the way. Let's hear what she has to say.'

Samartini greeted Jack like an old friend, but the sadness in her eyes was apparent when she embraced him.

'I was shocked to hear about Lorenza,' she said. 'Tristan must be devastated.'

'He is, and so are we all. But perhaps with your help, we can do something about it and catch those responsible.'

'We'll leave no stone unturned, that I can promise you. Especially after what happened yesterday. You think these matters are connected?'

'Could be. It's early days, but you know how these things go.'

Samartini nodded and turned towards the whiteboard. Cesaria, Samartini and Jack had been through a lot together two years earlier, and it was in no small way due to Samartini's ingenuity and tenacity that Tristan and Lorenza had been rescued in time, before falling victim to the deadly Ars Moriendi game conducted by the Mafia just outside Florence.

Jack smiled as he remembered meeting Samartini for the first time in Venice. Little had changed since. She was still the petite young woman with mousy-brown hair cut quite short, wearing thick glasses that amplified her eyes and gave her an almost comical appearance that reminded Jack of an earnest, short-sighted librarian. But appearances can be deceptive. With a PhD in IT from the University of Bologna, Samartini was one of the brightest members of Squadra Mobile's Forensics team, specialising in cybercrime and surveillance. She was also a black belt in karate.

'Perhaps before we begin, a few words about the dark web could be useful,' said Samartini. 'To put things into perspective, as there are so many misconceptions out there. Put simply, the dark web – or dark net as it is often called – is part of a much larger 'deep web', a network of secret websites that operate on an encrypted network that is not accessible via traditional search engines we are all familiar with.'

Samartini pushed back her glasses, which had slipped down her nose a little, and continued. 'What this means is this: the dark web is an ideal vehicle for illegal activities like black markets, drug dealing, child pornography, hackers, identity fraud, even murder, because the anonymity of the dark web provides a cloak of protection behind which the participants can hide. This has been a big problem for law enforcement agencies around the world for a long time now.'

'As you can imagine, the Mafia has used the dark web extensively,' said Grimaldi, stepping in. 'Especially with access to cryptocurrencies like bitcoin, which has made them a fortune, anonymously and safely.' Grimaldi stopped to light one of his small cigars. 'But thanks to talented officers like Clara here, we have made significant inroads into their activities; isn't that right, Cesaria?'

'It is. That's why I spoke to Clara last night after we got back and told her about Giuseppina, and what she had to say.'

'About making money on the dark web through gambling?' Jack weighed in.

'Yes, and I sent her the Landru video about that horror murder and as it turned out, that was the breakthrough.'

'In what way?' asked Jack.

'One of the most important features of the dark web is encryption,' replied Samartini. 'Like the notorious Tor encryption, which allows websites to hide their identity.'

'How?' said Jack.

'Without becoming too technical, Tor allows users to hide their location and identity. As you can imagine, this is very useful if you want to place yourself in a different country from where you actually are.'

'And Tor can do this?' said Jack.

'It can, very effectively. Individuals using Tor have their identifying information like their IP addresses encrypted, but using Tor can also be very dangerous – for various reasons I don't want to go into right now.'

'So, what have you been able to find out so far?' asked Grimaldi, blowing cigar smoke towards the open window.

'I contacted one of my colleagues in the US last night. She owes me a favour. They are much more advanced in these matters over there than we are.'

'*And?*' prompted Cesaria.

'She was able to trace parts of that video to an encrypted site that was active about the time Landru was convicted.'

'Really?' said Grimaldi, surprised.

'What kind of site?' asked Jack.

'An illegal gambling site. Not only bizarre, but also quite unique. Closed-group gamblers enjoying extreme violence like snuff videos, decapitations, torture and the like, with serious gambling on various aspects of the show and its ultimate outcome.'

'Unique in what way?' said Cesaria.

'The bets were not about the murder as such, but about the probability of someone other than the actual perpetrator being convicted of the crime.'

'Being framed, you mean?' asked Jack.

'Yes, and actually convicted in a court of law. The gambling had to do with the perpetrators getting away with the crime by blaming someone else. That's what made it unique and so exciting. And as we now know, that is exactly what appears to have happened with Landru; until now.'

'What do you mean?' said Grimaldi.

'Well, Cesaria tells me that Landru is likely to be released soon. Mainly because of this video, it has become apparent that he may not have committed the crime he was convicted of. An acquittal is therefore possible, and that presents a big problem for the parties behind the gambling site and, of course, the players as well.'

'What are you getting at?' Grimaldi asked.

'Can't you see? This upsets all the bets.'

'So? Surely, this is all academic by now, isn't it? Ancient history.'

A little smile spread across Samartini's face. 'Not necessarily.'

'What do you mean?' asked Grimaldi again.

'Hundreds of thousands of US dollars were gambled here and changed hands. All in anonymous cryptocurrency. This was the culmination of a long-running, carefully designed gambling project involving numerous brutal murders spanning several years. And it would now appear that it reached its climax in the wrong way. The winning horse wasn't the winner.'

'But isn't it all over?' said Jack. 'You just told us all about dark web encryption and anonymity.'

Samartini shook her head.

'What are you getting at?' asked Grimaldi impatiently.

'There's some information embedded in the video that may, I stress *may*, allow us to lift the veil of secrecy and encryption, and get to the source. In short, identify the original site, and possibly the individuals who were behind it and posted it, and expose them.'

'Seriously?' said Jack, looking incredulous.

'It would appear so.'

'My God, that would be amazing!' said Cesaria, who saw instantly where this was heading. 'Are you suggesting we could somehow let the cheated punters know about Landru's imminent release, and put this information *out there?*'

'Aha,' said Samartini, grinning. 'That's why the dark web is so dangerous. If the encryption fails and your identity is somehow revealed, anything can happen. These are dangerous people, and when there's so much money involved, well, you can imagine.'

'And we could perhaps embroil the Giordanos in this mess?' asked Grimaldi. 'Alessandro perhaps?'

'Possibly. After all, they were the facilitators. Accomplices in the, we would suggest, fraud, or at best deception and failure to deliver. And if we can put this out there on the dark web and expose those who benefited from this, all kind of disgruntled, dark people will come out of the shadows and go after them. I can guarantee it. We've seen this all before.'

Cesaria walked over to Samartini and gave her a hug. 'You are wonderful, you know that, don't you?'

'Can I be next?' asked Jack, holding out his arms.

Samartini held up her hand. 'Early days, Jack. Save it for later. There's still a lot to be done before this can work, but at least we have a plan, a promising one. Here, let me show you what I have in mind. We'll set a trap.'

'How intriguing, but please keep it simple,' said Jack and opened his notebook. 'Not all of us are IT wizards.'

Smiling, Samartini walked up to the whiteboard and picked up a felt pen. 'At least this should be a little less dangerous than your Calabrian escapades yesterday,' she said, and began to draw a diagram.

32

Palazzo da Baggio, Venice: 28 October, evening

Jack caught a water taxi from the railway station to the palazzo on the Grand Canal. He had arrived on the evening train from Florence after his meeting with Grimaldi, Cesaria and Samartini, and it was already quite late. As the taxi passed under the Rialto Bridge, a wave of sadness washed over him as he remembered the many times he had travelled the same route with a smiling Lorenza at the steering wheel of her beloved boat, showing off her driving skills. *How quickly life can change*, thought Jack as the taxi pulled up at the jetty in front of the palazzo.

Countess Kuragin and Bartolli were waiting for him in the salon on the first floor. Jack had asked Bartolli to meet him in Venice because he had something important to discuss that could change the direction of the entire case. He put down his duffel bag and walked over to greet them.

'How is he?' he asked.

'Quiet. He was worried about you,' said the countess, giving Jack a hug.

'You heard?'

'It was all over the news, but Tristan knew something bad was going to happen hours earlier. He was fretting all morning. You know what he's like when he keeps seeing things. Having Francesca here helped. I'm glad you asked her to come and keep us company.'

'Where's Leonardo?'

'Gone to bed early,' said the countess with sadness in her voice. 'He's taking it very badly. Dark moods ...'

'Hardly surprising.' Jack nodded and walked over to the sideboard. 'Drink anyone?'

'No, thank you,' said Bartolli. 'How did it go?'

'You mean apart from being caught in the Mafia crossfire at the airport? You both know what I'm like when I keep following my breadcrumbs.'

'Stubborn, reckless, determined. What do you think, Katerina? Have I left anything out?'

'All of the above, but I would add one more,' said the countess.

'Incorrigible?' said Tristan, who had just walked in and overheard the remark. 'And on this occasion, very lucky.'

'I would agree with that,' said the countess.

Jack walked over to Tristan and embraced him. 'How are you, mate?'

'Is that why you didn't want me to come along? Could you sense something too?'

'No. It's more complicated. I just didn't want you to face the mother of the man who most likely ordered the hit. I didn't think that would have been a good idea. For you, or for her.'

'You mean I would have been an embarrassing distraction, and she might have decided not to talk?'

'That too,' conceded Jack, surprised by Tristan's insight.

'I could have warned you about the assassination attempt.'

'Perhaps. We can't change the past, but we can plan the future. And I have a lot to tell you about that. And we have a lot of planning to do if we want to solve this mystery and catch the monster behind it.'

'We do?' asked Bartolli. 'I think I'll have that drink after all.'

'Yes,' said Jack as he opened a bottle of wine. 'I think things will move very fast from now on.'

'What makes you say that?' said Bartolli.

'Dupree called me this afternoon. Landru is about to be released on bail.'

'*What?* So quickly?' asked the countess.

'Yes. As you can imagine, this entire matter is a great embarrassment for the French authorities and they are in damage control. That's why they are moving so fast. Public opinion is a powerful tool and the elections are very close. They offered Landru a deal.'

'What kind of deal?' asked Tristan.

Jack put the bottle of wine and four glasses on a silver tray, and carried it across to the fireplace. 'I'll tell you. And some of it involves you, Katerina.'

'*Me?* In what way?'

'You are part of the bail conditions,' replied Jack, smiling.

'You can't be serious!'

'But I am. You'll see why in a moment. But first, let's have a glass of wine.'

Jack took a sip of wine, let himself sink into the comfortable chair facing the fireplace, and looked at the countess sitting opposite. 'Before I tell you about our meeting with Giuseppina, Giordano's wife, let's talk about Landru and his imminent release. As you can imagine, his lawyers have been working round the clock and applied for a judicial review of the entire case. Because this process can take quite some time, they argued that their client should be released on bail immediately, or else—'

'Or else, what?' interjected Bartolli.

'As you know, that house of horrors has attracted a lot of media attention, and the notorious Death Mask Murders are once again dominating the headlines. In short, Landru is back in the news, but this time not as the monster from before, but as a possible victim, wrongly convicted of a crime he didn't commit. And this is a big problem for the authorities that they can't just brush under the carpet and bury.'

'I can imagine,' said the countess.

'Lapointe, in particular, is in the firing line. He was the arresting officer who – it would now appear – arrested and convicted the wrong man. What this means, of course, is that the real murderer is still out there, and that is a major embarrassment.'

Jack paused to let this sink in and took another sip of wine. 'And that's why the authorities have suggested a deal.'

'What kind of deal?' asked Bartolli.

'In return for releasing Landru on bail, with some strict conditions attached, they want two things ...'

'What kind of things?' asked Tristan.

'No contact with the press, and his full cooperation in solving the case quickly, which Lapointe and his superiors see as the only way out of this mess.'

'Interesting,' said Bartolli. 'And Landru has agreed to this?'

'It would seem so. And in a way it doesn't surprise me. You want to know why?'

The countess nodded.

'Because that is exactly what Landru wants too, albeit for different reasons, and joining forces with the police can only enhance his chances.'

'Please explain what you mean,' said the countess.

'What drives Landru is an obsession. He wants to continue his quest. He wants to find the Llanganates treasure he's been searching for most of his adult life, but at the same time he wants to expose those who set him up, sent him to jail and ruined his life. In that regard, his aims and the interests of the French police overlap.'

'How fascinating,' said Bartolli. 'So, what are these bail conditions?'

'Ah. To begin with, a substantial surety: money. Of course, Landru hasn't got anything. I've agreed to put up the money. So, that's not a problem, but there's more.'

'What else?' said Tristan.

'He has to be released into the – how did the court put this? – "care of a reputable person who will report to the police on a regular basis". Dupree has agreed to be that person. I suppose Lapointe asked for his help here. As you know, they go back a long time. And besides, it's very clever because this way they can keep an eye on Landru and tap into what he knows.'

'But there is more, isn't there?' said Bartolli.

'Yes.' Jack turned to face the countess. 'The tricky bit.'

'I have a bad feeling about this,' said the countess. 'Tell me.'

'Landru has to live with Dupree. Under the same roof. The court imposed this as a strict condition that must be adhered to.'

'*What?* Landru is to live with Dupree in *my* Gatekeeper's Cottage next to the chateau? Is that what you're suggesting?'

Jack nodded.

Stunned silence.

'A convicted murderer out on bail released into the care of a retired police officer is to be my neighbour living in the grounds of my family estate?' said the countess quietly. 'That's absurd!'

'Uh-huh. That's about it,' said Jack, a sheepish grin on his face. He reached for the bottle and refilled the glasses.

'And you are recommending that I agree to this?'

'Yes, I do.'

'*Why*, Jack?'

'Because I'm convinced that Landru didn't commit those crimes. He may be many things, but he isn't a murderer.'

'I agree with Jack,' said Bartolli.

'And you will continue to be involved in this case?' asked the countess.

'Absolutely! Especially in light of what Giuseppina told us, and what the police in Florence have in mind. They too, want to solve this case, albeit for different reasons altogether. They are interested in the Mafia connection. That's the overlap. And there's more,' added Jack quietly.

'There is?' asked Tristan, his sixth sense aroused.

Jack hesitated, instantly regretting the comment, and bit his lip.

'Come on, Jack, what is it?' prompted Bartolli.

'There's a possible connection between this case and Lorenza's.'

'What do you mean?' Tristan almost shouted.

'Not now, please. I shouldn't have raised it.'

'You can't just—'

'It's better that way, trust me.'

'Let's leave it for now,' said the countess, stepping in. 'What if I don't agree?'

'I suppose Dupree will have to find alternative accommodation. He's determined to go through with this, but it wouldn't be the same. The cottage is perfect. Secluded, private, close.'

The countess took a deep breath and looked at Jack. 'Let me think about it.'

'Of course,' said Jack, relieved. 'What are you going to do? Are you staying here for now?'

'I am. I can't leave Leonardo here by himself. I will help him run the place, at least for a while. What about you?'

'I must go back to France straight away. I want to be in Paris when Landru is released.'

Jack turned to Tristan. 'And I was hoping that you would come with me, mate. What do you say?'

'You know the answer, Jack,' said Tristan, sounding his old self again for the first time since the funeral.

Will do him good, thought the countess. She knew he couldn't stay in Venice by himself. The grief would crush him. 'I will give you my answer in the morning, Jack,' she said.

'Very well.'

'What about the meeting with Giuseppina?' said Bartolli. 'And the Squadra Mobile in Florence?'

'It's late,' said Jack, sidestepping the question. 'Let's wait and see what Katerina decides first.'

'I understand.'

Jack turned to Bartolli. 'Would you come with us to Paris? It would be great to have you there when Landru is released.'

'I thought you'd never ask,' said Bartolli, smiling.

'Hooked?'

'What do you think?'

'Could be dangerous.'

'I'm used to it. I'm living with two teenagers, remember?'

'Ah. That explains it.'

33

Gatekeeper's Cottage, Kuragin chateau: 30 October

The unmarked police car pulled up at a side entrance of the Fleury-Mérogis Prison. It was just before eight am, and an icy wind was blowing in from the east.

Jack turned to Dupree sitting next to him. 'This is it. Ready?' he said and opened the door. Jack got out, turned up his collar and hurried to the entrance.

Dupree joined him moments later. 'Definitely a first.'

'What do you mean?'

'A convicted killer released on bail into the care of a retired police officer involved in the investigation that led to his conviction, which is now under appeal? How does that sound to you?'

'Weird, I know, but it's a good idea, don't you think?'

'For Lapointe and the authorities with egg on their faces and terrified of the media, definitely. But for us? I'm not so sure.'

'Getting cold feet?' asked Jack.

'No. Just feeling a little uneasy.'

'Understandable.'

'I'm surprised Katerina agreed to this. You must have been very persuasive.'

'Not really. She's a very generous person with a tremendous sense of right and wrong. She thought this was the right thing to do. And so do I.'

'Let's hope he won't disappoint us.'

'I don't think he will.'

'Let's go and find out, shall we?' said Dupree.

Just before leaving that morning, Jack had decided it would be best if Bartolli and Tristan stayed at the chateau and waited for Landru there, rather than coming to the prison. As soon as Jack walked through the doors and was met by the stony-faced prison officials, he knew he had made the right decision. The procedure to have Landru released was painfully tedious and full of frustrating bureaucratic red tape administered by officers who clearly resented what was happening, and did their best to make the procedure as difficult as possible. Dupree had to fill out countless forms and sign wads of documents; he was treated more like a new inmate being processed for admission than someone taking charge of a former prisoner being released.

While Jack had to use all his self-control not to let his frustration get the better of him, Landru appeared calm and just sat there quietly in his ill-fitting civilian clothes that appeared several sizes too big, and waited patiently for his release. No-one looking at him would have guessed that behind the controlled facade, he was almost bursting with jubilation as he counted down the minutes to the moment he had dreamed about for almost five years: *freedom*. The turning point had arrived, and Landru was ready to embrace it.

He was certain that inside his head he carried information that would not only set him free and clear his name, but also expose those who had destroyed his life and make them pay. In order to achieve that, he needed Dupree and Bartolli, and especially the French police, who desperately wanted to salvage their damaged reputation by solving the Death Mask Murders – quickly.

For Landru, however, there was more. A lot more. He was looking at a different, much bigger picture: solving the mystery of the Llanganates treasure, which would be the culmination of his life's work and vindicate everything he had done to achieve this. And most importantly, it would justify his many failures and mistakes. And for that, he needed Jack. For now, all the pieces seemed to be falling into place better than he had hoped, and all he had to do was walk through those intimidating prison gates a free man, albeit with temporary strings attached.

As soon as the gates closed behind him, Landru stopped and took a deep breath before getting into the waiting car. The man on the motorbike watching the car from the far end of the deserted lane, pulled down the visor on his helmet, started his powerful machine, and then followed the car as it pulled away and turned into the main street.

Landru barely spoke on the way back to the chateau and just stared out of the window. Just before the car turned into the long driveway leading to the chateau, he turned to Jack sitting next to him in the back. 'Thank you both for everything. My lawyer explained what happened behind the scenes to make this possible. I can't express how I feel right now. To see colours and life after five years behind drab prison walls designed to crush the spirit, is a liberation.'

'I understand,' said Jack.

'No doubt your lawyer would have explained that this is a temporary arrangement,' said Dupree, anxious to put the unusual relationship on the right footing from the very beginning, 'with strict conditions attached. And he would have told you about the urgency—'

'What urgency?' interjected Landru, frowning.

'As soon as we get to the cottage we'll have a talk,' said Jack, trying to diffuse the rising tension.

Landru nodded. 'If there's one thing I've learned over the years, it's this: nothing in life is free.'

'You are absolutely right about that. In the end, it's all about the price. It's all about what we are prepared to pay,' said Jack.

Dupree looked over his shoulder at Jack and raised an eyebrow. 'Chief Superintendent Lapointe will join us later today and explain everything.'

'Lapointe wants to talk to me?' said Landru, surprised.

'Yes. There's a lot at stake here, as you will see.'

Landru didn't reply and stared out of the window again as the car crossed the little bridge leading to the chateau. This was definitely turning out better than expected.

The man on the motorbike stopped at the park gates and watched the police car cross the moat. *A chateau close to Paris; very neat,* he thought. Then he pulled out his phone and called O'Hara.

Lapointe arrived two hours later. Landru had settled into his room in the Gatekeeper's Cottage and had devoured an early lunch prepared by cook. After five years of bland prison fare, the sandwiches and the tea cake tasted like a feast. So as not to overwhelm Landru, Jack had asked Tristan to stay in the background for the time being. Bartolli, however, had joined them for lunch. She was carefully observing Landru and analysing his demeanour when Lapointe walked in, followed by Clara Samartini, who had arrived early that morning from Florence. This was a surprise no-one had expected.

Lapointe took off his trench coat and hat, put them on a chair next to the fireplace and introduced Samartini. Then he reached for his pipe and lit it.

He looks more and more like Maigret, thought Jack, smiling.

Used to working under pressure and dealing with the unexpected, Lapointe knew exactly how to broach the subject that had brought him so suddenly face to face with Landru. 'I will not comment on the case under review,' he said quietly, looking at Landru who was watching him intently. 'That's a matter for the courts.'

Landru realised Lapointe was dancing around the main question. *Interesting. I wonder what he wants*, he thought, but didn't respond.

'We have more important and urgent matters to address,' continued Lapointe. He watched his pipe smoke curl towards the fireplace like exhaled breath on a cold winter's morning. 'As you no doubt know, your early release on bail was authorised by the Prefect of Police personally, and approved by the court,' continued Lapointe. 'And as you also know, nothing happens without good reason.'

Landru nodded.

'Apart from the bail conditions you are obviously aware of, there's another, more urgent subject here that concerns us all,' continued Lapointe and drew on his pipe. 'An opportunity.'

'What kind of opportunity?' asked Jack.

'Dr Samartini can explain that much better than I. But before I ask her to do that, I must insist that you keep everything you are about to hear totally confidential. Under no circumstances must any of this get out. You will see why in a moment. Lives depend on it.'

Everybody nodded.

Satisfied, Lapointe turned to Samartini. 'Dr Samartini. Please ...' he said and stepped back.

Samartini began by outlining the pending court case against the Mafia in Calabria about to get underway, and the part played by the women in making the groundbreaking prosecutions possible. 'In case you are wondering what all this has to do with the Death Mask Murders, there is a surprising connection, and it has to do with that anonymous tape sent to Chief Superintendent Lapointe that has triggered Mr Landru's release.'

Samartini paused to let this sink in. 'But more importantly, it has to do with what Jack discovered about it that really matters here,' she continued quietly. '*Spiridon 4.*'

'Can you please explain?' asked Landru.

Jack, who had heard it all before leaving Florence, was wondering how Landru would react to this, because everything depended on that. He was the essential link that could make it all come together and work.

Samartini took a deep breath and continued, 'About a year ago, the Squadra Mobile in Florence came up with a bold strategy that would allow them to infiltrate the Mafia and break the code of silence that had so effectively protected the key players for generations.'

'What kind of strategy?' asked Dupree, surprised by the direction the unusual briefing was taking.

'My colleagues and I developed a unique, encrypted messaging app designed to allow safe communication among a closed group that had exclusive access to the app. We knew that such an app would have huge appeal to the Mafia, always on the lookout for secure ways to communicate with one another. Suspicious by nature and almost paranoid about secrecy and security, the Mafia had experimented with several encryption devices before, but none of them had taken off. For that reason, the Mafia preferred personal contacts and face-to-face meetings. Needless to say, that had made surveillance extremely difficult. However, as business became more complex, stretching over continents and multiple time zones, such meetings became increasingly problematic. To cut a long story short, through a network of informers, we have been able to successfully infiltrate the Mafia and introduce this app to key players. So successful has this become, and so widespread the uptake, that the app – known as Omerta – is now the preferred method of communication between even the highest Mafia echelons.'

Samartini looked around the room before delivering the punchline. 'But, of course, what the users don't know is that the police are listening to every word spoken, every message sent, and have a precise record of it.'

'*Seriously?*' said Dupree, shaking his head as the staggering implications of what Samartini had just said began to sink in.

'Are you suggesting that this has gone unnoticed and is continuing to this very day?' asked Landru.

'Yes. And that has made this huge prosecution about to begin in Calabria possible. It is based almost entirely on evidence collected through this app. Hundreds have been arrested and millions of euros seized, together with tonnes of drugs both in Italy and overseas. The Mafia has been dealt a devastating blow.'

'Extraordinary,' said Dupree.

'It is,' said Samartini. 'But like all good things, it is about to come to an end.'

'Why?' Dupree asked.

'Because of the court case I mentioned. As soon as the case starts, the app and its implications will be introduced into evidence and therefore become public.'

'But before that happens, we have a unique window of opportunity,' said Lapointe calmly. 'We want to use this app to expose whoever is behind these Death Mask Murders and engaged Spiridon 4.'

'And we, that is the Squadra Mobile, want to nail one of the Mafia kingpins connected to these murders,' said Samartini. 'Because they were the facilitators who made them possible.'

'How exactly?' asked Landru.

'Let me explain,' Jack cut in. 'As you know, I've just returned from Italy. Cesaria and I met with the chief prosecutor and one of the key witnesses involved in the Calabrian trial, and we were almost killed in the process. Looking objectively at everything we have recently discovered so far, and taking into account what we know about Spiridon 4 and what they were capable of, it is reasonable to conclude that Spiridon 4 was involved here and committed the last murder at least, and quite possibly some of the others as well. So much seems clear. What isn't clear is this: who was behind it all, financed it, and more importantly, *why.*'

'I still don't understand,' said Landru, pretending ignorance. 'Where do I fit into all this?'

'We believe you can help us solve these cases,' said Lapointe softly.

'How?'

'By leading us to those responsible.'

'You can't be serious! I've just been released from prison, for Christ's sake!' said Landru, becoming agitated.

'Exactly. And that is precisely what will help us here, but I'm sure you already know that.'

'Please explain.'

Lapointe emptied his pipe into an ashtray on the mantelpiece and then turned slowly towards Landru. 'Let's stop playing games and put our cards on the table, shall we? I hate wasting time.'

'All right by me,' said Landru. He was beginning to see Lapointe in a different light, grudging respect overshadowing resentment and growing by the second. 'What's on your mind, Chief Superintendent?'

Lapointe picked up his pipe and pointed it at Landru. 'Here's the deal: You help us solve these murders, and in return you get your freedom and public exoneration.'

'Solve? How?'

'By setting a trap.'

'What kind of trap?' asked Landru, looking puzzled.

'One that will ensnare the key players in this deadly game.'

'What kind of bait will you use?'

'Greed and retribution.'

'How curious. Is that all?' said Landru, the sarcasm in his voice unmistakable.

'No, there's more.'

'More bait perhaps, Chief Superintendent? Tell me.'

Lapointe slipped his pipe into his pocket. 'Yes. *You,*' he said quietly and reached for his coat and hat.

34

Kuragin chateau: 30 October, evening

Apart from the conservatory where Jack did most of his writing, overlooking the manicured gardens and the pond, the rustic kitchen in the basement of the chateau, with its large fireplace and huge wooden refectory table rubbed smooth and shiny by elbows of generations past, was Jack's favourite place where he felt most comfortable and at home. In a way, it reminded him of the kitchen in the remote Queensland homestead where he grew up and had spent some of his happiest childhood moments, before the relentless drought had overwhelmed the family and driven a bitter wedge between his parents.

Jack opened another bottle of wine, a 2012 Domaine Rene Cacheux et Fils Chambolle-Musigny 'Les Argillères' – one of Countess Kuragin's favourites – and walked around the large table filling up the glasses. It was the end of a long, eventful day, and already quite late.

Bartolli pointed to the bottle in Jack's hand. 'What a splendid wine,' she said.

'You should see the cellar. It's quite extraordinary.'

'And Katerina left you in charge?'

'Something like that.'

'Was that wise?'

Jack shrugged. 'Good wine is to be enjoyed, not hoarded.' He turned to the cook clearing away the plates. 'Isn't that right, Antoinette?'

'*Oui, certainement!*' said the cook, a chubby woman in her fifties, beaming.

'As you can see, Jack's very popular down here,' said Tristan. 'He always praises the cooking, and never leaves a morsel of food on his plate.'

'I noticed,' said Bartolli, laughing. 'My mother told him he could come for lunch in our home any time. He ate two bowls of her pasta and sang its praises all afternoon.'

'Apparently, he did the same the other day at lunch with Giuseppina in Calabria,' Samartini chimed in, shaking her head. 'Cesaria told me. It broke the ice.'

'Speaking of Giuseppina and what she told us,' said Jack, turning to Samartini, 'could you repeat what we discussed in Florence with Grimaldi just before I left?'

Samartini put down her glass. 'Sure,' she said, collecting her thoughts. What she had found out about Landru and discussed with Lapointe earlier that day was valuable information she wanted to factor into her answer.

'As we know, all of this began with Landru's lawyers making contact with the Prefect of Police here in Paris on twenty-four September. They claimed that their client had new vital information about his conviction. They also asked for permission for their client to meet someone urgently – Jack. On three October, Jack met Landru in the Fleury-Mérogis Prison and—'

'We know all that,' interrupted Jack impatiently.

Samartini held up her hand. 'I know. Please bear with me. It is important to follow the sequence of events closely here, otherwise what I'm about to tell you will make no sense.'

'Sorry,' said Jack, biting his lip. After an exhausting, eventful day full of unexpected surprises, Jack felt a little irritable and edgy, which wasn't like him at all.

'Apart from everything else Landru told us,' continued Samartini, 'several matters stand out that have a significant bearing on this extraordinary case so far. First, Landru cracking that cipher and finding out what that meant—'

'The Paris address,' Bartolli cut in. '"*Deep down in the cellar is a wall, behind it you will find all.*"'

'Yes. That chamber of horrors and what it revealed. Six death masks and various body parts pointing to unsolved murders.'

'A magnum opus of unspeakable crimes,' said Jack.

'Yes, but much more than that: a *challenge*,' said Bartolli. 'Quite unique, and diabolically clever. The brainchild of a deranged, yet brilliant mind marching to a different moral drum. A psychopath outside the textbook.'

Samartini nodded. 'Quite. This was then closely followed by another event: that anonymous video sent to Lapointe, graphically showing the brutal murder Landru had been convicted of.'

'Wrongly, it would appear,' Tristan added.

'Perhaps,' said Jack. 'But according to Lapointe, this still has a long way to go before Landru can be cleared and walk free.'

Samartini turned to Jack. 'And that's where that chance discovery by you comes into play. Something that the master puppeteer lurking in the shadows and pulling all the strings here didn't count on.'

'The wrist tattoo linking the killing to Spiridon 4 and the Florence Mafia,' said Bartolli. 'A vital link that could open many doors if we play our cards right.'

'Exactly. Apart from what Giuseppina told us, that's the most significant breakthrough in this case so far, and that's why Chief Prosecutor Grimaldi and the Squadra Mobile in Florence are so interested in this.'

'Because it could assist in the Mafia trial against Giordano about to get underway in Calabria?' Jack offered.

'Yes, and that's where our respective interests overlap. The Paris police desperately want to solve these murders and deal with Landru's alleged wrongful conviction, and we in Florence want to nail Giordano and his associates and put them away once and for all. Their participation in these sensational murders could be just what we need here to make this possible,' said Samartini.

'And, of course, Landru just wants to clear his name and be set free,' said Bartolli.

'Obviously. But these horrific murders and the role the Mafia played in them could easily turn into the most high-profile segment of the entire Calabria trials,' continued Samartini. 'The publicity this would create would be unprecedented and turn the spotlight on the Mafia like never before, galvanise law enforcement agencies across Europe and spur them into action.'

'And that strange dark-web gambling scenario referred to by Giuseppina could be the catalyst here, you think?' asked Jack.

'It certainly could, because it reaches across the whole of Europe and points to a particular site on the dark web that several agencies across the globe have been very interested in for quite some time.'

'Echoes of Ars Moriendi,' observed Tristan, as he remembered that fateful evening outside Florence two years ago. Run by the Mafia, Ars Moriendi was a bizarre, illegal gambling scenario dicing with death, which had almost cost Tristan his life.

'Fascinating,' said Bartolli. 'All the threads seem to be coming together.'

'A victory for Grimaldi and his team,' said Jack. 'If we pull this off.'

'A victory for justice,' said Samartini. 'And you of all people, Jack, would know exactly what that could mean.' Samartini pushed back her glasses and looked at Tristan. 'Think of Lorenza,' she said quietly. 'It's all connected. This tree of violence has many branches and can only be killed at the roots.'

Jack turned to Tristan sitting next to him and put his hand on his shoulder. 'Are you up to this, mate? Because once we get into this murky quicksand, there's no turning back. It's sink or swim.'

Tristan nodded, tears glistening in his eyes.

'Good. So, what's the plan?' asked Jack.

'I had a long talk to Lapointe this morning. He came up with a brilliant idea.' Samartini paused to let this sink in.

'What kind of idea?'

'A long shot, but we would have to work closely together as a team, and move very quickly because there isn't much time.'

'All right by me,' said Jack. 'We've worked together before.'

'That's one of the main reasons we are suggesting this, but I must warn you, it's not without danger. Just how big a danger is anyone's guess at the moment. The unknown is always dangerous, but what we do know is whoever is behind these murders is capable of anything.'

'Danger is nothing new to us. Just think of Cesaria, Conti, and Istanbul. The showdown with Belmonte in the Basilica Cistern. It doesn't come any more deadly and dangerous than that.'

Samartini nodded. 'Speaking of Cesaria, she's meeting with Grimaldi right now to work out the details—'

'Of that long shot you mentioned?' Jack cut in.

Samartini nodded.

'Can you tell us more about it?'

'It's all about Omerta, Landru, and setting a trap.'

'How intriguing. Can you give us details?'

Holding her breath, Bartolli leaned forward, her face flushed with anticipation and excitement. Tristan clenched his fists, his knuckles turning white.

'Cesaria has a meeting scheduled with Lapointe in Paris tomorrow morning, and they will join us here after that to explain everything. It would be better if you could hear this from them,' said Samartini quietly.

She's avoiding the question and letting us down gently, thought Jack. *Clever girl.*

'Makes sense,' he said, accepting Samartini's decision and trying hard not to offend her by showing his disappointment. 'And besides, it's getting late. Everything will look different in the morning. Nightcap anyone?'

<h1 style="text-align:center">35</h1>

O'Hara's alpine fortress, Obersalzberg: 31 October, morning

O'Hara was one of those rare people who needed virtually no sleep at all. His active mind craved stimulation and action, not rest. Living in self-imposed isolation surrounded by the levers of a cyber empire he had created spanning the globe, he could not bear to be away from it for more than a few hours at a time. That didn't allow for more than three to four hours' sleep a night.

Sustained by a carefully designed Eastern diet consisting of specific meals prepared by a resident Chinese chef, and a daily exercise regime overseen by his personal trainer that would have exhausted an athlete half his age, O'Hara lived a cerebral life that thrived on power and total control, and that included the power over life and death. Much of it was a high-stakes mind game where he made up the rules and set the challenges. In many ways, it was like he was playing a game of chess with himself, but the pawns were real people, and being captured or removed from the chess board could mean mayhem, destruction, or even death.

On rare occasions, however, outsiders participated in this game, most of the time unwittingly. Such adversaries were rare and much prized by O'Hara. In Landru, he had found such an adversary, and he was going to savour every moment of this high-stakes game that had lasted for years and had just taken on a new, exciting dimension since Landru's release from prison, which O'Hara had orchestrated.

O'Hara stood in his control room in front of the large window overlooking the mountains. Usually, the spectacular view would clear his mind and help him concentrate, but not that morning. Ominous and threatening, the mountains were hidden behind mist and dark, low-hanging clouds, and a rare morning thunderstorm provided a lightning spectacular that sent vibrations through even the steel-reinforced concrete and double-glazed windows.

In many ways, the turmoil outside reflected the excitement boiling within O'Hara, who could sense that the endgame he had been looking forward to was coming closer. The phone call from Petrinko had made that clear. Landru had been released on bail and was living with Dupree, a retired police officer, in a chateau just outside Paris. New players had just entered the game, and O'Hara had allocated each player a position on his imaginary chessboard. He would be the black king, as usual.

Landru, his principal adversary, was given the role of the white king, and Jack Rogan would be one of his white knights, with Lapointe taking on the role of one of the bishops. Dupree became one of the castles and Bartolli, with her cutting-edge insights and early defence of Landru, the white queen. Landru's chessboard was rapidly filling up with formidable opponents.

Since finding out about Jack's surprise involvement through his paid informants in the prison, who had kept a close eye on Landru for years, O'Hara had thoroughly researched Jack and his background on the Net. What he found filled him with excitement, because he knew that Landru would have carefully chosen Jack for a specific reason that could only be related to the Llanganates quest. He had no doubt that the how and why would soon be revealed; all he had to do was watch, listen and follow.

Recommended by the Mafia, Petrinko was turning out better than expected and would make an excellent black knight. Resourceful, ruthless, independent and reliable, he was the perfect choice because these were the attributes O'Hara was looking for in someone who would be his eyes and ears on the ground.

O'Hara had no doubt that other players would soon be added to make this game really interesting. Until then, all Petrinko had to do was watch and report what was happening at the chateau, and identify the people close to Landru. If and when further action was required, O'Hara could call on his Mafia contacts for backup and support. They were his trusty foot soldiers, the pawns who could easily overwhelm and defeat even the most resourceful opponent if sent into battle at the right time and in the right way.

For that reason, O'Hara had kept in close contact with Alessandro after his father's arrest. Before that, O'Hara had only dealt with Giordano senior, who had initially made the arrangements with Spiridon 4 that had worked so successfully for years.

Apart from Spiridon 4, there had also been another, more complex dimension to their unusual relationship: gambling. O'Hara had developed a unique gambling site with unusual reality games on the dark web, and Riccardo Giordano had provided well-heeled gamblers who were looking for the ultimate thrill: bizarre wagers involving death, mutilation and murder. With that, a successful partnership was formed that had made them millions.

The unfortunate disintegration of Spiridon 4 caused by the unexpected deaths of Teodora and her twin sister, and the arrest and conviction of Silvanus and his brother, Aladdin, had brought that relationship to an abrupt end. This had been further complicated by Giordano's sudden arrest and imminent trial in Calabria.

Because of this, a certain amount of improvisation would be required to bring this game to a successful conclusion, and O'Hara could barely wait for the action to begin. These were the challenges he lived for and thrived on, because the stakes and risks were about as high as they could get.

The prize was a priceless, legendary Inca treasure lost for centuries, which was just waiting somewhere in the Caribbean to be discovered. O'Hara had painstakingly collected most of the missing pieces of this puzzle to make it all possible, except for one crucial missing link that would help him make history. With that in mind, O'Hara was determined to make sure that nothing would stand in his way and stop him from reaching what he believed to be his destiny.

O'Hara reached for the Regan amulet he now wore around his neck, and smiled. It was a constant reminder of the quest that had consumed him for such a long time and was about to reach its destination. He ran his fingertips slowly along the tiny, heart-shaped map engraved into the whale's tooth fragment, certain that very soon he would find the missing link that had eluded him for so long. Once again, Landru would do his bidding and show him the way. As a resourceful master manipulator, O'Hara was looking forward to crossing swords with Jack, in whom he saw a new, worthy adversary who would help him reach his objective.

For a while, O'Hara watched the lightning bolts race across the dark morning sky like tongues of angry dragons fighting to conquer the heavens. Then he turned away, reached for his mobile and called Petrinko.

36

Gatekeeper's Cottage, Kuragin chateau: 31 October

Cesaria and Lapointe arrived at the chateau in the afternoon for the briefing everyone had been waiting for. Jack, Tristan, Bartolli and Samartini were waiting for them in the conservatory with sandwiches, coffee, and a chocolate gateau to die for that cook had prepared earlier. Because Cesaria had to catch an evening flight back to Florence, they got straight down to business.

Over the next two hours, Cesaria and Lapointe set out an ingenious but risky plan that left Jack and Bartolli speechless, and even Samartini, who played a major part in it, was somewhat taken aback. As the stakes were high and time was running out, acting quickly was of the essence.

At the conclusion of the briefing, Lapointe put down his pipe and looked around the room, expecting questions.

'Let me get this straight,' said Jack, looking at Cesaria. 'It is clear from what you've just told us that your entire strategy depends on the full cooperation of one man: Landru. Yet, you specifically asked that he not be present and stay with Dupree in the cottage. Why?'

'Let me answer this,' said Lapointe. 'This can only work if all of us here in this room, and that includes you, Tristan, work as a team. I wanted to hear your views first and get your agreement to what we are planning to do, before approaching Landru and Dupree.'

'But Landru is the one most at risk here. He's the bait, as you called him the other day,' said Samartini.

'That's correct,' replied Cesaria. 'And this can only work with his full cooperation and a clear understanding of what's at stake here.'

'But he hasn't heard any of this. He hasn't even been part of this conversation,' said Jack, shaking his head.

'We did this quite deliberately,' Lapointe cut in, and lit his pipe. 'How do you think he would react to all this, hearing it from the officer who was instrumental in putting him behind bars – namely me – or hearing it from Cesaria, a law enforcement officer from another country with obviously a different agenda? Eh? Not very well, I'd say.'

'I can see that,' said Jack. 'But surely he has to be told, sooner or later.'

'Absolutely,' said Lapointe. He hesitated and looked at Jack. 'But he has to hear it from someone he trusts; someone who can explain it to him in a way that makes sense and clearly sets out what's at stake here, for him and for us.'

Jack held up his hands. '*Oh no*,' he said, realising where this was heading.

'You are the only one who can do this,' continued Lapointe. 'He trusts you. No, I believe he *needs* you, Jack. Let's not forget how all of this started. He asked to meet *you*, remember? What does this tell you? There had to be a good reason for that.'

'Let's be clear about this,' said Jack. 'You want me to talk to Landru, explain all this to him and persuade him to come on board, risks and all, because he *trusts* me?'

'That's about it,' said Lapointe. 'The sooner the better. Time's running out.'

All eyes in the room were on Jack.

'Don't look at me like that, guys. You are putting the responsibility of this entire case on my shoulders. We all know this is a dangerous business. We are dealing with ruthless people here with a lot to lose, for Christ's sake. The risks are huge, especially with what Grimaldi intends to do about Giordano and the Mafia in Florence, and the humiliating way he wants to do it. There is real danger here; not just for Landru, but for everyone involved in this.'

'You are right, Jack,' said Cesaria. 'Obviously, it's your call. We all understand that. If you walk away from this we understand that too. But once we start this, we must see it through as a team. You can see that, surely.'

Jack nodded, but he didn't like being put on the spot, especially by people he admired and respected. However, at the same time he could clearly see the logic of it all. The pressure was on.

Realising the matter hung in the balance and a little gentle persuasion may be needed to get Jack over the line, Bartolli stood up, walked over to Jack and sat down next to him.

'Why don't you go down to Katerina's cellar, select the best Scotch you can find, and then walk over to the cottage and have a chat with Landru? See how you go.' Bartolli looked at Jack. 'And don't forget Lorenza,' she added quietly. 'Give us your answer once you've spoken to Landru. What do you think?'

Jack smiled at Bartolli. She had found his weak spot and put her finger right on it: *Lorenza*. 'There's a Macallan twenty-five-year-old sherry oak single malt in the cellar I've had my eye on for quite some time,' he said after a while. 'Perhaps this could be the moment?'

Bartolli reached for Jack's hand and squeezed it in silent reply.

Bartolli stood in front of the music room window and watched Jack walk across the courtyard towards the Gatekeeper's Cottage. 'There he goes,' she said to Tristan standing next to her, 'with his precious bottle of whisky under his arm. Quite a guy!'

'He's more than that,' said Tristan quietly. 'I knew he would do it … for Lorenza.'

'You make quite a team, you two.'

'I suppose we do,' said Tristan. 'I wonder where this will take us,' he added pensively. 'We are poking a wounded lion here, and we both know what happens when you do that, don't we?'

'You are talking about the Florence Mafia here?'

'Yes. We've seen firsthand what they are capable of, especially the Giordanos. They are particularly dangerous when their backs are against the wall, and bearing in mind what Grimaldi has in mind here, this will get ugly very soon. I just hope we are ready for this.'

'So do I,' said Bartolli quietly, and slowly walked back to her chair next to the piano.

Jack had waited until after dinner to go and talk to Landru. Lapointe, Samartini and Cesaria had left earlier, so that Samartini and Cesaria could catch their flight to Florence. Jack had promised to give them his answer in the morning, after he had discussed the matter with Landru.

When Jack walked in, Dupree and Landru were sitting in front of the fireplace in the small, cosy lounge next to the kitchen, talking. Landru looked up, the throbbing veins on his forehead the only sign of the turmoil that had been brewing inside him since Lapointe and Cesaria had arrived at the chateau earlier that day.

'The messenger comes bearing gifts,' said Dupree.

Jack put the bottle on the mantelpiece and went into the kitchen to fetch some glasses.

Dupree pointed to the label as soon as Jack returned and began to open the bottle. 'Rolling out the good stuff, I see. That important, eh?' he said.

'Something like that,' replied Jack. He poured two fingers of whisky into each of the glasses and put the cork back into the bottle.

Both Dupree and Landru were fully aware of the purpose of Lapointe's afternoon visit and what was riding on it, their anticipation growing.

'Well, are you going to tell us?' asked Dupree, sipping the delicious whisky.

Landru didn't say anything, but was watching Jack intently. He realised that his future may well depend on what Jack was about to say.

Deliberately taking his time, Jack held up his glass and looked at it. 'Let's see if maturing for a quarter of a century in oloroso sherry-seasoned casks makes such a difference,' he said. Then he brought the glass up to his nose before taking a sip. 'I can smell sherry, cinnamon and wood smoke, and taste dried fruits and spices. Exquisite. What do you think?'

'If what you're about to tell us is half as exciting as this whisky, we should have an interesting evening,' said Dupree. 'What did the bigwigs have to say? Maurice has been dancing on coals all afternoon.'

Jack turned to Landru. 'I can imagine. But before I tell you, I need to clear up a few things that have been bothering me.'

'Go ahead,' said Landru, who had been expecting something like this. The moment of truth had arrived and there was nowhere left to hide. And besides, deliberately holding back some vital information to pique Jack's interest had done its work. Jack was in the room, his curiosity aroused, and asking questions. It was time to put all the cards on the table to get him to commit. And as far as Landru was concerned, that was absolutely essential if his plan was to succeed.

Jack put down his glass, pulled his notebook out of his pocket and looked at Landru.

'Let's begin. The first time we met in prison, you told me that you had carefully followed the Ritz murder cases and that something in my latest book, *The Lost Symphony*, opened your eyes and helped you crack the cipher code.'

'That's right.'

'Could you please tell us what that was?'

'It had to do with Frieda Malenkova. She was the missing link, or to put it more accurately, I believe she *had* the missing link in her possession, because she acquired it a few years ago and didn't sell it on.'

Dupree gave Jack a meaningful look. 'Echoes of *Le Fantôme* and the Black Widow, perhaps?' he said and raised an eyebrow.

'Could be. This case is getting stranger by the minute,' replied Jack.

'I believe there was a close connection between Malenkova and Mademoiselle Darrieux,' said Landru, ignoring Dupree's remark.

'I'm intrigued,' said Jack. 'What connection?'

'It's complicated. A long story.'

'We have all night, and an excellent bottle of whisky to keep us company.'

Landru nodded. 'The Death Mask Murders, Spiridon 4, Malenkova and Darrieux are all connected. They are linked to that quest I told you about.'

'The legendary Inca treasure of the Llanganates,' said Jack, 'which you have been looking for all these years?'

'Yes.'

'In what way? Please tell us.'

'For you to understand this, I have to deal with Mademoiselle Darrieux first. The connection you asked about became clear to me when I read about her sensational "coming out" at Shakespeare and Company here in Paris in February last year. The papers were full of it. This is all about her extraordinary story.'

'Seriously?' said Jack. 'In what way?'

'It all began to make sense when I delved into that dossier of newspaper clippings she presented to the press with Isis on that fateful day she bared her soul. That's when I found out that she had been working as a young prostitute in New Orleans, when she was called Maurice Moreau—'

'Who later became Estelle Montplaisir after a sex change, and then reinvented herself again after spending some time in jail in Miami, and turned into Adrienne Darrieux a few years later?' interjected Jack.

'Yes. But the most important piece of information here as far as I was concerned, was the murder she had been accused of in New Orleans.'

'The killing of Armand Baudin, a coloured man from Santo Domingo?'

'Yes.'

'Why was this so important?'

'Because of who Armand Baudin was. I had been following certain clues that I discovered about a shipwreck in the Caribbean at the time, and Baudin was helping me find it.'

'And this was relevant and part of your treasure hunt?' asked Jack.

'It certainly was, and very much still is. That's where the matter rested until I read those newspaper clippings last year about his murder in New Orleans,' continued Landru, speaking softly.

'According to the papers, Baudin was stabbed to death by a young male prostitute – Maurice Moreau – in a brothel in New Orleans. But the most significant clue that pulled everything together was a brief reference to something during an interview Darrieux gave shortly after her "coming out" last year.'

'What kind of clue?'

'As we know, after Estelle Montplaisir was released from jail in Miami a few years after the murder trial in New Orleans, she changed her name again, became Adrienne Darrieux and went to live in Paris. She was asked by one of the reporters how she had managed that, and it was the answer to that question that rocked me at the time.'

'In what way?'

'She said that she sold a rare Inca artefact on the black market in Paris, a golden burial mask she had brought with her from the US. Apparently, it was worth a fortune. That was the way she financed her new life and set herself up as the Paris socialite we know today.'

'Extraordinary!' said Jack, shaking his head.

'The only thing that's still a mystery here is how Darrieux actually got hold of the mask. Baudin had it, of that I'm sure. He was on the run and ended up in a brothel in New Orleans, where he was killed. We know that too. After that? Who knows? In a way I suppose it doesn't really matter, because what we also know is that the mask surfaced here in Paris years later, and Darrieux sold it on the black market.'

'Why don't we talk to her about all this,' suggested Jack, 'and see what else she can remember? It could be helpful, don't you think? I'm sure she wouldn't mind, especially when we tell her what's at stake here.'

'You think that could be arranged?' asked Landru, looking stunned.

'Sure. She's a good friend of mine. We've been through a lot together last year with the lost symphony in Russia ... you would have read all about it in my book.'

Landru nodded. 'That would be most helpful,' he said, 'and could perhaps even solve the final ...' Landru stopped mid-sentence and reached for his glass. He realised he had almost gone too far. 'I need another drink, if you don't mind.'

Watching Landru carefully, Jack reached for the bottle.

'But it doesn't stop there,' continued Landru, changing direction. 'This was merely the first clue that helped me crack the code. The second, more important one came shortly thereafter – and that's where your book comes into play again.'

'In what way?'

'Frieda Malenkova, the famous Paris fence and shady art dealer you described so eloquently in your book, was the second clue that actually helped me crack the code. I put two and two together. Somehow, she had to have been the buyer of Darrieux' golden mask. It was a perfect fit. If not initially, then sometime later when the mask changed hands again. Everything was pointing in that direction.'

'And that helped you crack the code?' said Jack, unconvinced. 'Malenkova's dead. Her house burned down and her art collection with it. All gone.'

'Once again, it's complicated. But without becoming too technical and delving into cryptography, algorithms, information theory and how it all works, suffice it to say, these clues helped me come up with a solution that solved the puzzle.'

'All right. And you maintain that this golden mask is somehow connected to the lost Inca treasure?'

'Yes, it is. It is the last missing link, the most important clue that could show us the way.'

'The way to where?'

'The location of the treasure.'

'*Seriously?*'

'Yes. And in a way, Baudin was part of it all. He found the missing link and was killed because of it.'

Jack shook his head. 'Can you explain?'

'It all began with a pilgrimage two years after I published that fateful paper that started it all.'

'About *The Navarro Chronicles?*' said Jack.

'Yes. I was much younger then, and struggling to come to terms with my homosexuality, which in the lofty academic circles I now found myself in, was a big taboo. It could have cost me my career, which had just taken off. For that reason, I desperately tried to hide it. I suppressed who I really was.'

'Understandable,' said Dupree.

'But that made me vulnerable. Very vulnerable. Suppressing who you really are always comes at a price. In this case, a very big one. I had a nervous breakdown. That's when I went on a pilgrimage, to sort myself out.'

'What kind of pilgrimage?' asked Jack, wondering where this was heading.

'The Camino de Santiago in Spain.'

'Ah, the Way of Saint James.'

'Yes, the famous pilgrims' walk,' said Landru. 'Which, as you no doubt know, is a large network of ancient pilgrim routes that all lead to the tomb of Saint James in Santiago de Compostela in Spain. And that's where it happened.'

'What happened?'

'A revelation. The threads of my quest came unexpectedly together at the tomb of Saint James, just like the pilgrims' routes criss-crossing Europe.'

'How?'

'I met someone.'

'Who?'

'A monk.'

'And this is somehow connected to that quest of yours?' said Jack, shaking his head.

'Yes.'

'In what way?'

'It's quite a story. It all began in 1721.'

'What happened in 1721?'

'James Mascarino was killed.'

'Who was James Mascarino?'

'If you pour me another whisky, I'll tell you.'

37

Cathedral of Santiago de Compostela: 12 June 1993

Landru was kneeling in front of the magnificent main altar in the Cathedral of Santiago de Compostela, praying. His eyes were closed, his head bowed. Utterly drained and exhausted after the long journey that had lasted almost three weeks on foot through rugged terrain, he could barely move.

The old monk sitting in one of the pews facing the altar recognised all the signs. A lonely, desperate young man searching for answers, or perhaps asking for forgiveness. In a way, the man reminded him of his younger self, embarking on a similar journey a long time ago that had brought him to Santiago de Compostela, searching for salvation. He remembered kneeling in front of the tomb of Saint James the Great, located in the crypt just below the altar, seeking guidance. That was before he became a monk, and later an eminent scholar working in the cathedral archives located in the medieval treasury.

The cathedral was almost empty and was about to close. It was time to leave, but the man kneeling in front of him seemed unaware of this, or perhaps too exhausted to notice. The monk rose awkwardly to his feet, walked slowly over to Landru and placed a hand on his shoulder.

'It's time to go, my son,' he said quietly. Landru opened his eyes and looked up, surprised. The bearded face looking down at him radiated kindness and compassion.

'I'm sorry, I lost track of time,' said Landru and stood up.

'No matter. It's very easy to get lost in this place. It can be quite overwhelming.'

Landru nodded and reached for his backpack lying on the floor.

'Have you got somewhere to stay?' asked the monk.

Landru shook his head.

'I thought so. Come with me. I live in a monastery close by. I can offer you a hot supper and a bed.'

Landru looked at the monk gratefully and put on his backpack. 'Are prayers always answered so promptly in this place?' he asked.

'Sometimes.'

'Must be my lucky day,' said Landru and followed the old monk out of the cathedral.

Sitting at a large refectory table in the cathedral cloister, Landru was devouring his second bowl of a hearty soup with spicy chorizo. The old monk was sitting opposite, watching him carefully. He had earlier found out that Landru was a history professor at the Sorbonne, and asked himself why a man like this had undertaken such an arduous pilgrimage all by himself. His curiosity aroused, he decided to find out. He poured himself another cup of wine and began to make small talk about the cathedral's history, which he was certain would be of interest to Landru.

'Did you know that according to legend, the apostle Saint James brought Christianity to the Iberian Peninsula?' began the monk.

Landru nodded and dunked another slice of crusty bread into his soup. 'According to another legend, the hermit Pelagius saw strange lights in the night sky and rediscovered the tomb of Saint James,' replied Landru. 'That happened in AD 814. When Bishop Theodomirus of Iria heard about this, he informed King Alfonso II of Asturias and Galicia, who recognised this as a miracle and ordered the construction of a chapel on the site.'

The old monk looked at Landru, impressed. 'You know your history, but what you may not know is that according to yet another legend, the king was the first pilgrim who prayed at the shrine of Saint James. A few years later, the first church was built and became a major place of pilgrimage.'

'Unfortunately, in AD 997, the caliph of Cordoba had had enough of this Christian ritual in his domain,' continued Landru, chewing contentedly as he spoke. 'He ordered Al-Mansur Ibn Abi

Aamir – his illustrious army commander – to destroy the church. This he did, but before fire devoured the sacred site, he removed the gates and the bells and took them back to Cordoba, where they were incorporated into the Aljama Mosque. This was seen as another triumph of Islam over Christianity. Fortunately, the tomb of Saint James and relics were spared.'

The old monk pushed a cup of wine across the table towards Landru. 'You are well informed,' he said. 'Few know this, and fewer still know that in 1236, when Cordoba was retaken by King Ferdinand III of Castile and the Muslims were driven out, captives carried the very same gates and bells to Toledo, where they were installed in the Cathedral of Saint Mary of Toledo.'

'I didn't know that. Obviously, the battle of faiths continued with symbolic objects like church gates and bells, sending potent messages of struggle, triumphs and defeats far into the future.'

'Quite so,' said the monk and refilled Landru's cup.

'You asked me earlier what had brought me on this pilgrimage. In a way, it is also about a struggle that began a long time ago, and resonates until this very day. It too concerns empires and beliefs, and precious, sacred objects coveted by conquerors.'

'Care to tell me about it?'

Feeling well-fed and relaxed, Landru stretched out his aching legs and took another sip of wine.

'Sure. It's quite a story, which is also closely linked to Spain and its illustrious colonial history; in this case, its bloody conquests in the Americas.'

Over the next hour, Landru told the old monk about the legendary Llanganates treasure and his recent discovery of *The Navarro Chronicles* in Seville, and their significance. He also told him about his personal struggle that was troubling him and which he was hoping to address during the pilgrimage. He hinted at his homosexuality, which he'd desperately tried to cover up and keep a secret, and spoke about a recent blackmail attempt that threatened to expose him and destroy his career.

The old monk listened in silence. Not once did he interrupt because he realised that with this cathartic monologue, the healing of a damaged soul had already begun. He also realised that a higher force must have brought Landru to him that evening, as he remembered a certain document he had come across in the archives in his care, which had a direct bearing on *The Navarro Chronicles* and what his young guest had just told him about them.

The old monk didn't believe in coincidences, only faith and destiny, and that everything was connected and had meaning and a purpose. He reached across the table and placed his hand on Landru's. Translucent like parchment, the veins looked like little streams criss-crossing a dry landscape that spoke of hardship and toil. 'Do you believe in destiny?' he asked, speaking softly.

Landru looked at him in surprise. 'I'm not sure. Why do you ask?'

'Because tomorrow I will take you to the cathedral cloister,' said the old monk, smiling, 'and show you something in the Archive Library that will dispel any doubts you may have in that regard.'

* * *

Jack glanced at the whisky bottle next to the spluttering candle on the mantelpiece. It was almost empty and the candle was about to die. 'That's quite a story,' he said. 'But you still haven't told us about James Mascarino and what happened.'

'Ah. That has to do with what the old monk showed me in the Archive Library of the cathedral the next day,' said Landru.

'Care to tell us about that?' said Dupree. *Finally?*

'Sure. But in order to fully appreciate the impact of what I discovered in that library, you had to first understand how that find came about, because it changed everything and showed me the way.'

Jack nodded, appreciating Landru's storytelling skills. *He knows how to create curiosity and draw us in*, he thought, smiling, as he recognised similar tactics to his own that he employed when telling a tale.

'When the old monk took me to the cathedral library, he showed me something that gives me cold shivers even now when I think of it ...'

'What was it?' asked Jack.

'A letter sent by Francisco Rodriguez de Ledesma, colonial governor of Cuba to Charles II, King of Spain, in 1678.'

'What was it about?'

'A failed expedition to search for the wreck of the *San Cristobal*, and retrieve the legendary Llanganates treasure.'

'Seriously?' said Jack.

'Yes. But that wasn't all. The letter specifically mentioned Father Navarro and what happened to him.'

'Do you know?'

'Yes. He died in 1678 of injuries he suffered during that expedition, and this letter was sent by the governor to the king at his request shortly after he died. It was all about unfinished business – and a betrayal.'

'What kind of betrayal?' asked Dupree.

'A betrayal by someone Navarro trusted and held dear.'

'And this is relevant?' said Jack.

'Yes, it definitely is because of what happened shortly after Navarro's death. Once I had a name, I managed to do some more research and was able to find what I'd been looking for. I found out what happened and I discovered who betrayed Navarro, and why.'

'Can you tell us?'

'Yes. Once again, this is directly linked to the Llanganates treasure. Navarro was betrayed by James Mascarino, I mentioned—'

'Who *was* James Mascarino?' interrupted Jack.

'It was as if my pilgrimage was meant to be,' continued Landru, ignoring the question. 'I was meant to meet that old monk and find this extraordinary letter. He was right.'

'Right about what?' asked Dupree.

'Destiny. As soon as I set eyes on that letter, I realised that it was destiny that had brought me to the tomb of Saint James. As you can imagine, I was very excited. To discover another significant document that dealt with the treasure and what happened to it – especially after *The Navarro Chronicles* – was not only an academic coup that would have a major impact on my career, but also a significant piece of a puzzle, pointing the way to the treasure. And that's where James Mascarino steps into the arena.'

'Who was James Mascarino?' asked Jack again, becoming impatient.

'The only one who had reliable information about the location of the wreck of the *San Cristobal*.'

'How come?'

'Because of who he was.'

'Are you going to tell us?' said Dupree.

'Yes. He was the son of Mad Dog Regan, the notorious pirate who sank the ship in 1664 and was executed in Havana. The letter the old monk showed me in the library was all about him, and what happened during a failed search for the wreck.'

'You didn't mention any of this in your journal,' said Jack. 'Why?'

'No, I didn't, because what should have been another academic triumph, turned into one of the biggest mistakes of my life.'

'What kind of mistake?' asked Jack.

'One driven by ambition and pride.'

'Care to elaborate?'

'As soon as I returned to Paris after my pilgrimage with that extraordinary find, I published another paper, this time about the Rodriguez Letter to the king of Spain, and James Mascarino.'

'I don't understand,' said Jack, shaking his head. 'How could that have been a mistake?'

'Because it pulled me deeper and deeper into a dark web of violence and death that I couldn't escape from, a dark web that still ensnares me today. And you are now part of it, like it or not.'

'Can you tell us more about that?' said Jack, looking perplexed. For a moment he thought it must be the whisky talking, not Landru, but nothing could have been further from the truth, as he was soon to find out.

'I will, but first let me tell you about James Mascarino and his doomed search for the wreck of the *San Cristobal*.'

38

Morro Castle, Havana: 3 June 1678

Gasping for air and barely able to see, Navarro knew he was close to death. Marooned for three weeks on a barren, rocky island with little food and almost no water or shelter, had taken its toll. But what had drained his strength and will to survive more than anything else, was the unexpected betrayal by someone he had trusted and held dear. To have been so wrong and deceived was not only disappointing, but also a crushing realisation of failure, especially for an experienced cleric who prided himself on understanding human nature and the workings of the mind.

The sailors carrying Navarro up to the castle on a makeshift stretcher knew they had to hurry. The man they had rescued two days earlier was barely alive. Four other men rescued at the same time had already died, yet he had insisted on being taken to the castle as soon as possible. Well-connected in Havana with influence in high places, he had also insisted that the governor be immediately notified of his arrival and asked to come to his bedside, as he had important information to convey before it was too late.

Francisco Rodriguez de Ledesma, Governor of Cuba, looked at the man lying on the bed in the darkened room and gasped. He barely recognised Navarro as the refined, cultured friend he had played many a robust chess game with over the years. The physician attending to Navarro bowed. Reading the question on the governor's troubled face, he shook his head and stepped back.

'The Lord be praised, you have survived,' said the governor.

'Not for long, I'm afraid,' said Navarro, his voice barely audible.

'What happened?'

'Come closer and I'll tell you.'

After the execution of Mad Dog Regan fourteen years earlier, Navarro had advised the king, Philip IV of Spain, that he had reliable information about the location of the wreck of the *San Cristobal*. He urged the king to authorise an expedition to locate the wreck and retrieve the legendary Llanganates treasure lost at sea. Unfortunately, the king died a short time later, and it took Navarro almost fourteen years and a trip to Spain to persuade his successor, Charles II, to finance an expedition. When word finally reached Navarro to prepare a salvage operation, he was forty-six years old, and in poor health. That's why he had turned to James Mascarino for help.

After his notorious father's execution, Mascarino went to live with Navarro in a monastery in Havana, where he received an excellent education under the watchful eye of his Jesuit protector. Exceptionally bright and eager to please, Mascarino excelled and went to work for a wealthy merchant, where he quickly rose through the ranks and ended up in charge of a vast trading empire stretching from Cadiz to the Caribbean before he turned thirty.

When Navarro approached him with a daring plan to locate the wreck of the San Cristobal, Mascarino embraced the idea with enthusiasm. The governor provided a naval vessel, and Mascarino the needed diving equipment and experienced crew to operate it. What Navarro didn't know at the time was that he was embarking on a wild goose chase, because the directions on the map given to him by Regan were worthless. What he didn't know either was that Mascarino had been patiently waiting in the background for just such an opportunity ever since his father's brutal execution in front of Morro Castle in 1664. To suddenly have a fully equipped naval vessel at his disposal, financed by the governor and the king, to conduct the very search he had been dreaming about, filled him with elation. The time to avenge his father's death had finally arrived, and he was determined to do whatever it would take to do his memory proud.

Navarro looked at the governor with feverish eyes. 'We followed the map and directions given to me by Regan and found the island. However, it soon became clear that locating a wreck in the vicinity was unlikely because there were no reefs nearby, only deep ocean, which would make diving for a wreck virtually impossible.'

Navarro paused, trying to catch his breath as blood trickled from the corner of his mouth. The governor stepped back and looked at the physician, who averted his eyes.

'What happened then?' asked the governor.

'After circumnavigating the island, and several attempts to find a suitable spot to land, we called off the search. That's when it happened.'

'What happened?'

'The unthinkable.'

'What do you mean?'

'A mutiny.'

'*A what?*' exclaimed the governor, stunned. 'But we thought your ship was lost in a storm?'

'Not so,' said Navarro. 'Just before we decided to return home, several members of the crew appeared on deck, armed.'

'And?'

'Took the ship.'

'What!'

'It happened very quickly, and what was most surprising of all was the fact that everything appeared to be very well organised. In advance, so it seemed. The naval crew of the ship was disarmed virtually without resistance, and the officers arrested—'

'By *whom*? Who was in charge?'

Navarro closed his eyes, trying to deal with the painful memories. 'James Mascarino,' he said. 'He was the leader.'

'No! That's not possible!'

'But it is. He took the ship within minutes without a fight, and then addressed the crew.'

'What did he say?'

'He told them that they were following an illusion created by his famous father – Mad Dog Regan – and that he, his son, had the only reliable information that would lead them to the wreck and the lost treasure. After that, it was every man for himself.'

'So, there was no storm?'

'No. Only a despicable mutiny and betrayal. Mascarino took charge. He was the new, celebrated pirate leader, cheered on by his adoring partners in crime. The crew was given a choice: join him and follow the footsteps of Mad Dog Regan and find the treasure, or be left on a deserted island to perish. What a choice, eh? He even renamed the ship: *The Templars Revenge II*.'

'What happened then?'

'All the officers on our ship and a few loyal members of the crew chose the island over mutiny. The others followed Mascarino, blinded by the promise of gold. After that, we were taken to the island. That's when I managed to confront Mascarino about all this.'

'What happened?'

'Just before he returned to the ship, he came over to me.'

'And?'

'He told me that he had been waiting for this moment since his father's execution and that he was determined to continue what his father began.'

'What was that?'

'The Templars' revenge. He told me that he loathed the Catholic Church, what it stood for, and what it had done to the Templars. And then, just before he left, he told me the most painful ...'

Navarro's voice became faint and trailed off.

What? urged the governor, leaning forward to hear better.

'That his father had deceived me by showing me the wrong location of the wreck on the map. But that wasn't all. Worse was to come.'

'In what way?'

'Mascarino claimed that *he* knew exactly where to find the wreck.'

'How?'

'He held up an amulet – some kind of engraved tooth he wore around his neck – and said: "Because of this." Apparently, his father gave it to him during that farewell meeting I arranged on the morning he died. Gullible fool, me! I pleaded with Mascarino to leave us some water, but he just laughed, turned around and walked away.'

Exhausted, Navarro closed his eyes, his breathing shallow.

'Promise me that you will write to the king and explain how and why I failed,' he whispered. 'I must take full responsibility for this disaster and set the record straight!'

The governor reached for his friend's limp hand. 'I promise. I also promise that I will hunt down those responsible and bring them to justice. Mascarino will hang, just like his wretched father.'

Navarro opened his eyes and looked at the governor. 'And that, my friend, fills me with more sadness than I can possibly put into words.'

Three hours later, Navarro was dead.

* * *

'What happened to Mascarino?' asked Jack.

'He became an infamous pirate, just like his father. They called him *El Diabolo*, the devil.'

'And did the governor hunt him down as promised?' said Dupree.

'No. Mascarino joined forces with Amaro Pargo, one of the most famous corsairs of his time. A legend. For years they terrorised the Caribbean together, until they had a falling out over a woman. Amaro Pargo was a notorious womaniser.'

'What happened?'

'There was a duel. Mascarino was killed by Amaro. That happened in 1721 in San Cristóbal de La Laguna—'

'On the island of Tenerife in the Canary Islands?' interjected Jack.

'Yes. Amaro's hometown. Legend has it that Amaro wept at Mascarino's funeral and said that he wanted to be buried next to his friend when the time came.'

'And the treasure? Was it ever found?' asked Jack.

'No. Mascarino mounted several expeditions after the mutiny and kept searching for it for years, but the wreck of the *San Cristobal* was never found.'

'So that's the end of it, then?' said Dupree.

'Far from it. In many ways, it's just the beginning.'

'What do you mean?' said Jack.

'If you arrange that meeting with Mademoiselle Darrieux as promised, I'll tell you,' replied Landru, smiling. 'And what I have to tell you will surprise you both, perhaps even shock you, especially as I am supposed to be used as the bait here. You've been pussyfooting around this all night, Jack, admit it. This is all about catching the Death Mask killer, right? We all want that, albeit for different reasons.'

Jack shot Dupree a meaningful look. 'You're on,' he said, trying to diffuse the awkward moment. 'If I don't get some shuteye soon, I'll turn into a pumpkin. And that, I promise you, gentlemen, wouldn't be a pretty sight. And besides, the formidable Mademoiselle Darrieux would certainly not listen to a pumpkin. Trust me.'

'In that case, you better go,' said Dupree and stood up. He walked over to the mantelpiece and blew out the candles. 'See you in the morning. Hopefully, with the intrepid Mademoiselle Darrieux in tow.'

39

Kuragin chateau: 1 November

Darrieux arrived early. She hadn't slept a wink since Jack's phone call and had left Paris at first light. The reasons given for the urgent meeting were classic Jack: brief, lacking in detail, but tantalisingly intriguing. All he had said was that it was related to her sensational coming-out appearance with Isis the year before, which had rocked Paris society to the core and caused such a stir.

Darrieux pulled up in her beloved red 1980 Citroën 2CV in front of the main entrance to the chateau and adjusted her attire. As Jack had promised not only a big surprise, but also meeting some fascinating new people, Darrieux wanted to make sure she made an impression that lived up to her reputation as a Paris personality of note and a flamboyant dresser, impossible to ignore. Because Jack had referred to her meeting with Isis, which was obviously a hint, she had decided to wear a similar outfit.

François, the butler, met her at the door. 'You are early, Mademoiselle. Jack is still in bed.'

Darrieux raised an eyebrow and gave François a stern look. 'Really? No matter, I can wait. I could do with some breakfast.'

'Tristan and Signora Bartolli are having breakfast in the kitchen right now. Perhaps you would care to join them?'

'Excellent, thank you. I know the way.'

'Of course,' said François, unable to suppress a smile as Darrieux strutted past him dressed in the latest 'butch chic' style – a plain white shirt and thin black tie, a punkishly torn embroidered vest shouting 'look at me', baggy black trousers, and red vintage riot grrrl boots that would have been the envy of Patti Smith, queen of punk rock.

Bartolli looked up as Darrieux swept into the kitchen, walked over to Tristan standing by the stove, gave him a hug, and then turned around.

'You must be the Italian criminal psychologist with the fearsome reputation Jack's been telling me about,' said Darrieux. She put her tiny designer handbag, which was probably worth more than her car, on the table and extended her hand.

'That's her,' said Jack, who had overheard the remark as he walked into the kitchen, wearing pyjamas and a dressing gown that was sizes too big. 'Be careful, she can see into your soul.'

Darrieux spun around. 'I have nothing to hide, certainly not since I bared my soul in public last year. Now the whole of Paris knows everything about me. No secrets left.'

'Everyone has secrets,' said Jack, running his fingers through his unkempt hair.

'You think so? You look a wreck, Jack. You should see yourself. Late night? Obviously no secret about that!'

'Early morning, more likely,' cook chimed in. 'He was right here in the kitchen scrounging for food when I arrived just after five.'

'Is that true?' said Bartolli, giving Jack a coquettish look.

'It is. All in the line of duty, as you are about to find out.'

'You don't say.'

'It's all your fault.'

'How come?' said Bartolli.

'You told me to go down into Katerina's cellar, select the best Scotch I could find, and then go over to the cottage and have a chat to Landru, remember?'

Bartolli nodded.

'And that's exactly what I did.'

'How did it go?'

'Coffee first, report later,' said Jack and sat down.

Bartolli turned to Darrieux sitting next to her. 'Isn't it annoying when he does that?'

'I'm used to it. He can't help himself. It's this storyteller thing,' said Darrieux, lowering her voice. 'All about calculated anticipation and tension.'

'It's more than that,' said Tristan. 'He's preparing the way. And us.'

'All right, guys, if you're finished analysing my motives, we can have some breakfast. I'm starving.'

'You are always starving,' said Tristan.

'How true,' said cook and put a steaming plunger of coffee in front of Jack. 'That should do it for now. Baked beans with spicy sausage coming up.'

'Ah. A good start. I'm glad we are all here, because what I'm about to tell you is—'

'*Extraordinary?*' Bartolli offered, using one of Jack's favourite words.

'It is that, and a lot more. And it concerns you especially, Adrienne,' continued Jack. He poured some coffee into a cup and handed it to Darrieux sitting opposite.

'Is that why you've asked me to drop everything and come here?'

'It was Landru, actually, who asked for you.'

'He did?' said Darrieux, surprised. 'Do you know why?'

Jack was watching Darrieux carefully. 'He said it had something to do with Armand Baudin, a golden mask, and why and how he was killed.'

Darrieux sat up as if poked with a hot needle, and paled.

'How could he possibly know anything about that?' she said, her voice hoarse.

'No idea. Why don't we ask him? He wants to meet you and talk about this.'

'*Are you serious?*'

'Is that a problem? Surely not, now that there are no more secrets left in your life, as you keep telling us,' teased Jack and poured himself another cup of coffee.

'Has Landru given you his answer?' Bartolli cut in. 'Have you been able to persuade him? I'm sure Cesaria and Lapointe would like to know.'

'I bet they would. He will give us his answer once he's spoken to Adrienne. After that, all will become clear,' said Jack, enjoying himself. 'He promised, but let's have breakfast first.'

'For heaven's sake, someone give the man some food and let's get this over with,' said Darrieux, looking exasperated. 'He's obviously not going to tell us anything. The suspense is killing me.'

'Before we go and see Landru, there's something I want to share with you,' said Jack, turning serious. 'It explains why the Squadra Mobile, and especially Grimaldi in Florence, are so keen to become involved here.'

'You spoke to Cesaria about this yesterday, didn't you?' said Bartolli.

'Yes. She took me aside just before she left for the airport to fly back to Florence.'

'And?'

'Ah. Here comes my breakfast,' said Jack and looked longingly at the plate that cook placed in front of him. 'We have a small window of opportunity here, and it has to do with Omerta.'

'That encrypted app the Mafia is using and the police can monitor without them knowing?' said Bartolli.

'Yes, that's the one. As you know, that has been one of the main reasons this huge court case in Calabria is going ahead. The entire prosecution case depends on it.'

'What has that to do with us here?' said Tristan.

'A great deal, as you will see in a moment.' Jack looked at Tristan, unsure whether to tell him exactly why. 'Riccardo Giordano, Alessandro's father, is already in jail in Calabria awaiting trial. His son Alessandro, on the other hand, is still enjoying himself on his yacht in Monaco, directing what's left of the family business from there. Grimaldi is furious about this, especially after the Stolzfus matter.'

'We know that,' said Tristan.

'Yes, we do. We also know that Cesaria and Grimaldi strongly suspect it was Alessandro who ordered the hit in Venice ...'

Silence fell. Bartolli reached across the table and placed her hand on Tristan's. Tristan looked at her gratefully. 'Intended for me,' he whispered.

'Quite so. And for that reason, more than anything else, Grimaldi is determined to nail Alessandro and bring him to justice once and for all.'

'And how is he going to do that?' said Bartolli.

'By using Omerta. Cesaria believes that Alessandro and his father have been involved in these Death Mask Murder cases.'

'Through Spiridon 4?' asked Bartolli.

'Yes. And that's where the interests of the Italian police, Landru, and our French friends here in Paris overlap: they all want to find out who is behind these murders, albeit for different reasons.'

'And an encrypted app is going to make that possible? How?' asked Tristan, sounding unconvinced.

'Cesaria and Lapointe have something in mind. It's a gamble – quite literally speaking – high risk, but ingenious.'

'Are you going to tell us?' said Bartolli.

'Not now. After we've spoken to Landru, and he has given us his answer. Cesaria has to convince Grimaldi about using Omerta first, and she can only do that if Landru agrees to go along with all this. As you can see, it all depends on that.'

Bartolli nodded.

'And where exactly do I fit into all this?' asked Darrieux.

'As soon as we go and talk to Landru, we'll find out,' said Jack, munching happily.

Darrieux clenched her fists. 'You can be *so annoying!*'

'What else is new?' said Tristan.

40

O'Hara's Alpine Fortress, Obersalzberg: 1 November

Hidden from view in the bushes on top of a rise overlooking the Kuragin estate, Petrinko had an uninterrupted view of the chateau and its grounds, which made surveillance easy. This allowed him to monitor all outdoor activities at and near the chateau.

A powerful, clear-vision HD spotting telescope popular with birdwatchers made reading even car registration numbers possible, and the newly developed Nikon SR lens attached to his state-of-the-art camera took high-quality pictures he could safely transmit via his encrypted mobile phone connection. Face recognition and his contacts in various French government departments – including the police – gave him instant access to databases and confidential intelligence usually only available to high-level law enforcement and security agencies like Europol, MI5 and the CIA. This allowed Petrinko to process and interpret the information he collected, and add vital data to his reports before he sent them to O'Hara.

A demanding client, O'Hara insisted on being informed in real time as events of note unfolded. Petrinko called him regularly and made his reports, often as he was actually watching someone arrive or leave the chateau.

O'Hara put down his phone and looked pensively at the large computer screen in front of him. A new player had just entered the arena: Adrienne Darrieux. The fact she had arrived so early at the Kuragin chateau the day after Lapointe and two police officers from Florence had visited Landru and Dupree at the chateau was clearly significant, as there seemed to be an air of urgency about it.

Well pleased with Petrinko and the efficient way he was handling his assignment – it had taken Petrinko only minutes to find Darrieux' name and address through the registration number of her car – O'Hara was confident he could stay ahead of the game as usual.

With access to a network of powerful search engines on the dark web he had modified to fit his needs, it took O'Hara no time at all to find out what he needed to know about Darrieux. Because there was so much information about her on the internet, he formulated a number of pointed questions that worked as filters, cutting out the noise and irrelevant, often-confusing material.

As soon as he came across the dossier of newspaper clippings Darrieux had handed to the press during her 'coming out' appearance with Isis at Shakespeare and Company the year before, he smiled and began to drill down into Darrieux' fascinating past. One name in particular immediately attracted his attention: Armand Baudin from Santo Domingo.

Ah, so that's how he did it, thought O'Hara, who immediately recognised the significance of the name and its connection to the Llanganates treasure. He also realised how this name, and the fact that Maurice Moreau, Estelle Montplaisir and Adrienne Darrieux were one and the same person, could have helped Landru crack the cipher code. The only thing that was still a mystery was how Landru had made the connection in the first place, and how he had been able to track down Darrieux so quickly and arrange a meeting.

Has to be Rogan, thought O'Hara. He'd been part of everything that had happened so far since Landru cracked the code. He was the key here, no doubt about it, and he was staying at the chateau.

O'Hara didn't believe in coincidences, only purpose and logic, and decided to investigate Jack further. The involvement of the French police was predictable, but the interest of the police officers from Florence in the matter, and the participation of an eccentric Paris socialite like Darrieux, was still somewhat of a mystery. But both had to be important because an astute and desperate man like Landru had made it a priority to make contact with them at the earliest possible opportunity.

O'Hara walked over to the large window and watched the morning sun light up the snow-covered peaks like beacons showing the way to heaven.

It was time to make contact with Landru, establish the ground rules of this game and show him who was in control. As a master manipulator who moved people and their lives around on his cyber chessboard like puppets, O'Hara knew exactly how to do this and which buttons to press. The only thing he had to be careful of, he told himself, was not to push Landru too far. The man had lost everything, and therefore had nothing left to lose except his one shot at vindication and freedom. The fact he had worked so hard trying to crack the code for years, told O'Hara everything he needed to know: the flame that had kept Landru going all this time hadn't been extinguished in jail. On the contrary, he was certain that it was burning brighter than ever; all he had to do was fan the flames, and the best way to do this was to ignite hope.

Had O'Hara looked a little more closely at the stunning peaks, he would have noticed a threatening bank of dark clouds approaching from the south. But he had already left the breathtaking view behind, instead using his mind's eye to refine his strategy to wipe out his opponents and claim the victory that had eluded him for so long.

41

Gatekeeper's Cottage: 1 November, morning

If Landru was in any way surprised when Darrieux and Jack walked into the cottage, followed by Bartolli and Tristan, he certainly didn't show it. Ignoring Darrieux' loud, theatrical make-up and eccentric attire, he politely shook hands with her and showed her to a seat near the fireplace.

'Coffee anyone?' asked Dupree, well aware of the critical importance of the meeting and the sensitive nature of the subject about to be discussed. An experienced police officer used to tense situations, he knew how to put people at ease. 'Nice to see you again, Adrienne,' he said. 'I hear you're working on a new book?'

'I am. You must come to the launch. It will be at Shakespeare and Company.'

'Where else?' mumbled Jack. 'She's an adored celebrity there.'

Bartolli poked him gently in the ribs and gave him a stern look. Jack had quickly changed into a tracksuit and combed his hair, which did little to erase evidence of a late night on the booze. By contrast, Landru was neatly dressed and in control.

'Thank you for arranging this meeting so quickly, Jack, and thank you all for coming, especially you, Mademoiselle Darrieux. I have been looking forward to meeting you for a long time.'

'How come?' said Darrieux and lit a cigarette, trying in vain to appear calm and casual. She found Landru intimidating, not just because of his reputation, but because the man sitting opposite unnerved her.

Sensing the tension, Bartolli decided to step in and take over.

'You asked us to come here this morning, urgently. Well, here we are. Care to tell us why?'

'Certainly. It's quite a story, and like all good stories, it's always best to begin at the beginning. I'm sure you would agree with that, Jack?'

261

'Absolutely.'

'As there are a number of competing interests involved here, it would be helpful if we could examine them one by one, before going further.'

'Good idea,' said Dupree, who appreciated Landru's methodical and disciplined approach that mirrored his own, rarely found in a layman and even rarer still in a convicted murderer trying to prove his innocence.

'So, let's begin with my interests, because they are the most obvious and transparent. Having been convicted of a crime I didn't commit and languishing for several years in jail, I am determined to clear my name and prove my innocence.'

Landru looked calmly around the room, to make his point and watch for a reaction.

'But, as you are all aware by now, there's another, bigger picture involved here that is intricately intertwined with my wrongful conviction: the search for the legendary Llanganates treasure. In fact, it was my obsession with this subject that started it all. And that was almost thirty years ago. I was a young, struggling academic trying to make a name for himself when I stumbled across *The Navarro Chronicles* in Seville, which changed my life. How this came about is also significant, as it has a direct bearing on everything we are about to discuss. In a way, it was the first bloody domino to fall, causing a relentless chain reaction of connected events that have brought us here this morning.'

Bartolli was carefully watching Landru, impressed by his demeanour and measured, logical approach to a very personal subject that must have caused untold heartache and pain.

'It all began the night I met Louis Mendoza in a nightclub in Paris that was frequented by gays. He was without doubt the most handsome man I ever met.'

Transported by painful memories, Landru looked dreamily at something only he could see.

'Who was Louis Mendoza?' asked Jack, trying to break the spell.

'Louis was a librarian working at the Archivo General de Indias in Seville, arguably one of the most significant depositories of historical documents relating to the Spanish Empire in the Americas. He was also my lover, and the first victim in the infamous Death Mask Murders. One of the death masks found in that house of horrors you discovered recently, belongs to him.' Landru waited, to let this sink in.

'Seriously?' said Dupree.

'Yes. Louis was on holidays when I met him. I spent two of the most wonderful weeks of my life with him here in Paris, exploring museums and art galleries. We were strolling through the Tuileries Garden – hand in hand after spending a day in the Louvre – when I first told him about the Llanganates treasure and my quest to find out what happened to it. As it turned out, he knew a lot about the subject. A month after he went back to Spain, he called me and told me about an exciting discovery he had made relating to the treasure. That's how I came across *The Navarro Chronicles*. It was Louis who found them in the library. I travelled to Seville and the rest, as they say, is history, albeit very sad and tragic history. Six months later, I published a paper that propelled me, almost overnight, into the academic limelight.'

Landru reached for a glass of water on the coffee table in front of him, well aware that Bartolli was watching him carefully.

'What happened to Louis?' asked Jack.

'One month after I published my paper, he was dead. Murdered in the ancient merchants' exchange in Seville, where he had found *The Navarro Chronicles* buried in the archives. His body has never been found. It disappeared without a trace, and so did *The Navarro Chronicles*. Stolen. It was as if they had never existed. The only thing left behind on the steps of the merchants' exchange was a white plaster death mask. Despite its notoriety at the time, the case has not been solved. That was the beginning.'

'The beginning of what?' asked Jack.

'My nightmare.'

'Can you elaborate?'

'A few days after the murder, I received an anonymous phone call – with a proposal.'

'What kind of proposal?' asked Bartolli.

'To share whatever information I discovered about the Llanganates treasure.'

'Share with whom?' asked Dupree. 'And why?'

'I wasn't told and I never found out, to this very day. All I was told was that a Swiss bank account had been opened in my name with one hundred-thousand US dollars, a small fortune at the time, especially for a young, struggling academic like me. It was apparent that Louis' murder, *The Navarro Chronicles*, and this extraordinary proposal were somehow connected—'

'And you didn't question this?' interrupted Dupree.

Landru looked at Dupree, sadness in his eyes. 'It shames me to say that I didn't. Not a day goes by that I don't regret that decision. Instead of walking away, I accepted, and soon I enjoyed a lifestyle beyond my wildest dreams. Insane sums of money kept flowing into my bank account every time I made some progress in my investigations and reported it. I bought an apartment in Montmartre, I drove the latest BMW, holidayed in the Bahamas, and went on luxury cruises with my lovers. I became a celebrity in gay circles. Sex, drugs, designer clothes, endless parties and rivers of champagne ... I became totally dependent on this arrangement and intoxicated by my success. I became a slave of my own greed and ambitions, with no way back. That was in 1991. After Louis, other murders followed. All related to discoveries I made in connection with the Llanganates treasure. Shortly after Louis was killed, came another murder.'

'Gerhard Blumenthal, the anthropologist you mentioned in your journal?' said Jack.

'Correct. After some more research in Spain, I was able to trace the Morales khipu described in *The Navarro Chronicles* to a museum in Berlin. For several months, I was working with Gerhard Blumenthal – a renowned anthropologist at the museum – trying to decipher it. He was brilliant and eventually, we published a paper about this together, which added significantly to my reputation as an authority on the subject, and poured more money to my already bulging bank account. But as I was soon to find out, nothing in life is free.'

'What do you mean?' asked Dupree.

'Blumenthal was murdered shortly after we published our paper in 1992. His death mask was found on the steps of the museum in Berlin, and the Morales khipu disappeared. Stolen just like *The Navarro Chronicles* in Seville. Again, neither his body nor his killer have ever been found.'

'This is incredible,' said Bartolli. 'And no-one made a connection here, and followed this up?'

Landru shook his head. 'Obviously, different law enforcement agencies in Europe didn't cooperate in the way they do today. Blumenthal's murder became another unsolved case, and disappeared into the filing cabinets of the authorities. I almost had a nervous breakdown after that. A year later, in 1993, I went on a pilgrimage to sort myself out—'

'The Camino de Santiago?' said Jack.

'Yes, the famous Way of Saint James, the pilgrim's walk. I was hoping this would help me and show me the way out of this nightmare. I was wrong, as it turned out. While kneeling in front of the main altar in the Cathedral of Santiago de Compostela, seeking guidance, I met an old monk who worked in the Archive Library of the cathedral. His name was Junipero de Avila, a very learned man. He took me back to the monastery where he lived, and gave me shelter and a meal. That was in June 1993, two years after I discovered *The Navarro Chronicles*. The next day came another fateful encounter that led to the discovery of the Rodriguez Letter, which as you will soon see, is the reason I wanted to meet you, Mademoiselle Darrieux.'

Landru stopped and looked intently at Darrieux, who had difficulty holding his gaze.

'No doubt you will tell us why?' she said softly.

'Once again, I had accidentally, so it seemed, discovered a significant piece of the Llanganates treasure puzzle in the most unexpected way. I went back to Paris and published another paper – *The Rodriguez Letter* – which immediately caused a sensation in academic circles. This elevated my career at the Sorbonne to dizzying heights. However, a few weeks later, the old monk was murdered in the Archive Library. The only thing found was the monk's death mask left on the altar in the cathedral where I had been praying. Neither his body nor his killer have been found.'

Landru ran his fingers through his hair as if this would help him remember. 'There's something else you should know about the death masks left behind—'

'Oh?' said Bartolli.

'Each mask has a section attached at the neck that makes it clear how the victim died.'

'What do you mean?' asked Dupree.

'Once your Forensics team has a closer look, they will find that each of the masks displays clear markings – deep cuts at the neck showing signs of garrotting. Each victim died just like Atahualpa at Cajamarca on twenty-nine August 1553.'

'Seriously?' Jack exclaimed.

Looking incredulous, Dupree held up his hands. 'Stop it right there!' he said. 'Are you telling us that you knew about all these killings, how the victims died, and their connection to your work, *and did nothing about it?*'

'Yes. I was in too deep and totally dependent on the arrangement I mentioned. But there was more ...'

'What do you mean?' asked Jack.

'After the old monk had been murdered, I had enough and wanted out.'

'What happened?' said Bartolli.

'The voice on the other end of the phone line just laughed at me. I was told there *was* no way out. If I tried to terminate the arrangement, a dossier of compromising photographs would be sent to the chancellor of the Sorbonne, making it clear that I was a raging homosexual and drug addict who was on the take, and involved in murders connected with my sensational discoveries.'

He's closing the gaps, thought Jack. Landru was telling them about the missing bits in his journal that he'd obviously saved up for later. *Very clever. I wonder where he's going with this.*

'You were blackmailed; is that what you are telling us?' said Dupree.

'Yes. But I was also shown a way out.'

'What kind of way out?' asked Bartolli.

'I was told that if I managed to find the Llanganates treasure, everything would stop. From then on, that was all I could think about. The Rodriguez Letter had given me a vital clue I was convinced could help me achieve this.'

'What kind of clue?' asked Darrieux.

'James Mascarino—'

'The notorious pirate killed by Amaro Pargo on Tenerife, who you told us about last night?' Jack cut in.

'Yes.'

'And this is why you asked me to bring Mademoiselle Darrieux along this morning?'

'Correct.'

'You also said it was all about catching the Death Mask killer.'

Landru nodded.

'How so?'

'Because of what I found when I had Mascarino's body exhumed.'

Silence.

He's doing it again, thought Jack. This time, he was trying to pull all of them into his web.

'What did you find? Can you tell us about that?' asked Bartolli, leaning forward.

She's hooked. Jack was fascinated by Landru's tactics.

'I will. After all, that's why I've asked you all to come here. It is the missing link that will explain it all and, if the goddess Fortuna smiles on us and we work together as a team, will lead us to the Death Mask killer.'

'You're serious? said Dupree.

'Deadly. It happened in Tenerife in July 1997. I was on holidays and the weather was so beautiful ...'

42

Tenerife, Canary Islands: July 1997

Looking relaxed and sipping a cocktail, Landru sat by the resort pool overlooking the beach, enjoying the warm sun caressing his face. After an unseasonal stretch of bad weather in Paris, it was nice to see the sun again. Shielding his eyes with his left hand, he watched Salah Cherif, a young Spanish colonial history student from Tunisia he had recently met in a Paris nightclub, performing amazing dives from the two-metre board. Tall, well-built and incredibly athletic, Salah reminded Landru of Louis, his young lover who had been so tragically murdered in Seville six years earlier.

Landru's career at the Sorbonne had advanced rapidly after the publication of *The Rodriguez Letter* in 1993, which had opened a new, exciting chapter in his research into the fate of the lost Llanganates treasure, on which he was considered an authority without equal. Other publications followed in quick succession, and each time he discovered another piece of the puzzle he passed it on, as his pact with the mysterious stranger pulling the strings in the background demanded. Huge amounts of money then appeared in his bank account, which financed his extravagant lifestyle to which he had become accustomed and could no longer do without.

The trip to Tenerife was one of the many holidays he indulged in regularly with lovers during university breaks, but this one had a specific purpose. Marshalling all of his contacts and influence at the university, Landru had worked in vain for months trying to obtain permission from the local authorities in Tenerife to embark on some unusual research relating to the Llanganates treasure. Because the research concerned the legendary Amaro Pargo – a local hero – and more specifically, locating the grave of Pargo's friend, James Mascarino, who Pargo had killed in a duel in 1721, such reluctance was more than understandable.

Part of that research included permission to open Amaro's family tomb in the church of the Santo Domingo de Guzmán Convent in San Cristóbal de La Laguna. A big ask, for sure. Landru had all but given up when quite unexpectedly, the mayor of San Cristóbal de La Laguna, Miguel Barrera, granted permission. Excited, Landru had dropped everything and arranged a trip to Tenerife.

'You should join Cirque du Soleil,' said Landru and handed Salah a drink. 'You're a born acrobat.'

'You think so?' Salah dried his face with a towel and sat down in a deck chair next to Landru, his muscular body glistening like polished ebony in the morning sun. 'Well, tomorrow's the big day you've been waiting for,' he said, smiling.

'It is that. The Rodriguez Letter showed me the way, and everything I've discovered about the treasure after that has been pointing to James Mascarino.'

'And you think he's buried right here, somewhere close to Amaro Pargo? Is that it?'

'Yes. Everything hinges on that.'

'I hope you're right. Tell me about Amaro, this legendary corsair,' said Salah, sipping his drink.

'What would you like to know?'

'Why is he such a legend?'

'Well, he was without doubt one of the most successful corsairs of his time. You do know what a corsair is, don't you?'

'A pirate.'

'Of sorts, yes, but he's a lot more than that. He's a pirate with a *licence*.'

'What on earth do you mean?'

'Unlike pirates who attacked anyone they could find, regardless of nationality, a corsair like Amaro plundered ships in the name of the king, in this case the king of Spain. He was an incredibly successful trader with his own heavily armed fleet, which attacked ships belonging to enemies of the Spanish Crown – mainly British and Dutch – along the busy trade routes between Cadiz and Havana.'

'He had royal permission to plunder?'

'That's about it. He was a shrewd businessman and excellent negotiator who made a fortune and owned a lot of property right here in La Laguna, his hometown, and became the richest man in the Canary Islands. He also fought some of the most ferocious pirates of his time, like Blackbeard and notorious Turkish raiders along the Barbary Coast. But he also had a softer side and looked after the poor in prison, and made generous donations to the Church.'

'What a guy. A Spanish Francis Drake.'

'Something like that. As a reward for services to the Spanish Crown he was made a caballero hidalgo in 1725, and was elevated to the nobility in 1727 with his own coat of arms. You'll see it tomorrow, engraved on his headstone just above the famous skull with the winking right eye and two crossbones.'

'Wow. A pirate fairytale of the high seas?'

'Something like that.'

'I can't wait.'

With two bored-looking gravediggers by his side, Miguel Barrera met Landru and Salah in front of the church just after sunrise the next morning. The mayor wanted to get the annoying exhumation over with before it could attract too much unwelcome attention in the old town, where everyone knew everyone and gossip was a pastime to be enjoyed over a morning coffee, or a glass of wine before an afternoon siesta.

Short and portly, his oily black hair parted in the middle and wearing small, steel-rimmed Trotskyesque glasses that made him look like an ageing Russian revolutionary, he was clearly uncomfortable in his ill-fitting, dark-blue three-piece suit and tie, which would have been more appropriate for a formal council meeting or a funeral than supervising an exhumation on a hot summer morning.

'You must have friends in high places, Professor Landru,' said the mayor and extended his sweaty hand.

'Very good of you to meet us here in person,' said Landru affably. 'On behalf of my university, I thank you.'

Somewhat mollified, Barrera pointed to the doors leading into the church. 'Shall we go inside?'

'Let's do that,' said Landru and followed the little man into the church.

'Well, here it is,' said Barrera and pointed to the marble headstone on the floor. 'The family tomb. What exactly is your interest in Amaro Pargo, Professor?'

'James Mascarino.'

'Ah. The tragic duel between two swashbuckling friends in 1721. Over a woman; what else? According to legend, it had to do with a nun, Sister Mary of Jesus, who was close to Amaro and gave him spiritual advice.'

'You are very well informed,' said Landru, surprised.

'I am a historian,' said Barrera, puffing out his chest. 'I have written a book about Sister Mary of Jesus and Amaro.'

'Well, that explains it. A fellow scholar. How opportune. According to another legend, there could have been more to that relationship than merely devotional reasons.'

'Yes, those rumours have been around for a long time, but I couldn't find any reliable, historic evidence to support them.'

'I see. Just rumours then, as so often happens. I come across this all the time in my line of work too. The siren calls of tempting research conclusions trying to seduce us and lead us astray.'

'Quite. I have read your papers about *The Navarro Chronicles*, and the Rodriguez Letter and their connection to the lost Llanganates treasure. Is that what brings you here?' asked Barrera, watching Landru carefully.

Landru took his time before answering the question. He knew he had to tread carefully. Trying to hide the real purpose of his visit could be counter- productive. On the other hand, trying to harness Barrera's local knowledge, which was obviously considerable, could be advantageous and helpful in the circumstances. For that reason, Landru decided to make an ally out of Barrera rather than keep him guessing in the dark.

'Yes, my visit has to do with the Llanganates treasure. In fact, it's about a vital missing piece of information that could throw some light on where to find it.'

'Intriguing,' said Barrera, his interest aroused.

'Yes, and it's all about Mascarino. You know, of course, who he was?'

'Of course. He was the son of Mad Dog Regan, the notorious pirate who was hanged in Havana in 1664.'

'Correct. As you seem to be familiar with my paper about the Rodriguez Letter, you would know that Regan gave an amulet to his son just before he was executed, which allegedly had a map engraved on it showing the location of the wreck of the *San Cristobal*.'

'Yes. Treasure hunters have looked into this for years. We know from historical material that Mascarino and Amaro went to the island shown on the amulet several times. They were looking for the wreck but couldn't find it and gave up in the end. That's why this story has been dismissed as a dead end by scholars and treasure hunters alike.'

'That may be so, but the identity of the island has never been discovered.'

'No.'

'Well, I'm here to change that.'

'*How?*' Looking incredulous, Barrera took off his glasses and began to polish them with a handkerchief.

'I've recently come across a letter from Mascarino to his daughter, who lived in Havana. Apparently, they were very close. I was doing some research in the Archivo de Indias in Seville when I discovered the letter by accident. In it, Mascarino talks about the amulet and what it means to him. He tells her that he never takes it off and wants to be buried with it when his time comes because it was his only link to his father.'

'Interesting, but how is this relevant?'

'If you've written a book about Amaro, you are obviously familiar with that ill-fated duel we just talked about.'

'Of course.'

'Amaro and Mascarino were close friends, right?'

'Yes. Very close.'

'The duel took place right here in La Laguna, Amaro's hometown.'

'Correct.'

'Amaro wept at Mascarino's funeral and said that when his time came, he wanted to be buried next to his friend.'

'Yes, there are records about that in our archives here on the island.'

'Then surely you can see where I am going with this, can't you?'

Barrera looked stunned. He put his glasses back on and stared at the tombstone in front of him. 'There are several bodies buried down there next to Amaro that have not been identified—'

'You've seen what's down there?' interjected Landru, becoming excited.

'Yes. In fact, there are six additional bodies buried in there belonging to nephews or great nephews of Amaro. We are not sure.'

'So, it could be possible that—'

'One of those bodies belongs to Mascarino? Yes, I suppose it is. We have no records of where he was buried, although he died right here in La Laguna in 1721, and we know he was close to Amaro.'

'Then, why don't we find out?' said Landru.

Barrera signalled to the two gravediggers standing behind him. 'Let's do that. Please remove the stone.'

43

Gatekeeper's Cottage: 1 November, afternoon

Landru looked pensively at Jack. 'To cut a long story short, when we examined the remains of the bodies buried next to Amaro in the family tomb, we found it.'

'Found what?' asked Bartolli.

'The amulet I was talking about. It was next to one of the skulls. A curved piece of whale's tooth about the size of a man's thumb, with a leather thong still attached, threaded through two small holes at each end. We had evidently found Mascarino's final resting place right next to Amaro, the friend who had killed him.'

Jack shook his head. 'This is incredible. What happened to the amulet?'

'As you can imagine, Barrera became very excited as the implications of what we had just discovered began to dawn on him. To keep him on side, I promised I would acknowledge his contribution in any publication about this find that may eventuate. He seemed very pleased about that.'

'What happened to the amulet?' repeated Jack.

'Obviously, there was no way I could take it with me. It had to remain in La Laguna. Barrera said he would take it to the local archives. So, I did the next best thing: I took detailed photos that clearly showed what was engraved on it. As far as I was concerned that was what really mattered, apart from the circumstances of the find, of course. And bearing in mind what was to come, I was right.'

'What happened next?' asked Bartolli.

'Salah and I went back to Paris and I reported the find to my ...' Landru hesitated without completing the sentence, and looked sadly into the distance. 'It shames me to say, I even sent the pictures I took because I knew this would result in a generous payment,' he continued softly. 'Then I began to write a paper about the find – *The*

Mascarino Amulet – my next instalment in the Llanganates treasure saga, perhaps the most important one. And the most deadly.'

'*Deadly?* How so?' asked Jack.

'Because three months later, just before I published my paper, Barrera was murdered in La Laguna. His death mask was found in the church on Amaro Pargo's headstone, next to the winking skull and crossbones. Neither his body nor his killer have ever been found, and neither has the amulet. It was stolen from the archives at the same time.'

Dupree shook his head. 'Murder number four, and you did *nothing?*'

'What could I do?' said Landru, a troubled look on his face.

'I still cannot see what all his has to do with me,' said Darrieux and lit another cigarette.

'You will in a moment,' said Landru calmly. 'I published the paper, but without showing the engraving of the island, because I was planning to visit it myself. And that is where you come in, Mademoiselle ...'

'I can't wait.'

Landru looked at Darrieux. 'I fully understand your frustration, Mademoiselle, but as you will see in a moment, understanding everything I told you so far – especially about Mascarino – is absolutely essential before we can talk meaningfully about why, and how, you fit into all this. In short, we must first take a step back and try to see the bigger picture here before we can assemble the pieces of this complex puzzle and make sense of it all.'

'If you say so.'

'After I published my *Mascarino Amulet* paper, and all the hype that it created had died down, I was able to plan my next move,' continued Landru calmly.

'What was that?' asked Jack.

'Isn't it obvious? Visiting the island depicted on the amulet, of course.'

'To look for the wreck of the *San Cristobal?*' said Dupree.

'What else? Surprisingly, because of its distinctive shape, the small island was quite easy to identify. It is a tiny, uninhabited heart-shaped island south of Cuba. Pirates used it a lot to seek shelter during storms and to get water, because there are two springs on the island. Otherwise, it is very rugged and remote. It's known as Heart Island among the locals, and there are a number of shipwrecks on the reefs close by because the waters surrounding the island are treacherous. For that reason, it is said to have a heart of stone.'

Fascinated by Landru's story, Bartolli was again watching him carefully.

'You mounted a salvage expedition?' she asked. 'Is that what you're saying?'

'To call it a salvage expedition may be a little ambitious. Calling it a reconnaissance trip on a small boat would be more accurate. I wanted to go and see what the place looked like, that's all, and make up my own mind about the Mascarino amulet story.'

'But others like Mascarino himself, and Amaro Pargo, had been there before you to try to locate the wreck, and they found nothing,' said Jack. 'What made you think you could do better?'

'A fair question. Curiosity, I suppose, would be the best way to answer this. And remember, I was obsessed with finding the Llanganates treasure. I contacted a man in Santo Domingo I had been referred to, who apparently knew these waters well and had a suitable boat to take me to the island.'

Landru looked around the room. 'When I tell you his name, all will become clear, especially to you, Mademoiselle.'

Darrieux kept staring at Landru – a familiar feeling of dread rising up from somewhere deep within her – but she didn't say anything.

'The man who took me to Heart Island and helped me look for the wreck of the *San Cristobal* ... was Armand Baudin.'

Everyone in the room digested this bombshell in silence.

'The man who was killed in my room in New Orleans and I was accused of having murdered?' whispered Darrieux, shocked.

'The very same,' continued Landru. 'When I read Jack's book and found out that Maurice Moreau, Estelle Montplaisir and Adrienne

Darrieux were one and the same person, and then came across a newspaper article about an interview you gave in which you spoke about a precious golden Inca burial mask you sold on the black market in Paris to start a new life, well, you can imagine ...'

The person who got their head around the stunning implications of what Landru had just said faster than anyone else in the room, was Tristan. Used to strange coincidences that were difficult to explain through logic alone, he was far more receptive to accepting matters of fate and destiny than others. He locked eyes with Jack and nodded ever so slightly, the bond between them allowing communication on a level that simply eluded others.

'If the Armand Baudin who took you to Heart Island, and the Armand Baudin killed in that brothel in New Orleans, were in fact the same person, then it follows that you would most likely know why he was on the run, what the golden mask was all about, and why he tried so desperately to hide it,' said Darrieux, her heart beating like a drum. 'I've wondered for years.'

'I do,' said Landru. 'And that, my friends, is the key to it all, and the main reason we are all here.'

'Can you enlighten us?' asked Bartolli, barely able to hide her excitement.

'Do you believe in destiny?'

'I think in our own way, all of us here do,' replied Bartolli.

Landru nodded. 'Not surprisingly, our little expedition to Heart Island did not lead us to the wreck of the *San Cristobal*,' he continued. 'Others had tried before us, and failed. While quite small – you can walk around the entire island in a couple of hours – it's very rugged, with a number of caves and massive coral reefs surrounding it on all sides, except for a narrow entry into a small, sheltered bay. After two days on the island, we returned to Santo Domingo and I flew back to Paris, understandably disappointed. But then about a month later, I received a phone call from a very excited Baudin, which changed everything.'

Landru paused, collecting his thoughts as he watched a fly crawl slowly up a windowpane.

'During a storm, Baudin, who was working on a fishing trawler at the time, took shelter on Heart Island with the crew, and spent the night in one of the caves I mentioned. That's when he found it.'

'Found what?' asked Jack.

'The morning after the storm, he found something extraordinary, partially buried in the sand not far from the cave. It was an artefact of solid gold. An ancient Inca burial mask. It must have washed up on the beach during the storm the night before.'

'*And?*' prompted Dupree, leaning forward.

'Realising what this could mean, Baudin decided not to tell the others about the find, and concealed the mask. But before he did that, he did something remarkable.'

'What did he do?'

'Because he had nothing else he could use, he scratched some landmarks identifying the location of the find into the back part of the mask with the tip of his knife, before he walked back to the cave and joined the others.'

Again, silence.

'Are you suggesting that there's some kind of map engraved on the back of the mask showing where it was found, and Baudin did that because this could help locate the wreck?'

'Yes, exactly. The reasoning behind this was simple enough: a heavy gold object like this could not have travelled a long distance, and had most likely been dragged to the surface by a strong swell during the storm from somewhere on the ocean floor not far away.'

'Makes sense,' said Dupree, impressed.

'I still don't understand,' said Darrieux. 'How did Baudin and the mask end up in my room in New Orleans a few months later?'

Landru looked at her sadly. 'That, Mademoiselle, has to do with one of the biggest mistakes of my life. I reported the phone call, and what it meant to—'

Tristan could see at once where this was heading. 'The man in the shadows, and he decided to take matters into his own hands,' he said, completing Landru's sentence.

'Sadly, yes. I thought – quite naively as it turned out – that I could now join forces with Baudin and mount another search for the wreck. I even told him that this was what I would like to do as soon as I could get away. He was very enthusiastic about that and agreed. Then a few weeks later, I received another call from him. This time he sounded scared, desperate. Someone had broken into his house and pulled it apart, obviously looking for something. He guessed at once what it was. Then, before he could make it to his boat, he was attacked by two men, who began to question him about the golden mask. Fortuitously, the attack was interrupted when a group of his friends came along and rescued him. The attackers fled. Baudin managed to get on his boat, where the mask was hidden, and took off—'

'He sailed to New Orleans, didn't he?' interrupted Tristan.

'Yes,' said Landru, his voice barely audible, 'and became a desperate man on the run. You know the rest.'

Just then, someone knocked on the front door. Dupree got up to see who it was. It was François, the butler.

'Apologies for the interruption, but this has just been delivered by a motorcycle courier,' he said and handed a small parcel to Dupree. 'It's addressed to Monsieur Landru.'

Dupree walked back into the room and handed the parcel to Landru. 'Just been delivered. It's for you,' he said.

'*For me?* Delivered by whom?' asked Landru.

'A courier; express delivery.'

Holding his breath, Landru began to unwrap the parcel, his hands shaking. Inside, he found a cardboard box the size of a Paris telephone book.

Tristan locked eyes with Jack again and nodded ever so slightly, as a familiar feeling of foreboding began to wash over him. It was a sickening feeling he encountered every time he came across true evil, which made his stomach churn and the hairs on the back of his neck prickle.

Slowly, Landru opened the lid, looked inside and gasped. His own death mask was staring back at him. Peaceful and serene, yet terrifying at the same time, like a glimpse into an uncertain afterlife.

There was also a note: *Nothing's changed*, it said. *You know the rules.* Scribbled in the margin was an encrypted phone number Landru knew well.

PART IV
THE RETURN OF THE GOLDEN MASK

'The dead cannot cry out for justice; it is a duty of the living to do so for them.'

Lois McMaster Bujold

44

Kuragin chateau: 2 November

Jack sat in the gazebo by the pond – a favourite place where he did most of his writing in summer, weather permitting. His little notebook was open and he was going over his notations from the day before. Enjoying the sunshine, he was feeding the ducks with one of the leftover breakfast croissants, when Darrieux walked up to him. Wearing a stunning traditional Japanese silk kimono complete with belt and backband, she looked like an ageing geisha taking a morning stroll through a Kyoto palace garden after a long night of playing the shamisen.

'Wow! Coffee?' said Jack and pointed to the plunger in front of him.

'Champagne would be better, especially after what Dupree told us yesterday, but coffee will do, thanks.'

'You look like Go-Sakuramachi.'

'Who on earth is that?'

'The last reigning empress of Japan. She abdicated in favour of her nephew in 1771.'

Darrieux shook her head. 'The things you come up with. I certainly don't feel like an empress.'

Jack raised an eyebrow. 'A dazzling kimono this early in the morning? A little overdressed, perhaps?' he teased.

Darrieux shrugged. 'I don't often get to stay in a chateau like this. So I thought, why not? I rarely get to wear this stuff these days. My young admirers used to take me to posh places all the time ... not anymore. I now wear it as a dressing gown. *Merde!*

'Come on ...'

'You don't know what it's like being a middle-aged, single woman in Paris. In many ways you become invisible to men, and resented by women.'

Jack began to laugh, which scared the ducks. They took off and returned to the safety of the pond.

'One could call you many things, Adrienne, but invisible isn't one of them.'

'You think so?' said Darrieux. She gave Jack a coquettish look and adjusted her hair. 'I hardly slept a wink last night. The things Landru told us. You do wonder, don't you?'

'At least now you know where you fit into all this.'

'Sure do, but he did leave a lot of questions unanswered, didn't he? A bit scary, don't you think? Tristan would call it destiny, and then this death mask business on top of it all. Shocked everyone.'

'Weird, for sure, but good news in the circumstances.'

'What do you mean?'

'I just spoke with Cesaria in Florence and told her about Landru's decision.'

'To go along with it all?'

'Yes. I also told her about the death mask. She was in Grimaldi's office with Clara. Something like the delivery of the mask was exactly what they were hoping for.'

'In what way?'

'The man in the shadows we're after has made contact. That's what it means, and it happened sooner and in a more dramatic way than we could have imagined.'

'I suppose so.'

'And what does that tell you? Someone's watching everything Landru is doing, and that is what we were counting on. You can't be the bait if no-one's fishing, right?'

'No, you can't.'

Jack pointed to his notebook on the table. 'I have a few questions about yesterday. Do you mind?'

Darrieux shook her head and watched the ducks – forever hopeful – circling nearby.

'Let's go back to the beginning. Landru reads my latest book – *The Lost Symphony* – in jail and learns about your "coming out" with

Isis at Shakespeare and Company. From the newspaper clippings you handed to the press on that day and all that frenzied publicity that followed, he finds out about you and Armand Baudin and the trial. That's how it all started, right?'

Darrieux nodded.

'According to Landru, this put a thought process in train that allowed him to crack that mysterious cipher code. I have no idea exactly how, but it really doesn't matter.'

'I still don't understand how all that fits together,' said Darrieux, sipping her coffee.

'It's confusing, I know, but bear with me.' Jack picked up his notebook.

'It's all about who Armand Baudin was, and why he was on the run. That's the key here, and it's all connected to that golden Inca burial mask.'

'As far as I was concerned, he was just another punter who walked into that miserable bordello on Bourbon Street in New Orleans, looking for sex.'

'Perhaps, but as we now know, he was much more than that: he was a desperate man on the run, trying to hide.'

'I couldn't possibly have known that, could I?'

'Of course not.'

Jack turned over a page in his notebook. 'You said he was just paying you, when there was some shouting outside and someone banging on the door of your room?'

'That's right.'

'And that's when Baudin took something out of his backpack wrapped in a cloth and asked you to hide it quickly?' continued Jack.

'Yes. He looked terrified. And I did what he asked.'

'Just before the door was broken down and two men burst into the room and told you to get lost?'

'Correct again. I ran. In that place you didn't ask any questions, and violence wasn't uncommon.'

'But *murder*?'

'Well, that was something quite different. And, of course, there was more – much more.'

'Let me get this right: A short time after you left the room, someone found Baudin – your client – in your ransacked room, stabbed to death. The police came, you were arrested and charged with his murder.'

'That's what happened.'

'There was a trial and you were acquitted. Insufficient evidence.'

'Yes. I had no idea who Baudin was, or why someone was after him. I was just a young prostitute caught up in all this. Doing tricks in a cheap bordello.'

'After the trial, you went back to your old room and retrieved the item you had hidden just before Baudin was killed.'

'That's right. I had a secret hiding place that no-one knew about, under the bed, behind a loose brick in the wall; it was where I kept my money. That's when I discovered that fabulous golden mask Landru was talking about. I had no idea what it was, or that some important information was engraved on the back of it, as Landru was telling us. It looked valuable, that's all. Solid gold. Obviously, that's what the intruders had been after. I had no idea why, or who they were. None of this came out in the trial, you see.'

'Landru seemed quite rattled by the death mask delivery,' said Jack, changing direction.

'Can you blame him? It's not every day someone sends you your own death mask, obviously as some kind of warning? How was it made, anyway? Last time I looked, Landru was still very much alive,' said Darrieux.

Jack shrugged. 'Some form of digital printing, most likely. Tell me again, what did you do with the golden mask?'

'As you can imagine, after the trial I was desperate. I kept it and several years later, after I made my way to Paris and when I thought it was safe to do so, I sold it on the black market to a fence I met in Montmartre. As it turned out, it was worth a fortune. It was my ticket to a new life.'

'I understand,' said Jack. 'And as far as you were concerned, that was where the story ended, but in many ways – as far as Landru correctly pointed out yesterday – it was just the beginning. The violence continued, because a few weeks after the fence sold the mask to an unknown buyer, he was murdered, and his death mask was left on the steps of the Sacré-Coeur Basilica overlooking Paris.'

'You're right. And that was Death Mask Murder number five, and by no means the end of this remarkable story.'

'No, because the golden mask surfaced again years later in rather dramatic circumstances; twice in fact,' said Jack. 'And the dark forces in the background were watching.'

'Correct. And after the Baudin murder in New Orleans, Landru's nemesis took over the reins completely.'

'What do you mean?' said Jack.

'Well, let's have a closer look. Landru's discoveries were no longer needed. All that mattered now, was to find that last, vital missing link: the golden mask, right?' said Darrieux. 'The murders all had to do with only one thing: finding the Llanganates treasure. First, the fence in Montmartre I sold the mask to in 2005. Then came the murder of that prominent art dealer in Paris in 2011. The golden mask was about to be auctioned. The day before the auction, the art dealer was killed in his shop. According to Landru, his plaster death mask was found in front of an open safe that had been broken into. Neither his body nor the murderer have been found.'

'Just like the Montmartre case Landru told us about.'

'Quite. But, of course, Dupree only knew about these two cases, didn't he?' said Darrieux.

'Sure. All the other murders happened years earlier, and in different countries. There was no reason to make a connection, certainly not at that stage.'

'The golden mask hadn't been found either,' observed Darrieux. 'Not because it had been stolen from the shop at the time the art dealer was murdered, but because it had been sold before the auction to an anonymous buyer on the Net. The man in the shadows missed it again. The hunt for the mask continued.'

'That's where the matter rested until that famous robbery in Monte Carlo a year later. Do you remember what happened?' asked Jack.

'Sure. We heard all about it last year in connection with our Russian investigations. Dupree told us and you wrote about it in your book. Apparently, that's how Landru first found out about it. Quite recently, it would appear. A gambler – a high roller – had a long losing streak in a glitzy casino. He put up a valuable painting as security: a Russian painting by Nesterov—'

'*The Missing Little Shepherd*,' interjected Jack.

'The gambler was a Russian count, remember? But what we didn't know was that later that night, the desperate count put up another valuable item, a precious golden Inca burial mask, as additional security, to be allowed to continue gambling. It was the poker game of the year. The golden mask made one more, final public appearance – and headlines – before it disappeared for good.'

'Ah. But *did it?* Enter *Le Fantôme* and the Black Widow,' said Jack. 'The scheming Malenkova.'

'None other. The hapless count continued to gamble, and lost. The winner took his prize back to his room and put the golden mask into the safe.'

'That's when things become really interesting,' continued Jack. 'Don't you think? According to Dupree, *Le Fantôme*, the mysterious cat burglar, broke into the winner's room, opened the safe and stole the golden mask and the Nesterov painting, and disappeared.'

'And we do know that the Nesterov painting ended up with Malenkova and was sold by her to a Russian billionaire,' said Dupree.

'Correct; Sokolov. And that information was, of course, also in my book, and therefore available to Landru.'

'It was. And it would have been reasonable for him to put two and two together and conclude that the golden mask ended up with Malenkova as well, just like the painting we know of,' suggested Darrieux. 'Don't you think? After all, she was a famous albeit shady art dealer and fence, well known in the Paris underworld, and that brings us right up to date, doesn't it? Following the fascinating but tragic trail of the golden mask ends right here with her.'

'Looks that way. And as we both know, Malenkova's dead.' Jack closed his notebook and looked at Darrieux. 'Is there anything else you can remember about these extraordinary events? Especially about the golden mask?'

'As a matter of fact there is. Just before I went to sleep last night, I did remember something curious about the mask that the fence in Montmartre told me just before we concluded the sale.'

'Oh? What was that?'

'He explained that the mask was unique in a number of ways. Apparently, encased within the heavy gold and forming the part of the mask that would have made contact with the wearer's face – in this case most likely the deceased – was something very special and sacred to the Inca. '

'What?'

'The back of the mask wasn't just gold. It was a piece of meteorite they held sacred.'

Jack looked up, surprised. 'Are you serious?'

'Yes. That's what the guy said.'

'How did he come to that conclusion?'

'He had the material analysed and it was, I *think* he said, iridium something. Very rare.'

'What!' Jack almost shouted. 'And whatever was scratched into the back of the mask was engraved in *that* material, not the gold?'

'Yes. It was quite different from the gold, like some kind of strange metal or stone.'

'Good God!' said Jack and ran his fingers through his hair. 'This is amazing.'

'In what way?'

'If Landru and Dupree are right and the robbery in Monte Carlo was carried out by *Le Fantôme*, working for the Black Widow as the evidence strongly suggests ...'

'Malenkova?'

'Yes, and she kept the golden mask and didn't sell it on because it was so special, and it ended up in her private collection in that crypt of hers under her home—'

'Destroyed by fire,' interjected Darrieux. 'Nothing left, remember?'

'Not necessarily.'

'What do you mean?'

'Not now. I want to have all the facts at my fingertips before we go down this path,' said Jack, smiling.

'So, you'll just leave me hanging there, is that it? Boiling over with anticipation?'

'Yes, for now.'

'You can be so aggravating, you know, Jack!'

'I've been called worse. You know what they say: you have to be cruel to be kind. So why don't you get out of this striking kimono and change into something a little more comfortable, and we'll go and talk to Dupree and Landru, eh? By then, I should be in command of all the facts.'

Gritting her teeth and clenching her fists, Darrieux turned around in a huff and, shuffling almost as gracefully as a geisha, walked back to the chateau.

45

Madame Petrova's memory trees: 3 November

After the turbulent meeting the day before with Landru, Dupree, and Lapointe – who had joined them later that evening – Jack wanted some time out to reflect on what had been discussed and decided. A chance remark by Darrieux linking iridium to the golden burial mask had changed everything and opened the door to an opportunity no-one had expected.

At first, Jack's proposition was received with scepticism and dismissed as fanciful speculation by all except Tristan. But Jack persisted and put forward persuasive arguments that finally carried the day.

At Dupree's request, Lapointe arranged for two police officers to be stationed at the Gatehouse around the clock as a precaution. The delivery of Landru's death mask had clearly unsettled Dupree, and he was taking the implied threat seriously.

As everything was now moving very fast and had a momentum of its own – especially with Lapointe, Cesaria and Samartini in a great hurry to implement their daring Omerta plan before it was too late – Jack needed some time to think.

With the countess – Jack's usual confidante and sounding board – still away in Venice, Jack turned to his mother, Rahima, who was living in a luxurious retirement home nearby, for advice.

After the dramatic events in Bogota earlier that year that had almost cost her life, Rahima had settled into her new surroundings surprisingly well, and felt totally comfortable and at home in the apartment previously occupied by Madame Petrova, her aunt, who had passed away some time ago.

Somehow Jack always remembered his first meeting with Madame Petrova every time he drove through the wrought-iron gates leading into the grounds surrounding the retirement home – an imposing eighteenth-century chateau that had once belonged to one of Madame Petrova's close friends – the memories making him smile. A retired prima ballerina in her nineties, always dressed as if for a cocktail party, and refusing to wear glasses or use a walking stick because she thought that would make her look old.

Enjoying the warmth of the morning sun on his back, Jack walked along the familiar gravel path behind the chateau leading to Madame Petrova's famous memory trees. As he turned a corner, he could see his mother sitting on a bench facing a grove of oak trees, each one planted in memory of a dear departed friend or relative.

'The matron told me I would find you here,' said Jack. He bent down and kissed his mother on the cheek.

'What a pleasant surprise,' said Rahima, looking adoringly at Jack. She still couldn't quite believe that she had been reunited with the son she had left behind in outback Australia as a baby five decades ago, and thought she would never see again. 'What brings you here this early?'

'What a magnificent spot,' replied Jack, sidestepping the question. 'Madame Petrova's memory trees.'

'Oh yes. I come here often, especially in the morning. It's a magic time, just like now. This place is an extraordinary link to the past, brimming with memories … and regrets,' she added sadly. 'Come, sit with me.'

Jack sat down next to his mother and reached for her hand. 'You look troubled,' she said.

'Ah. Nowhere to hide.'

'I'm your mother, remember? We may not have seen each other for a long time, but that doesn't change anything.'

'Obviously.'

'Well?'

'It's difficult to explain.'

'Try.'

'It's about these Death Mask Murders.'

'Monsieur Landru and his mysterious cipher you told me about?'

'Yes.'

'What about it?'

'It's Tristan.'

'In what way?'

'He says he can sense something he has never come across before.'

'What?'

'Something malevolent reaching out of the distant past, threatening to engulf us all.'

Rahima looked at Jack and raised an eyebrow. 'Isn't that a little melodramatic? Can you be more specific?'

'Seven shocking murders. And they are all connected to an ancient lost Inca treasure. And now this ...'

'What?'

'The last missing link in an extraordinary quest that has already claimed so many lives.' Jack paused and watched a flock of birds land on one of the oak trees. 'And a remarkable coincidence,' he added quietly.

'What link? What coincidence?'

'It's all about a meteorite that hit the earth sixty-six million years ago, and an ancient Peruvian burial mask.'

'My son the storyteller,' said Rahima, rolling her eyes and squeezing Jack's hand.

'No, this is serious.'

'I'm sure it is. Tell me what's troubling you.'

During the next half hour, Jack told his mother how each of the murders was connected to a specific part of the treasure puzzle and how the golden mask found by Baudin on Heart Island could hold the final clue leading to the discovery of the lost treasure.

'But you just told me that Malenkova's house and her art collection were destroyed by fire,' said Rahima.

'True, but that doesn't necessarily mean that everything was destroyed without a trace, despite the fact the place was thoroughly searched by Forensics after the fire.'

'What are you getting at?'

'That's where that meteorite I mentioned steps into the picture.'

'How so?'

'It's all about the Alvarez hypothesis.'

'Never heard of it.'

'Few have. About sixty-six million years ago, a massive asteroid larger than Mount Everest hit the earth on the Yucatán Peninsula at Chicxulub in Mexico. According to the Alvarez hypothesis, which has now been endorsed by scientists around the world, this catastrophic event caused the mass extinction of the dinosaurs and many other living creatures, and left a large crater, the Chicxulub Crater, which we can still see today.'

'Fascinating. But how is this relevant?'

'When Adrienne sold the burial mask on the black market in Paris, the fence she sold it to had it examined and tested. That's when something curious was discovered.'

'What?'

'Not all of the mask was solid gold. Part of it consisted of something quite different.'

'What?'

'Iridium, the second densest metal and the most corrosion-resistant metal on earth, even at two thousand degrees Celsius.'

'I still can't see—'

Jack held up his hand. 'Iridium is found in meteorites and would have been quite prolific near the impact crater on the Yucatán Peninsula, and beyond.'

'Ah.'

'From the description Adrienne gave, the style of the mask strongly suggests a pre-Colombian origin that pre-dates the Inca. The mask was most likely a precious ceremonial object held sacred by the Chimu, who lived along the northern coast of modern-day Peru and were conquered by the Inca around 1470.'

'I can see you've done your research.'

'I had to. Otherwise, I wouldn't have been able to persuade Lapointe to go along with it.'

'With what?'

'Authorising a forensic search of the ruins of Malenkova's house.'

'*Why?*'

'Unlike gold, which has a melting temperature of 1,064 degrees Celsius, iridium doesn't melt until a temperature of 2,466 degrees C is reached. Now, a typical house fire would reach temperatures of around eight to nine hundred degrees Celsius. It can be several hundred degrees hotter at floor level, but would unlikely reach a temperature of 2,466 degrees. What it means is this: if Malenkova did in fact have the golden burial mask in her collection, it is very likely the iridium part is still intact.'

'With Baudin's markings?'

'Still visible; yes. That's why Lapointe has authorised a search of the premises. Apparently, the property hasn't been touched since the fire. An insurance claim by the estate is still pending and, of course, it was a crime scene for quite some time after the fire.'

Rahima turned to face Jack. 'Ingenious,' she said. 'If this comes off, it could be quite a breakthrough.'

'It could.'

'Then, why the troubled look?'

'Tristan thinks we should walk away – *now!*'

'Why?'

'Because he can sense danger, grave danger.'

'Something malevolent reaching out of the distant past?'

'Yes. Something like that.'

'What are you going to do?'

'What do you think I *should* do?'

'I think you've already made up your mind,' said Rahima, preferring not to answer the question.

'Hm.'

'Have you ever walked away from something like this?'

'Hm.'

'I think we both know the answer, don't we?'

'That's what Tristan said.'

'Not surprising. After all, he can hear the whisper of angels ...'

'Thanks, Mum,' said Jack, smiling.

'When are they going to search the house?'

'This afternoon.'

'Then you better run along and follow those breadcrumbs of yours, but please make sure you don't end up as one of Madame Petrova's memory trees here.'

Jack reached across and kissed his mother on the cheek. 'Not yet, anyway,' he said, and stood up to leave.

46

In the ruins of Malenkova's house, just outside Paris: 3 November

By the time Jack, Tristan and Dupree arrived at what was left of Malenkova's house – which wasn't much – Lapointe and the Forensics team had already entered the building and were at work. They were searching the crypt under the house where the deadly blaze had started and where Malenkova had kept her prized art collection.

Lapointe waved and walked over to Jack. 'An ingenious idea. A long shot, but worth pursuing. That's what the Prefect said.'

Jack shrugged. 'Perhaps it takes divine intervention to solve this riddle.'

'Stardust, you mean?' said Dupree. 'What do you think, Tristan?'

'Could be.'

'Perhaps if we listen carefully, we might hear the whisper of angels?' teased Lapointe.

'Showing us the way? Who knows? This place is full of voices,' replied Tristan, looking serious.

'What do you mean?' said Jack.

'So much has happened here.'

'Can you feel something?'

'Oh yes, and it's making my skin crawl,' said Tristan and began to take a closer look at the ruins.

'We even managed to rustle up a metallurgist from the university. She's downstairs,' said Lapointe. 'Shall we go and see how they are going?'

'Sure, let's do that,' said Jack and followed Lapointe inside.

'Barely recognisable,' said Dupree, as he remembered the fascinating meeting with Malenkova the year before. It had been on that occasion he'd noticed a painting by Anielka hanging on a wall in Malenkova's study. As it turned out, this had provided an important clue that ultimately led to Anielka's exposure.

'According to the insurance company, the loss assessors have already been through the building to collect anything of value remaining.'

'Do we know if they found anything?' asked Jack.

'Not really. The insurers were very tight-lipped about the entire matter and referred us to their lawyers. As you can see, the ruins have been secured and the entire property has been fenced off. Apparently, it's all part of some litigation between the estate and the insurance company.'

'Could take years,' said Jack.

'Probably will.' Dupree turned to Lapointe walking along next to him. 'A little different from last time we were here, don't you think?' He pointed to the stone steps leading down into the crypt. 'Be careful. No handrails.'

Lapointe stopped at the top of the landing and looked down into the crypt. 'As I remember it, Zuzanna's body was found at the bottom of the stairs, and Malenkova's was just over there. She still had a gun in her hand. What was left of it.'

'Must have been a hell of a showdown,' said Jack as he walked carefully down the slippery stairs. 'So much violence.'

'And a hell of a blaze,' said Dupree. 'An accelerant was used; petrol. The heat must have been ferocious down there. Nothing left but rubble and a shell.'

'Hm. But let's not forget the unique properties of iridium,' said Jack. 'After all, that's why we are here, gentlemen.'

'You are right,' said a woman at the bottom of the stairs who had overheard Jack's remark. 'I am Professor Flaubert, the metallurgist.'

'This is Jack Rogan. All of this was his idea,' said Lapointe, making the introductions and trying to distance himself from what he personally believed to be a harebrained idea. As a methodical man who strictly followed the trail of logic and evidence, the notion of finding anything of value in this singed rubble, as postulated by Jack, was an alien concept based entirely on speculation. But then again, he had to admit that Jack had come up with some surprising ideas and results in the past that simply defied logic and rational method. For that reason, he had reluctantly gone along with the proposal to search the premises again.

'What do you think, Professor; is it possible that a piece of meteorite containing iridium could have survived the blaze and in essence remained intact?' asked Jack.

'Sure, it's possible. But we are looking for a needle in a burnt-out haystack open to the elements, perhaps buried somewhere under this mountain of rubble here. We have no idea how big it is, or what shape it is. We don't even know if it's here at all. We could be standing right next to it and mistake if for a piece of masonry just like this one, because any gold would have melted for sure and was perhaps retrieved by the insurers, or just lost. The temperatures in this inferno must have been extremely high down here.'

'But not hot enough to melt iridium,' Jack cut in.

'Very unlikely.' The professor picked up a piece of blackened masonry and held it up. The piece we are looking for, could look just like this.'

Jack nodded, trying hard not to appear too dejected, as the enormity of the task became obvious. What had seemed plausible and a good idea in theory, looked very different under the microscope of reality.

'That's why I brought this along,' said the professor and held up a gadget that looked like a Dyson vacuum cleaner.

'What's that?' asked Dupree.

'A very sensitive metal detector,' said the professor, smiling. 'Once the rubble has been spread out on the concrete floor here a little, making it more even, we can go to work. This metal detector can potentially detect celestial rocks. It will certainly find any of the platinum-group metals, like osmium, palladium, rhodium and, of course, iridium – even just traces of it inside a piece of meteorite.'

'Excellent,' said Jack, feeling no longer quite so crestfallen. Forever the optimist, he would try running a ten-tonne truck on the smell of an oily rag if it meant getting a shot at what he was after.

Lapointe walked back up the stairs, lit his pipe and watched the Forensics team spread out the rubble below, as directed by the professor. It was obvious to Jack that he considered the whole exercise a waste of time. About an hour later, Professor Flaubert went to work with her metal detector. Countless twisted metal pieces of all sizes, or objects with traces of metal, were found and carefully placed into boxes as she methodically covered the floor from side to side. To her trained eye, none of the fragments came even close to what she was looking for. Aware that Jack was watching her intently, she was too polite to make a comment, and instead continued to work until she had covered the entire floor area.

Professor Flaubert turned off the metal detector, looked up at Lapointe, and shrugged. 'Perhaps it was kept in another part of the house?'

'Unlikely,' said Dupree. 'All of Malenkova's prized possessions were apparently kept down here. And besides, upstairs is a complete mess. I wouldn't even know where to start.'

'I would,' Tristan called out from above. He had spent the past hour exploring the ruins above the crypt.

'What are you getting at, mate?' asked Jack, recognising the familiar signs.

'Difficult to explain, but I felt something.'

'Where?'

'I'll show you.'

'Professor, would you mind?'

'No. Why not?'

Jack, Dupree and Professor Flaubert walked back upstairs and followed Tristan to the back of the house. Reluctantly, Lapointe followed a few steps behind, carefully dodging singed roof beams and twisted metal, all part of the collapsed roof structure. 'This used to be a church,' he said, 'before it was converted into a house.'

Jack turned to the professor. 'Tristan has a sixth sense,' he explained. 'I've seen it at work many times. He's a remarkable young man.'

The professor didn't reply.

'In here,' said Tristan.

'I think this was Malenkova's study, if I'm not mistaken,' said Dupree and turned to Lapointe. 'What do you think?'

'You're right. And her desk was just over there, as I recall it. In front of the fireplace.' Lapointe pointed to a partially collapsed wall.

Tristan held up his hand and closed his eyes. 'Can you hear it?'

'What?' asked Jack.

'Chanting.'

Lapointe turned to the professor. 'They say he can hear the whisper of angels.'

'Ah. In that case, let's see what they are whispering about,' said the professor and turned on the metal detector.

It took the professor only a few minutes before getting a loud signal from somewhere under a mound of ash near the fireplace. Jack knelt down and began to clear away the powdery ash with his bare hands. Tristan knelt down beside him and helped.

'The voices are getting stronger,' he whispered.

Jack's fingertips touched it first: something cold and smooth. Then Tristan's fingers touched it too, and together they carefully lifted from the ash a heavy object the size of Jack's hand, and held it up. It looked like a shiny piece of rock or metal.

Mesmerised, Lapointe watched as the professor held the metal detector against it, the beeping noise becoming louder and more urgent. Smiling, Jack handed the piece to the professor. 'What do you think?' he said.

'Could be, but to be sure, I would have to take it back to my lab and test—'

Jack held out his hand. 'No need. I can tell you right now if this is what we've been looking for,' he said.

'*How?*' said the professor, surprised, and handed the piece to Jack.

Slowly, Jack began to rub the smooth surface with the back of his sleeve, wiping away the soot and grime, his heart beating like a drum.

'Because of this,' he said quietly. Then he held the piece up like a trophy and pointed to some clearly visible markings scratched into the smooth, shiny surface.

47

Port de Fontvieille, Monaco: 5 November

No-one standing next to the distinguished-looking elderly gentleman waiting in line to buy an ice cream in his crisp linen jacket and straw hat, would have guessed that they were almost rubbing shoulders with one of the most dangerous, and wanted, hitmen in Europe. The man smiled at the young woman behind the ice-cream cart with its colourful sun umbrella, and ordered two scoops – one vanilla and one chocolate – and then continued to stroll past the ostentatious millionaires' pleasure craft moored along the famous waterfront of Port de Fontvieille, like badges of wealth to be admired by the less fortunate.

The largest and most imposing vessel by far was *Nike*, the Giordano family's motor yacht – a magnificent, thirty-metre customised Majesty 105 superyacht built by Gulf Craft in the United Arab Emirates – which was permanently moored in the harbour. Since his father's arrest, Alessandro had made *Nike* his home, and was running what was left of the family business from there. Since the recent collapse of the Giordanos' lucrative drug business caused by the Stolzfus fiasco that had brought down Spiridon 4, Alessandro felt safer on board the *Nike,* surrounded by his bodyguards and crew, than at the family home in Florence. Florence had become a dangerous cauldron of rivalry between Mafia families jostling for position in the ever-shrinking drugs market, which was slowly being strangled by Chief Prosecutor Grimaldi and the Squadra Mobile. Desperately short of money, Alessandro was always on the lookout for an opportunity to improve the family's declining fortunes.

Enjoying his ice cream, the man in the linen jacket stopped in front of the *Nike* and smiled at the man, one of Alessandro's muscle-bound bodyguards, standing at the gangway. *Why do they all look the same?* thought the man, shaking his head. He finished his ice cream and was about to step onto the gangway when the bodyguard held up his hand. 'That's far enough, grandpa,' he said. 'Move along.'

'I don't think so. Why don't you be a good boy and run inside, and tell Alessandro that Grandpa Dragan is here to see him, eh? That way you'll keep your job, and I won't have to blow your head off to get past you. What do you think?'

Nonplussed, the bodyguard stared at the grey-haired man in front of him, unsure what to do. But something about the man triggered alarm bells: he radiated confidence and danger. 'Did you say Dragan?' asked the bodyguard. '*You* are Dragan?'

'I am. Now, what will it be?'

'Wait here,' said the bodyguard and hurried up the gangplank.

Moments later, Alessandro appeared on deck. 'I didn't expect you until this evening,' he said, waving from above. 'Come on board.'

Alessandro had never met Dragan M, as he was known in certain Mafia circles, but he had heard a lot about him. His father had engaged him on several occasions over the years, but only in connection with the most sensitive and important assignments. All Alessandro knew about him was that he was Bulgarian, very expensive, and the best in the business. For that reason, his father had used Dragan for the very public assassination of Salvatore Gambio, the person thought to be responsible for the killing of Alessandro's brother, Mario, in Florence two years earlier.

In fact, it had been Dragan who had recommended Spiridon 4 for jobs that required more than one operative, as he preferred to work alone. With Spiridon 4 no more, Alessandro's father had suggested that Dragan be approached with the sensitive assignment that had come up unexpectedly.

'Thank you for coming so promptly,' said Alessandro and pointed to a white leather lounge in the corner of the opulent, wood-panelled salon. 'Drink?'

'Yes, please. Gin and tonic.'

'Coming up. I wouldn't have asked if it wasn't, you know, and with Father in jail—'

Dragan held up his hand. 'No need to explain. Your father and I go back a long way. We've done business together for many years.'

'I know. And it is for that reason Father suggested I should turn to you now. But there's also another reason.'

'What other reason?' asked Dragan, watching Alessandro carefully.

'Because this assignment is related to others you were involved in quite a long time ago.'

'Oh? Can you be more specific?'

'Louis Mendoza in Seville, Blumenthal in Berlin, Junipero de Avila in Santiago de Compostela, and Miguel Barrera in La Laguna.'

'The Death Mask matter? Are you serious? My God, that was years ago.'

'I know. But this is part of it.'

'Are you sure? How come?'

'Same – how shall I put this? – *client.*'

'The elusive man with the deep pockets we never met? Is he still around?'

'Yes, he is. And still doing business. The same business, it would appear.'

'Extraordinary,' said Dragan. 'After Barrera, things became more complicated, and then Spiridon 4 stepped in.'

'Yes, with the three Paris assignments. The client became more demanding and peculiar with his requests. The last one was the gay prostitute in Montmartre.'

'The Landru case, if I remember correctly,' said Dragan.

'Correct. But, of course, Spiridon 4 are now gone.'

'Sadly so,' said Dragan, who had not only recommended the group, but had actually trained them. He had first come across them at the end of the Kosovo war in 2000. Twin girls and two gypsy brothers drifting aimlessly through the Bulgarian countryside, begging for food after their families had been brutally murdered.

Dragan had taken them in and began to train them on his farm near the ancient town of Bononia. He could still remember training manoeuvres with the group in the ruins of the Babini Vidini Kuli fortress, the home of the last Bulgarian Tsar Ivan Sratsimir, who lost his country and his crown to the Ottomans. Dragan had shown them how to dispose of dead bodies without leaving a trace; one of his specialities that had kept him alive all these years, and out of reach of the law. A few years later, the group was ready and became Spiridon 4, one of the most successful and deadly hit squads in Europe.

'Another drink?' asked Alessandro.

'Yes, please. But before we go much further, I have to tell you that I am retired now. After Teodora and her sister died, I knew it was time for me to step back. I wanted to tell you this in person. That's why I'm here. Call me old fashioned, or over cautious, but like your father, I don't like discussing important matters over the phone, however secure.'

Alessandro nodded and handed Dragan another drink. 'I understand, but I cannot think of another person who could carry out this assignment successfully. Father said it has you written all over it and would be a fitting conclusion to something that began almost thirty years ago. And Petrinko is also involved. You recommended him, remember?'

'So, Bohdan accepted?'

'He did. He needed a change, and some money,' said Alessandro, watching Dragan carefully. In the end, everything usually came down to money. 'He left Kiev, and Azov, and is now in Paris, working for the "client" and making a fortune.'

'What kind of fortune?'

'Let me come straight to the point,' said Alessandro, pleased by the direction the conversation was taking. He paused and looked at Dragan. 'Petrinko cannot do this by himself. He needs someone like you by his side to make this work. I have already discussed this with the client, who understands your position. However, to make coming out of retirement worthwhile, I have been authorised to make you an offer.'

'What kind of offer?' said Dragan, trying in vain to look disinterested.

Alessandro took his time before replying. He could see that he had Dragan's attention. 'One million US, plus a success fee,' he said quietly.

Dragan whistled softly and reached for his drink. 'That's quite an offer,' he said, thinking of his rapidly shrinking bank account. Retirement had turned out to be far more expensive than he had thought. 'What's involved?'

'It's about an artefact that was recently recovered by the Paris police from the ruins of a house fire near Paris. The client wants to get his hands on this artefact at any cost. This assignment is about just that.'

'Where's that artefact now?'

'With the Paris police. Their Forensics department.'

Dragan began to laugh. 'As you know, I've taken on difficult assignments many times before, but never impossible ones.'

'This isn't impossible, only complex, requiring the imagination and daring that have been the hallmarks of all of your jobs,' said Alessandro.

'Can you be more specific?'

'May I take it that you are perhaps interested?'

'I'm talking to you, am I not?'

'Excellent. In that case, let me tell you.'

Over the next hour, Alessandro outlined a plan so bold that most rational operatives available on the market would have dismissed it outright as risky nonsense, and walked away. Dragan, however, listened attentively without interrupting, his mind racing as he tried to work out the logistical considerations involved in making such a project work.

What Alessandro didn't tell him was the real reason the plan had so many specific, seemingly unrelated, extravagant components insisted upon by the client. This had nothing to do with eccentricity, and everything to do with an ingenious plan. Not only did O'Hara want to get hold of the artefact; he wanted to do so as part of a huge, final computer game and gambling extravaganza on the dark net that would be a fitting conclusion to the Death Mask Murders, and answer all outstanding questions in one spectacular finale that would make him, and Alessandro, a fortune.

48

Kuragin chateau: 7 November

The police officer sitting in the car parked in front of the Gatekeeper's Cottage watched as the motorcycle rider crossed the bridge and approached the cottage. 'Let's see what he wants,' he said to his colleague, a young constable, and got out of the car.

Wearing a leather vest with the logo of a well-known Paris courier company on the back, Petrinko pulled up next to the police officer holding up his hand, and stopped his bike. 'Delivery for Monsieur Landru,' he said and pushed up the visor of his helmet.

'You can give it to me. I'll take it to him.'

'All right,' said Petrinko and opened his saddle bag. Smiling, he reached into the bag, pulled out a Glock 19 with a silencer attached, and shot the officer in the forehead without taking his eyes off the constable sitting in the police car, watching him. Even before the dead police officer hit the ground, Petrinko had fired two more rounds as he got off the bike. The first shot shattered the windscreen of the police car, the second hit the constable, a young woman, in the shoulder. Petrinko opened the driver's door and looked at the constable staring at him, her eyes wide with disbelief and fear. 'Nothing personal, love,' he said and shot her between the eyes, and then adjusted the GoPro strapped to his chest that had recorded it all.

As Petrinko turned around, he could see a black van cross the bridge. Realising that timing was critical, he hurried over to the van as it pulled up behind the police car. 'All clear,' he said.

'I can see,' said Dragan. He got out of the van and handed Petrinko a clown's mask. The instructions from the client had been quite specific. Then he quickly took a couple of photos of the two dead police officers with his iPhone, before putting on his own mask.

310

Dupree and Landru were drinking coffee in the lounge. It was late afternoon, and Dupree had just taken a pot of coffee out to the two police officers who had just started their shift. 'Someone at the door,' said Dupree. He got up, walked through the kitchen and opened the front door.

'If you don't do anything stupid, you will live. Make a noise and you will join these two out here,' said Petrinko pointing his gun at Dupree. Dupree could see the dead police officer lying in a pool of blood on the ground behind Petrinko.

His mind racing, Dupree was assessing the situation. *Pros*, he thought, processing the enormity of what he had just seen. *Two dead police officers. Mon Dieu! These guys mean business.* As a retired senior detective used to dealing with extreme violence and the unexpected, Dupree knew there was only one way to get through a situation like this: follow instructions to the letter, and show no fear. If they had wanted to kill him, they would have done so by now.

'First we say hello to Monsieur Landru, then we go over to the chateau and say hello to the others, clear?' said Dragan, who was standing behind Petrinko, holding a small submachine gun. Dupree noticed that both men were wearing gloves.

If Landru was in any way surprised or shocked when two armed men wearing clown masks walked into the room with Dupree, and one of them pointed a gun at him, he certainly didn't show it. He put his coffee cup calmly on the table in front of him and looked at the two men. 'What can I do for you, gentlemen?' he said.

He's good, thought Dragan, appreciating Landru's presence of mind and self-control, and was therefore dangerous. 'Get up!' he said.

Landru stood up.

'Now, we'll go over to the chateau together and have a chat with Mr Rogan and his friends. Clear?'

'Clear,' said Landru and locked eyes with Dupree watching him.

'Let's go,' said Petrinko.

François was in the kitchen eating a sandwich with cook when he heard the front doorbell. He pushed his plate aside, stood up, and walked upstairs to answer the door.

'Good afternoon, François,' said Petrinko. He stood behind Dupree with a gun pointed at François, who looked shocked. 'I know who's in the building. What I don't know is where everybody is right now, but I'm sure you can help me with that.'

'Cook's in the kitchen downstairs; the others are in the music room having afternoon tea.'

'Everyone?'

'Yes.'

Petrinko smiled. So far, everything was going exactly as planned. 'Please take us to the music room,' he said.

'This way,' said François and turned around.

Jack was sitting in front of the fireplace with Tristan. They were playing chess. Darrieux and Bartolli sat on a lounge near the grand piano, chatting and drinking tea. Jack was about to move a pawn when François walked into the room, followed by Dupree and Landru. Jack looked up in surprise, and froze when he saw two men with guns pushing past them into the room.

'Nobody move,' said Dragan, speaking calmly, which made the words coming out of the mouth of a clown even more chilling. Dragan held up his gun. 'This is an Israeli Uzi submachine gun. It can fire six hundred rounds per minute and could kill everyone in this room in seconds. And in case you're wondering,' continued Dragan, 'the two police officers outside are no longer on duty.'

There was stunned silence in the room as everyone struggled to digest what had just been said.

Dragan turned to François standing next to him. 'Please take my friend into the kitchen and fetch the cook. That way, we'll all be nicely together in here.'

No-one spoke until François and Petrinko returned with a frightened-looking Antoinette, the cook.

'I've heard a lot about you, Mr Rogan,' said Dragan, speaking softly. 'I've seen you once before, you know. In 2016. You were standing next to Chief Prosecutor Grimaldi in front of the Chiesa di San Marco in Florence after Mario Giordano's funeral. Admittedly, I saw you through the scope of my rifle, which isn't quite the same as seeing you in the flesh. It was a really difficult shot.'

Good God, it's the same man, thought Jack, remembering the Gambio assassination two years earlier, but he didn't respond.

Dragan took off his backpack, pulled out a laptop and placed it on top of the piano. He did all that without putting down his machine gun. Only after he had made sure that Petrinko, who was standing at the door, had everyone in the room covered, did he put the weapon down.

'Ah, Venice, such a beautiful city, especially when you see it from a boat,' said Petrinko, carefully watching Tristan.

Tristan froze without looking at Petrinko, a strange feeling of dread washing over him.

'You look different close up, Tristan,' continued Petrinko. 'Younger, more vulnerable. Last time I saw you was through binoculars. You were leaving the palazzo and went shopping to the market behind the Accademia. That was the day before Lorenza ... unfortunate—'

Dragan glared at Petrinko and held up his hand, the gesture obvious.

Jack reached across the table and squeezed Tristan's arm without taking his eyes off Petrinko, well aware that he was looking at Lorenza's killer hiding behind the mask of a clown.

'Then why don't you kill me now,' asked Tristan, his voice barely audible, 'and rectify your blunder?'

'Because I work for a different master now,' replied Petrinko calmly. 'And I only do what I'm paid to do.'

Well aware of the mounting tension in the room, Dragan opened his laptop, switched it on, and turned the screen towards Jack. 'Can you see the screen, Mr Rogan?'

Jack nodded.

'Excellent, because I've someone who would like to meet you.'

'Care to enlighten me as to who that might be?' asked Jack. 'Or will this turn into another big mistake?'

'Patience. You'll find out in a moment,' said Dragan, ignoring the sarcastic remark.

Facing his favourite window overlooking the mountains, O'Hara sat in front of his large computer screens. While he waited for the encrypted Zoom connection to Dragan's laptop to be activated, he stared dreamily out of the window as a rare optical phenomenon – alpenglow – illuminated the mountains just after sunset, giving them a stunning, reddish glow.

This rare, mysterious display was usually only visible before sunrise or after sunset, and was caused by light reflected off airborne ice crystals in the lower atmosphere. On this occasion it was particularly strong, and filled the entire room with an eerie, rosy light. O'Hara smiled, as he considered this to be a prescient omen of things to come.

In preparation for the Zoom conference call he had arranged with Petrinko and Dragan the day before, O'Hara had carefully laid out his precious Llanganates treasure items he had collected over the years on the desk in front of him. Apart from these and the amulet, one crucial item was still missing. *But not for long,* he thought. He took off the Mascarino amulet he wore around his neck, and placed it on the table next to the Rodriguez Letter.

Moments later, the connection crackled into life and the grinning face of a clown appeared on the screen. 'Good evening,' said the clown. 'Everyone's here, as you can see.' As the clown stepped aside, O'Hara could see everyone in the room, but no-one could see him because the camera was turned off at his end.

'*Bonsoir*, Mademoiselle Darrieux,' said O'Hara. 'I've followed your exciting life for quite some time. All the way from New Orleans to Paris. What a journey! And thanks to you, the last piece of this fascinating puzzle is about to fall into place.'

Darrieux bit her lip and said nothing.

'*Buona sera*, Signora Bartolli,' continued O'Hara, looking closely at Bartolli sitting next to Darrieux. 'Your surprisingly accurate insights into the Landru case have fascinated me for years. Pity the French police didn't find them equally useful, don't you think so, Monsieur Dupree? But you had your doubts from the very beginning, didn't you? Yet, you did nothing about it. Until now that is. I wonder why—'

'Are you at least going to introduce yourself?' interrupted Bartolli, staring at the empty screen. 'A one-sided conversation is not only impolite, it's boring.'

O'Hara began to laugh, appreciating the grit and the wit of the remark. 'I will, in due course,' he said. 'But first I would like to meet all of you. Ah, Monsieur Landru. We've known each other for almost thirty years now, albeit from a distance, but I've actually seen you once before. The night you were arrested in Montmartre and charged with a murder you didn't commit. I was there, you see, and saw you being taken away by the police.'

Like Darrieux, Landru also remained silent, trying desperately to come to terms with the surreal situation unfolding around him.

'And that brings me to you, Mr Rogan,' said O'Hara. 'What a fascinating man you are. I must congratulate you on your recent success. To find what has eluded me for such a long time, so quickly and with such ease, was quite something. And to do it all by using iridium as the means to find it among all that rubble. I must say, that was ingenious! You can obviously see what others can't. That's quite a talent.'

O'Hara paused, collecting his thoughts. 'In case you are wondering how I know all this, Monsieur Landru has kept me informed of everything that's been happening, you see,' he continued, lowering his voice. 'Just like he's always done, but at least now I know why he chose you to help him in his quest, Mr Rogan. An excellent choice. And, of course, it was you who helped him crack the cipher code in the first place, and that opened the door to all this and brought us here. Congratulations!'

O'Hara looked around the room.

'Destiny? What do you think, Tristan? You of all people would know. After all, they say you can hear the whisper of angels and glimpse eternity. Mr Rogan told us all about that in his books. Fascinating. I too believe in destiny, you see. And what is happening here right now, tonight, is an excellent example of destiny at work. Don't you think?'

O'Hara began to chuckle. In many ways, this was the ultimate chess game. A chess game like no other, with real people he could move around the board at will. It was the culmination of a long journey that was rapidly approaching its destination.

'I see, no-one has anything to say. No matter. You are no doubt wondering what this is all about and what will happen next. Understandable. Well, let me explain.'

With that, O'Hara turned on his camera, which was trained on his Llanganates treasure collection spread out on the desk in front of him in a way that allowed him to stay in the background and out of sight.

'I'm sure Monsieur Landru will recognise these items. After all, he was the one who found them. They made him famous, you see, and very rich. It all began with *The Navarro Chronicles* here,' said O'Hara, as the camera zoomed in on a bundle of handwritten pages spread out on the table. 'Discovered by Louis Mendoza in the Archivo General de Indias in Seville in 1991. We all know what happened to him, don't we?' O'Hara paused to let this sink in. 'Such a handsome young man, don't you agree, Mr Clown?'

Dragan held up his hand and nodded, the gesture chilling.

'Mr Clown here should know,' said O'Hara. 'He was the last one who saw him alive, you see.'

Landru, who stood next to Dupree, let out a gurgling sound and began to shake. Afraid that he might launch himself at the clown, Dupree put his arm around him and held him tight until the shaking stopped.

'And then came the Morales khipu,' continued O'Hara, enjoying himself. 'What a fascinating item, you must admit. Arguably the most important one in the entire collection here because without it, the Llanganates treasure would not have been discovered in the first place.'

Mesmerised, everyone in the room kept staring at the laptop screen on the piano as O'Hara continued to describe each piece in his collection, and where it fitted into the puzzle.

'But as you are obviously aware, one important item is still missing. Your recent find, Mr Rogan. As you can see, I've gone to a lot of trouble to put this collection together, and it would be a shame if it were to remain incomplete, don't you think? Well, I will make sure that doesn't happen because the Mascarino amulet here, and the remnants of the burial mask you found, belong together. Only when they are united will they give up their secrets and you, Mr Rogan, will help me achieve this—'

'How exactly?' Jack asked, trying to interrupt the monologue and engage with the speaker.

'With the help of Monsieur Landru, of course, who, like me, has coveted the golden mask for such a long time, but he knows that it belongs to me, just like all these related items here that he helped me find over the years. And he knows what happens to those who stand in my way, don't you, Monsieur Landru?'

As the camera swung slowly around, Jack noticed something in the background. It looked like some kind of picture behind glass facing the window. Before the camera zoomed in on the amulet, it came to rest on the picture. Reflected in the glass, Jack saw something that made him gasp. Illuminated by the rosy light of the alpenglow was the familiar silhouette of a famous mountain that he had seen before: the Watzmann, near Berchtesgaden.

49

Kuragin chateau: 8 November

Lapointe, a light sleeper, reached for the mobile on his bedside table and answered the call. It was the duty officer at the Prefecture. The alarm clock next to the phone told Lapointe that it was just after two am.

'Just to be clear, could you please repeat that?' said Lapointe, instantly awake, and turned on the reading lamp. *'Mon Dieu!* When?'

'One of the officers relieving the first night shift just phoned it in,' said the duty officer.

'And both are dead?'

'Yes. Shot in the head, point blank. GIGN are on their way. The Prefect has already been notified. He wants you to take over.'

'Understood. I want a chopper to pick me up at home ASAP.'

'Consider it done, sir!'

This is a catastrophe, thought Lapointe, feeling quite ill. What he had just been told was every police officer's ultimate nightmare: two colleagues killed on duty, on his watch. He stood up and hurried to the bathroom. *At least GIGN are already on their way*, thought Lapointe. *They should get there before I do.* He washed his face and then went back into the bedroom to get dressed.

By the time the police helicopter landed on the lawn next to the Gatekeeper's Cottage, GIGN – the National Gendarmerie Intervention Group, an elite police tactical unit – had already secured the site and floodlights had been set up, illuminating the area in front of the cottage. The officer in charge walked over to the helicopter and reported to Lapointe.

'Forensics are on their way,' he said.

'What about the cottage?'

'Empty.'

Bracing himself, Lapointe asked the question that had been foremost on his mind since the phone call with the shocking news. 'You secured the chateau?'

'Of course—'

'And?' interrupted Lapointe.

The officer could see the worried look on Lapointe's face and therefore decided to proceed with caution.

'The front door was unlocked. We went inside and began to search the premises. The lights were on, but the house appeared empty ...'

My God! thought Lapointe, fearing the worst, but he didn't interrupt.

'Then we heard it.'

'Heard what?'

'Loud banging on a door. Downstairs in the cellar.'

'Get to the point, man!' Lapointe almost shouted.

'They were in the wine cellar. Locked in.'

'Who?'

'Six adults. Three women and three men.'

'Where are they now?'

'In the music room.'

'Thank you,' said Lapointe and slowly walked over to the police car with the shattered windscreen, preparing himself for what he knew would be a very traumatic scene.

Everyone looked up as Lapointe walked into the room. Without saying a word, Dupree stood up, walked to the sideboard and poured some Scotch into a glass. Then he walked over to Lapointe, handed him the glass and just stood there looking at him, his face ashen.

'What happened?' said Lapointe and took a sip.

Step by step, Dupree described the extraordinary events of the night, from the moment the two armed clowns had burst into the Gatekeeper's Cottage until had they locked everyone into the wine cellar two hours later, and left.

'Where are Jack and Landru?' asked Lapointe quietly. He lit his pipe and watched the aromatic smoke curl slowly towards the ceiling.

'They were taken away. No doubt in that black van I mentioned earlier.'

'This is unbelievable,' mumbled Lapointe, well aware of the huge problems he was facing as he tried to piece together the various parts of the brazen, yet extremely well-planned and executed crime. Two dead police officers and two high-profile individuals abducted, thought Lapointe, while under police protection. All hell would break loose in the morning. He knew they had better get ready for the media storm and a desperate Prefect under pressure.

'Is there anything else any of you can remember that could be relevant here? Please, this is very important. *Think*, while these events are still fresh in your minds. Even the smallest detail could be significant here.'

'There was something,' said Bartolli.

'Yes?' said Lapointe.

'Something the mysterious man who spoke to us, but never introduced or showed himself, said about one of the clowns.'

'What did he say?'

'He remarked that one of the clowns in the room was the last one to see Louis Mendoza alive.'

'What? The very first murder victim?'

'Yes. The clown even identified himself by raising his arm.'

'Was he suggesting that *he* was the murderer?'

'That was my impression.'

'That was also the way Landru saw it. He was visibly shocked,' interjected Dupree. 'I was standing next to him.'

'But that was thirty years ago,' observed Lapointe.

'Everything about this is bizarre,' said Bartolli. 'But in a strange way, it all fits. The man who spoke to us was in total control and in command of all the facts, right down to the last detail. As far as I'm concerned, he's our best candidate for a psychopath here, pulling all the strings. He ticks all the boxes.'

'We know that Spiridon 4 couldn't have committed the early murders,' said Lapointe. 'Those murders were well and truly before their time. The three Paris murders, maybe, but not the others.'

'I watched the two clowns very carefully,' continued Bartolli. 'One of them was definitely an older man, I'd say. His demeanour, the way he spoke, the way he moved, suggested that.'

Lapointe nodded, taking it all in. The case was becoming stranger by the minute. 'Anything else?' he said.

'Yes. This might explain why Jack and Landru were taken away,' said Dupree. 'The man in the shadows obviously has something quite specific in mind for them.'

'What are you talking about?' asked Lapointe.

'After he showed off his collection, the man referred to the Mascarino amulet and that piece of the mask we just found in the ruins. He said they belonged together because only once they had been united would they give up their secrets—'

'And he also said,' interrupted Darrieux, 'that Jack and Landru would help him achieve that. I think those were the exact words.'

'Correct,' said Bartolli. 'That's how I remember it as well. It follows that Jack and Landru will be used as some kind of pawns in this high-stakes game, and it all revolves around that lost Inca treasure. The man was obsessed with this subject and hardly spoke about anything else.'

'Is that it?' asked Lapointe.

'There was one more thing,' said Tristan quietly.

Everyone in the room turned and looked at Tristan, who until then hadn't said a word.

'Just before we were locked in the wine cellar and Jack and Landru were told to stay outside, Jack said something to me as I walked past him. I have no doubt that this is hugely significant. The expression on his face made that clear to me.'

'What did he say?' said Lapointe.

'Two things: "Irish stutter", and "Berchtesgaden".'

'What did he mean by that, do you think?'

'Well, the man who spoke to us definitely had an Irish accent and spoke with a slight stutter. It was barely noticeable, subtle, but it was definitely there.'

'And the second thing?'

'Berchtesgaden is a place in Bavaria that Jack knows well. He's been there several times, following up leads in connection with the lost Monet painting in 2008.'

'And this could be relevant?' said Lapointe.

'Must be.'

'Any ideas?'

'Not yet.'

What Tristan hadn't told Lapointe was that there was a third thing of importance. Throughout the strange video call, Tristan could sense something profoundly frightening. Something malevolent was reaching out from the distant past, threatening to engulf them all.

<h1 style="text-align:center">50</h1>

Florence: 8 November

'This changes everything,' said Grimaldi. 'Two police officers shot dead, and Jack and Landru abducted under the very noses of the French police. I thought something like this could only happen here in Mafia-polluted Italy. I was clearly wrong. This is a disaster! Lapointe must be going out of his mind!'

'We no longer have the luxury of time,' said Cesaria, who had been up since the phone call from Lapointe at three am that morning. 'And just as well, because the trial in Calabria is about to start in a few days. And we both know what that means—'

'The end of Omerta,' Grimaldi cut in, and lit one of his small cigars.

'Our best lead,' said Cesaria.

'First Lorenza and now this. Jack abducted! What a mess! We all know what that could mean. The violence just goes on and on. Poor Tristan,' said Grimaldi.

'But if we move quickly, Omerta could give us the answers we are all looking for,' continued Cesaria, 'and perhaps put a stop to all this. I've asked Clara to join us. She should be here any moment. She has made some truly astonishing progress during the night, as you will see. And what Lapointe told me this morning, could bring us even a step closer.'

'We could certainly do with some good news because so far, the villains appear to be winning.' Grimaldi opened the window behind his desk and looked down into the street, bustling with early morning traffic. 'I could kill for a coffee.'

'Should I ...?'

'No, thank you. Perhaps later. Let's hear what Clara has to tell us first.'

Moments later, Samartini swept into the room, her face flushed with excitement. 'Sorry I'm late,' she said and put a bundle of files on a chair next to Grimaldi's desk. 'I've been up all night, but I think it may have been worth it. My American contacts have been most helpful.'

'Enlighten us,' said Grimaldi.

Samartini pushed back her glasses, which were sitting on the tip of her nose as usual, and picked up one of the files. 'Do you mind?' she said and pointed to the whiteboard next to Grimaldi's desk.

'Go right ahead.'

Fastidious and methodical by nature, Samartini wanted to put everything she had to say into its proper context first, and the best way to do that was to begin at the beginning. 'A lot has happened since Cesaria and I met with Lapointe and the others at the Kuragin chateau on thirty-one October.'

Samartini picked up a felt pen and wrote *Kuragin chateau meeting, 31 October* in the top left-hand corner of the board. 'That was the day it was decided to use Landru as the "bait", as Lapointe put it, and Jack was asked to persuade Landru to go along with that. As we now know, he was successful, and in light of what happened earlier today, perhaps too much so.'

Samartini wrote down *Landru bait* in the middle of the board, and drew a line between the two notations. 'But what really gave us an unexpected breakthrough in our strategy, was the delivery of Landru's death mask with that encrypted phone number the next day. The mysterious puppeteer in the background pulling all the strings here made contact much sooner than we dared to hope. A line of communication between Landru and the suspected killer was opened.'

Samartini wrote down *Landru death mask delivery, 1 November* in the top right-hand corner with the word *contact,* underlined, after it. 'This triggered a chain of unexpected events, with remarkable consequences we didn't expect.'

'Please explain,' said Grimaldi, carefully watching Samartini.

'First, Cesaria and I decided to use Landru's recent release from jail to cause trouble among the dark net gamblers who had followed the Death Mask Murders for years, and flush out a reaction. We did this by contacting a number of them through Omerta, anonymously, of course. These were all high rollers Giordano had introduced to the game. Huge sums were wagered here—'

'We know all this,' Grimaldi cut in impatiently. He too had been up half the night and was irritable.

'Perhaps so, but you may not know what happened late yesterday,' said Cesaria, stepping in to assist Samartini, who was beginning to look a little flustered.

'Sorry. Tell me.'

'Instead of putting Alessandro under pressure, as we were hoping to do, quite the opposite happened. We know that since his father's arrest, he's been running the family business from his yacht in Monaco. He's desperately trying to prove himself and make some money.'

'What happened yesterday?' demanded Grimaldi.

'Another Death Mask Murders computer game appeared on the dark net called *The Final Showdown*. It's all about online betting, but of a very sophisticated, extremely violent, and highly illegal kind,' said Samartini. 'Because much of the violence is *real*.' Samartini paused, collecting her thoughts.

'We found it through Omerta and actually have access to this site,' continued Samartini. 'We can monitor everything that's going on right now, in real time. In essence, this is a unique online-betting site available to a closed group of privileged, very rich and very depraved individuals with deep pockets, looking for the ultimate thrill. The site has turned into an instant hit and, just like before, huge amounts are already being wagered on various scenarios and potential outcomes.'

'The encrypted site that was used previously has been reactivated, and that's very fortuitous,' said Cesaria. 'According to the Americans, who are looking into this as we speak, it is the same site that was used to post the Landru murder video sent to Lapointe. As you know, the Americans have been after this operation for years – especially in connection with illegal arms sales to terrorists – and they have tried in vain to shut it down.'

'And this could be helpful?' asked Grimaldi.

'It could; very,' replied Cesaria. 'Because something discovered in that video could make it possible to break the encryption and trace the source. And if that happens, the shield of the dark net may no longer provide anonymity and protection, and instead lead us to those hiding behind it.'

Grimaldi shook his head. 'Cyber warfare,' he said. 'I'm an old-fashioned cop. Out of my league, I'm afraid.'

'But not out of mine,' said Samartini. 'And that's not the end of the good news.'

'There's more?' said Grimaldi.

'Yes,' said Cesaria. 'According to Lapointe, just before Tristan and the others were locked in the wine cellar, Jack said something to Tristan. You know what Tristan's like; very perceptive to say the least, and there's a special bond between those two. If we are right about this, what Jack said could be hugely significant here. It was clearly an observation about what was going on at the time.'

'Oh? What did he say?'

'Three words,' said Samartini. She picked up the felt pen again, and wrote down *Irish stutter*, and *Berchtesgaden* at the bottom of the whiteboard, and drew a circle around the words.

'You speak in riddles,' said Grimaldi. 'Please elaborate.'

'How about I go down to your favourite trattoria,' said Cesaria, 'and bring up some coffee and a few pastries, and Clara can then tell us a little story over breakfast that will explain it all?'

'You're on. Let's do that,' said Grimaldi. 'I'm starving.'

'All right, guys,' said Grimaldi, devouring his second cornetto. 'Story time.'

Samartini put down her coffee and reached for one of her folders. 'This is all about the dark net, a mathematical genius, a computer whizz, and a hacker extraordinaire, all wrapped into one.'

Samartini held up her file. 'I received this just an hour ago from Washington.'

Grimaldi looked expectantly at Samartini.

'After the 1993 World Trade Centre bombing, the CIA collected intelligence around the world about hundreds of suspected black market arms dealers who could be supplying arms and explosives to potential terrorists. This was considered a promising line of enquiry for detecting – and reaching – terrorist cells.'

'Makes sense,' observed Grimaldi.

'Obviously, a number of operators stood out and warranted further investigation,' continued Samartini. 'That's when the Dark Net Bazaar first came to the attention of law enforcement agencies in various countries.'

Samartini looked at Grimaldi. 'Does the Dark Net Bazaar, or DNB, mean anything to you?'

'Should it?'

'I thought so. For years the DNB was an online, illegal marketplace where it was possible to buy just about anything imaginable, for a price. It was banned in most countries and pursued by law enforcement agencies around the globe, trying in vain to close it down. At first, the Americans were only interested in arms deals, but soon other, more sinister activities appeared on the site, like snuff movies, real-time murders, extreme pornography, and especially gambling. But what really focused their attention was a failed assassination attempt on the United States Ambassador to Israel that was linked to the DNB, because Mossad strongly suspected that the assassin had been sourced through the site, which had acted as a go-between, a broker—'

Grimaldi held up his hand. 'Fascinating, but where are you going with this?'

'It's relevant, trust me,' said Cesaria. 'This is only the background.'

Grimaldi shrugged.

'Because of this possible connection, the Americans began to dig deeper,' continued Samartini, 'until they came up with a name: Ronan

O'Hara, an Irishman suspected of being the man behind the DNB. Because the DNB operated on the dark web, it wasn't possible to pinpoint where the operation was actually located, but MI5 suspected it was somewhere in the UK. As it turned out, they were right and began to close in on a farmhouse in Cornwall. Unfortunately, by the time there was a raid, O'Hara had gone to ground and disappeared. After that, the Americans lost interest.'

Samartini reached for her coffee.

'Is that it?'

'No. In many ways this is just the beginning. I contacted MI5. They have a comprehensive dossier on O'Hara and, as it turns out, he's been on their radar for years, but has never been found.'

'Something puzzles me,' said Grimaldi, shaking his head.

'What's that?' asked Cesaria.

'How did you come up with O'Hara in the first place? And why do you think he could have something to do with what happened at the Kuragin chateau this morning?'

Smiling, Samartini stood up, walked over to the whiteboard and pointed to the three words at the bottom. 'Because of this: *Irish stutter*, and *Berchtesgaden*.'

'Go on.'

'Remember I told you that my American contact detected something embedded in the encryption of that video sent to Lapointe about the Landru murder?'

Grimaldi nodded.

'That something raised a red flag that pointed to the DNB. And when I told her about the Irish stutter and Berchtesgaden – a place in Bavaria – that Jack mentioned this morning, and this information was run through a supercomputer together with the encryption point from before, one name came up: Ronan O'Hara. Simple.'

'And you really think this could help us?' said Grimaldi.

'It's early days and we must dig deeper, but yes, we think it's definitely a lead worth pursuing,' said Cesaria.

'What makes you say that?'

'While O'Hara did go to ground and disappeared off the intelligence radar, the DNB never stopped operating. In fact, over the years it became stronger and more sophisticated, especially in online gambling of a very special kind, which is its trademark and a huge money-spinner. As I said before, law enforcement agencies around the world have tried in vain to shut it down. It is operating right now, and Omerta has taken us right to it, because the online gambling involving the Giordanos we mentioned earlier, is operated by the DNB.'

Grimaldi looked stunned. 'Wow! You have been busy. Well done, guys. So, where to from here?'

'I think Clara and I should go to London, talk to our contacts there, and have a close look at the MI5 dossier on O'Hara. It's our best lead by far. The French police will throw everything at this disaster and follow up forensic leads on the ground. They have the resources. This could be *our* contribution.'

Grimaldi nodded. 'Good idea. When do you want to do this?'

'I've booked an afternoon flight,' said Cesaria.

'Then you better go. There's obviously a lot to attend to before you can leave.'

'Quite,' said Cesaria. 'But there's one more thing ...'

'What?' asked Grimaldi.

'I would like to ask Tristan to come with us to London. You know what he's like, and how close he is to Jack. He can see things we can't. It's quite a gift. And let's not forget, he was right there in the chateau when it all happened. What do you think?'

'*Do it!* We need all the help we can get in this.'

Cesaria made eye contact with Samartini. 'I better call him then,' she said.

'You do that,' said Grimaldi, lighting another one of his small cigars. 'And besides, we owe him. Lorenza, remember ...?'

51

In the salt mines near Berchtesgaden: 8 November

Heavily sedated and strapped to a storage frame in the back of the van, Jack had been in a comatose state throughout the entire ten-hour trip from Paris to Berchtesgaden. Taking turns at the wheel and using back roads wherever possible, Dragan and Petrinko had driven the eight hundred kilometres non-stop. By the time Lapointe arrived at the Kuragin chateau just after three am, the van had already covered more than half the distance.

Excellent, thought O'Hara. He adjusted his computer screen as he watched the black van being backed into a barn on CCTV. The barn was part of an old farmhouse he owned at the foot of the mountain, not far from the entrance to the famous Berchtesgaden salt mines, a popular tourist attraction just outside the township.

The reason O'Hara had bought the property was not because of its lush meadows, but because of something far more practical: access to an abandoned, labyrinthine section of the old salt mines under the house, where he kept the most sensitive parts of his dark net server. It was a secure, stable, underground environment where the temperature never varied and unwelcome intruders never ventured because no-one really knew that this section of the mine existed.

O'Hara picked up his mobile and called Petrinko.

'Well done,' said O'Hara. 'This will be your home for the time being. You will find everything you need inside the house. My men will take care of things from here. The van will disappear, and Rogan and Landru are no longer your responsibility.'

'What would you like us to do next? Anything?' asked Petrinko.

'Yes, of course. I have an important assignment for you.'

'When?'

'Soon.'

'And Dragan?'

'He's needed here. Just like you. A bonus has already been paid into your bank accounts.'

The first thing Jack could feel as he drifted back into consciousness was a sore neck, and a splitting headache that made him feel nauseous. He was lying on his back on something hard and uncomfortable. As he tried to move his legs, they wouldn't obey, neither did his arms or his numb fingers. Taking a deep breath, Jack opened his eyes. At first, all he could see were little white stars dancing in front of his eyes, which made his headache even worse. He quickly closed his eyes, hoping the stars would go away and ease the pain.

Where am I? he wondered, trying hard to remember what happened. The last thing Jack could recall was sitting in a van with his hands tied behind his back, unable to move. A smiling clown was kneeling on the floor next to him, holding what looked like a hypodermic needle in his right hand. After that, everything had gone blank.

Slowly, Jack opened his eyes again. The stars had disappeared and he found himself staring at rocks melting out of the darkness. Rocks were everywhere. The ceiling, the walls, everywhere. *A cave. I'm in a cave,* thought Jack as his eyes began to focus and follow a dim shaft of light coming from somewhere on his right. Jack turned his head and gasped. At first he thought his eyes must be playing tricks on him, because the sparkling water all around him looked surreal. Illuminated by a green light, the clear water looked like a mirror reflecting the rocks, and the water seemed to almost touch the low ceiling pressing down from above, with glistening droplets of moisture clinging to the rocks like eyes of demons, watching. But most sinister of all was the total silence.

As Jack tried to prop himself up on his elbows, the ground below him began to move, rocking gently from side to side, and the rock walls around him began to glide slowly past. After several attempts, Jack managed to sit up and look around. *I'm adrift* he thought, *in the middle of a lake inside a cave. How weird. Or perhaps I'm just dreaming?* Exhausted, Jack closed his eyes again as his elbows gave way and he fell backwards, making the narrow wooden raft he was lying on rock alarmingly from side to side.

Suddenly, sublime piano music parted the silence and began to drift across the still waters. Softly at first, but soon becoming stronger until music filled the whole chamber. *Chopin,* thought Jack, recognising the familiar bars of a famous nocturne – one of his mother's favourites – *how bizarre.*

After some crackling, the music receded and a voice echoed through the chamber. 'Do you like Chopin, Mr Rogan?' said the voice. 'So serene, don't you think? Just like this place.'

Jack opened his eyes, sat up and looked around. It was obvious that the voice was coming from concealed speakers and not directly from a person. *Same voice,* thought Jack as he recognised the Irish accent with a slight stutter, almost hidden behind the Gaelic intonation.

'And in case you're wondering where you are,' continued the voice, 'you are in an abandoned salt mine, and what you can see all around you isn't just water, but brine. Water with a very high salt content. If you were to drop a coin into it, the coin wouldn't sink to the bottom, but float. Salt has been mined here since the twelfth century, and this chamber here has been in use for a very long time. Its very size speaks for itself.'

'Fascinating,' said Jack, 'but I'm sure you haven't brought me here for a lesson in salt mining.'

Appreciating the humour, O'Hara began to chuckle. 'No, of course not. What I have in mind for you is something far more interesting: a *demonstration.* The salt in this mine was extracted through a method called wet-mining. Fresh water was pumped into chambers like this, which, of course, were much smaller in the beginning; no bigger than a small room. The rocks here have a high salt content and the fresh water removes the salt from the composite rock by dissolving it. That's how brine is created, which is then pumped out of the mine to a processing plant. Over the years, this chamber was enlarged by pumping more and more fresh water into it to allow more salt to be dissolved. The non-soluble material sank to the bottom. You can see it clearly down there if you look carefully. It would have taken many years to create a chamber of this size. As you can see, it's almost as big as a football field, deep inside a mountain. Amazing, isn't it?'

'What kind of demonstration?' asked Jack.

'Well, we will do exactly what was done by the miners in the past: pump more fresh water into this chamber. All the pipes are still in working order, and I have a very powerful pump we can use. We could fill this entire chamber right up to the ceiling within hours.'

Jack didn't like the direction the conversation was taking. 'And this demonstration would have a specific purpose, I suppose?' he asked.

'Definitely! You haven't been paying attention. I've already told you what it is.'

'Remind me.'

'You will help me complete my collection. The Mascarino amulet and the burial mask you found in Malenkova's house belong together. The amulet showed us the way to Heart Island, and the burial mask will show us the way to the wreck.'

'And how exactly will I help you with that?'

'I'm sure a smart man like you would have worked that out by now. I will keep pumping water into this chamber until Chief Inspector Lapointe returns to me what is mine. If he doesn't, well, we both know what could happen, don't we?'

'Where's Landru?' said Jack, changing the subject. He needed some time to consider his predicament.

'In a similar chamber nearby, but you shouldn't concern yourself with that. For him, I have something a little different in mind. To see him slowly drown in brine inside a claustrophobic underground cave like this wouldn't have quite the same persuasive impact – especially with the red-faced French authorities – as seeing you, an international celebrity, share the same fate. Here, in this place, all by yourself. And see it all they shall,' added O'Hara, laughing.

'What do you mean?'

'Everything that happens in here is on CCTV, and can easily be transmitted.'

'Like the Landru murder?'

'Yes. Just like that.'

'My life in exchange for the mask, is that it?'

'Very good, bravo.'

'Lapointe will never do this. You can't blackmail the French Republic.'

'We'll see. For your sake, Mr Rogan, I hope you're wrong. And one more thing: if you look carefully, you will notice that the brine is already slowly rising. Tick, tick, tick.'

As the voice trailed off, Chopin's haunting nocturne returned, echoing eerily through the chamber like some distant promise of hope and beauty, and a better place.

52

Thames House, MI5 HQ, London: 8 November

Tristan caught the afternoon Eurostar from Paris to London and met Cesaria and Samartini at Thames House, the MI5 headquarters. He paid the taxi driver and waved to Cesaria, who stood next to Samartini in front of the imposing entrance to the famous 'haunt of spooks' as it was known in the trade in Europe, which had featured in countless novels, TV series and movies.

'Just in time. Our appointment is at five,' said Cesaria, pointing to her watch.

'How did you manage to pull this off?' asked Tristan.

Cesaria shrugged. 'Phone calls in high places. This case has gone right to the top, not only in France, but also in Italy.'

'Then let's see what we can find out here, because so far, we certainly haven't got much to go on, have we?'

'Three words, that's all,' said Samartini and linked arms with Tristan. She thought he looked tired and dejected, which wasn't surprising in the circumstances. 'Let's see where they take us.'

'This is all about what Jack said just before—'

'Yes, our best lead so far,' interjected Cesaria, anxious to make her way through security, which always took longer than expected. She hated to be late, especially to a meeting that had taken so much string-pulling to arrange.

The meeting with the junior officer who met them on the first floor went badly from the very start. It was obvious he knew very little about the matter, and considered the whole thing a hastily arranged nuisance to placate two excited police officers from somewhere in Italy about a case that had been closed a long time ago.

Cesaria was becoming increasingly frustrated with the lack of cooperation from the haughty officer with an annoyingly patronising manner, who brushed her questions aside and kept looking at his watch. Tristan, who had been following the exchange without stepping in, turned to Cesaria.

'I think we're done here, don't you think?' he said quietly.

'What do you mean? But—'

Realising that Cesaria's fiery Italian temperament was about to get the better of her, Tristan held up his hand. 'There's another way, trust me.'

'I agree,' said Samartini, who could see where this was heading. Limping cooperation that could only end one way: a heated confrontation and storming out of the meeting, which would achieve nothing except suiting the aggravating little man just fine. Taking a deep breath, Cesaria began to calm down. 'You're right,' she said and stood up.

Tristan stood up as well. 'May I suggest you keep the files on your desk for now,' he said, addressing the smirking officer.

'And why should I do that?' said the man.

'Because it will save you having to get them out of storage again when your superiors ask for the files, which I expect will be quite soon. Thank you so much for your help.'

With that, Tristan turned around and headed for the door, followed by Cesaria and Samartini.

Cesaria caught up with Tristan in the foyer. 'What was that all about?' she said.

Tristan pulled his mobile out of his pocket. 'Phone call first, explanation later.'

Cesaria turned to Samartini standing next to her. 'What's he up to, do you think?'

'We'll find out soon enough.'

Tristan finished the phone call and slipped the mobile back into his pocket. 'There's a nice little Italian restaurant not far from here. Let's have an early dinner; what do you think, guys? I'm starving.'

'Have you noticed? He sounds more and more like Jack,' said Samartini, shaking her head.

'Another incorrigible rascal in the making? Is that what you're saying?' said Cesaria.

'I hope not. One's enough, don't you think?'

'I heard that,' said Tristan cheerfully. 'You'll thank me later, you'll see.'

'You're obviously up to something,' said Cesaria. 'But an early dinner is a good idea. Our flight back to Florence isn't until ten-thirty tonight. At least that way, it wasn't all a complete waste of time.'

'A lot can happen between now and then,' said Tristan, smiling.

'We'll see. Now, where's this Italian restaurant of yours?' asked Cesaria. 'Let's get out of this depressing place.'

Sir Charles Huntley walked into the restaurant just after seven-thirty pm. Impeccably dressed in a dark-blue pinstriped suit, white shirt and bow tie, he looked every part the prominent London lawyer he was. 'Ah, there you are,' he said and waved to Tristan in the back of the crowded room. 'I came as soon as I could.'

'This is Sir Charles Huntley,' said Tristan, making the introductions. 'Isis's personal lawyer and a good friend. Jack has worked with Sir Charles on a number of matters in the past.'

Cesaria looked stunned.

'The Stolzfus case earlier this year was one of them,' added Sir Charles. He looked at Cesaria and Samartini sitting opposite. 'You were both involved in that case, weren't you, Chief Superintendent?' he said breezily.

Cesaria nodded, wondering where all this was going.

'A glass of wine, perhaps?' suggested Tristan.

'Yes, please. We just have time before the meeting.'

'What meeting?' asked Cesaria.

'A senior agent at MI5 who has been assigned to assist in this matter will meet us in half an hour. I play bridge with his boss every Thursday.'

Tristan turned to Samartini. 'Jack has many friends here in London.'

Samartini pushed back her glasses, which had once again slipped down her nose, and looked at Tristan. 'I can see that.'

Daniel Cross was impatiently pacing up and down in his office, fuming. 'What a stuff-up!' he said to his assistant, the surly young man who had been so rude and condescending to Cesaria before. '*How could you?*'

The phone call from his boss couldn't have come at a worse time, just as Cross was about to sit down to dinner in his club, to impress his boyfriend. To be ordered back to work to clean up the mess created by his assistant was not only annoying, but also humiliating. And on top of all that, to find that the complaint had come from none other than Sir Charles Huntley – an old adversary – was rubbing salt into a wound that had been festering for a long time. The only good news in the fiasco was that the urgent inquiry concerned Jack Rogan, who seemed to be in some kind of trouble. Jack had caused Cross a lot of heartache over the years, which had almost cost him his job.

'Have you got the files?' demanded Cross, trying to compose himself.

'Yes. On your desk.'

'All of them?'

'I think so.'

'You *think* so? You are not paid to think, but to do as I tell you. Clear?'

'Yes.'

'Now, bring them in and try to be civil. This is a repair job in damage control. Your future depends on it. Do I make myself clear?'

'Yes.'

'Please accept my apologies,' said Cross trying to appear cooperative, but gritting his teeth underneath. 'My assistant clearly misunderstood the instructions I gave before I left. There was little time ...'

'No matter,' said Sir Charles, enjoying Cross's discomfort. Ignoring the fidgeting assistant who stood demurely behind Cross, he made the introductions.

'Two dead police officers and two abductions,' said Cross, trying to shift the attention away from his previous failure to give the matter his personal attention it had evidently warranted. 'I understand Mr Rogan is in a spot of bother,' continued Cross, unable to resist referring to Jack's predicament. 'This is serious. How can we be of assistance?'

Sir Charles looked at Cesaria and nodded. 'Chief Superintendent?'

'This is all about the Dark Net Bazaar and the man suspected to be behind it.'

'That old chestnut,' scoffed Cross and lit a cigarette. 'The Americans have been trying to shut down the DNB for years, but like a hydra, it keeps popping up in unexpected places with new heads from time to time.'

'Well, it looks like one of those heads has just popped up again. But it seems to be an old one: Ronan O'Hara.'

'Seriously? After all these years? He's still around, you think?'

'We believe so.'

Cross shook his head. 'If you're right, he must be well into his seventies by now.'

'Evil has no age limit.'

'True. What makes you think that O'Hara could somehow be involved in this matter of yours?'

Cesaria decided not to tell Cross that everything hinged on just three words that Jack had uttered before his abduction. 'It's complicated,' she said instead.

'I see.' Complicated was intelligence speak for *I cannot tell you; don't ask me again.* 'So, what would you like to know?'

'We understand that you have a comprehensive dossier on O'Hara. Left over from that unsuccessful raid in Cornwall thirty or so years ago. Just before he went to ground and disappeared.'

Cross pointed to the files on his desk. 'This is it right here,' he said. 'We did a lot of work on O'Hara at the time. We reconstructed his life from the very beginning. You know how these matters work. It's all about detail. To expose and catch someone like this, it's somehow always the little things that count.'

'Quite. And it's precisely those little things we're after. They could make all the difference here, especially when linked to those complicated matters I mentioned earlier.'

'I see,' said Cross and opened the file in front of him. 'In that case, let me tell you what we know about O'Hara and what we believed at the time made him tick, and why.'

Samartini opened her notebook, pushed her glasses back up, and looked expectantly at Cross.

They walked out of Cross's office two hours later. 'I can't thank you enough, Sir Charles,' said Cesaria as they left the building.

'Don't mention it. When Jack's involved, we leave no stone unturned. Isis owes him a lot ...'

'I understand.' Cesaria looked at her watch. 'Here goes our flight,' she said.

'No matter. He should be here any moment,' said Sir Charles.

'Who?' asked Cesaria, looking puzzled.

'Boris. Isis's driver. Look, here he comes now.' Sir Charles pointed to a black Bentley pulling up at the kerb. The car stopped and a big man got out.

'*Boris!*' said Tristan. He walked over to the big man and gave him a hug.

Cesaria turned to Samartini standing next to her. 'Can you believe this?' she said, shaking her head.

'Come on, guys, get in,' said Tristan.

'Where are we going?' asked Cesaria.

'To meet someone special who will help us find Jack.'

53

Time Machine Studios, London: 8 November

The Bentley turned into the underground garage of the Time Machine Studios, a large converted warehouse complex on the banks of the Thames, and stopped in front of the lifts where Lola, Isis's PA and personal pilot, was waiting. Tristan got out of the car first, walked over to Lola and embraced her.

'I am so sorry,' said Lola, barely able to speak. 'Isis and I were devastated when we heard about Lorenza. Jack called, and it was all over the news here. Horrible!'

'I still have to come to terms with it all. One way to do that is to find those responsible. That's why we are here, Lola. We need your help.'

'Understood. Isis is waiting upstairs.'

'This is a bit like a dream,' said Samartini as the glass lift emerged out of the garage into the open, and travelled up the side of the building to Isis's penthouse on the top floor. The view over the Thames, Tower Bridge and the Tower of London lit up in the distance, was breathtaking.

Sir Charles turned to Cesaria standing next to him. 'You haven't been here before, have you?'

'No, but Jack has told me a lot about Isis and her fabulous residence.'

'You're in for a big surprise. Ah, here we are,' said Sir Charles as the lift doors opened.

Dressed in a tight-fitting leopard-print bodysuit by Valentino that accentuated the carefully nurtured hourglass-figure of the ageing rock star, Isis looked like a fashion model on a photo shoot. The large stone Buddha next to the lift – Jack's favourite – and the Māori war canoe suspended from above could have been the setting for a cover of *Vogue*. As soon as Tristan stepped out of the lift, Isis held out her arms. Tristan walked over to her.

'I know all about loss,' whispered Isis, holding Tristan tight. 'I know how it feels.'

'I know you do. Lorenza's gone. We cannot change that, but Jack is still very much alive, for now. I don't think I could bear it if I were to lose him too.'

'That serious? Have you seen something?'

'Yes. We haven't got much time.'

'Then let's not waste any. How did you go at MI5?'

'I'll tell you, but first let me introduce you to Cesaria and Clara.'

'Jack's Italian friends from the Squadra Mobile in Florence whom I've heard so much about?' said Isis in perfect Italian. *Benvenuta.*' Isis let go of Tristan, turned to Cesaria and extended her hand. 'Would you like to go to your rooms first, or shall we have a glass of champagne?'

'I don't understand,' said Cesaria, looking a little confused.

'You are staying the night, of course. Too late to return to Florence. And besides, I want to hear everything about your MI5 meeting.'

Sir Charles sat back in the comfortable leather chair facing the floor-to-ceiling window, and looked wistfully at the river below.

'So, what did you manage to find out?' asked Isis.

'Cross was his usual arrogant self, but he had to eat humble pie because his assistant stuffed up—'

'You ended up with Cross again?' interjected Isis, shaking her head. 'He keeps popping up every time we have some business with MI5.'

'It's weird, I know. I'm persona non grata as far as he's concerned, and he absolutely detests Jack, and you aren't far behind.'

'Not surprising,' said Isis. She turned towards Cesaria sitting to her right. 'After my parents were killed in 2011, Charles, Jack and I had, let's call it a "robust" disagreement with Daniel Cross that almost cost him his job. Not surprisingly, he's never forgotten that. And then earlier this year, he popped up again in the Stolzfus matter and ended up with egg on his face. No wonder we are not popular!'

'That to one side,' continued Sir Charles, 'he did give us access to the MI5 files on O'Hara – reluctantly – and provided the information we were looking for.'

'Was it helpful?'

'I think so,' said Tristan, stepping in. 'But not for what was actually in the file as such, except for one obscure piece of information.'

'Care to elaborate?' said Isis.

'In a moment, but before I do, you need to get a picture of O'Hara as he was thirty years ago. Clara, would you mind telling us your take on O'Hara?'

'Certainly.' Samartini reached for her notebook and opened it. 'MI5 has done an excellent job digging into the background of this fascinating man, very thorough. Pity they didn't pursue it all later. Ronan O'Hara was one of those abandoned and abused children living in one of those dreadful "unmarried mother and child" homes run by the Catholic Church that were active during the 1950s in Ireland. They were just recently in the news again about some old scandal. Single mothers used to give birth in those homes, where child mortality and abuse were scandalously high, and no-one seems to have cared or did anything about it.'

'The boy had a dreadful childhood and grew up in one of those homes in Cork,' said Sir Charles. 'Abandoned by his mother, his father unknown.'

'Apparently, he had an unfortunate disability: a terrible stutter,' said Tristan. 'Please keep this in mind, because it is important.'

'However, he also had an extraordinary gift,' said Cesaria. 'Numbers. His astonishing mathematical abilities at an early age brought him to the attention of a local priest, who took the boy under his wing and gave him access to books like *Liber Abaci* by Fibonacci, which was the most influential mathematical work in Europe for over three centuries. O'Hara was reading sophisticated textbooks on complex mathematics and was capable of mathematical feats that astonished everyone who came into contact with the stuttering teenager, who could express himself better through numbers and complex equations than words.'

'At seventeen, the boy left the home. He ran away and somehow made it to London, where he fell in with a bad crowd and became part of the London criminal underworld,' said Samartini. 'He had a nickname, "Tartaglia", which means stammerer in Italian. However, this nickname was in fact a compliment because O'Hara was named after Niccolo Tartaglia, one of the most illustrious mathematicians of the sixteenth century.'

'Quite so,' said Cesaria. 'And Tartaglia is best known today for the Cardano–Tartaglia formula for solving cubic equations, which O'Hara used in ingenious ways in connection with the World Wide Web.'

'For almost two decades, he disappeared. No criminal record of any kind, nothing,' said Sir Charles. 'Until he came to the attention of the authorities in an unexpected way.'

'How?' asked Isis, fascinated.

'This was in the early 1980s,' continued Sir Charles. 'By now, O'Hara was doing research for CERN – the European Organization for Nuclear Research – in Switzerland, which resulted in the establishment of the World Wide Web, linking hypertext documents into a complex information system and making it accessible to the entire network. This was a revolutionary breakthrough that would soon change the way the world communicated.'

'How did he come to the attention of the authorities?' asked Isis.

'O'Hara left CERN and took valuable, confidential research material belonging to his employer with him, and disappeared.'

'What, he *stole* it?' said Isis.

'Yes,' said Cesaria. 'And that's where the matter rested, until years later, when he came to the attention of the authorities again – this time the Americans, FBI – in connection with illegal activities on the dark net, which was just emerging.'

'Fascinating,' said Isis. 'How did this end up with MI5?'

'The Americans traced the illegal activities on the dark net to Great Britain, and asked MI5 for help,' said Samartini. 'This was in the early '90s. By now, the Dark Net Bazaar – which was forerunner to the infamous Silk Road, a drug bazaar – was fully operational, and represented a serious headache for law enforcement authorities around the world.'

'The Silk Road website was shut down in 2013 by the FBI,' said Cesaria. 'And its founder, Ross Ulbricht, who operated the site under the pseudonym "Dread Pirate Roberts" was arrested on several charges, and convicted and sentenced to life in prison without parole. More than one billion dollars in bitcoin connected to Silk Road was seized.'

'Unfortunately, MI5 was not as successful pursuing the DNB in the '90s,' said Sir Charles. 'They traced the criminal online activities on the dark net to a farm in Cornwall. By the time they raided the farm, O'Hara had gone to ground and has never been found.'

'Perhaps until now,' said Tristan quietly.

'What do you mean?' asked Cesaria, looking at Tristan in surprise.

'It's all about that obscure piece of information I mentioned earlier.'

'What about it?' asked Sir Charles.

Tristan turned to face Isis. 'You still have that letter Jack received as a boy from Brother Francis in Australia that led to the discovery of the lost Monet, don't you?'

Isis looked at Tristan, perplexed. '*Little Sparrow in the Garden?* Sure, it's part of the Francis diary that came with the purchase at the auction.'

'Is it here?'

'Yes, of course. It's upstairs in my study, with the painting.'

'Could we see it?'

'Sure, but why?'

'I'll tell you later.'

'All right. Give me a moment. I'll go and get it.'

Isis stood up and walked over to the lift.

'You are a dark horse, Tristan,' said Cesaria. 'What did you discover during our session at MI5?'

'A name.'

'What name?' asked Sir Charles.

Tristan shook his head.

'Perhaps the angels whispered something in your ear?' teased Samartini.

'Perhaps. Let's wait until Isis comes back and see. But what we can do while we wait is talk about that name. Clara, can you remember what Cross told us about that further investigation into O'Hara's childhood and background after O'Hara went to ground and they tried to find him?'

Samartini looked at her notes. 'Yes. They managed to trace his parents. Apparently, his mother was Kate O'Hara, a young domestic servant who worked on a farm in Cork. She was a single mother when—'

'And the father?' interrupted Tristan.

'MI5 concluded that the father was a German Nazi officer who came to Ireland to disappear after the war. It was a good place to hide, especially when the resourceful Catholic Church helped. He was working on that farm as a labourer.'

'And do you remember his name?'

'Yes. I made a note of it here ...'

'Don't tell us,' said Tristan. 'Let's wait until Isis gets back, all right?'

'Fine,' said Samartini and closed her notebook.

'This is almost turning into a whodunnit worthy of Agatha Christie,' said Sir Charles, looking bemused.

'If I'm right,' said Tristan, 'it will be better than that. Why? Because this is *real*, not fiction.'

Moments later Isis stepped out of the lift, carrying a small book.

'This is Father Francis's diary, which was part of the Monet auction sale.' Isis held up the book.

'And Jack's letter I mentioned earlier is part of it?'

Isis opened the little book and took out a piece of paper. 'Yes, it's right here.'

'As I remember it,' said Tristan, speaking softly, 'the letter has some quite specific instruction on the back about a grave in a cemetery in Berchtesgaden; isn't that right?'

'Yes. Jack went there in 2008, found the grave and located this diary, which was hidden under the headstone.'

'Hm. Can you please tell us the name identifying the grave?'

'Sure. Berghofer.'

'Clara, could you please tell us the name you've written down?'

Samartini opened her notebook, her hand shaking, and stared at the page. *'Berghofer,'* she whispered after a while, and closed the notebook.

54

Isis's Penthouse, London: 9 November

Cesaria tiptoed into Tristan's room, which was next to hers, and sat down on the edge of his bed. It was just after three-thirty am. Gently, she put her hand on Tristan's shoulder, trying to wake him.

'I could feel you come in,' said Tristan. Instantly awake, he opened his eyes, reached for the bedside lamp and turned on the light. 'You look troubled. What's wrong?'

'This just came in. It's from Lapointe.' Cesaria pressed play on her iPad and and turned the screen towards Tristan.

'Jesus!'

Tristan peered at the screen. 'Play it again.'

The short video lasted for less than twenty seconds. The first scene looked like something out of *The Phantom of the Opera*. A still, mysterious lake inside what looked like a cave lit up by a ghostly green light appeared. Then the camera zoomed in on something at the far end of the lake, melting out of the darkness. A shape emerged, hazy at first, but becoming clearer as the camera moved closer.

A man was standing in the water, which reached up to his chest. The top of his head was only centimetres away from the rock ceiling. He had what looked like an iron collar around his neck, which seemed to be attached to the rock wall behind him. A heavy-looking chain was wound around his chest, pinning his arms to his body. At first it was impossible to see the man's face in the semi-darkness. Then a shaft of light appeared, illuminating the face. It was Jack.

Moments later, a voice: 'You have something that belongs to me, Chief Superintendent. I'm sure you know what it is. I want it. The water in this ancient chamber is slowly rising. Soon it will reach the ceiling. If you follow my instructions, it will stop and Mr Rogan will live. If you fail ... you know the answer. Your choice. More soon.' Then the voice trailed off, and the screen went blank.

'It's the same voice,' said Tristan. 'Irish accent with a slight stutter.'

'Are you sure?'

'Yes. Have you spoken to Lapointe?'

'I have.'

'What did he say?'

'Not surprisingly, he was shocked. This case is unsettling him. Like last time, this video was sent to his private email address. Scary, don't you think? He forwarded the video to the Prefect and is waiting for instructions. He's probably talking to him right now. This is crazy.'

'Hm.'

'You don't look surprised, Tristan. How come?'

'It all makes sense now.'

'What makes sense?'

'Just before I went to sleep, a strange feeling came over me. I could hear Jack's voice. At first I couldn't understand what he was saying, but then one word became clear and he repeated it over and over.'

'What word?' asked Cesaria.

'*Berchtesgaden*. But that wasn't all.'

'What do you mean?'

'I also *saw* something.'

'What did you see?'

'Something similar to what we saw in the video just now. Jack was standing in water. It came up to his chin and was rising quickly. Just before it reached his mouth he said something else.'

'What did he say?'

'Another word. Over and over.'

'What word?'

'Salt.'

'*Salt?* What's the significance of this, do you think?'

'Not sure.'

'What happened then?'

Tristan looked at Cesaria, pain clouding his eyes. 'He drowned,' he said quietly.

'What does it all mean?'

'Jack's sending me a message. This has happened before, in moments of extreme danger.'

'What kind of message?'

'Unless we do something and act quickly, he will die.'

Cesaria shook her head. 'What are we going to do?'

'I'll wake Lola. I know where her room is. We haven't much time.'

'What are we going to do?' repeated Cesaria, urgency in her voice.

'Not sure yet, but I have an idea,' said Tristan and got out of bed.

Lola had made some tea. 'Isis won't be long,' she said.

Everyone sat in the lounge, surrounded by Isis's eclectic art collection, waiting, the mood subdued. Sir Charles had gone home just before midnight and the rest of the staff hadn't arrived yet. Apart from Boris, who had his quarters on the ground floor, and two security guards on duty, the building was empty. The kitchen was closed. After Cesaria had woken Samartini in the early hours to show her the video, Samartini had promptly booked the first flight back to Florence and Boris had driven her to Gatwick at dawn.

Dressed in a stunning, embroidered vintage dressing gown once worn by Marlene Dietrich in a Berlin nightclub, Isis stepped out of her apartment on the top floor, and after stopping briefly on the landing, came walking slowly down the glass stairs leading into the open-plan lounge below.

Cesaria looked at Lola and raised an eyebrow.

'Give her time,' said Lola. 'She's not used to getting up this early. Interrupted beauty sleep ... early mornings aren't easy for megastars. But an entry, is an entry!'

Smiling, Cesaria nodded, appreciating a little welcome levity.

Looking pale without make-up – and older – her usually impeccably coiffured hair not quite as stylish, Isis walked over to the antique sideboard and poured herself a cup of tea.

'Lola showed me the video,' she said. 'This is dreadful. Where to from here?'

Tristan stood up, walked over to Isis who was sitting by herself on a couch, and sat down next to her. Then he reached for her hand and looked at her.

'Over the years, you and Lola have become part of Jack's life – mine too – and shared some extraordinary escapades and adventures with him. Remember Alistair Macbeth of Blackburn Pharmaceuticals, with its deadly medical experiments in Somalia?'

'That despicable man with his dark and deep desires?'

'Jack and I almost got killed on his ship before it sank and took that monster down with it into the deep. Lola came to our rescue and brought us back here to safety,' said Tristan. 'On your private jet.'

'While I was recovering in a Boston hospital.'

'Under the care of the enigmatic Dr Greenberg.'

'The medical genius who operated on my brain tumour and went where no other surgeon dared to go, and saved my life.'

'The same doctor who also helped Professor Stolzfus, after you and Lola came to Jack's rescue in Colombia, remember?'

'Ah, that concert in Bogota with the glass coffin.'

'Which helped us smuggle Jack's mother out of the country.'

'You're right, we've been through a lot,' said Isis, becoming emotional. 'But you know what? I wouldn't have missed any of it for the world. In a way, your friendship and being included in these adventures have helped me cope with ...'

Lola stood up and walked over to Isis. 'Would you like another cup?' she said, holding out her hand. She saw that Isis was drifting into a dark space, and tried to change the subject.

Isis looked at her and smiled.

'I was going to say mortality, and no longer being able to perform, which to a flamboyant exhibitionist like me who craves the limelight, is actually worse than death. Yes, thank you, Lola, I'll have another cup.'

Wow! That was honest, thought Tristan. 'I'll have one too, if I may,' he said. He let go if Isis's hand and then looked at Lola. 'You and Isis are two of my closest friends. You and Jack are part of my family.

You *are* my family. We have a special bond and all of us here believe in destiny. I believe what we are facing here, right now, is a moment of destiny, just like last night when we discovered that name on the headstone in Berchtesgaden—'

'Berghofer?' interjected Samartini.

'Yes. These are Jack's breadcrumbs he always talks about. The Monet auction in 2012, the discovery of Brother Francis's diary in the cemetery that showed us the way to the Imperial Crypt in Vienna, are all good examples. All we have to do now is *listen* and we'll find those breadcrumbs that will lead us to Jack. I'm convinced of it. Jack needs us. Right now. Without our help he'll die.'

'What makes you so sure?' asked Cesaria.

'I'm sure because we are dealing here with something I've never come across before. Something I've never *felt* before. Not in connection with Macbeth nor Malenkova. Not with that crooked Russian billionaire Sokolov, nor all the Mafiosi in Florence with their hired assassins. Not even Anielka, who almost killed Jack in Russia, comes close, neither does Lorenza's assassination that was meant for me,' added Tristan, the sadness in his voice palpable.

'Can you explain?' said Isis.

'The reason Jack's in such great danger is because we are dealing with something profoundly frightening – terrifying. Something without any moral compass whatsoever.'

'What are you talking about?' said Cesaria.

'True evil.'

'You obviously have something in mind,' said Isis, changing direction.

'Yes, and it involves all of us here.'

'Are you going to tell us?'

'Yes. Our most pressing problem is time. We have to act very quickly. I believe the last two words Jack uttered hold the key here.'

'Berchtesgaden and salt?' said Cesaria.

'Yes. And let's not forget that name on the headstone.'

'Berghofer? Why?' asked Isis.

'Because it could show us the way.'

'The way to where?' asked Cesaria.

'To Jack.'

'How exactly?'

Tristan held up his hand. 'One crumb at a time. Salzburg is the closest airport.'

'Closest to ...?' asked Lola.

'Berchtesgaden. Could we use *Pegasus*?'

'No problem,' said Isis. She pointed to Lola, a sparkle in her eyes. 'Get the plane ready.'

Lola stood up. 'Just like the good old days on tour, eh? I'll call the airport.'

Cesaria shook her head. 'You wouldn't perhaps be interested in joining the Squadra Mobile, would you?'

'We are strictly freelance, sorry,' said Tristan, smiling. 'And besides, as you can see, our methods aren't exactly by the book.'

'All right, Tristan,' said Isis. 'Show us the way, but first I need a hot shower and my hair done! Come, Lola. Let's get ready.'

55

Berchtesgaden: 9 November

Dr Gruber watched the sleek jet taxi along the runway and then turn into a designated spot reserved for visiting private aircraft. Gruber turned to the mayor of Berchtesgaden standing next to him.

'Isis was the mystery buyer of that painting we found in the Imperial Crypt in Vienna a few years ago, which made headlines around the world, remember? She paid millions for it and Professor Krakowski, the owner of the painting, donated all of it to charity. You do know who Isis is, don't you?'

'Of course. The billionaire celebrity rock star.'

'Exactly. It is vital that we provide every possible assistance we can, regardless of what it is.'

'I understand. I have one of our best local historians standing by. She will meet us at the cemetery as you requested.'

If the mayor thought that the entire matter was weird and over the top, he certainly didn't show it. When someone as influential as Oberregierungsrat Dr Otto Gruber from Vienna asked for a favour, you obliged. Careers depended on it.

'Excellent,' said Gruber, pleased. 'Here they come now.'

'That's him over there,' said Tristan and waved. 'The little man with the hat and the overcoat.'

'You go first and make the introductions,' said Cesaria and took a deep breath of the bracing but invigorating mountain air.

Oozing Austrian charm, Gruber shook hands with everyone and then introduced the mayor.

'I have arranged transportation,' said the mayor, oozing cooperation. 'Our maxi taxi with driver we use for council outings is at your disposal. We can go straight to the cemetery just as you requested, Mr Te Papatahi. It isn't far.'

'Excellent, we are indebted to you, Herr Gruber. Just like last time in Vienna. Thank you for acting so quickly and bringing the local mayor along. This really is a matter of great importance and urgency. I will explain everything on the way.'

Half an hour later, the car pulled up in front of the Franziskaner Kirche in the centre of Berchtesgaden.

'The cemetery in question is next to the church over there,' said the mayor. 'Ah, there is Frau Reiter, our local historian.'

Everyone got out of the car and followed the mayor into the cemetery.

Frau Reiter, a portly woman in her fifties wearing a Bavarian hat that had seen better days – her ruddy face almost hidden behind a thick woollen scarf – was waiting at the gates leading into the small, picturesque walled cemetery.

Tristan pulled a copy of the Brother Francis letter with the cemetery map on the back out of his pocket and showed it to Frau Reiter. 'Do you think you could find this grave?'

'Sure. It's just over there; come.'

So this was where Jack had found the diary on Christmas Eve in 2008, thought Tristan as he read the name *Johann Berghofer* on the headstone.

'This is definitely it, no doubt about it,' he said, a strange feeling washing over him.

'What would you like to know?' asked Frau Reiter. 'I've brought the cemetery records with me.'

'What can you tell me about the Berghofer family? I see Johann here died in 1932.'

'Well, the Berghofers have been prominent local *bauern* – how do you say? – farmers, for generations here in the Berchtesgadener Land. Dairy cows mainly. They had substantial landholdings on the Obersalzberg not far from here.'

'You say *had*? What about now?'

'The war had a devastating impact on many families around here. Almost a whole generation was wiped out. Look around you. You'll see many graves in here of young soldiers killed during the war. Johann Berghofer had two sons. Both went to war and didn't return.

Thankfully, he didn't know that. As you can see, he died in 1932. His wife, however, lived to a ripe old age. She died in her nineties.'

Frau Reiter pointed to a grave in the next row. 'She's buried just over there with her parents. May I ask what your interest is in this?'

'It's complicated. For now, I would like to know if any of their landholdings are still in the family.'

'I can help with this,' said the mayor. 'The farm on the Obersalzberg stayed in the family until just before Elfriede Berghofer died. She lived in a nursing home in Bad Reichenhall by then. That was in the 1990s.'

'What happened to the property?'

'It was sold.'

'To whom, do you know?'

'A security company from Munich called Adler bought it. They use it for some kind of training purposes. A distant relative, I believe ...'

Tristan shot Cesaria a meaningful look. 'Do we have a name?'

The mayor shook his head. 'I could find out.'

'You said earlier, Frau Reiter, that the property wasn't far. Could we go and have a look?'

'I don't see why not.'

Paris Police Headquarters: 11:30 am

Dupree was waiting in Lapointe's office for an answer. He was nervously pacing up and down, and kept looking at his watch. After having spoken at length to Cesaria earlier, he was desperately trying to buy time for her as she had requested.

Lapointe had arranged a meeting with the Prefect to discuss the strange ransom demand that had come in to Lapointe's personal email account earlier that morning. It was apparent that things were moving very quickly and the pressure for a breakthrough, especially regarding the two murdered police officers, was enormous.

The expression on Lapointe's face gave nothing away when he walked into his office and calmly looked at Dupree.

'*Well?*' said Dupree.

'It wasn't easy. We'll go along with it, but there are strict conditions.'

'We are? Seriously? Despite the vague and strange handover demands?'

'Yes.'

'And still nothing about Landru?'

'No. This is only about Jack.'

'Weird. How did you manage to persuade the Prefect?'

Lapointe reached into his pocket, pulled out his pipe and tobacco pouch, and began to fill the pipe.

'I told him that it was our best chance to get to the perpetrators. And in some way it is, but we have to play our cards right, or the whole thing will come crashing down and bury us.'

Lapointe paused to light his pipe.

'Can you imagine what the press would make of this one-sided ransom demand? Handing over a precious artefact in front of that obscene house of horrors in exchange for directions to find a celebrity author abducted on our watch? How would that look, do you think, eh? It's crazy, and I still can't believe we are actually contemplating something like this. But if it buys valuable time as you suggest, then who knows, something good could perhaps come out of all this. And besides, it's all we've got at the moment. We are obviously dealing with a madman here.'

'Or an evil genius. Let's not forget all the Death Mask Murders and that house of horrors, and how Landru's been framed. And don't forget the abduction. Anyone who can pull all that off ...'

'You're right. And this seems to be more of the same; madness! I already gave the necessary instructions. Everyone's getting ready. You should too. The whole area will be sealed off. Not a mouse will be able to get near the place or leave it without us knowing about it. The Prefect insisted on it despite the exchange conditions. Strictly no police, remember? There isn't much time. I want you right there when it all happens.'

'Any more conditions?' asked Dupree.

'Yes. You won't like them, but I had no choice. It's all about that mask.'

'Tell me.'

'I will.'

56

Obersalzberg: 9 November, 11:30 am

The drive up to the Obersalzberg took less than half an hour.

'What a view,' said Isis as they approached a cluster of picturesque farmhouses surrounded by lush meadows and towering mountains.

'Look, a high fence, electric I think, and a boom gate at the end of the lane leading to the property. Security? Here, in this isolated place?' said Cesaria. 'I wonder why?'

As they approached the gate, a man dressed in what looked like some kind of uniform appeared and held up his hand. 'Can I help you?'

The mayor wound down his window. 'I am Hans Weindorfer, the mayor of Berchtesgaden. We would like to have a word with the owner.'

'May I ask what about?' said the man politely.

'It's about Johann and Elfriede Berghofer, who used to own this place and live here.'

'Please wait a moment,' said the man in the uniform. He pulled his phone out of his pocket, turned away from the car and made a call. He returned moments later and handed the mayor a business card. 'I cannot admit you right now. We have manoeuvres. It isn't safe. Please call this number and make an appointment. You can turn around over there.'

'Did you see the logo on his beret?' said Cesaria.

'It looked like a lightning bolt,' said Tristan. 'Echoes of the SS perhaps?'

'There's something you should know about this place and Adler Security,' said the mayor, who had overheard the remark.

'Oh? What?' asked Tristan.

'We've suspected for some time that this place is being used by some neo-Nazi organisation, and that the security firm is merely a cover,' said the mayor, lowering his voice. 'I tell you this in confidence, because Europol and our local police are looking into this right now.'

Cesaria reached for Tristan's arm and squeezed it. 'I don't think we'll get into that place in a hurry to check it out. So, where to from here?' she asked.

'I would like to find out a little more about the Berghofers and their neighbours,' said Tristan. 'And the history of this place.'

Gruber turned to the mayor sitting next to him. 'Could that be done?'

'I know someone who could help,' offered Frau Reiter.

'Who?' asked the mayor, annoyed. He had hoped that the whole matter had come to an end, and they would return to Berchtesgaden to have lunch in a cosy *Gasthaus* where he could play the generous, jovial host showcasing Bavarian hospitality. The neo-Nazi matter was a highly sensitive issue, especially in Berchtesgaden, which he didn't want to get involved in. He preferred to leave that to the police.

'Leopold Wagner. He knows everything about this place, and the people. Especially the Nazi era,' said Frau Reiter.

'Good idea. He's in charge of Dokumentation Obersalzberg,' said the mayor.

'What's that?' asked Tristan.

'A museum with an extensive permanent exhibition dedicated to the history of the Obersalzberg,' said the mayor. 'There's even a model of the entire former Nazi complex, complete with secret tunnels and bunkers. It's all about Nazi Germany and especially Hitler and the time he spent up here in Fortress Obersalzberg. He directed a significant part of the war from the famous Berghof, his alpine residence.'

'Hitler bought the Berghof in 1933,' said Frau Reiter and pointed out the window. 'It stood just over there, not far from the museum. There's a lot of history here, and Wagner knows it all. He's an expert on the Nazi installations that are still here – underground.'

'Then let's go and talk to him,' said Tristan, feeling better.

He's following his breadcrumbs, thought Cesaria, who had been watching Tristan carefully. *Like a somnambulist. I wonder where they will take us. Amazing.*

* * *

Standing at the window in his control room, O'Hara watched the car turn around at the gate. He didn't like unannounced visitors. He liked the reason given for the visit even less. O'Hara didn't believe in coincidences, only reason and purpose.

Why now? he thought, feeling uneasy, and sensing danger. At this critical time? Who were the others in the vehicle? What were they doing here? What did they really want?

O'Hara turned to the monitors on his desk, and like an admiral on an aircraft carrier directing a combat mission, he evaluated what was happening in his own private theatre of war, with several moving parts interacting with one another within a tight, precise timeframe. These were challenges he thrived on.

He was campaigning on two fronts, and both involved the lives of his two prisoners he held in his hands and could snuff out at will. This gave O'Hara a tremendous sense of power and satisfaction that was accessible only to a privileged few.

First, there was Landru. His fate was closely linked to the dark net gambling extravaganza that was in progress at that very moment, with huge amounts being wagered. The first video relating to that had just been posted on the dark net and, judging from the size of the bets coming in, it had been very well received, resulting in a betting frenzy.

A second video was being prepared to ramp up the excitement, and would be posted shortly. It would record Landru's dying moments and drive the betting to dizzying heights, netting O'Hara and Alessandro millions. Real death always came with a premium.

Then there was Jack and the Paris ransom demand. The purpose of that battle was quite different, and more personal. The unique instructions relating to that had been sent out earlier, and O'Hara was waiting for a response from Lapointe.

O'Hara considered himself to be a master criminal and tactician who used his huge wealth, intellect, and the latest technology to pursue his dark, psychopathic desires, where the boundaries between reality and fantasy had been blurred to an extent where it was no longer possible to tell the two apart. A final video featuring Jack had also been prepared, and would be released if necessary.

O'Hara was determined to get his hands on the last remaining piece of the Llanganates puzzle that had eluded him for so long, and complete his collection. He also wanted to make the final Death Mask Murder as memorable and exciting as possible. Letting Landru get away, and live, wasn't an option. It was a matter of pride. Letting Jack go wasn't an option either. That was a matter of common sense because he knew too much.

Landru's whole life, just like the lives of those who had gone before him, was closely intertwined with what was happening in Paris right at that moment. Gamblers who had been following the Death Mask Murders on the dark net for years, were well aware that the game was entering its final stage, with an enormous final prize worth a fortune almost within reach.

O'Hara turned on the CCTV camera showing what was happening to Landru in the death chamber deep inside the mountain. Satisfied, he turned on the other camera showing Jack's predicament in a different part of the mine.

That should do it, he thought, smiling, confident that Lapointe and the Paris police would do his bidding and accept his conditions regarding the handover, however strange. The handover plan was as daring as it was ingenious, using surprise and the latest technology to outwit a sophisticated, well-equipped police force that would leave no stone unturned to catch the perpetrators, to save face. And all that would be accomplished by one anonymous man pulling all the strings from the safety of his distant mountain retreat on the other side of Europe.

What O'Hara was counting on was human weakness, in this case fear, which in his view was always predictable. Lapointe and his superiors were desperate for results, and would agree to almost anything in the hope of avoiding further embarrassment and humiliation. O'Hara turned on the speakers and contacted Dragan, who was at the bottom of the mountain in a farmhouse that had underground access to the mine.

'Everything ready?' asked O'Hara.

'Yes. Landru hasn't much time left. The wheels are turning.'

'Neither has Mr Rogan. The water keeps rising.'

'Relentlessly. It's almost at the ceiling.'

'Make sure the video shows it all. I want close-ups.'

'Understood. Petrinko is down there working on it right now.'

'Excellent. Not long now.'

'What do you want us to do when, you know ...'

'It's all over? We flood the mine and close it for good. Monsieur Landru and Mr Rogan will disappear in a watery grave and eventually turn to stone, embedded in salt, once the water evaporates. They will become like the *Mann im Salz*, the man in the salt.'

Der Mann im Salz, a historical novel by Ludwig Ganghofer, was one of O'Hara's favourite books and had been the inspiration for *The Final Showdown* that was about to take place deep inside the ancient salt mine. It was the culmination of a long journey of violence and death he had shared on the dark net with a group of wealthy, deranged punters looking for the ultimate thrill, who couldn't get enough of it and were prepared to spend a fortune just to be included.

'All clear? You know what to do?'

'Yes.'

On a high, O'Hara took a deep breath. 'Excellent,' he said, turned off the speakers and called his man in Paris to finalise the arrangements for the handover.

Grimaldi's office, Florence: 11:45 am

Samartini burst into Grimaldi's office and held up her iPad. 'We've done it!' she said, out of breath. 'We got it!'

'You managed to get access?'

'Yes. The Americans just cracked the encryption. We now have access not only to the Omerta phone calls, but to the dark net gambling site as well.'

'Show me.'

'You won't like it.' Samartini turned on her iPad, called up a video and showed it to Grimaldi.

'Good God! And this is happening right now?'

'Yes, in real time. You can see the clock counting down on the side here. That's what the gambling's all about. They are betting on when Landru will, you know …'

'Be garrotted by this contraption?'

'Yes.'

'This is madness!'

'Perhaps so, but it's real.'

The video showed Landru sitting in a rusty iron chair below a huge wooden waterwheel turning slowly above him. His wrists were strapped to the hand rests and a thick rope wound around his chest tied him to the back of the chair. He looked like a condemned man waiting to be executed in an electric chair in some godforsaken American prison. Only this was taking place in an underground mine, with water trickling from the ceiling onto the wheel, turning it slowly each time one of its buckets filled with water. Attached to the wheel was a mechanism of smaller wheels and pulleys that slowly tightened the wire noose around Landru's neck each time the wheel turned. It was obvious that he didn't have long to live. His eyes were bulging and he had difficulty breathing.

'With the encryption removed, can the origin of the site be identified?' asked Grimaldi.

'Yes. The Americans are working on it right now. Early indications are it's all coming from somewhere in Bavaria—'

'That's where Cesaria and Tristan are right now,' interrupted Grimaldi.

'Exactly! I think they are on the right track, and all they need is time. You know Tristan and his sixth sense.'

'And are our French friends helping with that?'

'Looks that way. Despite everything, they are going ahead with the handover, but on their terms.'

'What does that mean?'

'Don't know, but Dupree is keeping me informed.'

'Good work, Clara. I hope we catch the bastards who are doing this.'

'So do I, but for now, keeping Jack alive is all that matters. As for Landru, well ...'

'Sure,' said Grimaldi. *I don't like our chances*, he thought, shaking his head, and lit one of his small cigars.

<h1 style="text-align:center">57</h1>

Dokumentation Obersalzberg: 9 November, 12:00 noon

The museum was Wagner's world. He knew every exhibit and could talk for hours about the meaning of every photograph, document or artefact on show in *Dokumentation Obersalzberg*, visited by thousands every year.

Wagner, a retired schoolteacher, looked up in surprise. It wasn't often that the mayor of Berchtesgaden paid him a visit.

'We need your help,' said the mayor.

'Certainly. How can I assist?'

With his long, unkempt white hair and steel-rimmed glasses, Wagner reminded Tristan of a caricature of Einstein on a poster he had seen at university.

'My guests here would like some information about the Berghofers and their property,' said the mayor.

'No problem. What would they like to know?'

'We've just come from the Berghofer place. Couldn't get near it.'

'Ah. Adler, the security company, right? Well, that's a joke, isn't it, Herr Weindorfer? We know better, don't we? The Obersalzberg here is a shrine for neo-Nazis to worship on. It is an ideology magnet that is raising its ugly, dangerous head again.'

The mayor held up his hand, keen to stop the unwelcome tirade. 'I think what my friends would like to talk about is the Berghofer family who used to own the property, and their neighbours.'

'I understand two of the sons went to war and didn't return,' said Tristan.

'Quite. Like so many of the boys from around here. But the Berghofer lads were different.'

'In what way?' asked Cesaria.

'They joined the Hitler Youth and then the Nazi party quite early, and advanced rapidly in the SS. In fact, there was a whole group of them, all neighbours from the Obersalzberg here. Close friends. They were known as the wolf pack. Thick as thieves, they were. Excellent mountain climbers and skiers. Outdoor types.'

'Any names? Apart from the Berghofer boys?'

'Yes. Three families were very close. The Steinbergers, the Hoffmeisters and the Berghofers. All had sons around the same age who joined the Nazis and went to war.'

'And their farms?'

'Adler Security bought up most of them over the years. The ones that were next to each other. They are now all part of that compound you saw.'

'The company also owns one further down the mountain that used to belong to the Steinbergers,' said Frau Reiter.

'That's right,' said the mayor. 'Close to the salt mine.'

Tristan locked eyes with Cesaria and nodded. Everything was beginning to come together. The video, his dreams and intuition were all intersecting and showing the way. 'That's another thing I wanted to talk about: *salt*,' he said.

'What about it?' said Wagner, surprised. 'Salt has been part of Berchtesgaden for centuries. It has been mined here inside this very mountain for over a thousand years. We are standing on the Obersalzberg, the upper salt mountain.'

'I would like to show you something,' said Tristan. 'It's confronting, but very important. It's the reason we are here.'

Tristan turned to Cesaria. 'Would you mind showing us that video you received from Lapointe this morning?'

Cesaria reached into her briefcase, pulled out her iPad and turned it on. Then she called up the short video showing Jack standing in the water with a chain wound around his chest and an iron collar around his neck.

'Good heavens!' said Wagner. 'What is the meaning of this?'

'I would like to know that too,' said the mayor. 'Did you know about this, Herr Gruber?'

'Yes, I did. It was shown to me earlier. In confidence.'

'Please forgive me, but there's no time to explain. I have one question, Herr Wagner, an important one.' Tristan pointed to the video. 'Could this small lake be part of the salt mine? Somewhere inside this mountain?'

'Sure. There are large chambers like this inside the mine. There's a lake just like this one in the mine that's open to the public. A boat ride across the lake is part of the tour. It's one of the main attractions, together with the wooden slides used by the miners to quickly go down into the mine. Tourists love it, especially the children. Some of the slides are more than fifty metres long and quite steep. Your bottom gets hot sliding down on the polished wood; that's why the miners had leather aprons as part of their uniforms, which they could sit on.'

'Apart from the entry into the mine used by the tourists, are there other entries or access points into the mine?'

'I don't know of any, but quite possibly,' said the mayor. 'The underground mining complex here is huge, with many levels and countless tunnels. Most of them are closed, of course, and only a small part of the mine is open to visitors.'

'The Steinberger property you mentioned earlier that's owned by the security company, is it close to the mine entrance?'

'It is,' said Wagner.

Tristan turned to the mayor. 'Could we go and have a look?'

'Sure. It's almost on our way back to Berchtesgaden.'

Tristan closed the iPad and gave it back to Cesaria, convinced that he had just found another one of Jack's breadcrumbs of destiny that would show him the way. *Perhaps the most important one of them all,* he thought, desperately hoping it wasn't too late.

'House of horrors', Paris: 12:30 pm

Dupree looked at his watch. It was 12:30 pm precisely. Adjusting his earpiece, he got out of his car, opened the iron gate and walked up to the front door of the deserted house, which was still a crime scene.

Taking a deep breath, he opened his briefcase, took out the piece of iridium Professor Flaubert had given him earlier, and placed it on the front step as instructed. Then he turned around, left the courtyard and got back into his car.

'All done,' he reported, talking into the microphone attached to his collar.

'Now leave,' said the officer in charge of the GIGN conducting the operation. He was watching the house of horrors from a building nearby. 'And leave the rest to us.'

Dupree started his car and slowly drove away.

The powerful camera attached to the drone hovering high above the house had recorded it all. Sitting in the back of a van in a quiet back street a few kilometres away, the operator of the drone – a trusted member of the Adler Security company – was watching Dupree's movements on his laptop.

Sitting in his control room on the Obersalzberg, O'Hara was watching the live transmission from the drone on his monitor. The drone, a sophisticated prototype equipped with robotic arms sensitive enough to carry out an eye operation, and powerful electronic devices capable of detecting, recording and transmitting the movements of a grasshopper on the ground, ensured that the complex manoeuvre would not only take the Paris police by complete surprise, but render them powerless and incapable to respond.

'*Do it now!*' said O'Hara.

The man in the van adjusted the controls, which looked like buttons on a PlayStation, and began to guide the drone down into the courtyard. For a moment it hovered above the house, and then descended slowly and approached the front step like some alien beast stalking its unsuspecting prey.

'What on earth is that?' mumbled the officer in charge, watching through his binoculars as the drone moved slowly towards the front door.

First, the robotic arms carrying Landru's death mask reached out and placed it on the step next to the iridium piece, like a sinister visiting card from another world.

'*Move! Move!*' shouted the officer into the microphone attached to his chin just before the drone turned, the arms reached out and picked up the iridium piece with its steel claws. Holding it firmly in its grip, the drone moved away from the step and, rising quickly, turned in mid-air and flew away, the entire manoeuvre lasting less than a minute.

Moments later, armed commandos descended on the house from all sides and burst into the courtyard, only to find it empty.

'*Perfect!*' said O'Hara. 'You know what to do?'

'Yes,' said the man operating the drone. He opened the back door of the van just as the drone approached, and watched it fly slowly inside and land perfectly at his feet.

58

**Salzbergwerk Berchtesgaden,
on the way into the salt mine: 9 November, 12:30 pm**

'That's it over there,' said Frau Reiter. 'Haus Alpenblick.' She pointed to a picturesque, traditional Bavarian farmhouse with wooden balconies and flowerboxes facing the view, a sloping shingle-covered roof with large stones on top, and a spacious barn attached at the back.

The council car turned into the driveway and stopped at the entrance. There were no parked vehicles and the house looked deserted. No-one came to the door.

'I'll see if anyone's home,' said the mayor and opened the car door. Tristan looked at Cesaria. 'Let's have a quick look around.'

'Can you sense something?'

'I can; come.'

While the mayor knocked on the front door, Tristan and Cesaria walked along the side of the house to the barn at the back. Lola followed a few paces behind.

Standing at the kitchen window, Dragan, the only person in the house, was watching them from behind the curtain. The two Adler Security guards who usually stayed at the house had been called up to the compound on the Obersalzberg for a briefing, and Petrinko was down in the mine, shooting a video. Dragan turned off the laptop on the kitchen table, reached for his machine gun and went to the back door.

For some reason he couldn't explain, Tristan was drawn to the barn. 'Let's have a look,' he said and began to push against the heavy barn door with his shoulder. Slowly, the door opened. Tristan looked inside.

'*This is it*, look!' Tristan pointed to a dark van with a French number plate. Cesaria stepped forward and had a look. 'I'll tell the mayor to call the police, quickly! This is a dangerous place.'

Cesaria was about to turn around when she felt something hard pressing against her back. 'Not so hasty,' said a voice from behind. 'Go inside, both of you!'

Pressing the barrel of his gun against Cesaria's back, Dragan pushed her inside and quickly closed the barn door behind him. 'Hold up your hands where I can see them, *now!*'

Tristan and Cesaria raised their hands.

Lola, who had seen Dragan walk up to Cesaria from behind, had the presence of mind to press herself against the farmhouse wall. As Isis's former bodyguard, personal trainer, and a hand-to-hand combat champion, Lola reacted instinctively to what was happening. Taking deep breaths to calm herself, she evaluated the situation. Instead of running back to the car and raising the alarm, which would only have put Tristan and Cesaria in greater danger, she decided on a different approach.

The biggest threat by far was Dragan and his gun. If she could somehow disarm him by using surprise and her karate skills, that would be the best outcome. Lola looked around. She could see a side door leading into the barn. Staying low, she quickly made her way to the door and looked through a crack in the wooden slats to see what was happening inside.

Tristan and Cesaria stood next to the van – hands in the air. Holding his Uzi, Dragan stood behind them with his back towards Lola.

'First, I want your phones,' she heard him say. 'Where are they?'

'Mine's in my right back pocket,' said Cesaria calmly. She knew from experience that in dangerous, unpredictable situations like this where anything could happen, the best thing to do was to cooperate and stay calm, without trying something reckless, stupid, or both.

As Dragan stepped forward towards Cesaria, Lola quickly opened the door a little and, crouching down, slipped inside. She knew that her best chance to disarm the attacker would be when he was reaching into the back pocket of Cesaria's jeans to take out her phone. That would be the moment he was distracted.

Her training told her what she had to do to make this work, but her experience told her just how risky such a manoeuvre really was. At the same time, she realised that to do nothing was riskier still, as Jack's life, should he in fact be as close as Tristan seemed to think, could be hanging in the balance.

Some of the most important decisions in life are often made in a split second, instinctively, and without planning or preparation. This was such a moment. As Dragan reached into Cesaria's back pocket with his right hand and pulled out her phone, Lola moved silently forward like a cat, and pounced. She managed to wrench Dragan's left arm sideways, away from Tristan and Cesaria. This dislocated Dragan's shoulder, causing excruciating pain. The gun went off, the bullets missing Tristan's head by inches, as Lola delivered a karate blow to the back of Dragan's neck before he could turn around. Feeling dizzy, Dragan dropped the gun.

'*Cesaria, pick it up!*' shouted Lola as she continued to twist Dragan's left arm backwards. Dragan – well into his sixties – was physically no match for Lola, who was supremely fit and agile. Once he dropped the gun it was all over.

Hearing the shots, Gruber and the mayor ran towards the barn, closely followed by Isis. The mayor was already on the phone calling the police as Gruber opened the barn door and looked inside. Disorientated and dizzy, Dragan was sitting on the floor, holding his limp left arm. Cesaria stood next to him with the gun pointing at his head.

'One clown down, one to go,' said Tristan, grinning. He had recognised the Uzi and the voice from the chateau.

'My God, what happened here?' said Gruber.

'Tell you later. We have to act quickly, there isn't much time,' said Cesaria.

'The police will be here shortly,' said the mayor.

'We can't wait.'

Tristan knelt down beside Dragan and, holding him by the collar with both hands, looked at him. 'Remember me?' he said. 'We met just the other day at the Kuragin chateau. Where's Jack Rogan?'

'Fuck off!' mumbled Dragan.

'Lola, I think that shoulder needs some more attention,' said Tristan.

Lola reached for Dragan's limp arm and began to twist it backwards. Dragan cried out in pain. 'Over there, the trap door,' he croaked, his eyes turning glassy.

Tristan let go of the collar, went over to the trap door, opened it and looked inside. 'A ladder,' he said. 'An entry into the mine, I'm sure of it. Cesaria, come. Bring the gun. We're going down.'

'I'm coming too,' said Lola and let go of Dragan's arm. 'This guy's not going anywhere in a hurry. Herr Gruber, would you please make sure it stays that way until the police get here?'

The mayor walked over to Gruber. 'Leave him to us,' he said, standing over Dragan holding an iron bar he had just picked up from the floor.

'If you think you are leaving me behind,' said Isis, 'you are gravely mistaken, guys. I didn't come all this way to miss this. Lola, lead on!'

Cesaria slung the machine gun over her shoulder and followed Lola down the shaft leading into the darkness below.

Grimaldi's office, Florence: 12:30 pm

'Call them again!' said Grimaldi, without taking his eyes off the screen of the laptop.

'It's no use,' said Samartini. 'No-one's answering. They must be somewhere out of range.' Samartini had tried in vain to get in touch with Cesaria and Tristan all morning.

'Great! Can you believe this? A brutal murder is happening somewhere out there right now, and we are watching it live on the dark net while some obscene betting is going on, and we are unable to do anything about it?'

'The Americans are doing everything they can to track the site.'

Mesmerised, Grimaldi kept watching the screen and lit one of his small cigars. 'This is *insane!*'

The waterwheel above Landru's head kept turning slowly, tightening the noose around his neck. It was obvious the end was near. On the left of the screen, the seconds on a clock kept ticking over until abruptly, the clock stopped and the camera moved in for a close-up, showing Landru's contorted face. The noose had just broken his neck. The ordeal was over.

'Look at this,' said Samartini. She pointed to a flashing number under the clock that had just appeared on the screen: 2,456,300. It was the dollar amount the winner who had picked the time closest to Landru's death would take home.

'Incredible,' said Grimaldi as the screen went suddenly blank. 'That's it, I suppose.'

'No, *look!*' said Samartini and pointed to the screen. The short video that followed was the sequence taken by the drone as it approached the house of horrors in Paris, placed Landru's death mask at its door, and then picked up the piece of iridium left there by Dupree, before flying quickly away and disappearing into the distance.

'Can you believe this?' said Grimaldi, staring at the blank screen. Then he reached for his phone and called Lapointe.

* * *

O'Hara looked at the screen on his workbench and watched the drone disappear into the distance. The amounts that had been wagered had surpassed expectation and had made him a fortune. With Landru's death, the game that had lasted for more than thirty years had come to an end, and the final missing piece of the puzzle that would show him the way to the lost Llanganates treasure was finally within reach.

As far as the dark net punters were concerned, the betting was over, but before O'Hara could declare himself the overall winner in this bizarre game where he set the challenges and made all the rules, one final move on his imaginary chessboard was required: the white knight who had teamed up with Landru and almost foiled his victory at the very last minute, had to perish.

O'Hara turned on the CCTV camera showing Jack standing in the lake. The brine had almost reached the ceiling and Jack had to press his face against the smooth rock above him to be able to breathe. As instructed by O'Hara, Petrinko had set up a video camera on the steps inside a narrow tunnel leading down to the lake, and was recording Jack's final moments with close-ups of his face.

Unlike all the other video footage posted on the dark net, this one was for O'Hara's eyes only. He had used Jack to defeat the French police and bend them to his will. They had followed all his instructions to the letter, without getting anything in return. The fear of embarrassment and public humiliation he had caused had been too great, O'Hara thought, pleased with himself.

Over the years, he had committed seven spectacular murders without being caught, and was about to add one more before declaring himself the overall winner, and disappearing. Apart from France, he had outfoxed and outmanoeuvred law enforcement agencies in Germany and Spain, the UK, and even in the Canary Islands.

O'Hara turned on the speakers, with music playing in the background. A stickler for detail, he liked it that way.

'Goodbye, Mr Rogan,' he said. 'Pity we didn't meet earlier. I really enjoyed your company, your books, and especially our recent conversations, albeit under difficult circumstances.'

O'Hara began to chuckle. 'You would have made an admirable adversary,' he continued. 'And just like me, you like Chopin.'

With that, O'Hara turned up the volume, sat back in his chair, and listened to his favourite nocturne echo through the underground chamber while his last opponent was about to depart from the chessboard, defeated, and he could finally declare himself the undisputed winner.

59

**Salzbergwerk Berchtesgaden,
inside the salt mine: 9 November, 1:00 pm**

Descending into the old mine was like entering a different world, where time stood still and echoes of a distant past could still be heard by those who knew how to listen. Tristan was one of those who could. For hundreds of years miners had toiled underground, facing danger every day in order to find new, more efficient ways to rob the mountain of the precious salt it had guarded for aeons.

Not surprisingly, many miners had lost their lives inside the mine due to frequent roof collapses, and catastrophic flooding that occurred from time to time due to faulty pipes and equipment failure. It was therefore hardly surprising that Tristan could hear many voices reaching out, trying to tell their stories. With each step, the voices became louder and more urgent, but Tristan was focused on one in particular.

The landing at the bottom of the ladder was narrow, with barely enough room for them all to stand next to each other, shoulder to shoulder.

'At least there's some light down here,' said Lola. She pointed to a lantern dangling from a rusty hook at the entrance to a narrow shaft. The walls and the low ceiling were lined with crumbling timber beams, and other lanterns could be seen in the distance lighting the way.

'My guess is this is part of the old mine, and the entry we've just used is much more recent,' said Cesaria. 'Electricity is coming from the house above us. You have seen the cables in the shaft coming down?'

Tristan held up his hand and closed his eyes, intense concentration on his face. He was trying to hear what the remaining voice was telling him, as the confusing gibberish of the other voices faded away. 'Jack is close,' he said. 'I can hear him, but his voice is very faint.' Tristan opened his eyes and looked into the distance at something only he could see. 'It sounds like someone speaking under water.'

'What are you saying?' asked Isis, who had seen Tristan's extraordinary intuition at work before.

'I have never felt anything like this,' continued Tristan quietly. 'It's very scary.'

'What are you talking about?' asked Lola.

'Difficult to explain.'

'Try.'

'It's as if part of me is ...'

'What?' asked Isis.

'Dying,' whispered Tristan, his eyes misting over.

'Right. There's only one way to go,' said Lola, trying to break the spell. She pointed to the shaft. 'That way. Shall we?'

They followed the shaft for about a hundred metres until it turned sharply right, and they found themselves in a large chamber with a high ceiling that looked like an underground chapel. The only thing missing was an altar.

'Wow! What an amazing place,' said Cesaria, and began to look around. 'The end of the road, you think?'

'I think not,' said Lola. 'Come, have a look at this.'

'What is it?'

'Looks like one of those slides Herr Wagner told us about. It's the only way out of here, unless we go back,' said Lola.

Everyone walked over to have a look at the steep, polished wooden rails reaching down deep into the mountain below.

'More lights down there,' observed Isis.

'All right, who'll go first?' said Lola.

'We go down together,' said Tristan. 'There isn't much time; come.' He sat down, straddling the wooden rails. 'Sit behind me, and hang on.'

'Sounds like fun,' said Cesaria and sat down behind Tristan. The others did the same.

'Now hold on to the one in front of you; ready? We used to do this as kids in the park.'

Tristan leaned back and lifted up his feet. 'Here we go!'

After an exhilarating fifty-metre ride to the bottom, the wooden rails they were sliding down turned upwards, bringing them gradually to a standstill.

'Wow! Can we do this again?' said Isis.

'We could, but you have to walk up these stairs first.' Lola pointed to a steep, narrow set of stairs next to the slide, leading to the top.

'Ah. Perhaps later,' said Isis. 'What's that over there? Something's moving!'

'I'll have a look,' said Lola and walked over to investigate. 'Good Lord! Come quickly! *It's Landru!*'

Wedged into a crevasse above an alcove almost hidden from view, a large waterwheel was turning slowly. Illuminated by a ghostly light from behind, its wooden spokes sent crazy shadows creeping along the uneven, wet floor every time it turned, like claws of a demon looking for a victim.

'Who could do something like that?' said Cesaria, barely able to speak, staring at the headless body strapped into a rusty chair below the wheel. Landru's head – glassy eyes wide open – had been severed, and was lying in his lap, with water dripping down from the wheel above turning crimson as it ran along the floor past his feet.

'A deranged psychopath trying to show the world that he is smarter than anyone else,' said Tristan. 'Death Mask Murder number eight, only this time, the death mask was sent to Landru in advance. Crazy!'

'This is bizarre,' said Isis. 'It looks like some scene in a fairground ghost train diorama to frighten children and young lovers. Only this is real.'

'It sure is. Just like that house of horrors Jack found was real. Someone's gone to a lot of trouble to kill Landru this particular way. Very theatrical. Once again, the attention to detail is remarkable. It's like a signature.'

'What does this tell you?' asked Isis.

'The human mind is a strange place,' replied Tristan. 'It also tells me we have to hurry. This happened just a short while ago. Look at the blood. It's too late for Landru, I just hope it's not too late for Jack.'

Tristan paused and held up his hand. '*Shhhh*. Can you hear it?'

'Music?' said Lola.

'Chopin,' said Isis. 'Here? This is crazy!'

'No, it isn't! We are close,' said Tristan. 'Hurry!'

As they followed another narrow shaft leading deeper into the mountain, the music became louder.

Cesaria, who was leading the way, saw it first: a dark shape in the distance that appeared to be moving. She stopped, held up her hand and pointed ahead. 'Wait here,' she whispered. 'I'll go and have a look.'

Holding the machine gun with both hands, Cesaria walked slowly towards the dark shape.

Petrinko sat on one of the stairs leading down to the flooded lake below. He was holding a video camera aimed at something in the distance. *Not long now*, he thought, looking through the viewfinder.

With only his nose above water, Jack was barely able to breathe. His eyes were closed, the bleeding tip of his nose pressed against the rock ceiling above. Realising the end was near, Jack found himself drifting back to the Queensland cattle station where he grew up and had spent some of the happiest times of his youth with Gurrul, his Aboriginal friend and mentor.

Petrinko didn't notice the moving shadow until Cesaria was almost upon him. He turned his head and looked straight at the barrel of Cesaria's gun pointing at him. 'Come quickly!' shouted Cesaria and looked around, trying to evaluate the situation.

Tristan was the first to emerge out of the shaft. In his mind's eye he had already seen something similar and was therefore quick to grasp what was happening. '*Jack!* He's over there – alive!' he shouted. He quickly took off his shoes and plunged into the water. As he waded towards Jack at the back of the small lake, the low rock ceiling began to slope downwards.

Jack opened his eyes and looked straight at Tristan coming towards him out of the gloom. *I must be dreaming,* he thought. *Or perhaps I'm already dead …*

But then he heard Tristan's voice: 'Hold on mate. I'm coming!'

As Tristan moved closer, the water became noticeably deeper and he had to swim until the ceiling almost touched the water and he ran out of space. Taking a deep breath, he dived and quickly swam over to Jack to investigate. The chain around Jack's chest was impossible to move, and the iron collar around his neck wouldn't budge. Running out of air, Tristan had to swim back a few strokes where there was more headroom, and he could hold his head above water and breathe.

'I need some help here!' he shouted, waving his arms. Then he took another deep breath, took another dive, and swam back to Jack under water.

Lola kicked off her shoes, waded into the lake and quickly swam over to Tristan to help. As he came up for more air, he told her what he had found.

'I think I know how to loosen the chain, but we have to do it together.'

'All right. Show me. Let's go.' Lola took a deep breath and followed Tristan over to Jack.

Petrinko had dropped the camera and was holding up his hands. 'The water is obviously rising,' said Cesaria. 'Can it be stopped? *Tell me!*' she said and pushed the nozzle of the gun against Petrinko's chest.

'No idea,' said Petrinko.

'Liar!'

'Go to hell!'

'The only one going to hell here is you, I promise!'

Isis, a strong swimmer, had taken off her shoes and jumper and swam over to Jack to assist. By now, Tristan and Lola had gone back and forth several times and had managed to free Jack from the chain. That only left the iron collar, which seemed to be a problem.

'How's it going? asked Isis as Tristan came up for air. 'The collar. We can't take it off! He's about to drown.'

'Let me have a look. Isis took a deep breath and, passing Lola on the way, swam over to Jack under water.

'It's no use,' said Lola to Tristan, gasping for air. Both were totally exhausted.

Isis was gone for a long time. 'Can she stay under water this long?' asked Tristan, treading water.

'She can. She's a remarkable swimmer.'

As Isis ran her fingers along the iron collar around Jack's neck for a second time, she found it: a hinge at the back. As she pushed back the hinge, the collar parted, releasing Jack's neck from its iron grip. Holding Jack under his arms, Isis kicked hard against the rock wall, pulled him free and swam back to Tristan and Lola.

'My God, *look!*' said Tristan as Isis surfaced next to him, holding Jack's head above water.

'I think he just went under,' she said. 'Help me, quickly!'

* * *

O'Hara kept staring at the CCTV screen showing the small green salt lake inside the mine, his mind racing. What he had just witnessed was not only a game changer, but a serious threat not to be underestimated. How a group of strangers had managed to enter his secret, private world, find his last remaining foe moments before his death and rescue him, was not only a mystery, but a matter of great concern to a man used to being in total control and always winning.

Something had gone terribly wrong. The chess game was far from over. The white knight was back on his horse and ready to attack. And he didn't come alone. He had powerful allies who could turn the tide.

O'Hara realised there was only one way to deal with a situation like this: go on the attack. He was a man who recovered quickly. His analytical brain evaluated the unexpected setback, and like a seasoned general directing his troops on the battlefield, he worked out a strategy to defeat his enemies and secure victory. And he had plenty left in his arsenal to do just that. The old salt mine was his territory, his turf, and anyone trying to fight him there better be prepared for the unexpected.

Smiling for the first time since he saw the strangers invading his private domain, O'Hara called up the computer program that remote-controlled all the sophisticated installations inside the mine, and prepared to send his elite soldiers he had kept in reserve, into battle. Only these soldiers didn't fight with conventional weapons, but with something far more powerful: *water.*

60

**Salzbergwerk Berchtesgaden:
Escape from the salt mine, 9 November 2:30 pm**

With Tristan's help, Lola turned Jack onto his back and was about to apply CPR, when water gushed out of Jack's mouth, and he began to breathe. Moments later, he began to cough, opened his eyes, and looked at Tristan.

'What took you so long?' whispered Jack and tried to sit up.

Tristan pushed him gently back down, leaned forward and kissed him tenderly on his forehead. 'We almost didn't make it. Never frighten me like this again.'

'How do you feel?' asked Isis.

'All right. Incorrigible rascals are tough—'

'Do you think you can walk?' interjected Lola, frowning.

'Perhaps not that tough, but I'll give it a go.'

'We must get out of here, *fast*!'

'Good luck!' said Petrinko.

'No-one asked you!' snapped Tristan.

'You have no idea what you're dealing with here.'

'Ah, the other clown,' said Tristan. 'Just as I thought.' He recognised the voice from the recent encounter at the chateau. 'You're the one who killed Lorenza!'

'Shit happens,' said Petrinko, who had been watching carefully and was biding his time. Slowly lowering his right arm, he reached into his pocket. He always carried a flick-knife; an old habit. When Cesaria turned to look at Jack lying on the ground in front of her and momentarily lowered her gun, he knew he had his chance. A street fighter since his teens with extensive military training and combat experience, he knew exactly what to do.

Cesaria's right arm was closest to him. Holding the knife firmly in his right hand, Petrinko lunged forward and stabbed Cesaria in the arm.

384

Taken by surprise, Cesaria gasped in pain and dropped the gun, lost her balance and, slipping on the wet step, fell into the water. Carried forward by the momentum, Petrinko, a solid, powerful man, fell on top of her.

Petrinko surfaced first. His eyes firmly fixed on the gun lying on the step in front of him, he tried to lift himself out of the water to reach it. Tristan, who had seen it all, was closest to the gun. A split second faster than Petrinko, he reached it first and pulled the trigger. Hit in the chest at close range, Petrinko was dead before he fell back into the water.

'For Lorenza,' said Tristan. 'You should have killed me while you had the chance!'

'Not bad for someone who listens to the whisper of angels,' said Lola, and helped Cesaria climb out of the water.

* * *

O'Hara, who had seen it all on CCTV, punched in the code on his laptop that would open the large sluice gate valves on one of the upper levels. This would allow water from two small salt lakes to drain into the lower tunnels and shafts, to quickly flood the mine.

* * *

Supporting Jack under his arms, Isis and Tristan almost had to carry him because he was too unsteady on his feet. Both realised that this was the easy bit. The real challenge would come later: how to get Jack to the top of the miners' slide by navigating the steep, narrow stairs wouldn't be easy.

As they dragged Jack past the alcove with the waterwheel, Jack turned his head and looked inside.

'*Jesus!* I think drowning would have been easier,' he said. 'We can't just leave him here.'

'Let the police deal with that. This is a crime scene. Landru's gone. You're still very much alive. We've got to get out of here.' said Tristan. 'Quickly!'

Just before they reached the wooden slide, Cesaria, who had walked ahead, held up her hand. 'What was that?' she said. 'Did you hear?'

'What?' asked Lola, who was bringing up the rear.

'Hush! *Listen.*'

'Sounds like water,' said Isis.

'You're right,' said Cesaria and looked up. At first, water came rushing down the slide and ran along the floor towards the tunnel leading to the lake below. Moments later, the noise intensified, and water came rushing out of the tunnel above and cascaded down like a waterfall. Cesaria realised at once what was happening: water from above was flooding the area below. It would quickly reach the lake and then back up, filling the tunnel and the entire chamber completely.

'*What now?*' shouted Isis as the water kept rising. It had almost reached her knees. 'We certainly can't go up there!'

'We can't stay here either, or we'll drown!' said Tristan and let go of Jack's arm. 'As we walked past Landru just now, I think I saw something behind him.'

'What did you see?' Lola had to shout to make herself heard, the cascading water echoing through the chamber almost drowning out her words.

'I'll go back and have a look. Hold on!'

As Tristan turned to leave, the lights went out and plunged the chamber into darkness, making the rushing waters sound louder and more threatening.

'That's all we need!' he said. He reached for his iPhone, turned on the torch, pointed the cone of light at the rising water and then waded back to the alcove.

Tristan returned moments later. By now, the water was reaching their waists. 'There's another way out,' he said. 'Come – hurry!'

The first police car had just arrived at the farmhouse. Others were not far behind and the fire brigade was on its way.

'They went down there,' said the mayor, pointing to the open trap door. He was addressing the officer in charge, a burly Bavarian with a crew cut who had served in Afghanistan. 'You better go down and see what's happening.'

The police officer looked down into the shaft. 'The boys from the fire brigade should be here any moment. I think this is a job for them, don't you?'

'I'm worried,' said Gruber. 'My guests should have been back by now. They only went down for a quick look.'

The officer turned to Wagner, who had just arrived after the mayor had called him and asked for his help. 'What do you think's down there, Leo?' he asked. 'You know this place better than all of us.' The officer knew Wagner well. They shared the same *Stammtisch* in a *Gasthaus* in Berchtesgaden.

'Part of the old mine. It reaches all the way across to here, but this entrance is definitely new. Ah, here are the rescue boys now.'

Wagner pointed to the fire truck. 'Let's go and talk to them.'

'All right, but first let me have a word with this guy here.' The officer pointed to Dragan, sitting on the floor in front of the mayor. 'He must know something.'

The officer crouched down next to Dragan and looked at him. *Tough guy*, he thought, recognising all the signs. 'I don't have to tell you about the amount of trouble you're in. I'm sure you know. You can improve your situation by telling me what's down there, or things will get worse. Your choice.'

'Your show, your problem, *boy*!' hissed Dragan, pursing his lips in contempt.

'All right, Gramps, have it your way.'

Nodding, the officer stood up and turned to one of his men. He realised it was pointless to pursue the matter further. 'Handcuff him, put him in the car and search the house.'

With Gruber and the mayor anxiously watching at the trapdoor, three young firefighters, all mountain climbers with alpine rescue training, climbed down into the shaft to investigate.

'What happened up here is bad enough,' said Gruber, 'but if something's happened to them down there, well …'

'I understand. You should have told me!' said the mayor.

'About the video?'

'Of course. There's a lot more to all this than we know, right?'

'Looks that way,' conceded Gruber, forever the pragmatist. 'But now that we know, we have to deal with it and minimise the damage,' he added.

'I suppose so. Let's see what the lads come up with. They are the best we have.'

A few minutes later, one of the firefighters appeared at the top of the ladder. 'We have a problem,' he said, a worried expression on his face.

'What do you mean?' demanded the mayor.

'It's a mess down there. Water. It's coming from everywhere and flooding the old tunnels. Part of the roof has already collapsed. There's no way we can get through them from here. We were lucky to get out.'

'What about the people who went down …?'

The firefighter shrugged and took off his helmet.

'This is a catastrophe!' said Gruber, his mind racing. He could already see the headlines, and his career going up in flames.

'Perhaps I can help,' said Wagner, who had overheard the conversation.

'What do you mean, Leo?' said the mayor.

'There could be another way into the mine further down.'

'Can we get to it?' asked the firefighter.

'Access has been closed for years, but yes. I think so.'

'How?'

'From the mine that's open to the public.' Wagner pointed over his shoulder. 'I could show you. It's just over there.'

'Here, look,' said Tristan, and pointed to a narrow shaft leading into the mountain under the waterwheel. The entry to the shaft was a few feet above the water racing past them down to the lake below.

'It's our only chance,' said Cesaria. 'I'll go in first.' She handed the gun to Lola, and turned on the torch on her phone. 'Let's go, guys.'

'Just when I thought I've been rescued,' said Jack. *This?*'

'Count your lucky stars, mate,' said Tristan. 'At least this shaft is pointing up, not down.'

'That's something, I suppose,' said Jack, trying to sound cheerful. 'You don't know what it's like standing in this salt water for hours.'

Tristan turned to Isis holding on to Jack's arm next to him. 'Can you believe this guy?' he said.

Isis shook her head. 'Certain rascals are like that. That's why they call them incorrigible. Come on, let's go.'

As Cesaria moved deeper into the mine shaft, it gradually narrowed and she had to get down on all fours. Ten metres further in, she had to get down on her belly and crawl until her head almost touched the low ceiling and she could barely move. Taking a deep breath, she raised her head a little and looked ahead. 'A chamber,' she shouted. 'I can see a chamber!'

'How far?' asked Lola, who was just behind her.

'Not far. I'm almost through. Tell the others.'

Manoeuvring Jack through the narrow opening was difficult, but with Tristan pushing from behind, and Lola pulling at the front, they managed to get him through. Exhausted, his wet clothes torn and his knees and elbows bleeding, Jack lay on the ground. 'You know what, guys?' he said. Looking up at Tristan.

'What?' said Tristan.

'I think I prefer the water.'

'Ignore him, he's just winding you up,' said Isis, rubbing her aching back, well aware that Jack was using a little humour to make everyone feel better. She had seen him do this often before. 'That's better. At least I can stand up again.'

Pointing her torch at the steep rock walls, Cesaria was exploring the chamber for a way out. 'Here, look,' she said. 'Another shaft; a big one.'

Lola walked over to investigate.

'*Oh no!*' said Cesaria, sounding exasperated.

'What is it?'

'Come.'

Holding a rusty iron bar with both hands, Cesaria was furiously shaking a solid grate reaching from floor to ceiling, blocking her way.

'The shaft's been closed off,' said Lola, running her fingers along a chain attached to an iron ring set into the rock wall. 'It's not moving. We can't get out!'

Looking defeated, Lola sank to her knees and buried her face in her hands. Jack crawled over to her and put his arm around her. 'Don't worry, Lola. We'll get out of here, you'll see,' he said.

'How can you say that?' Just look at this!' Lola began to rattle the grate with the chain.

'It's not our time.'

'He's right,' said Tristan.

'Come on, not you too!' said Lola, tears in her eyes. 'How can you be so sure?'

'Because of that,' said Tristan and pointed into the shaft on the other side of the grate. As Lola turned her head, she could see lights flickering in the distance. Then she heard voices. What Lola could hear were the voices of the firefighters coming towards them out of the darkness.

61

**Adler Security Company compound,
Obersalzberg: 9 November, 4:30 pm**

Ignoring the thunderstorm raging outside, O'Hara put down his binoculars and stared out of the window. He knew exactly what would happen next. More police, two additional fire engines and an ambulance had arrived at the farmhouse at the foot of the mountain. Dragan had been arrested and it was therefore only a matter of time before the authorities came knocking.

The lights inside the salt mine had gone out some time ago as the water kept rising and the tunnels collapsed, making the CCTV cameras inoperative, but O'Hara had seen enough. Landru and Petrinko were both dead, and the unwelcome intruders would have drowned by now in the flooded mine.

Instead of feeling concerned, O'Hara felt strangely energised and elated. It was all part of the high-stakes game he lived for and, once again, he was clearly winning. In many ways, he had carefully prepared for a moment just like this, and it was time for the final masterstroke.

O'Hara picked up his mobile and called his pilot standing by in the next farmhouse.

'Get the chopper ready, we are leaving,' he said. Then he took a last look at his much-prized Llanganates gems spread out on the desk in front of him, and smiled. These were the precious trophies collected over many years that would show him the way.

Beginning with *The Navarro Chronicles*, he packed them carefully into a small metal case, as a bright bolt of lightning illuminated the control room with a ghostly light, and a loud clap of thunder rolled across the mountain, rattling the windows. To many, it would have sounded like a warning, but to O'Hara it was just the opposite: applause. He was about to leave the stage, leaving nothing behind for his opponents but unanswered questions and speculation. O'Hara, the master tactician and manipulator, wouldn't have it any other way.

The pilot opened the tall barn doors and activated the turntable. Slowly, the helicopter moved outside into the open, ready for take-off.

Fully aware of the staggering implications of what had taken place inside the mine, Gruber had taken control of the situation. First, he had made sure that the paramedics carefully examined everybody as they came out of the mine. The firefighters and Wagner had done an outstanding job in bringing everybody out safely, and so quickly. Apart from some superficial cuts and bruises everyone seemed fine. Even Cesaria's stab wound wasn't too serious as it turned out, and stopped bleeding once a bandage was applied. Jack was the weakest, but he too would recover quickly. All he needed was rest and a hearty meal.

Because no-one was allowed to leave, the mayor had arranged accommodation in the prestigious Kempinski Hotel on the Obersalzberg. The Kempinski was an excellent choice. Privacy and discretion were assured and because of the high-profile celebrity status of his guests, both were needed.

Gruber realised that if only part of what Cesaria had told him about their escape was true, the matter would quickly become a sensation, involving law enforcement agencies from a number of countries. And that could quickly escalate and propel Berchtesgaden and the notorious Obersalzberg into the international spotlight, especially as some form of neo-Nazi involvement was a distinct possibility.

A shrewd and experienced public servant, Gruber quickly recognised this was a golden opportunity to advance his career. And what was happening around him was the opportunity of a lifetime he had to take advantage of. He was in the right place at the right time, and could therefore influence events and be noticed before Europol and detectives from Munich arrived and took over.

The police officer in charge had been instructed by his superiors to secure the site, treat it as a crime scene, and wait for the detectives coming from Munich to arrive.

Gruber walked over to the mayor, who was talking to the firefighters, and took him aside.

'I think we should go back up to the Adler compound and have another look around. Whatever has happened down here is linked to Adler Security. They own this place.'

Gruber was watching the mayor carefully. 'We could do something useful before the detectives get here; what do you think? You mentioned a possible neo-Nazi connection ...'

The mayor, also an ambitious man, nodded. He realised at once where Gruber was going with this: initiative was the key to advancement.

'Why don't you talk to the police officer in charge here, and ask him to come with us?' suggested Gruber. 'You seem to know him well. We could even take the firefighters along to add a little clout, in case they don't let us in up there.'

'Good idea. I'll talk to them.'

O'Hara stood at the window and watched two police cars and a fire engine approach the closed gate. It was raining heavily and dense mist was rolling in from the valley below, which almost obscured the view.

Here they come, thought O'Hara and closed the metal case on the bench in front of him. Then he checked the detonator – a complex device – and carefully put it into his shoulder bag. Taking a last look out the window, he saw the fire engine crash though the boom gate. *Definitely time to go*, thought O'Hara. Then he hurried down to the basement and walked through the tunnel leading to the farmhouse where the helicopter was waiting.

The police officer in charge was driving the car that followed the fire engine through the shattered gate. Gruber tapped him on the shoulder. 'That was bold,' he said.

'In Bavaria we do things differently,' said the officer, grinning.

'Well done,' said the mayor, who sat in the back of the police car. 'After all, you were told to secure the crime scene. I have no doubt that all this here is part of it.'

'Let's see if you're right,' said the officer. 'Once we talk to whoever's in charge here, we'll know. Here we are.'

'Can you hear it?' said Gruber and held up his hand. They were standing in front of the house in the driving rain. The place looked deserted, and the mayor had just rung the doorbell.

'*A helicopter!*' said the officer and ran to the back of the house to investigate.

Sitting next to the pilot, O'Hara listened to the powerful engine roar into life as the helicopter took off. 'Fly over my house,' said O'Hara and looked down. He could see two police cars parked in front of the house and several people standing in the rain, looking up. Smiling, O'Hara reached into his shoulder bag and activated the detonators. Moments later, there was a massive explosion. The roof of the house was blown apart and a fireball almost reached up to the helicopter as it gained altitude and turned away.

Lying on the ground next to the police officer, covered in shards of glass, the mayor watched the helicopter disappear into the mist.

'You were right,' said the officer and stood up. 'It's a crime scene all right.'

62

Kempinski Hotel Berchtesgaden, Obersalzberg: 10 November

Cesaria turned to Tristan sitting next to her in the private breakfast room the manager had made available for their exclusive use. Gruber had just arrived with the mayor and was giving an update. 'Jack should really hear this,' she said. 'How is he; do you know?'

'Still sleeping, I think. He had a big meal last night, and then went straight to bed. I'll go and have a look.' Tristan stood up and left the room.

He returned a few minutes later with Jack. Wearing a bathrobe and slippers, his dishevelled hair and grey stubble accentuating the deep rings under his eyes, Jack looked like someone who had spent a week in an Oktoberfest beer tent without sleep.

'How do you feel?' said Gruber. He stood up and walked over to Jack.

Jack put an arm around Gruber's shoulder and looked at the others having breakfast. 'I would like to say something,' he said. 'How do I feel? Grateful. In more ways than I can express right now. What you did yesterday was extraordinary.' Jack looked first at Lola, then Isis sitting next to her, and then Cesaria. 'I wouldn't be here without you guys, and that includes you, Herr Oberregierungsrat Gruber, and you, Mr Mayor.'

'That's quite a speech on an empty stomach,' said Isis, who noticed that Jack was becoming emotional. 'I think you could do with some breakfast. Would you like some?'

'I thought you'd never ask. I'm starving.'

'Herr Gruber, could you please repeat what you've just told us? For the starving latecomer's benefit?' said Cesaria, a sparkle in her eyes.

'Certainly.'

While Jack was devouring his breakfast, Gruber described what had taken place at the Adler compound.

'Not only did the explosion and the fire completely destroy the house, it also blew up extensive installations under the house,' said Gruber. 'Obviously all of this was quite deliberate. A huge amount of explosives must have been used and detonated by a timer, or somehow from a distance. No bodies were found in the ruins.'

'What kind of installations?' said Cesaria.

'Bunkers left over from the war.'

'What was inside them; do we know?'

'The Forensics team is there right now investigating all this. There isn't much left after the blast, but I understand it was all sophisticated electronics gear.'

Jack looked at Cesaria. 'Could be the dark net server,' he said.

'That's what I've been thinking.'

'And there was a helicopter that got away?' said Isis.

Gruber turned to the mayor. 'You know more about this than I do. Could you tell us?'

'Yes. Just before the explosion, a helicopter took off from one of the farmhouses further up. I saw two people in the chopper. The pilot and someone sitting next to him.'

'Incredible! And they got away?' said Lola.

'What I'm about to tell you must stay in this room, at least for the moment,' said the mayor, lowering his voice. 'I was told in confidence.'

'Understood,' said Jack, looking up.

'The helicopter crashed—'

'*What?* exclaimed Jack and wiped his mouth with a serviette. 'Where? How?'

'The exact circumstances are still under investigation, but it would appear that the chopper crashed into a mountainside near Koenigssee and plunged into the lake. Police divers are there right now. The lake is very deep there and surrounded by mountains.'

Silence.

'Obviously no survivors. The storm?' said Cesaria.

The mayor shook his head. 'It's not that simple.'

'What do you mean?' said Jack.

'According to an eyewitness, the chopper landed briefly next to a remote farmhouse close to the lake.'

'Interesting,' said Jack.

'It gets better,' continued the mayor. 'Moments after it took off again, the eyewitness heard an explosion and saw the chopper plunge into the lake.'

'Are you suggesting it didn't crash into the mountainside but exploded in mid-air?' said Isis.

The mayor shrugged.

'What about that farmhouse?' asked Jack. 'Do we know anything about it?'

'We do, but please remember this is strictly confidential. You'll see why in a moment.' The mayor looked around the room, apparently seeking assurance.

'Are you going to tell us?' asked Cesaria quietly.

'No-one is living in the farmhouse. It's empty, but that's not the interesting bit.'

'What is?' said Jack.

'The owner.'

'Adler Security?' suggested Tristan.

'Exactly,' said the mayor, surprised. 'How did you know?'

The detectives from Munich arrived later in the morning and began to interview everybody and take statements.

'Clearly this will take some time,' said Isis. They were having coffee with Gruber in the lounge while they waited their turn. Isis pointed to her tracksuit the manager had provided from the stores of the wellness centre. 'We obviously need some clothes, don't you think?'

'I will make arrangements with the concierge,' said Gruber.

'I have no problem with mine,' Jack chimed in, contentedly devouring a delicious piece of cake. 'I love tracksuits.'

'All right for you, my friend,' said Isis. 'Not everyone is a rugged outdoor type like you who doesn't mind standing in salt water for hours. Some of us are little more refined.'

'Ah. Is that what it is?'

'Absolutely. I would be grateful if you could arrange that, Herr Gruber,' continued Isis, undeterred. 'Perhaps a pair of *Lederhosen*, or a Bavarian *Dirndl*? What do you think?'

'Why not both?'

'Why not indeed. How exciting!'

'If I'm the rugged type, you are a hopeless fashion aficionado. A rather snobbish one at that,' said Jack, starting on his second slice of sachertorte.

'I can live with that,' said Isis. She crossed her legs and sat back in her chair.

'By the way, Chief Superintendent Lapointe and Monsieur Dupree are on their way,' said Gruber, tactfully changing the subject. 'They should be here around midday.'

'Our French contingent. That should be interesting,' said Jack. 'The hostage exchange.'

'I just had a long conversation with Katerina in Venice,' said Tristan, who had overheard the remark. He sat down next to Jack and slipped his phone into his pocket. 'She made a suggestion.'

'What kind of suggestion?' asked Jack.

'She has invited us all to Venice. She said after all we've been through, a couple of days in the Palazzo da Baggio would do us good. As you know, the hotel is still closed. The funeral ...'

'What an excellent idea!' said Isis, becoming excited. 'We have the plane right here. I haven't been to Venice in ages. We could be there in a couple of hours. What do you think, Jack?'

'Great. We could all do with a little time out. Let's ask Bartolli and Mademoiselle Darrieux to fly down and join us there. I know they would hate to miss out.'

'In that case, I need a new wardrobe,' said Isis, turning serious.

'Can't let Darrieux outshine you,' mumbled Jack.

'We might have to go into Salzburg. Could that be done, Herr Gruber?' said Isis, ignoring the remark.

'I don't see why not. Salzburg is only half an hour or so from here.'

'Excellent. Did you hear that, Lola?'

'I did. I'll tell the boys to get the plane ready, and we can leave as soon as the police let us go.'

'Sure, but first, we go shopping!'

63

Kempinski Hotel Berchtesgaden, Johann Grill: 10 November

After a gruelling interview with the detectives from Munich who had taken over the case, Jack headed straight to the Johann Grill, the famous hotel restaurant. He had invited Wagner to join him for lunch. Because of Wagner's extensive knowledge of local family history, especially during the Nazi era, Jack wanted to follow up on the three families Wagner had mentioned: the Berghofers, the Steinbergers and the Hoffmeisters.

Smartly dressed in a Bavarian *Janker*, white shirt and traditional tie, Wagner was wearing his Sunday best. It wasn't often that he got invited to one of the most exclusive restaurants in the area, albeit one that was very close to Dokumentation Obersalzberg, where he worked.

'Firstly, I wanted to thank you for yesterday. Without your invaluable knowledge of that mine labyrinth down there, the boys from the fire brigade wouldn't have found us, and I wouldn't be sitting here with you.'

'I'm glad I was able to help.'

'You did more than that. You saved us.'

Wagner smiled. 'Be that as it may, I'm sure you didn't invite me to this posh place just to talk about that. I saw your reaction when I mentioned a possible neo-Nazi link between the Berghofer place and Adler Security.'

'Very perceptive of you. You're right. As you know, I'm a writer—'

'I do know that; a very famous one,' interjected Wagner. 'Is that what this is all about?'

Jack waved dismissively. 'No, it goes much further than that. You seem to have a keen interest in family histories from around here, especially during the Nazi period, which, of course, featured very dramatically up here on the Obersalzberg.'

Wagner nodded. 'Comes with the territory. My job.'

'Forgive me for saying this, but to me it sounded like more than that. It sounded personal.'

'I'm impressed, Mr Rogan. You're right. My grandparents owned property almost exactly where we are sitting right now. This here was part of their dairy farm: milk and cheese. The best. It had been in the family for generations until the Nazis confiscated it. Hitler's Berghof, Martin Bormann's house, and Goering's "mountain lodge" as he liked to call it, all stood on land once owned by my family. They tried to resist the Nazis, but lost. The Berghofers, the Hoffmeisters and especially the Steinbergers embraced the Nazis and did much better. Their sons joined the Nazi party and advanced rapidly.

'And one of them was Sturmbannfuehrer Wolfgang Steinberger, isn't that right? He was very active in Auschwitz.'

Wagner looked at Jack, surprised. 'That's correct. You are very well informed. Yes, he was one of the boys from here who had an illustrious career in the SS. He often came here to the Obersalzberg in his chauffeur-driven Mercedes. Not just to visit family, but on official business with Hitler and his cronies.'

'To do with gold shipments to Switzerland. Dental gold from the concentration camps. Horrendous stuff like that. That's how the Nazis financed the war and feathered their nests, and later their getaway, right?'

Wagner nodded, impressed. 'He was very well connected. Right up to the top. Money talks, you see. Nothing's changed.'

'Do you know what happened to him? After the war, I mean,' said Jack.

Wagner shrugged. 'Not really. He disappeared like so many of them.'

'I can tell you what happened to him.'

'*You can?* How come?'

'You are right, he was very well connected, and not just in Germany. After the war he stayed for a while in Rome. Protected by the Vatican. He was helping other high-ranking Nazis to go abroad with new identities. He had access to money – huge Nazi money. And then, he reinvented himself.'

'What do you mean?'

'He became Dr Erich Neumueller, an aeronautical engineer, and migrated to Australia. A new, albeit stolen identity; the real Dr Neumueller was killed in an air raid in Dresden. A new life and a new start made possible by the Vatican. A few years later, he changed his name to Newman and became a prominent banker. He was even knighted and became Sir Eric Newman—'

'How do you know all this?' interrupted Wagner.

'It's a long story. He was prosecuted in Australia for war crimes and went on trial. That's how I became involved. It all began with a famous violin, the Empress. A Stradivarius. I even wrote a book about it.'

'You are a dark horse, Mr Rogan. Do you know what happened to him?'

'Yes. He had a heart attack in court and died shortly after that. The court case was closed. He was in his eighties by then, but there's a lot more to all this. And then, of course, there was his brother, Dr Erwin Steinberger, the infamous Auschwitz surgeon who experimented mainly on twins. For a while, he was also Goering's physician. Erwin and his brother were staying at the Ritz in Paris at the time. That was in 1941.'

'This is astonishing,' said Wagner, looking stunned. 'Few around here know about that. It's a terrible part of history that many want to forget and pretend it never happened.'

'In that case they certainly wouldn't know what happened to him after the war, would they?' said Jack, enjoying himself.

'Are you suggesting that you do?'

'Yes. And how that came about is another remarkable story. I wrote a book about that too. He went to live in Kenya and changed his name to van Der Hooven. But a leopard doesn't change its spots. He continued with his despicable medical experiments, mainly using trusting natives. This time it wasn't for the Nazis, but for wealthy drug companies with deep pockets that didn't ask too many questions about the how, and were only interested in results. But this didn't end well, either. He was killed by the Mau on his farm in 1960.'

'You amaze me, Mr Rogan. Well, at least now I know what happened to the Steinberger boys. Another chapter to add to the sad Obersalzberg story. No happy endings. Hard to believe when you look around up here today. Look at this hotel. Five-star luxury built on a spot where some of the most shocking crimes in history were planned. Millions died. The timeless beauty of the spectacular landscape here hides many tears.'

'It does, but the scars remain, don't they?'

'They do. That's why I'm so passionate about the museum. The world must never forget.'

'You are right. I can tell you what happened to one of the Hoffmeister boys as well,' said Jack, smiling. He reached for his glass and looked at Wagner.

'You can? You are full of surprises. Which one?'

'Anton Hoffmeister.'

'Incredible. The Hoffmeister farm was just over there, next to ours.' Wagner pointed pensively out the window, the hurt in his eyes apparent.

'After the war, Hoffmeister also ended up in Rome and linked up with Wolfgang Steinberger,' said Jack.

'They grew up together, you know. Up here. They were all part of the wolf pack I mentioned.'

'That explains it. Steinberger and the Vatican helped Hoffmeister to migrate to Argentina and start a new life there. He became Don Antonio, a nightclub owner. Tango clubs. I visited him there.'

'You did? You met him?'

'Yes.'

'Why?'

'It's complicated. It all had to do with the Steinberger prosecution. Hoffmeister was going to give evidence in the case, but it all went wrong.'

'What happened to him, do you know?'

'He died a broken man, in Buenos Aires.'

'As I said, no happy endings. This is astonishing, to say the least. Especially in light of what happened yesterday.'

'It is. And it doesn't end there. I would like to talk about the Berghofer family, especially Johann Berghofer, who is buried in Berchtesgaden, and his son who joined the Nazis.'

'I can help you there, but why?'

'Do you believe in destiny, Herr Wagner?'

'A strange question, but yes I do. Very much in fact.'

'I thought so. So do I.'

Jack pointed to the burnt-out ruins of the cordoned-off farmhouse in the distance.

'In a way it's all about destiny. I believe what happened yesterday over there at the Adler compound is all linked to the past we just discussed. The Berghofers.'

'Intriguing. What would you like to know?'

'I'll tell you, but let's order first, shall we?'

Jack had asked Tristan to come with him into Berchtesgaden. He wanted to visit the cemetery before it got dark. It was his only opportunity because they had been given permission to leave the next day after the last of the police interviews. Lola had made the necessary arrangements for their short flight to Venice, and the plane was standing by.

'You spent a lot of time with Wagner this afternoon,' said Tristan. He was sitting next to Jack in the hotel limousine taking them into Berchtesgaden.

'He was very helpful.'

'In what way?'

'He provided the missing breadcrumbs that showed me the way.'

'Way to where?'

'Ronan O'Hara. I believe I know who he really is, and where he fits into all this.'

'You do? Care to explain?'

'I will, as soon as we get there.'

'Where are we going?'

'The cemetery. The same one you visited with Frau Reiter yesterday.'

'Why?'

'Look, we are almost there,' said Jack, ignoring the question as the car pulled up in front of the Franziskaner Kirche. 'Wait here, please,' he said to the driver. 'We won't be long.'

'It's all coming back to me,' said Jack as they walked through the cemetery gates next to the church.

'What exactly?' asked Tristan.

'Christmas Eve 2008. It was snowing and candles had been lit on most of the graves here. It was a magical moment, very emotional. I was looking for the grave of Brother Francis.'

'Described in his letter?' said Tristan. He reached into his pocket and pulled out a piece of paper and handed it to Jack. 'This one?'

Jack looked at it, his eyes misting over. It was the copy of Brother Francis's letter that Tristan had brought with him from London. 'You are a remarkable young man, Tristan, you know this, don't you? You too recognised that the Berghofer grave here held the key to all this, didn't you? Both of us sensed it, perhaps for different reasons.'

Jack walked along the narrow gravel path between the rows of graves and stopped. 'Here it is, just as I remember it. Johann Berghofer. This is where I found the Francis diary concealed under the headstone.'

'That showed us the way to the Imperial Crypt in Vienna.'

'And led to the discovery of the lost Monet hidden in that sarcophagus you identified because you could see and feel what others couldn't,' said Jack. 'The whisper of angels ...'

'It's all about voices reaching out from the past. All you have to do is listen.'

'Few know how. And that's why I've asked you to come here with me, because I want you to listen to what this grave is telling us. Not only this one, but one other as well. The important one.'

'Oh?'

'The grave of his wife, Elfriede, who died in 1984.'

'Did Wagner tell you about that?'

'Yes.'

'How is this relevant?'

'I'll tell you in a moment. You'll remember a while back I thought I had finally discovered who Brother Francis really was.'

'Yes. You concluded that he must have been SS Sturmbannfuehrer Franz Berghofer, the son of Johann Berghofer.'

'Yes. It all made sense at the time, but as it turns out, I was wrong. Franz had a brother, you see: Heinrich, also SS.'

'Oh?'

'In light of what Wagner told me, I think I now know who Brother Francis really was and why, and how, he ended up on the Coberg Mission in Australia with Sister Elizabeth.'

'Your grandmother?'

Jack nodded.

'Are you going to tell me?' asked Tristan.

'Yes. It's all about Elfriede Berghofer. Come.' Jack pointed to the next row of graves. 'She's buried with her parents in the family grave over there.'

Slowly, Jack walked over to the grave, his eyes moist with emotion.

'Here it is. Elfriede Berghofer. Born in 1890.' Jack reached into his pocket, pulled out a box of matches and a small candle and lit it. Then he bent down and placed it carefully into the small lantern attached to the headstone.

'Now let me tell you a remarkable story about Elfriede Berghofer and her other son, Heinrich,' said Jack. 'And while I do, I would like you to listen and tell me if you can hear the whisper of angels, because what I'm about to tell you is all about destiny.'

64

Palazzo da Baggio, Venice: 11 November

Isis was greeted with great fanfare at Marco Polo airport as soon as *Pegasus* landed. She was well known in Italy and still had a huge following. Customs officials and excited airport staff came running from all sides, asking for an autograph from their idol. Dressed in an Austrian designer *Dirndl* and a cute hat with eagle feathers she had bought in Salzburg, Isis was enjoying the attention. For an ageing rock star who craved the limelight, this was the oxygen that kept her creativity, and her memories, alive.

Countess Kuragin was waiting with Bartolli and Darrieux on the small pontoon in front of the palazzo, with its traditional striped gondola mooring posts, for the water taxi to arrive. Darrieux and Bartolli had arrived on an earlier flight from Paris. Having only heard snippets of the dramatic events of the past few days, they could barely wait to hear the full story.

The kitchen staff had assembled on the terrace facing the Grand Canal, and waved excitedly as soon as Isis stepped off the taxi. Delighted by the warm welcome, Isis waved back and blew kisses to her adoring fans.

Countess Kuragin, the consummate host, was in her element. After showing her guests to their rooms, pre-dinner drinks were served in the large salon on the first floor. It was the same room where only a short time ago, Lorenza had been farewelled by mourners. Because the palazzo and the restaurant, Osman's Kitchen, were still closed to the public after the funeral, the countess had the kitchen staff's undivided attention and had therefore been able to arrange a feast fit for a doge. She knew that Lorenza would have wanted it that way. After lengthy consultation with the head chef, a special menu had been chosen, with Hunkar Begendi, Osman's Kitchen's famous signature dish, the centrepiece.

When Bartolli heard what was planned for dinner, she was in raptures. She was shown the famous Ottoman recipe gracing the restaurant walls, introduced to the kitchen staff, and given a tour of the kitchen.

Dupree, who had arrived in Berchtesgaden with Lapointe the day before to join the investigation, had spent the whole day, and half the night, in meetings with the police, interviewing Dragan. They were trying to arrange his extradition to Paris to face trial for the murder of two police officers and related offences. When Dupree heard that Jack, Isis and even Cesaria were going to Venice with Isis, he asked Lapointe for permission to accompany them. Lapointe agreed, as Dupree was no longer needed in Berchtesgaden and the rest of the complex matter would now be up to him and the Prefect in Paris to unravel. And besides, he had a special assignment in mind for Dupree.

Cesaria, who was urgently needed in Florence because the Mafia trial in Calabria was about to start, had come along for practical reasons. She could stay overnight in Venice, and then catch an early train to Florence. And besides, she didn't want to miss what she realised would be a special occasion. She had seen enough of the Palazzo da Baggio and Countess Kuragin's hospitality to realise that this would be a celebration dinner not to be missed.

The countess walked over to Jack standing by the open window overlooking the canal. 'You and your escapades, Jack. Must have been quite something. Cesaria just told me all about the rescue. Sounds unbelievable, like a movie. It's a miracle you made it out alive.'

Jack shrugged. 'I'm here. That's all that counts.'

'You don't want to talk about it?'

'Not really.'

The countess handed Jack a glass of champagne. 'I understand. Welcome back, Jack. You look remarkably well, all considering.'

They touched glasses.

'Anna looks happy,' said Jack. 'I haven't seen her so animated for a long time.'

'She loves it here. It's an artist's paradise. She hasn't stopped painting. Something to do with wonderful childhood memories, I think; we often visited here during the holidays, and she and Lorenza were close. And Bobby loves school ...'

'You are staying here, then?'

'I'll tell you later.'

'Leonardo seems much better.'

'You think so?'

'Definitely. You bring sunshine wherever you go, Katerina. It's a gift.'

The countess leaned across to Jack and kissed him on the cheek. 'Thanks Jack. Tristan hinted that there's something you want to—'

'Get off my chest? Perhaps. I'm still thinking about it.'

'It's wonderful to see everybody here, don't you think?' said the countess, changing the subject because the expression on Jack's face told her not to probe further. 'Especially after all that's happened. I still can't believe that two police officers were gunned down in front of the cottage, and Landru ...'

'That was dreadful. We are dealing with some very dark people here. That's why I'm still hesitating.'

'What about?'

'Getting certain things off my chest.'

'I see.'

Dupree, who was standing in front of the fireplace, tapped a small spoon against his glass. 'May I have your attention please?' he said. 'I have something important to tell you before we go and have dinner. It's a message from Chief Superintendent Lapointe. He just called me and sends his regards, and regrets not being able to be here tonight. But there was another reason for his call: a disconcerting breakthrough in the investigation,' said Dupree, speaking softly.

Everyone in the room stopped talking and looked at Dupree, the tension growing by the second.

'What kind of breakthrough?' asked Jack, sounding apprehensive.

'The police divers have just found the wreck of the helicopter in the lake. That by itself is unremarkable, but what they *didn't* find, is.'

'What didn't they find?' asked Tristan, who already knew the answer.

'A second body.'

'What are you suggesting?' said Jack quietly, breaking the silence.

'Most of the cabin was still intact. The body of the pilot was still strapped into his seat, but the seat next to him was empty, with the seatbelt still attached. The passenger wasn't there.'

'Could he have been thrown out of the cabin during the explosion?' asked Isis.

Dupree shook his head. 'The experts don't think so. As I said, the cabin was more or less intact.'

'What does this mean?' asked Cesaria.

'The current thinking is this: we know that the helicopter made a brief landing at a farmhouse close to the lake, and then exploded moments later while making a turn over the lake. An eyewitness saw it all.'

'The passenger got out before the helicopter disintegrated and plunged into the lake. Is that what you're saying?' asked Jack.

'That's exactly what I'm saying,' said Dupree. 'According to the Adler staff at the compound, who have now all been interviewed, the passenger was a "Tobias Berghofer", an electronics genius and managing director of Adler Security, who lived in the house that was blown up. An eccentric recluse, so it seems. People rarely saw him; some of them didn't even know what he looked like. I believe by now Europol has every country in Europe looking for him,' said Dupree.

'So, the man we believe was behind the Death Mask Murders, the Dark Net Bazaar with all that depraved gambling, and everything that happened in the salt mines, got away *again*?' said Cesaria, shaking her head.

'Looks that way,' said Dupree.

'Astonishing, but in a way it all fits,' continued Cesaria. 'According to Samartini, the DNB and the gambling site she was monitoring went off the air at about the same time the house in the compound exploded—'

'Destroying the dark net server,' interjected Jack. 'Are we saying that blowing up the house with all its underground installations, and then blowing up the chopper after this Tobias Berghofer got out and disappeared was all part of a sophisticated, well-planned getaway?'

'That's the way the police are looking at it at the moment.'

Reading the mood in the room, Countess Kuragin, an experienced host, could see her dinner plans drifting in the wrong direction. It was time to intervene and restore the congenial atmosphere before gloom and doom spoiled the evening. Bad news rarely enhanced the appetite. She clapped her hands together, trying to break the spell.

'We can talk about all this later, my friends. Dinner is about to be served. Please follow me.'

65

Palazzo da Baggio, Venice; the dinner: 11 November

The dining room with its original seventeenth-century solid-oak dining table and intricately carved high-backed chairs was lit entirely by candles, making the large room with its paintings and tapestries appear intimate and inviting. The shadows dancing along the walls as the waiters served the food, made the da Baggio ancestors come to life in their portraits lining the walls, witnesses one and all of a memorable evening about to unfold in the dining room where cardinals, European royalty and even two popes had enjoyed da Baggio hospitality over the centuries.

A floral display in the middle of the table added colour, and the rare Meissen china plates and stunning antique Austrian solid silver-gilt and enamel cutlery added opulence and style, ensuring that the dinner would be a truly memorable occasion.

'You must have culinary magicians working in the kitchen, Katerina,' said Bartolli after Hunkar Begendi, the main course, had been served. 'I have never tasted anything quite like this. Amazing.'

'That's what the pope said,' said Jack, smiling.

'He should know,' added Tristan. 'It saved his life, after all.'

'All the dishes served this evening are Lorenza's creations,' said the countess, ignoring the remark. 'She found ways to fuse classic Ottoman cuisine with contemporary Venetian cooking.'

'Genius,' said Bartolli, enjoying her second serving.

'I thought we'd have a little break before dessert is served,' said the countess. She knew that breaks between courses were not only essential to allow the palate to adjust, but added to the enjoyment of the dishes by encouraging conversation between courses.

Tristan turned to Jack sitting next to him. 'Are you going to tell them? This would be a good moment, don't you think?'

Jack had been in two minds all night about whether to talk about the disconcerting discovery he had made in Berchtesgaden the day before that had rocked him to the core, and he was still struggling to come to terms with. The reason for his hesitation was due to the fact that some of the conclusions he had reached were still speculative. Not everything was clear. He knew that interpreting the past was never black and white, only shades of grey at best.

Discovering what has been hidden for so long and interpreting it correctly is always fraught with danger. It is easy to fall into error because of what one *wants* to see rather than what one *should*, based on the facts. Because of the staggering implications – should his interpretation of the facts turn out to be correct – Jack had hesitated. Yet he knew that Tristan was right. Everyone present had played a part and therefore deserved to know. It was the right moment. The breadcrumbs of destiny might never align again, and missing that moment could result in serious regrets later.

When Jack looked at Lorenza's coffin photo on the mantelpiece, he thought he could hear her whisper: 'Tell them, Jack. Now's the time. Do it for me.'

'You're right, Tristan,' said Jack and stood up. 'May I have your attention for a moment please, my friends.' Jack looked pensively around the dining table, collecting his thoughts. As his eyes drifted from Isis sitting opposite, to Lola, Cesaria, Bartolli and Darrieux looking at him expectantly, and then came to rest on Dupree, Anna and Countess Kuragin sitting next to Leonardo at the head of the table, he knew that he had made the right decision.

'I have something important to tell you. Something very personal that is a direct result of the extraordinary events we have witnessed recently. Tristan and I went to a little cemetery next to the Franziskaner Kirche in Berchtesgaden last night. You will remember that I visited that cemetery on Christmas Eve in 2008, and retrieved Brother Francis's diary hidden in a grave identified by him. You all know what followed after that. Tristan and I discovered the hidden Monet in the Imperial Crypt in Vienna.

'The grave in Berchtesgaden belonged to Johann Berghofer and what I'm about to tell you has to do with the Berghofer family, with destiny, and with fate. It's all about four friends who lived on the Obersalzberg we just visited. All four left their farms and their families, joined the Nazi party and went to war. They were dazzled by Hitler's charisma, followed the siren call of the Third Reich and had illustrious careers in the SS.'

Everyone around the table was listening intently, captivated by Jack's storytelling.

'As all of you are familiar with my books,' continued Jack, 'you already know what happened to three of them. Wolfgang Steinberger migrated to Australia; his brother Erwin, a surgeon, went to live in Kenya; and Anton Hoffmeister ended up in Argentina. All were senior SS officers with blood on their hands, who received help from the Vatican to leave Europe after the war and start a new life. You know their remarkable stories, so I will not repeat them. But what you do not know is the story of the fourth one, Heinrich Berghofer.'

I wonder where he's going with this, thought Countess Kuragin, watching Jack carefully.

'Ever since I met Brother Francis at the Coberg Mission in Queensland as a boy, and then years later located his diary hidden in the Berghofer grave I just mentioned, I wondered who he really was. At the Coberg Mission he was known only as Brother Francis, a gentle man who had joined the Pallottines after the war, worked in the fields, and was close to Sister Elizabeth, my grandmother. How I found out about that is another story most of you are familiar with, and I will not go into again right now. Brother Francis's real name and identity, however, had remained a mystery for years, until after some careful digging I concluded that he must have been Franz Berghofer, the son of Johann Berghofer. The diary hidden in the grave in Berchtesgaden strongly supported this. But as it turns out, I was wrong.'

'In what way?' asked Countess Kuragin, who knew how much all this meant to Jack.

'Franz Berghofer had a brother, Heinrich. Both joined the SS and rose rapidly through the ranks. SS Sturmbannfuehrer Franz Berghofer was close to Hitler and died in Berlin during the Russian advance. His brother, Heinrich, also a Sturmbannfuehrer, escaped and ended up in Vienna—'

'Do you know what happened to him?' interrupted Isis.

'Yes, I only found out during our recent visit to MI5 in London. Buried in the files dealing with Ronan O'Hara was a name that started it all: Heinrich Berghofer, a high-ranking SS officer wanted for war crimes who, helped by the Vatican, ended up in Ireland after the war. He was working on a farm in Cork as a labourer. That's where he met Kate O'Hara, a housemaid. They had a son, Ronan. Kate O'Hara gave birth after Heinrich did a runner and disappeared. There was nothing further about him in the files. MI5 had no idea what happened to him after that, nor did they care ... but Wagner knew.'

'How?' asked Isis.

'Heinrich's father, Johann, died in 1932. His mother, however, died many years later, in her nineties. Wagner, whose family had lived on the Obersalzberg until they were evicted by the Nazis, knew her well. She spent her last years in a nursing home, and Wagner visited her often. As I told you, he is very passionate about local history, especially the Nazi era. It was during one of those visits that she told him.'

Jack hesitated and took a sip of wine, steeling himself for what was to come.

'What did she tell him?' asked Cesaria.

'That her son had visited her briefly after the war. He was a wanted man by then because of his involvement in putting down the Warsaw Ghetto revolt. Effectively, he was a war criminal on the run. He told his mother that the Vatican was making arrangements for him to join the Pallottines and go to live in Australia. He also told her about two children: a girl born in Paris just before the end of the war, and a boy born in Ireland two years later. Different mothers—'

'What are you telling us, Jack?' asked Countess Kuragin, who could see where this was heading.

'What I'm about to tell you is somewhat speculative. I'm trying to fill in the gaps in the story so far the best I can, but as you will see in a moment, the conclusions are compelling. There is no doubt in my mind that Heinrich Berghofer became Brother Francis after he joined the Pallottines and went to live on the Coberg Mission in outback Queensland, where I met him. I have no doubt that it was Heinrich Berghofer who was hiding from the Russians in the Imperial Vault in Vienna and buried the Monet in the sarcophagus. After escaping from Vienna he made his way to Berchtesgaden to visit his mother, and went into hiding. He stayed there until the Vatican arranged the trip to Australia and it was safe to leave. And while he was in Berchtesgaden, he hid his diary in his father's grave in the little cemetery I just mentioned.'

'Why do you think he did that?' asked Isis.

'He obviously didn't want to take the diary with him to Australia because it was highly incriminating. Neither could he bear to destroy it because it was a link to the past. At bit like the story of the stolen Monet, I suppose. As an art teacher who valued art, he couldn't bring himself to destroy the painting. He couldn't keep it either, so he hid it safely instead.'

'As an artist myself,' said Anna, 'I can understand that.'

Momentarily overwhelmed by the memories, Jack sat down and covered his face with his hands.

'As you know, I went with Jack to visit the cemetery yesterday,' said Tristan, stepping in. 'It was there, standing in front of Elfriede Berghofer's grave – she's buried with her parents in the next row – that all of this became clear. Standing at the grave, Jack told me this story, and while he was talking, everything fell into place. I could sense things and even hear voices reaching out from the past. We know that Sister Elizabeth, who joined the Pallottines before Heinrich and went to work on the Coberg Mission, was Anastasya Petrova, who gave up her daughter and left Paris with her lover during the German evacuation. The daughter she had left behind in Paris, Natasha, grew up at the Kuragin chateau, cared for by her grandparents.'

Tristan turned to Jack.

'As we now know, Natasha was your mother, Jack.'

Jack nodded without looking up.

'What Jack is telling you is this,' continued Tristan. 'Looking at everything he has found out so far objectively, it is reasonable to conclude that Heinrich Berghofer was Jack's grandfather.'

Stunned silence.

'But that would make Ronan O'Hara ...' said Isis.

'My uncle,' replied Jack quietly, choking with emotion.

The room went deathly quiet as everyone tried to come to terms with the sensational revelations, and even the da Baggio ancestors appeared to stare disapprovingly down into the silent dining room.

Trying to break the spell, Isis stood up. 'Facing the truth is never easy,' she said. 'Facing it in public, as you, Adrienne, have done recently, is brave and takes courage. Sharing it with friends and family is honest, and perhaps the most difficult thing to do because that's where we are at our most vulnerable. Love makes us vulnerable, and what Jack has just shared with us makes him vulnerable. Why? Because he is baring his soul for all of us to see.'

Isis walked over to Jack and embraced him in an expression of genuine affection. The ice was broken and everyone began to talk excitedly all at once. Then Isis held up both hands in a theatrical gesture. 'I too, have an announcement to make,' she said. As a seasoned performer, she knew how to command a stage, and at that moment, the dining room was her stage, and those sitting around the table, her audience.

'Thanks to Jack, the last missing piece of the Llanganates treasure puzzle – the burial mask – has been found and has given up its secrets. If the treasure does in fact exist, we now know where to look in order to find it.'

Isis paused, to make her point.

'For that reason, my friends, I now ask for your permission and support to launch a salvage operation as soon as possible to go to Heart Island, follow the clues we have just discovered, and see if the treasure is in fact waiting at the bottom of the sea, where Baudin found the golden burial mask washed up on the beach.'

Isis paused again, enjoying the ripple of excitement washing across the room.

'But in light of what Jack has just told us,' continued Isis, 'we must act quickly – because it seems we are not the only ones who know where Baudin found the mask. Remember what Claude told us on the plane about the handover in Paris that had taken everyone by surprise? The drone flew off with the mask and it is safe to assume that the villain who left his lair and appears to have just escaped, has added it to his collection and now has all the information, as we do, to locate the treasure—'

'Not necessarily,' interrupted Dupree, smiling. He reached under the table, opened his briefcase, took out a small parcel wrapped in brown paper, and placed it on the table in front of him. 'I have something for you, Jack. It is only because of you and your friends here that we have been able to apprehend one of the killers who murdered those two police officers. And for that, the entire French police force is grateful. But that isn't all. You did much more than that. From the moment Landru contacted you and made you his confidant, you joined him in a quest to find the Llanganates treasure, and in doing so, you have solved the mystery surrounding the notorious Death Mask Murders reaching back more than thirty years. It was you who found that crucial final missing link buried in the ruins of Malenkova's house.

'And as for that lost treasure, it was you who found that piece of meteorite that fell from the heavens long ago and became a sacred object revered by in Inca, who made it part of a sacred burial mask that will now show us the way.'

Dupree reached for the parcel and handed it to Jack, sitting opposite. 'This is a token of appreciation from Lapointe and a grateful Prefect for services rendered to the French police. They are sure you will make excellent use of it.'

'What is it?' said Jack.

'Open it and see.'

Slowly, Jack peeled back the brown paper, looked inside the parcel and gasped.

'I don't believe it! *It can't be!* How ...?' he mumbled.

'What is it, Jack?' asked Tristan. 'Show us.'

Jack peeled back the paper completely and held up something heavy that gleamed in the candlelight. Tristan recognised it at once. It was the piece of iridium he and Jack had found buried in the ashes of Malenkova's house.

'Is this the original?' said Jack, barely able to speak.

'Yes, it is,' said Dupree.

'*How is this possible?* You said the drone—'

'What was handed over at the house of horrors and the drone flew away with,' said Dupree, 'wasn't the original, which is right here, but something Professor Flaubert created.'

Dupree pointed to the parcel in front of Jack. 'It was a piece of iridium just like this one. It was a sample from her lab she engraved with similar markings. The only difference being that those markings do not identify the spot where the golden mask was found, but an insignificant cove on the opposite side of the island.'

'That was clever,' said Tristan, turning to Isis. 'No need to hurry then; what do you think?'

Visibly moved, Jack stood up and reached for his glass. 'I would like to propose a toast.' Jack picked up the piece of stardust that once was the sacred part of a burial mask intended to grant a murdered king entry into the afterlife, and held it up. 'This may lead us to a great treasure, but I have the greatest treasure of them all right here: *your friendship.*' Jack looked around the table as the others rose to their feet. '*To friendship,*' he said quietly, and lifted his glass.

66

Mexico City: two months later

Benito Juarez International Airport was chaotic as usual. Boris was waiting for Jack at Customs and took him straight to Isis's home in the centre of Mexico City. It was the spectacular house Isis had inherited from Dolores Gonzales, her grandmother, in 2011. It was also the place of Jack's first meeting with Isis, the legendary rock star.

Isis had relocated to Mexico soon after leaving Palazzo da Baggio in Venice, to arrange the salvage operation on Heart Island. It was a project she knew her grandfather, a prominent archaeologist and art dealer, would have given his right arm to be part of.

Jack remembered the stunning home well. Set into the side of a small hill, the house was built directly on top of the ruins of an Aztec temple. The clever architecture incorporated the features of the ruins into the modern structure without altering or in any way disturbing their integrity. No restoration of any kind had been carried out. Ingenious glass panels and concealed lighting gave the house a surreal, almost stage-like appearance, with stairways and corridors leading in all directions, where rare statues of bloodthirsty gods and mythical creatures lurked around every corner, ready to frighten the unwary.

The only thing visible from the busy road was an elaborate wrought-iron gate, which opened all by itself as soon as the car pulled into the driveway. Everything else was hidden behind high walls and lush, jungle-like vegetation.

'It's just as I remember it,' said Jack as Boris drove into the underground garage. 'This is where I met Isis for the first time; unforgettable.'

'I remember picking you up from the airport,' said Boris. 'A lot of water under the bridge since then.'

'You can say that again. Isis was waiting for me in a huge, underground cave-like chamber entirely lit by candles. It looked like a stage. I think it was once part of a temple forecourt.'

'Correct. She's waiting for you there right now.'

'Perhaps listening to baroque music like last time? And trying on exotic costumes under the watchful eye of her French dress designer fussing over her?'

'Who knows? You'll find out in a moment. Here's the lift now, come.'

Moments later, the lift doors opened and Jack was looking straight at Isis waiting for him.

'What, no tight-fitting costume accentuating the figure? No elaborate helmet-like headdress made of colourful feathers like those worn by Aztec priests?' said Jack after they had embraced. 'How disappointing!'

'Last time you caught me during my dress rehearsal for the big concert here, remember?'

'How can I forget? It certainly made for an unforgettable first meeting. You looked like a goddess. Very intimidating.'

'You think so? Not like the old crow I've turned into, you mean? Look at me now!'

'Come on. Don't be too hard on yourself. You look stunning, as always.'

Mollified, Isis shrugged. 'I thought something a little less dramatic was in order this time. How was your flight?'

'I came as soon as I could. Despite the fact you told me very little. "Drop everything and come", I think were your words. It was just after two in the morning. And before I could ask any questions, you were gone.'

'She didn't want to spoil the surprise,' said Lola, coming down the stairs. 'A bit like you, I suppose. She's been on the phone all night, preparing the way.'

Jack kissed Lola on both cheeks. 'Preparing the way for what?'
'She'll tell you.'

'Come, let's sit,' said Isis. She took Jack by the arm and guided him towards the middle of the chamber.

'Ah, the gruesome Coyolxauhqui stone,' said Jack and sat down on a wooden bench facing a large, exquisitely carved circular stone. 'The Aztec legend of a decapitated and dismembered mythical being. Just when I thought we had left that house of horrors behind for good ...'

'You are one of the very few who've seen this and knew exactly what it was. We were off to a good start.'

'I hope you have better news for me this time,' said Jack. 'Last time you told me about how your parents had been attacked in their home in London. That too was a house of horrors.'

'It was. Happier news this time, don't worry.'

Jack sat back and looked expectantly at Isis sitting demurely next to Lola on a bench opposite, fidgeting. She was trying in vain to hide the excitement boiling within.

'I think we found it,' said Isis softly, her voice quivering with emotion.

'*Seriously?*'

'Yes.'

'Any confirmation?'

'Yes. Marcos Chavero, the marine archaeologist in charge, just confirmed it. I talked to him for over an hour on the phone last night. I know him very well—'

'Isis is a huge benefactor of the Museo Nacional de Antropologia where he works, and has sponsored several digs,' said Lola. 'And as you know, she's quite a collector ...'

'Ah. That would have helped.'

'It sure did. That's the only reason we were able to secure the services of a Florida-based private salvage company: Triton Maritime Archaeological Exploration. Something like that. They are supposed to be the best in the business. Chavero introduced us.'

'After two weeks of disappointments, a result at last? You were just about to give up. What happened?'

'Unfortunately, the engraved landmarks on the mask just weren't precise enough.'

'How so?' asked Jack. 'Photos of the amulet Landru found in Amaro Pargo's grave showed us the way to Heart Island, and the golden mask found on the island by Baudin was supposed to show us the way to the wreck.'

'True, but there were several spots on the island the engraved landmarks could have referred to. We tried them all; nothing! Then Triton brought in a small submarine from Canada the other day. They also used LiDAR, which has recently revolutionised underwater archaeology. That made all the difference. They could actually see—'

'But that's fantastic!' interrupted Jack, excited.

'It is. They found the wreck of the *San Cristobal*, but it was much further out to sea than expected—'

'And the gold?' interrupted Jack.

Isis looked at Lola. 'Tell him.'

'The wreck is stuck on a reef in shallow seas, well preserved. Less than twenty metres down; clear water with excellent visibility. A diver's dream. Easy salvage—'

'And the Llanganates treasure?' interrupted Jack, biting his lip.

Lola turned to Isis. 'How did Profesor Chavero put it?'

'He pronounced it one of the greatest finds in maritime history. The maritime equivalent of Howard Carter finding Tutankhamen's tomb,' said Isis quietly. 'He believes there are thousands of gold artefacts down there. Even parts of the original trunks are still well preserved. Not to mention a whole shipment of silver from the Potosi mines. It's incredible.'

'Good heavens! So, what's next?'

'We go and have a look, of course, what else?' said Isis. 'But we have to move fast. You can't keep a discovery like this under wraps for too long. Word will get out quickly.'

Jack nodded. 'Then what?'

'All hell will break loose.'

'I can imagine. The vultures will be circling.'

'You bet. For that reason, we must beat them to it.'

'What do you mean?'

'How far did you get with your book?'

'About the Death Mask Murders?'

'Yes.'

'I went straight back to the Kuragin chateau with Adrienne, and began to work on it immediately.'

'Good. You have all the material at your fingertips then?'

'Sure, but why?'

'We'll make an announcement, a big splash. The world will hear this story from us – from you, to be more precise – and I know just the person who will broadcast it to the world.'

'Celia Crawford?'

'Who else? I spoke to her this morning. She'll meet us in Havana.'

'*Havana?*'

'Sure. We'll fly to Havana. Plane's ready. From there it's about a four-hour boat ride to Heart Island. Lola chartered a fast boat for us already. It's waiting in Havana Harbour as we speak. If we leave right now, we could be in Havana in under three hours.'

'You have been busy.'

'The archaeological find of the century waits for no-one.'

'I suppose so. Thanks for waiting for me.'

'We wouldn't leave without you, Jack. Not after what we've been through in those salt mines just to keep you alive. Ready?'

'Sure.'

'Then let's go. Lola, ring the airport.'

Isis stood up and looked around. 'Boris, where are you?'

Heart Island, somewhere in the Caribbean

Celia Crawford, a senior correspondent at the *New York Times* who knew Jack and Isis well, was pacing nervously up and down in front of a sleek motor yacht moored in Havana Harbour. It was the spot Isis had designated for their meeting. Celia had dropped everything after receiving Isis's cryptic phone call earlier that day and, after speaking briefly to her editor in New York, she'd headed straight for the airport. When Isis called and promised the story of the century, Celia came running.

They should have been here by now, she thought. When she looked again at her watch, she noticed a huge red convertible – a 1956 Chevrolet Bel Air – coming towards her. Someone in the back seat was waving furiously and the horn began to blare as the car came closer, almost mounting the kerb before coming to a sudden stop.

'I should have known,' said Celia, laughing. 'The whole gang.' She embraced Jack, who got out of the car first. 'You too? I thought you were in France working on your book.'

'I was, until yesterday. Then Isis called in the middle of the night and here I am.'

'Thanks for coming,' said Isis, kissing Celia on the cheek. 'Where were you when I called?'

'In New Orleans doing an interview about cyclones.'

'Lucky. Quite close then. We could have picked you up on the way. Lola would have loved that. Anything to do with flying, she's your girl. Do you like the car?'

'Fabulous. Typical Cuba.'

'Sure is. They have sixty thousand of these beauties on the island. It's a classic car paradise.'

'What's all this about?' asked Celia, linking arms with Jack. 'Where are we going; do you know?'

'Let's get on board first,' said Isis, pointing to the yacht. 'And then Jack will tell you the whole story. It's best if you hear this from our resident storyteller; isn't that right, Lola?'

'Definitely,' said Lola and followed Isis up the gangplank.

Half an hour later, the powerful motor yacht left the Bay of Marimelena and headed out of the harbour into the Gulf of Mexico. As they were leaving the narrow entry into the harbour and approached Morro Castle, Jack joined Celia on deck.

'Isn't it spectacular?' he said. 'All these fabulous fortifications are still intact. That over there is Morro Castle. Have a good look at it because it played a major role in the story I'm about to tell you.'

'You and your stories, Jack,' said Celia, shaking her head. 'I can't believe we are doing this. First the Stolzfus matter earlier this year, and now this ... whatever "this" is.'

'Brace yourself. It's quite a story.' Jack pointed to the massive fortifications extending right down to the water's edge, as they passed Morro Castle. 'On the morning of seven July 1664, there was a public execution over there in front of the castle. Mad Dog Regan, a notorious pirate, was hanged.'

'Fascinating.'

'It is, because that hanging put a series of unique events in train that have a direct bearing on what we are doing right now.'

'Seriously, Jack, no wonder your books are so successful. You're a born storyteller!'

'Coming from one of the most celebrated and acclaimed journalists in the US, that's quite a compliment.'

Over the next two hours, Jack told Celia the whole story of the Death Mask Murders, Landru, and the Llanganates treasure. Beginning with *The Navarro Chronicles*, the Morales khipu, and the Rodriguez Letter, he told her about James Mascarino and the amulet with the engraved map, Baudin, and the golden burial mask showing the way to the wreck of the *San Cristobal* off Heart Island.

'Come on, Jack, are you suggesting that all of this is *real*, and not just a romantic tale of lost treasures and pirates fit for a thriller and a great movie with Jack Sparrow?'

'It's real all right,' said Isis, who had overheard the remark as she joined them on deck. 'I must admit it sounds a bit like fact stranger than fiction, but you know us well enough by now, Celia. We wouldn't be here if this was merely fantasy, or chasing some shadow from the past.'

Shielding her eyes from the glare, Isis looked out to sea.

'Well, in a moment you can judge for yourself. We are almost there. That's Heart Island over there, and that's the Triton vessel doing the salvage right now.'

A very excited Profesor Chavero, a man in his sixties sporting a spectacular moustache, met them on board the salvage vessel and took them straight to the control room to introduce them to the captain in charge of the salvage.

'I have been in this business for almost thirty years,' said the captain, 'but I haven't seen anything like this before. This is history. What is down there, is almost unimaginable.'

'Let's show them,' said Chavero.

The captain walked over to a table by the window and pointed to a steel box. 'This has just been recovered this morning,' he said. 'Come, have a look.' The captain opened the lid and stepped aside.

Isis gasped.

Holding his breath, Jack stared into the box as Celia squeezed his arm so hard, he almost cried out.

In the centre of the box was a crown of solid gold fit for a king. Next to it were several exquisite gold and emerald necklaces, pectorals, ear plugs and heavy gold bracelets. But the most stunning item by far was a golden mask of great beauty that had once covered the face of an Inca noble, preparing his passage into the afterlife.

'There are thousands of items like this down there, and fortunately for us, not in very deep water. To appreciate the scale you have to go down and have a look,' said Chavero.

'Could that be done?' asked Isis.

'Yes. In the submarine,' said the captain. 'I can arrange it right now, if you like. Interested?'

Isis turned to Jack standing next to her. 'What do you think?'

'I'm in,' said Jack.

'So am I,' said Celia.

'You can't leave me behind,' said Lola.

'You have your answer, Captain. Let's do it!'

The compact, state-of-the-art submarine looked like a curious puffer fish with huge eyes surveying the deep. Instead of fins, it had retractable robotic arms that allowed it to retrieve objects from the ocean floor with surprising agility and precision. Sitting next to the captain at the front, Lola, as a pilot, was particularly fascinated by the controls of this unique vessel, which had great manoeuvrability and a diving capacity to great depths. On this occasion, however, the shallow dive with excellent visibility was more of a sightseeing trip than an expedition to the bottom of the sea.

'I feel like Captain Nemo,' said Jack, as the vessel glided slowly through the water towards the wreck of the *San Cristobal* resting on a reef nearby.

'You're in for a big surprise,' said Profesor Chavero. 'There she is, well preserved as you can see.'

'This must have been a huge ship,' said Isis, pointing to a jumble of massive, barnacle-encrusted timbers illuminated by a shaft of sunlight from above. While most of the ship had fallen apart, it was still possible to make out its overall shape and dimensions.

'Look, there!' said Celia. She was pointing ahead as the barrel of a massive eight-pounder gun came into view. Tiny, colourful fish darted in and out of the safety of the barrel, looking for food. 'And over there – more guns!' continued Celia excitedly.

'Here we are,' said Chavero as the submarine slowed down and, hovering just above the wreck, almost came to a stop. Three divers were working on a section of the wreck below that had once been the huge cargo hold of the galleon. 'The artefacts you saw earlier were in those trunks you can see over there. There are dozens down here, all filled with priceless solid gold pieces. Some of the trunks have fallen apart and there is gold everywhere you look.'

'This is like a dream,' said Jack, looking at the surreal scene in wonder.

One of the divers looked at them and waved. Then he reached into the trunk in front of him in slow motion and pulled out what looked like a golden cup. Swimming towards them he stopped in front of one of the large circular windows, and held up the cup with both hands like a trophy. With his face only centimetres from the window, Jack could make out embossed shapes of faces and strange-looking animals decorating the cup. Then the other two divers arrived, each carrying a golden artefact in what looked like some strange underwater ballet.

Isis turned to Jack sitting next to her. 'Congratulations, Jack, you found the Llanganates treasure.'

'I didn't find it, *we* did. This was a team effort.'

'Perhaps. But what comes now, definitely will be. In many ways, this was the easy bit.'

'What do you mean?'

'The big challenge now is to decide what to do with all this, and how. A find like this will make headlines around the world. It will cause a media storm and attract competing claims of ownership. The salvage is well underway and in expert hands with Profesor Chavero and Triton. But what comes next will be a legal minefield—'

'That's correct,' said Chavero. 'I've been in similar situations before, but nothing on this scale.'

'Is that why you've asked me to come along?' said Celia.

'That's certainly part of it. We have to plan this very carefully. It will be a balancing act between the media, and our legal team. Public opinion is a powerful tool and, of course, so is a court of law,' said Isis.

'*Legal team*? What do you mean?' asked Jack.

'We'll need a team of maritime law and international law specialists to deal with this explosive situation, and I know just the man who can help us there,' said Isis.

'Who?'

'Charles, of course. I had a long discussion with him already and he has some excellent suggestions. But we have to move fast. I asked him to come here and see it all firsthand, but he declined. He said he was much more effective with both feet planted on terra firma. He also said that the only way to keep a clear head was to keep it *above* water.'

'I know what he means,' said Jack laughing. 'You told him about the salt mine?'

'Of course.'

'That's Sir Charles all right. Typically English. He doesn't want to get his bow tie wet, I suppose. So, what's the plan?'

'He will meet us in Havana. In fact, he should be at our hotel when we get back,' said Isis.

'I've booked rooms for us in the Hotel Ambos Mundos,' said Lola.

'Excellent choice. Hemingway lived there for several years,' said Jack, 'in room 511, and began writing *For Whom the Bell Tolls* in that room in 1939.'

'You are well informed,' said Celia.

'Hemingway's one of my favourite writers. He spent a lot of time at the Ritz in Paris, as well. During the war. Madame Petrova actually met him there.'

'I chose the hotel because I knew you would like it,' said Isis. 'And besides, I think it will be the perfect place to discuss the Llanganates find, and what to do with it.'

'I'm impressed,' said Jack. 'You've really given this a lot of thought already, haven't you?'

'Come on, Jack, this is the opportunity of a lifetime. We'll make history with this, can't you see?'

'And I will help you write some of it?' said Celia. 'Is that why I'm here?'

'You will; trust me,' said Isis.

'Hm. You obviously have something quite specific in mind,' said Jack. 'Can you tell us what it is?'

'Later. Look, we're going back,' said Isis, changing the subject as the submarine began to rise slowly, leaving the divers behind at the bottom. 'We must return to Havana as quickly as possible. Every hour counts.'

Hotel Ambos Mundos, Havana

Located in Old Havana, the Hotel Ambos Mundos was popular with tourists mainly because of its famous long-term tenant, Ernest Hemingway, who had lived there for seven years in the 1930s. He'd enjoyed the views over Old Havana from his room on the fifth floor, and the proximity to the harbour where he kept his yacht, *Pilar*.

It was already dark by the time they arrived at the hotel. Dressed in his customary dark-navy pinstriped suit, white shirt and bow tie, Sir Charles was waiting in the bar on the ground floor.

'You do get around, Jack,' said Sir Charles, shaking Jack's hand. 'Last time it was MI5 in London, and now this. I love this hotel. I've been here several times before. Great history. Wonderful location. Drink? You should try the rum.'

'Before we get too comfortable,' said Isis, 'may I suggest we go up to the terrace on the top floor? We can have dinner there, and the view is to die for.'

'Great idea,' said Sir Charles. 'Airline food just isn't my cup of tea!'

Jack turned to Isis standing next to him. 'You seem to know this place well,' he said on their way up in the lift.

'I came here often with my grandmother,' said Isis quietly. 'She loved this place, especially the food and the music.'

'Ah, Dolores Gonzales. She was a formidable lady.'

'She certainly was that, and you discovered secrets of her past just before she died and gave her peace. And for that, I will always be grateful, Jack. And a lot of it had to do with Madame Petrova and the Ritz in Paris you mentioned earlier. Strange, how everything is so interconnected, don't you think? Serendipity?'

'Tristan would call it destiny.'

'And you? What would you call it, after all we've seen today?'

'Destiny, of course, what else?' said Jack as they stepped out of the lift.

After a fabulous dinner of traditional Cuban fare including tostones rellenos and ropa vieja, a popular entree blending Cuba's Spanish and African influences and flavours, and plenty of fresh seafood ordered by Isis, who knew all the dishes well, everyone began to relax.

'As the submarine left the wreck of the *San Cristobal* this afternoon and returned to the mother ship, Jack asked me a question,' began Isis, introducing the subject that was on everyone's mind: what to do about this extraordinary find on Heart Island. 'Do you remember what it was, Jack?'

'Sure. You said that retrieving the Llanganates treasure was the opportunity of a lifetime and that we would make history. It was clear to me that you had something quite specific in mind. I asked you to tell us what it was, but you said you would explain it all later.'

'Exactly. And sitting here with you right now, looking across to Morro Castle just over there where Mad Dog Regan was hanged, is the right place, and the right time, to tell you what I have in mind.'

Isis looked pensively across to Morro Castle lit up in the distance like a stage set for a play. 'As you know, I have a great interest in Mesoamerican and South American civilisations and indigenous cultures. The Llanganates treasure we have just discovered inside the wreck of the *San Cristobal* belongs to the people it was stolen from, no-one else. It can never belong to an individual or a corporation, not even a museum. What I think we should do, is return the treasure to where it belongs.'

'What exactly do you mean by that?' asked Jack.

'I have discussed this with Charles already. I believe that the treasure should be returned to Cajamarca in northern Peru, where Atahualpa was captured and murdered by the Spanish invaders. After all, it was assembled by his people as a ransom payment for a humiliated and defeated king. It was about to be handed over by Ruminahui, his faithful general, when Atahualpa was brutally murdered by the Spanish conquerors. Because of this treachery, the treasure was hidden by Ruminahui somewhere in the Llanganates Mountains and disappeared – until now.'

'Do you think that's possible?' asked Jack quietly, breaking the silence.

'I will let Charles answer that,' said Isis. 'Charles?'

'The greatest piece of luck in this extraordinary saga so far, is the fact that the find is in international waters, and the treasure had obviously been stolen by the Church, as there is no trace of it anywhere in any of the historical records we could find, like a ship's manifest or similar. The Spanish were usually very meticulous with their record keeping, especially when huge amounts of money were involved. This has significant legal and practical implications that should help us. Tiny Heart Island is more like a reef than an island, and with global warming and rising sea levels it will most likely disappear altogether in the not-too-distant future. I have already retained legal experts in the US to begin preparing a submission.'

'What kind of submission?' asked Jack.

'Our strategy will have several parts: the legal matters speak for themselves. They will start almost immediately, and unfold in the background. As you will see, they have a momentum of their own.

'Then we'll have the all-important media. That's where you come in, Celia. Just as you've done so effectively with the discovery of lost Monet, the return of the sacred icon to Russia, and more recently the Stolzfus matter, your articles – strategically released – will not only create huge international interest, but also set the scene for what we have in mind and are hoping to achieve.'

'And what exactly is that?' asked Jack.

'Just as Isis said, the return of the treasure to where it belongs. And the book you are writing about this right now, Jack, will add further gravitas to our arguments. Why? Because it will explain the extraordinary journey of the treasure and the circumstances of its creation and discovery, which you will no doubt present to the world in your inimical style. Just as you've done with the lost symphony and the Russian icon, and their return to where they belong. It will be a bestseller, for sure. And then, of course, there's Isis's tour.'

'*Tour?* What tour?' asked Jack, frowning.

'Let me answer that,' said Lola, stepping in, as Isis seemed a little uncomfortable. 'That's my idea. We all saw the huge success of Isis's concert in Bogota in July. So I thought, why not put together a South American tour for Isis and the Time Machine in support of the return of the lost treasure, and raise awareness, and money, for the project?'

'What an excellent idea!' said Jack, who could see where this was going. 'As we've seen, Isis is incredibly popular in South America. And besides, a tour would do her good. All big egos need a little massaging from time to time.'

'Thanks, Jack. I knew I could count on you,' said Isis, relieved by the levity and the way the suggested tour had been received. 'I can dig out my old feathered temple costumes you so admired and recycle them. I only hope they still fit.'

'All jokes aside,' said Sir Charles, 'such a tour could be immensely useful and could be of great help with the third part of our strategy.'

'*Third part?*' asked Jack.

Sir Charles adjusted his bow tie. He often did that in court when he collected his thoughts and needed a little time. It was an endearing habit well known to his friends and colleagues.

'The third component of our strategy is political. In my view, this could easily turn out to be the most effective weapon in our arsenal, because it will give us a unique platform for presenting our arguments. It will add credibility and reach a worldwide audience.'

'Could you please elaborate?' said Celia.

'Certainly. I think as part of our strategy, we should involve UNESCO straight away and prepare a proposal.'

'What kind of proposal?' asked Jack.

'As you know, the United Nations Educational, Scientific and Cultural Organization – it goes something like this on its website – seeks to build peace, eradicate poverty through international cooperation, intercultural dialogue, education, the sciences, culture, and communication.'

'That's quite a mouthful,' said Jack. 'And how exactly are you intending to use this?'

Smiling, Sir Charles turned to Isis. Jack had just given him the opening to allow Isis to take centre stage. 'Georgie,' – Sir Charles always called Isis 'Georgie' because her real name was George Edward Elms, and Lord Elms since her father's death in 2011 – 'could you please tell us what you have in mind?'

'As you know, I am bankrolling the salvage. Profesor Chavero here is in charge and will document the find according to accepted archaeological principles. He has an outstanding reputation and is, in my view, the best man for the job. He, and the Museo Nacional de Antropologia, the largest museum in Mexico visited by millions each year, will stand behind this venture and give it professional standing and prestige in political and academic circles. As part of our plan to return the treasure to Cajamarca, I would like to conduct an international design competition for a suitable museum to be built to house the legendary Llanganates treasure on the site of Atahualpa's imprisonment, *El Cuarto del Rescate*, the Ransom Room.'

'What a wonderful idea,' said Chavero, who had heard this for the first time.

'My foundation will finance the construction of the museum, which hopefully will become an iconic building like the Grand Egyptian Museum being built right now close to the Giza Pyramid complex. That is a UNESCO site that incorporates the Great Sphinx and the Giza Necropolis. This could become something similar, and attract millions of visitors each year.'

'That's incredible,' said Celia. 'And you want me to write about all this *and* break the story?'

'Absolutely. I couldn't think of anyone better. What you did with the lost Monet and the auction was outstanding,' said Isis.

'Involving UNESCO from the beginning would be a good idea,' continued Sir Charles. 'In fact, placing the Llanganates treasure into the custody of UNESCO may be the best way to go, and then having the site of the museum declared a UNESCO World Heritage site would give our plan the best chance of success. I have friends in UNESCO,' said Sir Charles, lowering his voice, 'and I know they would be delighted to assist us in this. This could easily turn out to be one of UNESCO's most important and prestigious projects, made possible because of the tenacity of Jack and his friends in finding the treasure in the first place, and Isis's generosity to finance its recovery, and build a suitable place to house and display it. In short, a perfect partnership.'

'I'm speechless,' said Chavero.

'What do you think, guys?' said Isis.

'If Charles thinks we can pull this off, then it certainly has my vote. I have no doubt that the others who were involved in solving this mystery would feel the same way. I am specifically talking about Tristan, Francesca Bartolli, Dupree and Darrieux.'

'We still have a long way to go,' said Sir Charles, 'but I think we can get there.'

'In that case, I would like to propose a toast,' said Jack. He stood up and pointed to Morro Castle with his glass.

'To begin with, I would like to suggest that we change the name of our find from Llanganates Treasure to Ruminahui's Ransom. After all, it is only because of the courage of that Inca warrior that the treasure survived and didn't fall into the hands of the rapacious conquerors. At least not straight away. What do you think, guys?'

'I'm all for it,' said Isis, standing up as well.

'Much more appropriate,' said Chavero, straightening his moustache.

'Certainly has a much better ring to it,' said Celia.

'In that case,' said Jack, lifting his glass, 'may Ruminahui's Ransom finally return to where it belongs, and bring much-deserved self-esteem and recognition to a proud people who have lost so much. To Ruminahui's Ransom!'

67

Cajamarca: 26 July 2019

'Well, what do you think?' said Isis, pivoting slowly in front of a mirror inside one of the vans used by the television crew.

'Stunning,' said Lola, helping Isis straighten her tight-fitting dress. Inspired by the traditional chaplet worn by the Sapa Inca as King of Cusco, the dress was made of exquisite layers of multicoloured braid and red tassels affixed to gold tubes.

'Losing those few kilos definitely helped, don't you think?'

'Absolutely; you look fabulous.'

Beginning the South American *Ruminahui's Ransom* concert tour in Cajamarca by announcing the winner of the international museum design competition sponsored by Isis had been an inspired idea. And to do so on the anniversary of Atahualpa's murder was a master-stroke that brought the historic aspects of the occasion into focus.

Jack had suggested this after the release of his book – *The Death Mask Murders* – in Mexico City one month earlier. Because of Celia's articles in the *New York Times* about Jack and Isis, and the historic find off Heart Island, the book launch inside the Museo Nacional de Antropologia had attracted huge media attention around the world. Everyone wanted to know more about the fabulous Ruminahui's Ransom treasure, the Cajamarca Museum design competition, and Isis's upcoming South American tour to promote the return of the treasure to Peru.

Arranged by Profesor Chavero, the televised book launch was cleverly used to showcase a few stunning pieces of the treasure and introduce it to the public. As Jack's book dealt with the extraordinary journey of the treasure and its discovery, this was most appropriate as it prepared the way for the planned handover of Ruminahui's Ransom to Cajamarca and its people as soon as the new museum was ready.

Sir Charles' UNESCO campaign had been surprisingly successful. After some complex negotiations, a great deal of lobbying and several court cases, it had been agreed that the treasure would be housed temporarily in the Mexican museum under the auspices of UNESCO, but supervised by Profesor Chavero and his team. Chavero, together with archaeologists from Peru who had joined his team, were documenting the thousands of gold artefacts retrieved from the wreck, and were painstakingly restoring them to their former glory after four hundred and eighty-five years under water; a daunting task and not for the fainthearted.

'Wow!' said Jack, who had been standing quietly in the background with Tristan. 'This is even better than the costume you wore when we first met.'

'You think so?'

'No question.'

'So, what's the drill? You know I hate making speeches. I'm a musician, remember? My mind's on tomorrow's concert, not this!'

Jack looked at Lola and winked. 'All you have to do is look fabulous, announce the winner, and lay the foundation stone. I'll do the rest. A few local dignitaries will be present, but definitely no crowds as this is mainly a television event, preparing the way for your concert in Lima tomorrow. Sold out months ago, just like all the others ...'

'That's a relief!' said Isis, adjusting her hair. 'Good to know that I'm still popular down here.'

Tristan tried hard not to laugh.

'Tonight's merely a tribute to your philanthropy,' continued Jack, 'featuring the museum design competition and marking the beginning of construction. Small private function tonight, cheering crowds tomorrow. All part of the tour. I understand that some kind of performance by indigenous locals is planned, no doubt to entertain us.'

Isis took a deep breath. 'The things an artist has to do. All right, guys, let's go.'

A small wooden stage had been erected directly in front of *El Cuarto del Rescate*, the Ransom Room. According to the competition brief, the historic Ransom Room had to be the centrepiece of the new museum complex. As soon as Isis and Jack stepped onto the stage and were welcomed by the mayor, the haunting sounds of flutes and panpipes made of bone began to drift across the empty square, lit entirely by torches. Shaped like a human skull, a large ceramic brazier stood in the centre of the square, which had been closed to the public. Flames darting out of the eyes and mouth gave the skull an eerie, almost lifelike appearance.

After a brief welcome by the mayor, Isis announced the winner – a Swedish architect well known for his Gaudiesque style of extravagant shapes and unique use of materials – and unveiled a model of the stunning design as the TV cameras zoomed in. Then Jack stepped forward and made a short speech about the lost treasure's remarkable journey. He had brought the iridium piece with Baudin's engraved landmarks with him up on stage, and used it to illustrate the story. He had done something similar during the recent book launch to great effect, as the intriguing artefact had attracted a lot of media attention.

As Jack made a point and held up the piece of stardust, a group of Quechua men wearing traditional dress – loincloths and simple tunics – began to dance around the brazier, their athletic bodies casting strange shadows against the ancient stone walls of the unassuming building. Moving slowly out of the shadows, a group of drummers moved into the circle of light surrounding the brazier, and joined in the dance.

Mesmerised by the beat of the drums echoing across the square, Tristan glimpsed fleeting images of a brutal slaughter four hundred and eighty-five years earlier, which had humiliated a king and defeated an empire.

Then one of the dancers walked up to Jack, took him by the hand and guided him towards the brazier. Smiling, Jack followed and was immediately surrounded by the dancers, who formed a protective circle around him as the drum beat intensified.

'*The chosen one has returned*,' chanted the dancers in Quechua. '*The time has come!*'

Tristan turned to the mayor standing next to him on the stage. 'What are they saying?' he asked.

'This is an important local ceremony,' said the mayor, side-stepping the question. 'Very soon the Villaq Umm will arrive and all will become clear.'

'Who is the Villaq Umm?'

'A high priest. A direct descendant of Atahualpa and the guardian of ... here he comes now, look.'

A strange sense of wonder descended on Tristan as he watched a procession of torchbearers enter from one of the narrow side alleys and walk slowly towards the brazier.

'The one at the front is Villaq Umm,' said the mayor, bowing his head.

Wearing a traditional royal coat of colourful textiles and a spectacular woven hat trimmed with gold and topped with feathers, the Villaq Umm looked like an emperor. Walking behind him, four men carried on their shoulders what looked like some kind of a statue hidden under a colourful blanket covered with exotic-looking feathers, reminiscent of the religious processions parading effigies of saints through the streets during religious festivals, introduced by the Spanish after the conquest.

The Villaq Umm walked up to Jack and bowed. 'Welcome,' he said in perfect English. 'We have been waiting for you for a long time. Please follow me.'

Lola walked over to Tristan standing at the front of the stage. 'What do you think's going on?' she asked.

'No idea. But whatever it is, it's fascinating; look.'

The Villaq Umm had taken Jack by the hand and was leading him up a set of rough stone steps towards the Ransom Room behind the stage, a small, stark building that looked mysterious in the semi-darkness. The men carrying the statue followed, but the men with the torches stayed behind at the brazier, chanting.

'Please come inside,' said the mayor. 'You are about to witness something unique only seen by a privileged few. No cameras are allowed inside the *El Cuarto del Rescate*. This is strictly for your eyes only.'

Isis looked at Tristan. 'You look like you've seen a ghost,' she said.

'Perhaps I have. Let's go inside and see what this is all about, shall we?'

* * *

Despite the significant time difference – Venice was seven hours ahead of Cajamarca – Countess Kuragin and Leonardo were watching the Cajamarca transmission on TV in the palazzo salon.

'I don't know how he does it,' said the countess, 'but the stories certainly seem to find Jack wherever he goes. Just look at this!'

'I know why.'

'You do?'

'He's something very rare and special,' said Leonardo.

'What's that?'

'A just man.'

The countess looked at Leonardo, surprised. 'You put it very well,' she said. 'That's exactly what he is.'

Leonardo reached for the countess's hand and squeezed it. 'Thanks, Katerina.'

'What for?'

'For staying with me. I don't think I could have coped with Lorenza's death without you.'

'You are one of my dearest and oldest friends. And you heard what Jack had to say about friendship.'

'He got that one right. How long are you planning to stay?'

'As long as you want me to. Why do you think I asked Adrienne to run the chateau hotel for me once we open it up again?'

'Seriously?'

'Absolutely.'

'In that case, how does forever sound?'

The countess looked at Leonardo, her eyes moist with tears, and squeezed his hand in silent reply.

* * *

Bartolli and her mother sat on the terrace above the bustling market in Travestere, where the stallholders were already busily setting up their wares. They were having an early breakfast and were watching the Cajamarca transmission on the television in the kitchen.

'You like him, don't you?' said Bartolli's mother.

'He's a very charming man.'

'That's not what I asked.'

'My life is complicated enough. Two teenage daughters, a mother who fusses over me, a demanding conductor, and a faithful dog who doesn't leave my side. That will do it for me. What more can a middle-aged single mother want? I'll settle for friendship.'

'Smart girl. Broken hearts never mend. Trust me, I know.'

* * *

'No cameras allowed inside,' said Darrieux. 'How weird. Why do you think that is?'

'No idea,' said Dupree, and turned up the volume on the TV. They were sitting in front of the fireplace in the Gatekeeper's Cottage having an early cup of coffee while watching the Cajamarca transmission. The strange procession had just gone into the Ransom Room and the camera was swinging around to show the dancers moving slowly around a large brazier in the square to the beat of the drums.

'Katerina is an extremely generous person, don't you think?' said Darrieux.

'She sure is that. Without her, I wouldn't have had a home after my son died in the fire. But she's more than that. She radiates love, and this affects everyone around her.'

Darrieux looked at Dupree, surprised. 'You are absolutely right. That's exactly what it is. Look at me. An eccentric, middle-aged trans woman who still struggles with her identity after all these years, has been asked by a sophisticated lady like Katerina, a countess, to run her boutique hotel for her? She has entrusted this chateau into *my* hands. Can you believe that? Someone like me, who started out as a teenaged male prostitute in New Orleans and told the whole world about it?'

'Oh, I can. Do you want to know why?'

'Tell me.'

'Because she's also an excellent judge of character, who believes, just like Jack, that friendship is the greatest treasure of them all.'

'And you, what do you believe?'

'I agree with them. Another coffee?'

* * *

Grimaldi had arrived in his office early that morning. He didn't want to miss the Cajamarca ceremony on TV. Cesaria and Samartini joined him for breakfast just before the transmission was due to start.

'This is a momentous day for us,' said Grimaldi. 'What Jack and Isis are doing in South America is truly remarkable, and we — especially you, Clara, with Omerta — have played an important part in all this; congratulations. Not only have the notorious Death Mask Murders been solved and at least one of the killers arrested — making the French happy — thanks to Giuseppina's evidence, Riccardo Giordano got life, and so have many other Mafiosi in Calabria. Effectively, the notorious 'Ndrangheta has been wiped out, and that is a big feather in your cap, Cesaria.'

'Pity we couldn't get Alessandro,' said Cesaria. 'I have no doubt that he was behind that botched assassination in Venice that cost

Lorenza her life, yet he's still swanning around on his yacht in Monaco—'

'Not anymore,' interrupted Grimaldi, smiling.

'What do you mean?' said Cesaria.

'I just received word from Port de Fontvieille. There was a huge explosion on board *Nike*, the Giordano yacht, in Fontvieille harbour last night. The yacht was obliterated. There are no survivors.'

'Was Alessandro on board?'

'Yes. There's a rumour that the Lombardos were behind it. Payback for the drug supply fiasco last year that cost them their business, and a lot more.'

Cesaria looked at Grimaldi, stunned. 'How did they know that Alessandro was responsible for that?'

'In the end, justice always finds a way …'

'*You told them!*' said Samartini.

Grimaldi shrugged. 'Tristan would call it destiny.'

* * *

Built entirely of stone, *El Cuarto del Rescate* was an empty rectangular chamber lit by hundreds of candles. It reminded Jack of an underground burial vault somewhere in the catacombs in Rome.

The Villaq Umm stood in silence as the four men entered, carefully put down what they were carrying on the stone floor and stood aside.

Tristan kept staring at what looked like someone sitting on the floor under a blanket. The shape suggested that. For some reason he couldn't explain, it was as if something was reaching out to him, trying to tell him something he couldn't quite understand. Then the Villaq Umm stepped forward, put his hands on the exquisite blanket and looked at Jack.

'Those of us who know what happened, stand here and remember a great wrong that was committed not far from here a long time ago.' The Villaq Umm began to slowly lift the blanket to expose what was hidden under it. 'And you, Mr Rogan, have the power to set it right. You can allow a lost soul who has been wandering in the wilderness all these years, to finally enter the afterlife.' With that, the Villaq Umm quickly lifted the blanket and knelt down. The four bearers did the same.

'Behold, Atahualpa, the Sapa Inca, last king of Cusco and Emperor of the Tahuantinsuyo,' he said.

Holding his breath, Jack was staring at what looked like a well-preserved mummy sitting on the ground. Only the face and a full head of hair were visible. The eyes were closed, the expression on the face serene. The elongated earlobes had heavy gold earplugs inserted, but the rest of the body was tightly wrapped in coloured textiles. However, the most striking object by far was a stunning chaplet on top of the mummy's head, made of layers of coloured braid and gold – the Mascaipacha – the imperial symbol worn only by the Sapa Inca.

Tristan too, kept staring at the mummy when suddenly, he could understand the whispers and hear some strange noises in the background. It was the sound of battle and the desperate cries of the maimed and dying, pleading for mercy.

Isis turned to the Villaq Umm kneeling on the ground in front of her. 'Are you telling us that these are the remains of Atahualpa, who was killed here almost five hundred years ago?'

'Yes. After his murder, Atahualpa was taken from here to a sacred cave high up in the mountains, where his body was prepared for his journey into the afterlife. But one important item was missing: his sacred burial mask, which had been stolen by Pizarro.' The Villaq Umm paused and looked at Jack. 'But which thanks to you, has now found its way back here to where it belongs. There has only ever been one such sacred burial mask in the empire that contained a piece of the sun god Inti, which had fallen from heaven. It belonged to the Sapa Inca and would ensure his entry into the afterlife.' The Villaq Umm turned around on his knees and looked at Jack.

'On behalf of my people, I plead with you to return the sacred mask to where it belongs, and place it on the face of Atahualpa, so that he may finally join his ancestors and become one with the sun god.'

Deeply moved, Jack reached into his shoulder bag and, holding it with both hands, lifted the piece of the burial mask found on Heart Island out of the bag. Then he bent down – his hands shaking – and placed it carefully on the upturned face of the mummy in front of him.

For an instant Tristan thought he saw Atahualpa's lips move ever so slightly, and something drift out of his mouth. Was it his restless spirit finally escaping with the help of his burial mask, to find peace in the afterlife? Tristan wondered. Or was it merely a shadow reaching out from the distant past?

The Villaq Umm stood up and began to chant. Then he reached for the blanket and covered the mummy. The four bearers stood up as well, lifted up the mummy and slowly carried it outside. The Villaq Umm followed and together, they disappeared into the night.

* * *

The old house just outside Minsk in Belarus was shrouded in mist. It was just before sunrise.

O'Hara wasn't used to losing. He had just watched the Cajamarca ceremony and turned off the TV. Then he looked pensively at his precious Llanganates collection spread out on the table in front of him. Beginning with *The Navarro Chronicles*, he let his fingertips glide from one item to the next, each one having cost a man's life. When he came to the last one, the iridium piece handed over by the police in Paris, he remembered the white knight on his imaginary chessboard. *Never underestimate a knight*, he thought. *He can defeat you.* Slowly, he pushed the piece to the edge of the table until it overbalanced and fell to the floor. *This doesn't belong here. I will never make that mistake again.*

True evil never dies, it just finds a new home.

A PARTING NOTE FROM THE AUTHOR

As a writer, authenticity and accuracy are paramount. Without that, it isn't possible to create a seamless storyline where the boundaries between fact and fiction are blurred, so that the reader is never quite sure where one ends, and the other begins. This is quite deliberate, as it creates the illusion of truth and reality in a work that is pure fiction. In my view, a successful work of fiction is a balancing act: reality must rub shoulders with imagination in a way that is both entertaining and plausible, and this can only be achieved through meticulous research and attention to detail.

Interpreting the past is never easy and is often fraught with danger. However, all the historical material dealt with in the storylines has been carefully researched and is, to the best of my knowledge, based on primary sources like original letters, court documents and accepted academic texts, articles and related source material.

In addition, I draw quite heavily on current affairs and events that have some relevance to the storylines and characters featured in the book. This gives a further dimension of 'reality' to my work, as these often well-known and documented events further underpin the illusion of reality in a work of fiction. To put it another way, the story must appear plausible and have the 'ring' of truth.

The best way to illustrate this is by way of a few examples:

Zodiac

An unnamed serial killer known only as 'the Zodiac', who had killed at least five people in the 1960s, sent letters to newspapers in San Francisco providing evidence of his crimes, including a code known as the 340 cipher that apparently would reveal his name. For more than fifty years some of the best cryptologists in the world had tried in vain to solve the encrypted message. This code – considered one of the holy grails of cryptography – has recently been cracked by Australian cryptologist Dr Blake, and two others, on a Melbourne supercomputer known as 'Spartan'. While the decoded cipher revealed a lot about the killer's state of mind, it did not reveal his name.

This fascinating story has become the inspiration for the cipher sent to Landru in prison that, once cracked, would reveal the address of that house of horrors at the beginning of the storyline and reignite the quest for the lost Llanganates treasure.

ANOM

ANOM is an encrypted messaging app developed by law enforcement agencies, which was covertly distributed by the FBI among the criminal underworld via informants with links to the Mafia. So successful was this operation, which allowed police around the world to monitor conversations among senior crime figures, that it was described by Europol as the 'biggest law enforcement operation against encrypted communication' ever. This ingenious sting, which was made public in June 2021, involved eight thousand police officers, resulted in countless arrests in more than sixteen countries, and the confiscation of tonnes of drugs and millions of dollars in proceeds of crime.

ANOM was the inspiration for the app Omerta, used in the book by Clara Samartini and the Squadra Mobile in Florence to expose Lorenza's killer and lead them to O'Hara. It was also instrumental in convicting Riccardo Giordano and many others at the Calabrian Mafia mega-trial that effectively wiped out the notorious 'Ndrangheta.

Italy's largest Mafia trial

In January 2021, the largest Mafia trial in decades against members of the feared 'Ndrangheta, involving more than 900 witnesses and 350 high-profile accused, began in Lamezia Terme in Calabria, in a purpose-built courtroom with cages to hold the defendants, and room for a thousand people and four hundred lawyers. This historic trial and its far-reaching ramifications features in the book and introduces the concept of '*Vedo, Sento, Parlo,*' 'I see, I hear, I speak', a movement by Mafia women who'd had enough. This extraordinary trial has been the inspiration for such characters as Giuseppina, Riccardo Giordano's wife, who gave evidence at his trial, and prosecutor Donizetti, who was injured in an assassination attempt at the airport in Catanzaro after Jack and Cesaria visited Giuseppina in a Calabrian safe house.

Amaro Pargo

Amaro Rodriguez-Felipe y Tejera Machado, known as Amaro Pargo, was a famous Spanish corsair who features prominently in the book. As a historical figure, a great deal is known about him, and all the historical material used in the book is, to the best of my knowledge, accurate and based on the most reliable historical records. This includes the famous winking skull and crossbones on his tombstone in the Church of Santo Domingo in San Cristóbal de la Laguna, Tenerife.

These records reveal that he was buried next to his parents and a black servant. However, in November 2013, forensic scientists and archaeologists carried out a detailed study on the notorious pirate, including DNA tests and even a reconstruction of his face. This study resulted in an exhumation, during which it was discovered that Pargo was laid to rest next to six additional people, some of them thought to be nephews of Amaro Pargo.

What is interesting to note is that the exhumation was funded by a French video game company and used to promote its famous *Assassin's Creed* video game. All of this factual material served as further inspiration for various twists and layers in the storyline, and in particular O'Hara's involvement in sophisticated video games on the dark net.

Finally, please keep in mind that I am not a historian nor an academic, but a thriller writer with a legal background, whose aim is to entertain and tease your intellect and imagination with questions, interpretations and scenarios that are both realistic and plausible, but are of course pure fiction intended for the thinking reader and culturally curious.

More Books by the Author

Jack Rogan Mysteries Series Starter Library
The Empress Holds the Key
The Disappearance of Anna Popov
The Hidden Genes of Professor K
Professor K: The Final Quest
The Curious Case of the Missing Head
The Lost Symphony
Jack Rogan Mysteries Series Box Set Books 1–4

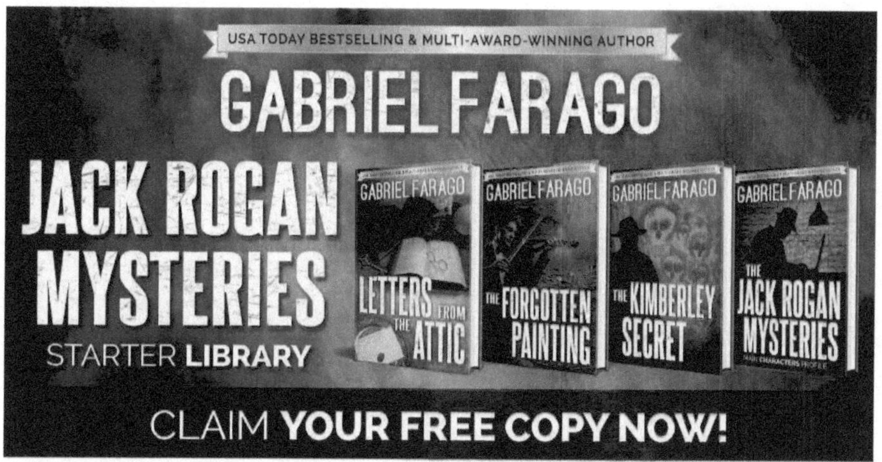

So, what exactly is a STARTER LIBRARY? Well, it's a way to introduce myself and what I do, to new readers, and create interest in my writing. How? By providing little insights into my world, and the creative process involved in becoming an international thriller writer.

The Starter Library consists of four short books:
1. *Letters from The Attic* – a delightful collection of auto-biographical short stories;
2. *The Forgotten Painting* – a multi-award-winning Jack Rogan novella, providing insights into Jack Rogan's character and background;
3. *The Kimberley Secret* – a novella delving into Jack Rogan's earlier life;
4. *Jack Rogan Mysteries Main Characters* – a glossary that provides some exciting background stories and insights into the main characters featured in the series, and acts as an aide-mémoire to place and follow the many characters featured in the series.

The Starter Library is available right now, and can be downloaded for FREE by following this link: https://gabrielfarago.com.au/starter-library2/

Please share this with your friends and encourage them to download the Starter Library.

In 2013, I released my first adventure thriller –
The Empress Holds the Key.

THE EMPRESS HOLDS THE KEY

A disturbing, edge-of-your-seat historical mystery thriller

Jack Rogan Mysteries Book 1

Dark secrets. A holy relic. An ancient quest reignited.

Jack Rogan's discovery of a disturbing old photograph in the ashes of a rural Australian cottage draws the journalist into a dangerous hunt with the ultimate stakes.

The tangled web of clues – including hoards of Nazi gold, hidden Swiss bank accounts, and a long-forgotten mass grave – implicate wealthy banker Sir Eric Newman and lead to a trial with shocking revelations.

A holy relic mysteriously erased from the pages of history is suddenly up for grabs to those willing to sacrifice everything to find it. Rogan and his companions must follow historical leads through ancient Egypt to the Crusades and the Knights Templar, to uncover a secret that could destroy the foundations of the Catholic Church and challenge the history of Christianity itself.

Will Rogan succeed in bringing the dark mystery into the light, or will the powers desperately working against him ensure the ancient truths remain buried forever?

The Empress Holds the Key
is now available in ebook and paperback

Encouraged by the reception of *The Empress Holds the Key*, I released my next thriller –*The Disappearance of Anna Popov* – in 2014.

THE DISAPPEARANCE OF ANNA POPOV

A dark, page-turning psychological thriller

Jack Rogan Mysteries Book 2

A mysterious disappearance. An outlaw bikie gang. One dangerous investigation.

Journalist Jack Rogan cannot resist a good mystery. When he stumbles across a hidden clue about the tragic disappearance of two girls from Alice Springs years earlier, he's determined to investigate.

Joining forces with his New York literary agent; a retired Aboriginal police officer; and Cassandra, an enigmatic psychic, Rogan enters the dark and dangerous world of an outlaw bikie gang ruled by an evil master.

Entangled in a web of violence, superstition and fear, Rogan and his friends follow the trail of the missing girls into the remote Dreamtime-wilderness of outback Australia, where they face their greatest challenge yet.

Cassandra has a secret agenda of her own and uses her occult powers to conjure up an epic showdown where the stakes are high, and the loser faces death and oblivion.

Will Rogan succeed in finding the truth, or will the forces of evil prevail, causing untold misery and destroying even more lives?

The Disappearance of Anna Popov
is now available in ebook and paperback

My next book, *The Hidden Genes of Professor K*, was released in 2016.

THE HIDDEN GENES OF PROFESSOR K

A dark, disturbing and nail-biting medical thriller

Jack Rogan Mysteries Book 3

A medical breakthrough. A greedy pharmaceutical magnate. A brutal double-murder. One tangled web of lies.

World-renowned scientist Professor K is close to a groundbreaking discovery. He's also dying. With his last breath, he anoints Dr Alexandra Delacroix as his successor and pleads with her to carry on his work.

But powerful forces will stop at nothing to possess the research, unwittingly plunging Delacroix into a treacherous world of unbridled ambition and greed.

Desperate and alone, she turns to celebrated author and journalist, Jack Rogan.

Rogan must help Delacroix, while also assisting famous rock star Isis in the seemingly unrelated investigation into the brutal murder of her parents.

With the support of Isis' resourceful PA, Lola; a former police officer; a tireless campaigner for the destitute and forgotten; and a gifted boy with psychic powers, Rogan exposes a complex web of fiercely guarded secrets and heinous crimes of the past that can ruin them all and change history.

Will the dreams of a visionary scientist with the power to change the future of medicine fall into the wrong hands, or will his genius benefit mankind and prevent untold misery and suffering for generations to come?

Outstanding Thriller of 2017
Independent Author Network Book of the Year Awards

The Hidden Genes of Professor K
is now available in ebook and paperback

My next book, *Professor K: The Final Quest*,
was released in October 2018.

PROFESSOR K: THE FINAL QUEST

An action-packed historical medical mystery

Jack Rogan Mysteries Book 4

A desperate plea from the Vatican. A kidnapped chef. An ambitious mob boss. One perilous game.

When Professor Alexandra Delacroix is called in to find a cure for the dying pope, she follows clues left by her mentor and friend, the late Professor K, which lead her on a breathtaking search through historical secrets, some of them deadly.

Her old friend Jack Rogan must step in to assist while also searching for kidnapped Top Chef Europe winner Lorenza da Baggio.

He joins forces with his young friend and gifted psychic, Tristan; a dedicated Mafia-hunting prosecutor; a fearless young police officer; and an enigmatic Egyptian detective who is on a perilous hunt for a notorious IS terrorist.

Together, they stand off with the head of a powerful Mafia family in Florence and uncover a network of corruption and heinous crimes reaching to the very top.

Will Rogan and his friends succeed in finding Lorenza and curing the pope, or will the dark forces swirling around them prevail in their sinister plots?

**Gold Medal Winner in the Fiction
Thriller - Medical Category**
Readers' Favorite 2019 International Book Awards Contest

Professor K: The Final Quest
is now available in ebook and paperback

My next book, *The Curious Case of the Missing Head*,
was released in November 2019.

THE CURIOUS CASE OF THE MISSING HEAD

A gripping medical thriller

Jack Rogan Mysteries Book 5

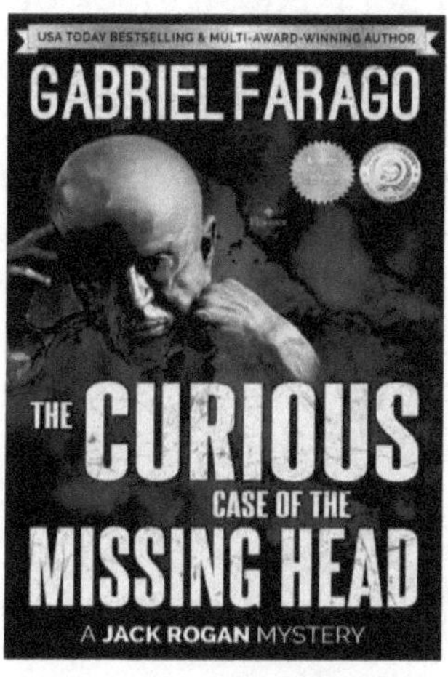

A headless body on a boat. An international conspiracy. Can a kidnapped genius survive a controversial scientific discovery?

Esteemed Australian journalist Jack Rogan is on a mission to solve the disappearance of his mother in the 70s. But when a friend needs help rescuing a kidnapped world-renowned astrophysicist, he doesn't hesitate. Struggling with more questions than answers, his investigation leads them aboard a hellish hospital ship, where instead of finding the kidnap victim, he's confronted with a decapitated corpse.

As the search intensifies, Jack bumps up against diabolical cartels with hidden agendas. And when his research reveals dubious experiments, a criminal on death row, and a shocking revelation about his mother's fate, he must uncover how it's all linked.

Can Jack unravel the twisted connections and catch the scientist's killer, or will the next obituary published be his own?

**Gold Medal Winner in the Fiction
Thriller – Conspiracy Category**
Readers' Favorite 2020 International Book Awards Contest

Outstanding Thriller/Suspense of 2020
Independent Author Network Book of the Year Awards

The Curious Case of the Missing Head
is now available in ebook and paperback

My latest book, *The Lost Symphony*, was released in November 2020.

THE LOST SYMPHONY

A historical mystery thriller

Jack Rogan Mysteries Book 6

A murdered tsarina. A lost musical masterpiece. A stolen Russian icon. Can Jack honour a promise made a long time ago, and solve an age-old mystery?

When acclaimed Australian journalist and author Jack Rogan inherits an old music box with a curious letter hidden inside, he decides to investigate. As he delves deeper into a murky past of secrets and violence, he soon discovers that he's not the only one interested in solving the puzzle.

Frieda Malenkova, a ruthless art dealer, and Victor Sokolov, a Russian billionaire with a dark past, will stop at nothing to achieve their deep desires and foil Jack's valiant struggle to uncover the truth.

Joining forces with Mademoiselle Darrieux, a flamboyant Paris socialite, and Claude Dupree, a retired French police officer, Jack enters a dangerous world of unbridled ambition, murder and greed that threatens to destroy him.

On a perilous journey that takes him deep into Russia, Jack follows a tortuous path of discovery, disappointment and betrayal that brings him face to face with his destiny.

Will Jack unravel the hidden clues left behind by a desperate empress? Can he save the precious legacy of a genius before it's too late, and return a holy icon revered by generations to where it belongs?

**Gold Medal Winner in the Fiction
Mystery - Historical Category**
Readers' Favorite 2021 International Book Awards Contest

**Award-Winning Finalist in the Fiction
Thriller - Adventure Category**
The 2021 International Book Awards

**Outstanding Mystery of 2021
Mystery Category Winner**
Independent Author Network Book of the Year Awards

The Lost Symphony
is now available in ebook and paperback

Jack Rogan Mysteries
Box Set Books 1-4

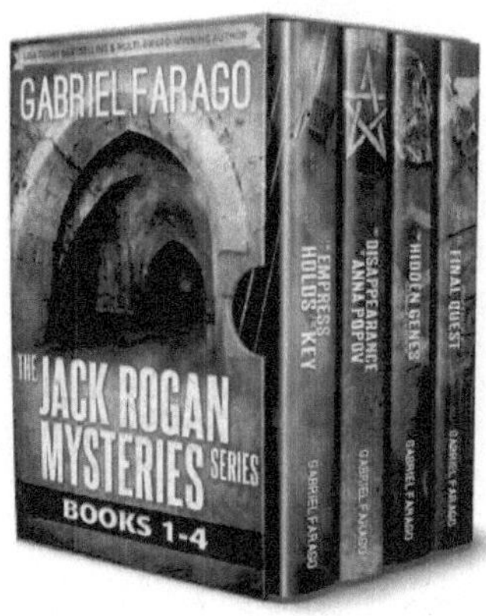

The Jack Rogan Mysteries Box Set
is now available in ebook

ABOUT THE AUTHOR

Gabriel Farago is the *USA TODAY* best-selling and multi-award-winning Australian author of the *Jack Rogan Mysteries Series* for the thinking reader.

As a lawyer with a passion for history and archaeology, Gabriel Farago had to wait for many years before being able to pursue another passion – writing – in earnest. However, his love of books and storytelling started long before that.

'I remember as a young boy reading biographies and history books, with a torch under the bed covers,' he recalls, 'and then writing stories about archaeologists and explorers the next day, instead of doing homework. While I regularly got into trouble for this, I believe we can only do well in our endeavours if we are passionate about the things we love. For me, writing has become a passion.'

Born in Budapest, Gabriel grew up in post-war Europe and, after fleeing Hungary with his parents during the Revolution in 1956, he went to school in Austria before arriving in Australia as a teenager. This allowed him to become multi-lingual and feel 'at home' in different countries and diverse cultures.

Shaped by a long legal career and experiences spanning several decades and continents, his is a mature voice that speaks in many tongues. Gabriel holds degrees in literature and law, speaks several languages and takes research and authenticity very seriously. Inquisitive by nature, he studied Egyptology and learned to read the hieroglyphs. He travels extensively and visits all of the locations mentioned in his books.

'I try to weave fact and fiction into a seamless storyline,' he explains. 'By blurring the boundaries between the two, the reader is never quite sure where one ends, and the other begins. This is, of course, quite deliberate as it creates the illusion of authenticity and reality in a work that is pure fiction. A successful work of fiction is a balancing act: reality must rub shoulders with imagination in a way that is both entertaining and plausible.'

Gabriel lives just outside Sydney, Australia, in the Blue Mountains, surrounded by a World Heritage National Park. 'The beauty and solitude of this unique environment,' he points out, 'gives me the inspiration and energy to weave my thoughts and ideas into stories that in turn, I sincerely hope, will entertain and inspire my readers.'

Gabriel Farago

Author's Note

I hope you enjoyed reading this book as much as I enjoyed writing it. I'd be very grateful if you'd post a short review on your favourite online bookstore and Goodreads. Your support really does make a difference.

Connect with the Author

Website
https://gabrielfarago.com.au/

Goodreads
https://www.goodreads.com/author/show/7435911.Gabriel_Farago

Facebook
https://www.facebook.com/GabrielFaragoAuthor

BookBub
https://www.bookbub.com/profile/gabriel-farago

Signup for the author's New Releases mailing list and get a free copy of *The Forgotten Painting** Novella and find out where it all began ...

https://gabrielfarago.com.au/free-download-forgotten-painting/

* I'm delighted to tell you that The Forgotten Painting has just received two major literary awards in the US. It was awarded the Gold Medal by Readers' Favorite in the Short Stories and Novellas category and was named the 'Outstanding Novella' of 2018 by the IAN Book of the Year Awards.